Surrounded by the exotic beauty and
heat of a desert kingdom…
An ordinary woman fights her own desires
and the indomitable will of the handsome
king who has decided he wants her!

THE DESERT

Sheikh's

DEFIANT QUEEN

Two passionate, sensual novels by favourite
authors Jane Porter and Annie West

THE DESERT SHEIKHS
COLLECTION

THE DESERT

Sheikh's

DEFIANT QUEEN

JANE
PORTER

ANNIE
WEST

MILLS &
BOON

Harlequin Mills & Boon Limited, Eton House,
18-24 Paradise Road, Richmond, Surrey TW9 1SR

THE DESERT SHEIKH'S DEFIANT QUEEN
© Harlequin Enterprises II B.V./S.à.r.l. 2011

The Sheikh's Chosen Queen © Jane Porter 2007
The Desert King's Pregnant Bride © Annie West 2008

ISBN: 978 0 263 88753 2

025-0311

Harlequin Mills & Boon policy is to use papers that are
natural, renewable and recyclable products and made from
wood grown in sustainable forests. The logging and
manufacturing processes conform to the legal environmental
regulations of the country of origin.

Printed and bound in Spain
by Litografia Rosés S.A., Barcelona

The Sheikh's Chosen Queen

JANE
PORTER

Jane Porter grew up on a diet of Mills & Boon® romances, reading late at night under the covers so her mother wouldn't see! She wrote her first book at age eight, and spent many of her school and college years living abroad, immersing herself in other cultures and continuing to read voraciously. Now Jane has settled down in rugged Seattle, Washington, with her gorgeous husband and two sons. Jane loves to hear from her readers. You can write to her at PO Box 524, Bellevue, WA 98009, USA. Or visit her website at www.janeporter.com

Don't miss Jane Porter's exciting new novel, *A Dark Sicilian Secret*, available in May 2011 from Mills & Boon® Modern™.

For my mother-in-law, Jackie Gaskins.
God has a new and feisty angel in heaven.

PROLOGUE

How did a king ask for a favor?

In the palace courtyard, King Sharif Fehr broke the rosebud off the stem and held the half-opened bud in his palm, the blush petals almost pink against his skin. Roses were difficult to grow in his country's desert heat, which only made them more rare and beautiful.

So how did a king ask for help?

How did a king get what he needed?

Carefully, he answered himself, his thumb stroking a tender petal. Very carefully.

CHAPTER ONE

THE LOW heels on Jesslyn Heaton's practical navy pumps clicked briskly against the sidewalk as she left the administrative office.

It was the last day of school and mercifully the students had finally been sent home stuffed full of cupcakes and gallons of shocking red punch. All she had to do now was close her room for the summer.

"Going anywhere fun for holiday, Miss Heaton?" a student asked, his thin, reedy voice breaking on her name.

Jesslyn glanced up from the paperwork she'd pulled from her faculty mailbox. "Aaron, you haven't left yet? School ended hours ago."

The freckle-faced teen blushed. "Forgot something," he mumbled, his flush deepening as he reached into his backpack to retrieve a small package wrapped in white paper and tied with a purple silk ribbon. "For you. My mom picked it out. But it was my idea."

"A present." Jesslyn smiled and adjusted the pile of paperwork in her arms to take the gift. "That's so thoughtful. But Aaron, it's not necessary. I'll see you next school term—"

"I won't be back." His shoulders rose and he hunched miserably into the backpack he'd slung again onto his thin back.

"We're moving this summer. Dad's been transferred back to the States. Anchorage, I think."

Having taught middle school at the small private school in the United Arab Emirates for the past six years, Jesslyn had witnessed how abruptly the students—children of ex-pats—came and went. "I'm sorry, Aaron. I really am."

He shoved his hands deeper into his pockets. "Maybe you could tell the other kids? Have them e-mail me?"

His voice cracked again, and it was the crack in his voice along with the way he hung his head that nearly undid her. These children went through so much. Foreign homes, foreign lives, change the only constant. "I will, of course."

Nodding, he turned around and was gone, rushing down the empty corridors of the school. Jesslyn watched his hasty departure for a moment before unlocking the door to her deserted classroom with a sigh. Hard to believe that another school year had ended. It seemed like only yesterday she was handing out the mountain of textbooks and carefully printing children's names in her class register. Now they were gone, and for the next two months she was free.

Well, she'd be free as soon as she closed up her classroom, and she couldn't do that until she tackled her last, and least-favorite task, washing the chalkboards.

Twenty minutes later her once-crisp navy dress stuck to the small of her back, and perspiration matted the heavy dark hair at her nape. What a job, she thought, wrinkling her nose as she rinsed out the filthy sponge in the sink.

A knock sounded on her door and Dr. Maddox, her principal, appeared in the doorway. "Miss Heaton, you've a guest."

Jesslyn thought one of her students' parents had shown up, concerned about a grade on a report, but it wasn't Robert.

Heart suddenly racing, she stared stunned at Sharif Fehr. *Prince* Sharif Fehr.

She convulsively squeezed the wet sponge, water streaming through her now-trembling fingers.

Sharif.

Sharif, here?

Impossible. But he was here, it was without a doubt Prince Fehr standing in her doorway, tall, imposing, real. She stared at him, drinking him in, adrenaline racing through her veins, too hot, too cold, too intense.

Dr. Maddox cleared her throat. "Miss Heaton, it is my pleasure to introduce you to our most generous school benefactor, His Royal Highness—"

"Sharif," Jesslyn whispered, unable to stop herself.

"Jesslyn," Sharif answered with a slight nod.

And just like that, her name spoken in his rich, deep voice made the years disappear.

The last time she'd seen him they'd been younger, so much younger. She'd been a young woman in her first year of teaching at the American School in London. And he'd been a gorgeous, rebel Arab prince who wore jeans and flip-flops and baggy cashmere sweatshirts.

Now he looked like someone altogether different. His baggy sweatshirts were gone, and the faded, torn jeans were replaced by a *dishdashah* or a *thoub*, as more commonly known in the Arabian Gulf, a cool, long, one-piece white dress and the traditional head gear comprised of a *gutrah*, a white scarflike cloth, and the *ogal*, the black circular band that held everything together.

He looked so different from when she'd last seen him, and yet he still looked very much the same, from the piercing pewter eyes to his chiseled jaw to his dark, glossy hair.

Confused, Dr. Maddox glanced from one to the other. "You know each other?"

Know? *Know?* She'd been his, and he'd been hers and their lives had been so intertwined that ending their relationship had ripped her heart to shreds.

"We…we went to school together," she stammered, cheeks heating as she unsuccessfully tried to avoid his eyes.

But his gaze found hers anyway and held, the corner of his mouth sardonically lifting, challenging her.

They didn't go to school together.

They weren't even enrolled in school at the same time. He had been six years older than her, and although he hadn't dressed the part, he had been a very successful financial analyst in London when they met.

They'd dated for several years, and when she broke it off, she walked away telling herself she would never see him again. And she hadn't.

That didn't mean she hadn't hoped he'd prove her wrong.

Finally he had. But why? What did he want? Because he did want something. Sharif Fehr wouldn't be in her Sharjah classroom without a very good reason.

"We went to school in England," she added, striving to sound blasé, trying to hide how deeply his surprise appearance had unnerved her. There were boyfriends in life from whom you parted on good terms and then there were the ones who had changed you forever.

Sharif had changed her forever, and now, despite all the years that had passed, just being in the same room with him made her nerves scream, Danger, danger, danger.

"What a small world," Dr. Maddox said, looking from one to the other.

"Indeed," Sharif answered with a slight inclination of his royal head.

Jesslyn squeezed the sponge even tighter, her pulse leaping as she wondered yet again what he was doing here. What did he want?

What could he want with her?

She was still a teacher. She still lived a simple, rather frugal life. She still wore her brown hair at her shoulders in virtually the same style she'd worn nine years ago. And unlike him, she hadn't ever married, although the man she'd been dating a couple of years ago had proposed. She hadn't accepted the proposal, though, knowing she didn't love him enough, not the way she'd loved Sharif.

But then, she'd never loved anybody the same way she'd loved Sharif.

Abruptly turning, she dropped the sponge in the sink, rinsed her hands and used one of the rough paper towels to dry them. "What can I do for you, Sharif?"

"I suppose I'm not needed here anymore," Dr. Maddox said with a sigh of disappointment. "I'll head back to my office. Good afternoon, Your Highness." And with a respectful nod of her head, she left them, gently closing the door behind her.

Jesslyn heard rather than saw her classroom door close, and she drew a quick painful breath realizing they were alone.

Alone with Sharif. After all these years.

"Sit, please," Sharif said, gesturing for her to sit down at her desk. "There's no reason for you to stand for me."

She glanced at her chair but didn't think her legs could carry her across a room, at least not quite yet. "Would you like a chair?" she asked instead.

"I'm fine," he answered.

"Then I'll stand, too."

His expression never changed. "I'd be more comfortable if you sat. *Please*."

It wasn't a request, though, it was a command, and Jesslyn looked at him, curious as well as surprised. He would never have used such an authoritative tone with her before. He'd never raised his voice or issued commands when she knew him. He'd always been gorgeous, confident, comfortable in his own skin. But he'd never been regal, never formal. He was both now.

Studying him more closely, she realized his face had changed more than she'd initially thought. His face was different. The years had subtly reshaped his features. His cheekbones were more pronounced, his jaw wider, stronger, his chin and brow also more defined.

Not a young man anymore but a man.

And not just any man but one of the most powerful leaders in the Middle East.

"Okay," she said, her voice suddenly husky, betraying her nervousness, "let me just clean up and I'll be happy to sit down."

Turning back to the sink, she quickly tucked the bucket and sponge beneath the sink, wiped the sink down with another paper towel and then threw it away.

"You have to wash the chalkboards yourself?" Sharif asked as she made her way to her desk, stepping carefully around a crate of athletic gear and a stack of books that still needed to be put away in the closet.

"We're responsible for our own boards."

"I would have thought the janitor would take care of that."

"We're always trying to save money," Jesslyn answered, kneeling down to pick up a misplaced paperback novel. She'd taught at this school, a small private school in Sharjah for four years now, and her classrooms were always warm, and downright sweltering in May, June and September.

Sharif's eyes narrowed. "Is that why it's a hundred degrees in here?"

She grimaced. So he'd noticed. "The air conditioner is on. Unfortunately, it doesn't seem to put out as much cool air as warm air." Taking a seat behind her desk, she prayed she looked more put together than she felt. "Is that why you're here? To make a list of our school's needs and then make a contribution?"

"If you help me, I'd be happy to make a contribution."

There it was, why he was here. He wanted her help. Jesslyn felt a heavy weight in her chest and realized she wasn't breathing.

Jesslyn forced herself to exhale and then inhale, trying to keep from dissolving into a state of panic. There was no reason to panic. She owed him nothing. Their relationship had ended nearly ten years ago.

Her attempt at cool, calm and collected ended when she caught sight of his expression. He was observing her intently, assessing her from head to toe.

Flushing, she shuffled papers nervously. "What kind of help do you need?"

"The kind you're good at." He was walking toward her, very slowly.

She tried to concentrate on what he was saying instead of his proximity, but he was coming too close, moving too quickly. "I'm a teacher, Sharif."

"Exactly." He stood over her, tall and imposing.

Had he always been this tall? "It's been a long time," she said.

"Nine years."

"Nine," she repeated, finding it nearly impossible to tear her gaze from his fiercely handsome features, features that had only grown harder and more beautiful over the years. The handsome prince had become a man. But then, he wasn't merely a prince anymore. He was Sarq's king.

With one hand she smoothed her skirt, feeling miserably dowdy, all too aware that her wardrobe and hairstyle were basic, practical, no nonsense. She'd never been a fashionista to start with, and nine years in the classroom had reduced both her wardrobe and her sense of style to nil.

She forced her lips into a professional smile. "After nine years, what could I possibly do to help you?"

"Teach," he answered simply.

She felt a funny flicker of emotion, an emotion that fell somewhere between unreasonable fury and tears. "That's right. I'm a teacher and you're a king."

Sharif's gray eyes held hers, his expression enigmatic. "You could have been my queen."

"You were never serious, Sharif."

A spark flared in his eyes, and explosive tension whipped the room. "Neither were you."

And just like that they were adversaries, on opposite sides of an insurmountable wall.

"Unfair and untrue," she said through gritted teeth, anger making her chest too hot and tight. "There was no room for me—" She broke off, unable and unwilling to continue. It was history, so long ago it shouldn't matter. The fact that they were even discussing events of nine years ago struck her as tragic, especially as she had someone else in her life, someone who mattered a great deal to her. "So what *really* brings you here, King Fehr?"

His jaw hardened and his narrowed gaze ruthlessly swept her, head to toe. "I've told you. You do. I've come to offer you a job."

He was serious, then. This was about a job. *Teaching.*

Heat rushed through her, heat that left her deeply shaken.

Swallowing, she looked up at him, her smile so hard it felt brittle even to her. "I have a job."

"Apparently not a very good one," he answered, indicating the old chalkboards and battered room fixtures.

She wouldn't stoop to his level, wouldn't let herself be ridiculed, bullied or criticized. "It's one I like very much, thank you."

"Would you feel better if I told you the position is just for the summer?"

Her chin tilted even more defiantly. "No."

"Why not?"

It was on the tip of her tongue to tell him that she didn't have to answer to him, she didn't owe him anything. But that was a pointless exercise. It wasn't even the past holding her back, it was the future. She had plans for the summer, a wonderful eight and a half weeks of gorgeous, lovely travel—two weeks to beaches in Australia's Queensland, ski slopes in New Zealand, and lots of museum and theater excursions highlighted by great food in Sydney, Melbourne and Auckland. "Because…no."

"You'd be back here before school started in September," Sharif persisted, his tone so cool and smooth and relentless that goose bumps peppered her flesh.

"You remind me of my students when they're not listening."

He just smiled, grimly. "You haven't even considered the proposal."

"There's nothing to consider," she countered, amazed at his arrogance. "I've plans that can't be changed. Not even for you."

She saw his eyes narrow at her tone. She hadn't meant to be sarcastic, but there was a definite edge in her voice, an edge due to her discomfort. She didn't like the way he was towering over her desk, issuing dictates as though he were in his palace instead of her classroom, didn't like the way he pushed, didn't like his disregard for her, her feelings or her interests. "I appreciate you thinking of me, and I thank you for the invitation, King Fehr, but the answer is no."

"I'll pay you twice your salary—"

"Stop!" Her voice rang out as she slapped a heavy textbook down on her desk. The book thudded loudly, echoing in the classroom. "This isn't about money. I don't care about money. I don't care if you were to pay me two thousand dollars a day! I'm not interested. Not interested. Understand?"

Silence descended, a silence that felt positively deafening.

But it wasn't her fault she lost her temper, she reminded herself. He wasn't listening. "I'm going on holiday," she added, squaring her shoulders, refusing to be intimidated, even as her gaze clashed with his. Their relationship ended years ago, and there was no reason to start anything again—professionally or personally. "I leave tonight."

His features hardened, his expression so flinty his cheekbones and jaw looked as though they'd been chiseled from stone. "You can go on holiday next summer. I need you."

Jesslyn couldn't stifle a hysterical laugh. "You *need me?* Oh, that's a good one, King Fehr. Very funny indeed."

He wasn't laughing. His brows flattened over glittering gray eyes. "Give me one good reason why you won't even consider the position."

"I can give you three," she answered, impatiently stacking the teacher editions on her desk, one on top of the other. "I've just finished a year of teaching and need a break. I've planned a wonderful holiday traveling in Australia and New Zealand and everything's paid for. And last, and perhaps most important, having once been your girlfriend I've no desire to be—"

Jesslyn wasn't able to finish the rest, drowned out by the blare of the school fire alarm.

It was a loud, piercing sound, and for a moment Jesslyn stood transfixed. Normally she'd snag her attendance book and swiftly march the students out, but there were no young charges to lead to safety.

The door to the classroom flew open and two hulking men appeared, dressed in dark clothes, their weapons cocked and ready. One of them spoke quickly, loudly to Sharif who just nodded and looked back at Jesslyn.

"Happen often?" he shouted over the deafening blare.

"No," she shouted back, reaching for her purse, briefcase and blazer, momentarily taken aback by the quick action of Sharif's security detail, but not totally surprised as Sharif had security even when they lived in London.

"I imagine it's a false alarm," she added distractedly. "One of those end-of-year student pranks the graduating seniors like to pull. But we still have to leave until the fire inspector gives us the okay to return."

She'd just lifted her blazer from the back of her chair when the ceiling sprinklers came on, drenching the classroom in a torrent of warm water.

Sharif grabbed her briefcase and purse from her desk. "Let's go."

The hallway connecting the classrooms was slick with water, and as they dashed down the hall they could hear sirens in the distance and a lot of yelling in Arabic.

By the time they reached the front steps of the main administrative building, the fire trucks were pulling into the parking lot and the rest of Sharif's security team, another half-dozen men, were on full alert.

As his men spotted Sharif they moved toward him, but Sharif quickly checked their progress.

Dr. Maddox, who'd been pacing the school's front steps,

rushed toward them. "I'm sorry," she said, wringing the hem of her skirt and then her hands. "I'm so terribly sorry about all this. We pride ourselves on our school and yet here you are, absolutely soaked—"

"We're all soaked," Sharif said, "and we'll dry." He glanced past her to the school where the firemen had gone to do a formal check to make sure there wasn't a fire anywhere. "Miss Heaton's classroom was drenched. Are all classrooms that wet?"

"I imagine they are. It's a new sprinkler system, put in this year on recommendation by our school board. And they work—" Dr. Maddox paused, pushed back wet gray hair from her forehead "—a little too well."

"But it's worth it if it'll save lives," Jesslyn interjected as she took her things from Sharif. "We can replace books and carpeting, and fortunately the school is insured. With nearly three months before classes resume, there's time to fix everything."

"Are you volunteering to give up your holiday, Miss Heaton?" Dr. Maddox asked irritably. "Because to get everything done, someone will have to be here overseeing the repairs."

"Miss Heaton has plans, I believe," Sharif answered smoothly, and turning his back on Dr. Maddox he focused his full attention on Jesslyn. "I'll walk you to your car."

"I don't have a car," she said, shouldering the strap of her purse. "I take a taxi home."

Sharif frowned. "But you drive."

"Cars are expensive, and I'm happy taking taxis. No one bothers me." And no one would, she knew, not in Sharjah.

Jesslyn loved her adopted country. Sharjah might not have the same glittering nightlife of Dubai or the mad hustle bustle of the business world, but it retained a charm and elegance not found so easily in Dubai's sleek skyscraper-studded skyline and artificial island paradise.

In her mind Sharjah was quieter, smaller, less splash and cash. She adored the stately palm-tree-lined boulevards and the handsome tall buildings in the center. It was always a pleasure to walk or take a taxi to wherever she needed to go. And she didn't have to worry about the parking, either. She felt welcome here. Welcome and wanted.

"I'll take you home, then," Sharif announced, and with a nod toward his guards, he indicated he was ready to leave. "My car is waiting just there."

Jesslyn had already spotted the limousine and two black escort vehicles, but she wasn't about to accept a ride. "I'd prefer to hail a taxi," she answered, with a swift glance at her wristwatch. "And if I leave now, I can just avoid the afternoon rush hour."

She's walking away.

Walking away from me.

Incredulous, King Sharif Fehr bit down so hard he felt as if he was choking on his own tongue, but it was that or say something he might regret.

Not that he thought he'd regret it.

In fact, right now he was certain he'd derive a great deal of pleasure from putting Jesslyn Heaton in her place.

"I shall take you," he repeated, teeth flashing in a barely civil smile. "I insist."

Her brown eyes lifted, met his. He saw her full lips compress, her mouth a dark rose.

Hot sparks lit her eyes. Leaning forward she whispered so only he could hear. "I do not work for you, King Fehr, nor am I one of your subjects. You can't insist. I'm afraid you forget, Your Highness, that you have no jurisdiction over me."

Once again she'd told him no. Once again she'd flat-out rejected him.

He frowned, trying to digest her rejection.

It'd been years since anyone had refused him so absolutely. People didn't say no to him. People needed him. People came to him wanting favors, assistance, support.

Studying her pale, oval-shaped face, he let his gaze drift from her dark, winged eyebrows to the heat in her warm eyes to the set of her firmly molded chin. He'd never noticed just how firm that chin was until now. He'd never noticed her backbone until now, either.

When he'd first known her she'd been a broken girl, literally broken from the accident that had taken his sisters. Jesslyn had been in the hospital, all white plaster and gauze and pins.

She wasn't broken anymore.

"You don't like me," he said, almost amused. On one hand he was angered by her cool dismissal, and on the other hand he was surprised and intrigued, which was a novelty in and of itself. As king of a Middle Eastern country enjoying its tenth year of peace and economic stability, these days he found himself surprised by little and intrigued by even less.

Jesslyn eyed him steadily, her feelings for him definitely mixed. "Perhaps it would be more accurate to say I don't trust you."

"Why on earth wouldn't you trust me?"

She again shouldered her purse, her damp coat dripping over her arm. "You're not the Sharif I knew. You're King Fehr."

"Jesslyn." His voice suddenly dropped, turned coaxing. He didn't like his integrity being questioned. "Obviously, I've offended you. That wasn't my intention. I've come to you to ask for help. At least let me explain."

She glanced toward his limousine and then his half-dozen men who stood at attention, their eyes shielded by dark glasses. "I'm catching a redeye flight tonight, and I'm going to be on that plane."

"So you'll let me drive you home?"

She turned her head, looked up at him, her damp dark hair forming soft ringlets around her face. "I'm going to be on that plane," she repeated.

He liked the way the dark-chestnut curls framed her pale face, liked the stubborn press of her lips and the defiant lift of her chin. "Then let me take you home."

CHAPTER TWO

AFTER giving Sharif's driver her address, Jesslyn placed her purse and briefcase on the floor and laid her damp coat on her damp lap as she tried to ignore the fact that Sharif was sitting so close.

Unfortunately, he was impossible to ignore. He was the kind of man who dominated a room, drawing light, attention, energy. And worse, sitting so close to him she could feel his warmth, smell a hint of his fragrance, and it threw her back to the past, filling her with memories of his skin. She loved his skin. He'd always known how to hold her.

Her heart turned over, and her fingers curled into her coat as the strangest pain shot through her.

Sorrow. Grief. Regret.

He was awakening memories and feelings she didn't want or need, memories and feelings of a past—a life—she'd accepted was gone.

"You don't look at me," he said, as the car started.

She couldn't exactly tell him that looking at him made her hurt worse. Made her realize all over again how foolish she'd been when she'd left him. She hadn't really meant to walk away, not forever. Instead she'd thought he would have come running after her, had hoped he would have pursued her, beg her to reconsider, pledge undying love.

"Endings are awkward. It was awkward then, and it's awkward now."

"But you're happier. Look at you. You're living your dream."

Her dream. She inhaled softly, a quick gasp of protest. She'd never dreamed of being single at her age. Her dream had always been to have a family, a family of her own. Having been raised by an elderly aunt after her parents' deaths—three years apart—made her realize how much she needed people to love and people to love her. Instead here she was still single, and still teaching other peoples' children.

"Yes," she agreed, hiding the pain his words caused her. "It's wonderful."

"I've never seen you this confident," he added.

Jesslyn glanced out the window and watched the fire trucks and school buildings fall away as the limousine exited the parking lot and pulled onto the street. "It's not hard being stronger or more confident," she said after a moment, turning to look at him. "All those years ago I was a different person."

He knew immediately what she alluded to. His eyes darkened. "It was a terrible accident."

She nodded, and suddenly the accident wasn't eleven years ago, but yesterday, and the loss was just as fresh. "I still dream about it sometimes," she said, knotting her hands, her fingers interlocking so tightly the tips of her fingers shone pink and the knuckles white. "I always wake up on impact. I wake up before I know what's happened."

Sharif didn't speak, and she fought the enormous heaviness bearing down on her chest. "But when I wake I know what happened."

"You weren't at the wheel."

"But Jamila did nothing wrong. No one in our car did anything wrong."

"That's why they're called accidents."

Tragedies, she whispered in her mind.

"Otherwise, you've healed," he said. "You're lucky."

His sisters hadn't been.

Hot tears stung her eyes, and Jesslyn swiftly reached up and brushed them away before they could fall. It'd been a long time since she'd talked about the accident, and still she carried the grief and loss in her heart. Jamila and Aman had been her best friends. She'd met them when she was ten, and they'd become instantly inseparable.

But the past was the past, she reminded herself, trying to focus on the present. She could only live right now, in the present time, a time where she could actually make a difference. "You've changed, too, but I suppose you had to, being a…"

"Yes?" he prompted when her voice faded away without finishing the thought.

Jesslyn shifted uncomfortably. "You know."

"But I don't. Why don't you tell me."

She didn't miss the ruthless edge in his voice, and suddenly she wished she'd never said anything at all. "You have to know you've changed," she said, dodging his question even as she looked at him, really looked at him and saw all over again how much harder, fiercer, prouder he'd become. Beautiful silver into steel.

"You don't like me now, though."

Her shoulders shifted. "I don't know you now."

"I'm still the same person."

But he wasn't, she thought, he wasn't the man she knew. He'd become something other, larger, more powerful, and more conscious of that power, too. "Maybe what I should say is that I don't see the man anymore, I see the king." She could see from the hardening of his expression that he didn't like what she'd said, so she hastily added, "But of course you've changed. You're not a young man anymore. You're now… what? Thirty-eight, thirty-nine?"

"Thirty-seven, Miss Heaton." He paused, his voice deepening. "And you're thirty-one."

Something in his voice made her look up, and when she did, she stared straight into his stunning silver-gray eyes, eyes she'd once found heartbreakingly beautiful.

Eyes that seemed to pierce her heart now.

The air left her in a rush, forcing her to take a quick breath and then another.

Her prince had become a king. Her Sharif had married and then been widowed. Her own life with him had been a lifetime ago.

"You're displeased with me, and yet it's the opposite for me. You're more than I remembered," he continued in the same deep, husky voice, "more confident. More beautiful. More of everything."

Once again her chest tightened, her heart feeling as mashed as a potato.

He made her feel too much. He made her remember everything.

Inexplicably she suddenly wanted to seize all the years back, the nine years she'd buried herself in good works and deeds, the years in higher-education courses and summer school and night school, arduous activities and pursuits designed to keep her from thinking or feeling.

Designed to keep her from regretting.

Prince Sharif Fehr, her Prince Sharif Fehr, her first lover, her only love, had married someone else only months after they broke off.

Shifting restlessly, she glanced out the window, saw they were less than a mile from her apartment and felt confusing emotions of disappointment and relief.

Soon he'd drop her off and be gone.

Soon she could be in control of her emotions again.

Sharif's gaze still rested on her face. "So tell me more about your school, your current job. Are you happy there? What is the faculty like?"

This Jesslyn could answer easily, with a clear conscience. "I love being a teacher. I always end up so attached to my students, and I still get a thrill teaching literature and history. And yes, the school is very different from the American School in London, and the American School in Dubai where I taught one year, but I have a lot more control over my curriculum here and I get to spend more time with my students, which is what I want."

"*Your* students," he repeated.

She smiled, finally able to breathe easier. Talking about teaching put her firmly back in control of her emotions, and she wanted to keep it that way. She *had* to keep it that way. "I do think of them as my kids, but I can't help it. I have such high hopes for each of them."

"If you love children so much, why don't you have any of your own?"

Immediately she was thrown back into inner chaos, her sense of calm and goodwill vanishing. *Did his mother never tell him? Did he still really not know?*

Her fingers balled into fists as she felt anger wash through her, anger toward his cold, manipulative mother, and anger toward Sharif. Sharif was supposed to have loved her. Sharif was supposed to have wanted her.

"Haven't met the right person," she answered tightly, looking into his face, seeing again the hard, carved features, the way his dark sleek hair touched his robe, and the shadow of a beard darkening his jaw.

That face…

His eyes…

Heat rushed through her, heat followed by ice because she could never have been his wife. She could never have been the one he married and cherished. She was, as his mother had put it so indelicately, a good-time girl. Someone frivolous and fun to pass the time with.

"You've never married?" he asked.

"No."

"I'm surprised. When you left all those years ago I was sure there was someone, or something, you wanted."

No, there was nothing else she wanted, but she hadn't known how to fight then. Hadn't known how to keep, protect, what she loved. "We're almost to my apartment," she said numbly, gesturing to the street.

"My girls need a teacher this summer. They're home from boarding school and lagging academically."

They were so close to her apartment, so close. Just another block and she could get out, run away, escape.

"I'll pay you three times your annual salary," he continued. "In ten weeks you could make three times what you make in a year."

She wanted to cover her ears. She didn't want to know about the job, didn't want to hear about his children—children he'd had with his fabulously wealthy and stunningly beautiful princess—or their academic deficiencies. "I'm going on holiday, Sharif. I leave tonight."

"I thought you cared about children. I thought you wanted what's best for children."

But these weren't her children and she wasn't going to get involved. "I've plans," she repeated woodenly.

"Plans you could change," Sharif said so pleasantly that Jesslyn felt a prickle beneath her skin. She didn't trust Sharif when he used that tone of voice.

But then, she didn't trust Sharif at all.

Maybe that's because she didn't know the real Sharif. The Sharif she'd dated and adored would have never married a Dubai princess just to further his career and kingdom, much less married that princess less than six months after they'd broken up. But that's what he'd done. His wedding had been covered by virtually every glossy magazine in the UK, and in every article about the wedding, below every photograph the caption read, Prince Sharif Fehr Marries Princess Zulima of Dubai after a Year-Long Engagement.

Year-long engagement?

Impossible. Six months before the wedding Jesslyn was still dating Sharif.

The car had stopped but Jesslyn didn't wait for the driver to appear. Gathering her things, she flung the door open. "Good luck, Sharif," she said, sliding her legs out and standing. "Goodbye."

And Jesslyn rushed to the entrance of her building, racing to the lobby and the entrance as though her life depended on it. And in a way it did, because Sharif would annihilate her if she gave him the chance.

She wouldn't give him the chance.

In her apartment Jesslyn forced herself to focus on finishing packing. She wasn't going to think about Sharif, not again, not anymore. She had more pressing things to think about, things like her passport, sunscreen and extra batteries for her digital camera.

Her trip required more luggage than she would normally take, but ten weeks and radically different climates meant swimsuits and shorts for the warmer temperatures in Northern Queensland, slacks and elegant blouses for the big Australian cities, and then down jackets and fleece-lined boots for the ski slopes in New Zealand.

She was just zipping the biggest suitcase closed when her phone rang.

"Hello," Jesslyn said, answering the phone as she dragged her big suitcase into the hall.

It was Sharif. "I've news I thought you'd want to hear."

She straightened, leaving the suitcase by her door. "I've a million things to do before the flight, Sharif—"

"It concerns one of your students." He hesitated. "Perhaps you'd like to sit down."

"Why?" she asked suspiciously. "What's happened?"

"I just had a call from Mahir, my chief of security, and he's on his way to the Sharjah police station. They've arrested one of the school students for vandalizing the campus this afternoon. It was thought that I'd want to press charges."

She walked into the small living room and leaned against the back of her couch. "Are you pressing charges?"

"Mahir is handling the matter."

"But what does that mean?"

"It means that Mahir makes those decisions. He's responsible for my security."

Jesslyn's hand shook as she held the phone to her ear. "Which student?"

"Aaron."

Aaron?

She frowned, bewildered. It couldn't have been Aaron. Aaron wasn't like that. Aaron didn't pull pranks. He was a good kid, a serious kid, almost nerdy. "He didn't do it," she said faintly, folding one arm across her chest to fight the icy weakness in her limbs. "He wouldn't pull the fire alarm. He wouldn't."

"They caught him running from the scene."

"It just…it's not…it's not what he'd do…" And then her voice faded as she pictured the small gift Aaron had brought her earlier that day, after school had ended. She could see the white paper, the colorful silk ribbon. She'd left it on her desk when the sprinklers turned on.

"Wait." Jesslyn chewed on her mouth. "He *was* on campus after school, but that's because he had a goodbye gift for me. He's moving back to the States."

"Which probably explains his stunt," Sharif answered. "I may be in my thirties but I remember being a teenager, and kids do things to get attention—"

"So you will forgive him?" she interrupted eagerly.

"If that's all he did, the punishment would be light. But he didn't just pull the fire alarm. Apparently he also broke into the vice principal's office and stole copies of exams from a filing cabinet. Dr. Maddox intends to prosecute." He paused. "She's asked me to press charges as well."

"Don't," she whispered.

"It's not just me, though. The police are involved, as well. Theft is a serious crime."

Swallowing, Jesslyn felt her heart lodge up in her throat. There was absolutely no way Aaron did what they said he'd done. "Sharif, he didn't steal anything. He brought me a gift. It's on my desk. We can go to school, retrieve that—"

"A janitor spotted the boy running away."

"He was running to get home, not running away!"

"Jesslyn, there's nothing we can do right now."

She continued to shake her head. It wasn't true. She wouldn't believe it until she talked to Aaron herself. "I must see him. Take me to the jail, Sharif, please take me right now."

"They won't allow you to see him. They've called his parents, but the police must finish questioning him first."

Jesslyn closed her eyes and drew a deep breath. "You're telling me they won't let you in? You're telling me they won't let Sheikh Sharif Fehr in to see a child?"

He sighed. *"Jesslyn."*

Her heart was racing so hard it hurt. "You can get me in to see him, Sharif."

Silence stretched over the phone line. "I know how protective you are of your students—"

"Sharif. Please." Her voice broke. "Please."

Again silence answered her request, a silence that just grew longer, heavier until she heard him sigh again. "I'll send my car for you, *laeela*, but understand this is serious. Understand he's being formally charged."

Sharif's car arrived for her within the hour, and while sitting in the back of the dark Mercedes sedan, Jesslyn replayed the afternoon scene with Aaron in her mind again and again.

He'd been upset when he gave her the gift, touchingly emotional. But had he been acting? Or was it a ruse? The gift of the present an opportunity to cover his crime?

She didn't know and still couldn't decide when the car pulled up in front of the station. Sharif was already there, appearing from the police station to meet her at the car.

Jesslyn had changed before the car arrived for her, selecting a conservative, loose-fitting chocolate linen dress with long sleeves and a simple skirt. It was a dress she wore when she didn't want to draw attention to her figure as she knew both men and women traditionally wore robes to hide the body. Sharif, she noticed, had changed, too.

He offered his hand to her as she stepped from the car. She didn't want to take it but couldn't refuse him, not with so many of his men watching.

Reluctantly she put her hand in his, felt his fingers wrap around hers.

"You're cold," Sharif said, as she stepped onto the pavement.

"I'm nervous," she confessed, worriedly glancing up into the sky. It was beginning to grow dark. Her flight would board in a little more than three hours.

His expression sharpened. "You think he did do it, then?"

"No." She shot Sharif a desperate look. "I'm certain he didn't, but I'm afraid for him. If his parents have been called they'll be upset. He'll be upset." She shook her head. "Oh, I wish none of this had happened."

"But it has. Now we just have to see what the situation is."

They headed for the police station's entrance, Sharif's security detail surrounding them. The bodyguards were everywhere tonight—in front of them, behind them, beside them, and while the security had been with them earlier today, it unnerved her tonight.

Or maybe it was Sharif who was unnerving her by walking so close.

Inside the station Sharif was received with great respect. The entire station staff, from desk sergeants to detectives to the chief of police, made a point of welcoming Sharif, and after ten minutes of warm greetings, the police chief and Sharif stepped aside to have a private talk.

Jesslyn waited anxiously for them to return, praying that Sharif could convince the police chief to let her see Aaron. Finally Sharif summoned her. "We have been granted permission to speak to your student, and you may ask him whatever you'd like, but you must understand they've a good case against him." He looked at her, his gray gaze shuttered. "Jesslyn, the consequences would be severe."

Another one of her fears.

Sharjah was Jesslyn's second home and she was loath to criticize any of it, much less the government and the very good police force that worked so hard to protect both Western expats and Arab citizens, but there were dangers here, particularly for careless or reckless American teenagers who failed to heed the law.

Fortunately, teenage boys didn't go to prison for stealing or destroying private property, but the punishment wouldn't be light and could be emotionally scarring.

"I understand," she whispered.

They were escorted to a small office, and while they waited for Aaron, Jesslyn nervously twisted the ring on her third finger, a ring given to her by her grandmother when she'd turned eighteen. She'd always called it her good luck ring and she played with it now, praying for good fortune.

The door finally opened and the police chief appeared, escorting young Aaron.

She was devastated that he was handcuffed, but before she could say a word the police chief removed the boy's handcuffs and pulled out a chair for him.

Aaron tumbled into the chair, his head hung so low he couldn't see anything but the floor.

"Aaron." She said his name softly.

His head lifted slightly but she could at least see his face.

He'd been crying. His cheeks still bore traces of tears and his nose was red and shiny. "Miss Heaton," he choked.

Her heart contracted. He'd always been one of her favorite students and to see him like this made her feel absolutely desperate. She didn't even know what to say.

As if he could read her mind he shook his head. "I didn't do it, Miss Heaton. I swear I didn't. It wasn't me. It wasn't."

She wanted to comfort him but didn't know how, not when she knew she couldn't reassure him that everything would be fine. It was impossible to promise him anything. "They found you on campus," she said carefully. "They said they caught you running."

He groaned. "I was on campus because I'd taken you a gift."

"But why were you running?"

"I was late getting home. I didn't want my father to know I'd missed the school bus."

She bit her bottom lip, bit down to keep her emotions in check. "Apparently someone saw you running from the office—"

"Not me." He looked at her, eyes brilliant with unshed tears. "And maybe someone was running from the office, and maybe someone had stolen papers, but it wasn't me."

Sharif glanced from Jesslyn to the boy. "What do you know about the papers?"

Aaron's jaw hardened and yet his eyes were filled with pain. "I can't tell you."

"Why not?"

"I can't." And then he dropped his head, his shoulders slumping.

Jesslyn moved forward on her chair. "Aaron, if you know who did it, it would save you from serious trouble."

"And if I tell you, he'd be in serious trouble and I can't do that. His mom is already dying—" Aaron broke off on a soft sob. His head hung so low that a tear fell and dropped onto the floor.

Jesslyn inhaled sharply, knowing who he was referring to. Only one boy in the upper grades had a mom dying, and it was Will. Will McInnes. Will's mother had just been moved to a hospice facility, and Will's father was coping by drinking too much and then terrorizing the children.

She turned to Sharif. "I need to talk to you." They stepped out of the room and stood in the narrow hall.

She told Sharif everything, about Will and Aaron's friendship, how Aaron's parents had done their best to include Will in their family life as Will's family life unraveled. "Will is barely getting by," she said, her eyes stinging. "He's had such a hard year, and the only person who's really been there for him is Aaron. And now Aaron's leaving."

"But why steal?" Sharif replied. "And why pull the alarm? He flooded the school, which destroyed nearly every classroom. He's going to have a criminal record and his family will have to pay for the damage, damage that will be in the thousands."

"Then we can't tell anyone it was Will. We'll deal with Will ourselves."

"*We* will?" Sharif repeated.

"We *have* to. His dad has a fierce temper. I can't bear to think what he'd do to Will if he found out about this afternoon."

"So you'll let Aaron, who just might be innocent, pay for the crime instead?"

Jesslyn could picture Aaron in her mind, could see his ashen face and the tear that trembled on his lower lash before spilling and falling to the cement in a wet plop. "No. We get Aaron off."

"Jesslyn."

She lifted her shoulders. "He didn't do it, he can't be punished. Will did do it—"

"So he should be punished."

"But he's a child, Sharif, in the process of losing his mother. She doesn't have long. Not even a month. It's all about pain management for her now, and imagine what Will is going through, imagine how helpless he feels, imagine his rage."

Sharif gazed down into Jesslyn's upturned face.

It wasn't hard for him to imagine what Will was going through, he thought, nor was it difficult to imagine the grief, the fury, the pain as his children had lost their mother just three years ago. Unlike Will's mother, Zulima's death had been sudden, and there had been no time for goodbyes. One moment she was resting in her room after her cesarian section and the next gone, dying from a blood clot.

"My children also lost their mother," he said roughly. "It's not fair for children to lose their mother so early in life, but it does happen."

"But if we can do something, change something, make it more fair—"

"We can't."

"We can." She took his arm with both her hands, pleading. "Please, Sharif. Please help me help these children. Get Aaron released. Help me find Will, let me speak with him. Perhaps we can get the papers back, get them returned."

"You're asking for a miracle."

Her hands gripped his arm tighter. "Then give me a miracle, Sharif. If anyone can make this happen, you can. You can do anything. You always could."

Sharif stared down into her upturned face, fascinated by the pink bloom in her cheeks and dusky rose of her lips. Emotion lit her features; passion and conviction darkened her eyes.

She looked at him with such faith. She looked at him with

all the confidence in the world. She was so certain he could do all this, certain he *would*.

Her fierce faith in him made his breath catch. Her fire made something in his chest hurt. In all his years of marriage Zulima had never once looked at him that way.

"I'd have to pull a million strings," he said, even as his brain already worked through the possibilities of getting Aaron released and Will sorted out. It'd be complicated, far from easy, but he did know the right people and he could put in calls...

"Then pull them," she answered, dark-brown brows knitting.

"It's more than a snap of my fingers," he answered, intrigued by this Jesslyn Heaton standing in front of him. This woman was neither naive nor helpless. In fact, this Jesslyn Heaton had grown into something of a warrior and a defender of the young.

"I understand that, but I love these kids and I know these kids. I've taught them for years. Will's acting out and Aaron's protecting him, and yet in the end, they're just boys. Just children."

He'd never heard any other woman but Jesslyn speak with so much feeling, but that was the kind of woman Jesslyn had always been. From the time he met her she wore her heart on her sleeve, and eleven years after first meeting her he realized her heart was still there for everyone to see.

Impulsively he reached out and touched her smooth, flushed cheek. Her skin was warm and surprisingly soft. He dropped his hand quickly and hardened himself to her pleas. "It'd be better to let the boys take the blame and accept the consequences. That way they'd learn from this."

"Maybe," she argued, "maybe in other circumstances they would learn. But not now, not when Will's mom is nearly gone." She held his gaze, held it long, her expression beseeching. "Do this for me, Sharif, do this and I will do whatever I can for you."

His pulse quickened. His interest sharpened. "What exactly are you offering?"

Shadows chased through her eyes, shadows of worry and mistrust, and then she shook her head and her expression cleared. "You need me," she said firmly. "You came to me today because you wanted me for the summer. Well…" her voice wavered for a moment before she pressed on. "Help me sort the boys out, and then I will help you for the next two weeks—"

"No. Not two weeks. The summer."

The clouds were back in her eyes, and some of the pink faded from her cheeks. "But the trip. My trip…"

"So what do you want more? Your holiday or your children rescued?"

She stared up at him, her lips pressing grimly, and he could see her thoughts, could see her frustration and resentment but also the realization that he alone could do what she needed, wanted, done.

"You love children," he added quietly, surprised by the sudden tightness in his chest. Pressure and pain. "And my children need you. My children need you as much as these two."

And still she looked up at him, weighing, judging, deciding. She didn't trust him, he could see it in her eyes and that alone made him want to drag her back to Sarq. She was the one who had betrayed him, not the other way around. She had no right to mistrust him. He was the one who'd been deceived.

He was the one who was owed not just an apology but the truth. And he'd have the truth. After nine years he was going to have that truth.

Jesslyn touched the tip of her tongue to her upper lip. "So, if I give you the summer, you will make this problem go away?"

"The entire summer," he said.

If Jesslyn felt any trepidation she didn't show it. Instead her eyes flashed and her chin jutted up. "We have a deal, then?"

His lashes dropped and his gaze drifted slowly across her face. "Your head for his?" He paused, considered her. "I don't know if it's fair, but I'll take it."

CHAPTER THREE

AN HOUR and a half later Sharif stood in the shadows of the McInnes house and listened to Jesslyn give Will McInnes the talking to of a lifetime.

If Sharif hadn't heard Jesslyn's severe tone, he wouldn't have known she had it in her. But apparently she did, for she let Will know in no uncertain terms that she knew what he had done, and he was in serious trouble.

Not only did she want all the stolen tests back—tonight—but he should also consider himself on probation. If he so much as broke a pencil or stepped on a bug, she'd have his head. That is, if she didn't go to his father right now and tell him what Will had done this afternoon.

When Jesslyn returned to the car twenty minutes later, she carried a stack of exams and handed them to Sharif before getting in the car. "There. Yours. Mission completed."

"You weren't easy on him," he said.

Seated in the car Jesslyn sighed and rubbed the back of her neck, her head aching. The day felt positively endless. "No, I wasn't. I was angry and disappointed, and I let him know it."

One of the guards closed the door behind her. "Is that why he was crying when he brought you the tests?" Sharif asked.

Her lips pursed. "He was crying because I told him if he ever did anything stupid like that again that you'd have him arrested and thrown into prison, and who knew what would happen to his family."

Sharif's eyebrows lifted. "You didn't."

"I did." She wrinkled her nose as she reflected on what she'd said and done. "Was that so terrible?"

"Not if you can save him from a life of crime."

"My thoughts exactly." She turned to look out the tinted window. The limousine was again winding through the quiet downtown streets, but this time they were heading the opposite direction from which they'd come, away from her apartment and on toward Dubai. "We're not going back to my apartment?"

"No. We're going to stay at a hotel in Dubai tonight and then fly out in the morning."

"But my things…"

"I've taken care of that. A courier picked your suitcase and travel bag up from your apartment. You'd left both by the front door."

She shot him a cool glance. "You left nothing to chance."

The corner of his mouth lifted, but it wasn't much of a smile. "I try not to."

So that was that, she thought. There'd be no holiday this summer. Instead she was going back to work.

Tired tears started to come, but she squeezed her eyes closed, forced them away, refusing to feel sorry for herself. She'd done the right thing. She knew she had. How could she possibly have gone on holiday when Aaron would have faced horrible fines and stiff charges? Better to miss some beaches and skiing and live with a clear conscience.

"You must be hungry," Sharif said, his voice deep in the

car's dark interior. "It's nearing eleven, and I can't imagine you've eaten since noon."

"No, but I haven't been hungry. Too many emotions," she answered, sinking back deeper against the impossibly soft leather seat. She was tired and thirsty and virtually numb from the roller-coaster day.

When she'd woken up this morning she'd thought she would be flying to Brisbane tonight. Instead the plane had taken off without her and she was facing the prospect of a long summer in Sarq.

The thought alone sent prickles of fresh panic up and down her spine.

How could she do this? How could she spend ten weeks with Sharif and his family? The fact that he was widowed changed nothing for her.

"I know nothing about this job I've accepted," she said. "You'll have to tell me about your children. How many…their names, their ages, as well as your objectives."

"I will," he answered. "But first things first, and that's a proper dinner, because I know you—you need to eat. You always skimp meals to get things done, but in the end, it backfires. You just end up irritable."

"I don't."

"You do. And you are already. You should see your face. You're famished and exhausted."

She bit back her immediate retort. It wouldn't help to get into a hissing contest with Sharif. The fact was, they were going to spend a considerable amount of time together. Better to try to get along with him than become adversaries. "So, distract me from my hunger. Tell me something about your family. How many children will I be teaching?"

"Three."

"Boys and girls, all boys…?"

"All girls." His expression never outwardly changed, but Jesslyn sensed tension and didn't know why or what it was.

"They're bilingual?" she asked, knowing her Arabic would get her by on market day but wouldn't be considered proper Arabic by any stretch of the imagination.

"Yes, but you'll discover all that tomorrow when we head home."

Home. His home. Sarq. A country she'd visited only once, and very briefly, to attend Aman's funeral. She'd flown in and out the same day, and in her grief, she remembered nothing but the heat. It was summer after all and hot, so very very hot.

But they weren't in Sarq yet. No, they were heading for the glossy and busy city-state of Dubai.

A 200-year-old city, once populated by pirates and smugglers, today Dubai was a cosmopolitan melting pot, teeming with more foreigners than locals. The city had blossomed overnight with the discovery of oil and now had so much money that the powers that be kept coming up with the most interesting ways to put it all back into the country and boost tourism. Jesslyn hadn't quite gotten used to the idea of man-made islands shaped like the world, or the snow ski facility in the desert. There were already plans underway for a huge theme park called Dubailand, along the lines of Disneyland and even an underwater hotel.

Dubai Creek ran through the middle of the city-state with the business district Deira to the east, and Bur Dubai, the commercial and historic district, to the west.

But the driver wasn't going to Deira or Bur Dubai, he was destined for Jumeriah Beach, the playland for the rich, royal and beautiful.

Despite living in the Emirates for six years Jesslyn had

spent very little time at Jumeriah Beach's posh waterfront resorts. For one, you couldn't even get into some of the hotels unless you were a hotel guest, and "treating" oneself to a night at the Burj Al Arab, reportedly the most luxurious hotel in the world, wasn't in the budget, not when rooms started at $1,280. But obviously that wasn't a problem for a man with Sharif's wealth.

"We're eating here?" she asked Sharif as the car turned into the hotel's private drive.

"And staying here. I've my own suite reserved for my exclusive use."

"That's nice."

He merely smiled at her, the smile of a king who'd become used to having his way.

As they stepped from the car, Jesslyn felt as if she'd entered a production of *Arabian Nights*: gilded doors magically opened, overhead lights dimmed, lush green fronds parted.

The uniformed staff scrambled to assist Sharif, and while Jesslyn knew hotel staff were exceptionally attentive in Dubai, she personally found the attention overwhelming. There were too many people, too much bowing, too much of everything.

"You'll have your own suite," Sharif said. "And the hotel manager has promised to see you there and make sure you've everything you need."

Jesslyn glanced around. "My luggage—"

The hotel manager nodded. "It's already there, ma'am."

While Sharif took one elevator, she took another, escorted by the hotel manager and a young woman in a fashionable robe and veil. The hotel manager described the hotel, explained where everything was, including the numerous restaurants and lounges. "You'll have your own butler," he added, gesturing to the veiled young woman, "and anything you should need will be taken care of. Also, you will be dining with His Highness in thirty minutes. Meena will escort you to the restaurant where you'll be joining Sheikh Fehr."

Jesslyn barely had time for a quick bath, a change into a simple black skirt topped by a soft silk pearl-gray blouse and a quick brush of her hair before it was time to go.

She followed the robed woman back to the elevator where they went to a lower level, transferred to a different elevator, which went straight to the restaurant at the very top of the luxurious hotel.

Jesslyn had to skirt a group of robed men who were in animated discussion. She caught bits and pieces of the conversation—impossible not to as they were talking quite loudly—and discovered their conversation had to do with Sheikh Fehr. Apparently two or more of the men had daughters and each father was quite adamant that it was his daughter who would be marrying King Fehr next September.

Jesslyn froze and stiffened as though she'd just been doused with a bucket of ice water.

Was Sharif getting married again? Were plans in the works for another Dubai princess?

Her head practically throbbed. Jesslyn put a hand to her temple, closed her eyes, wondering all over again just what kind of personal hell she'd agreed to. Tragically, she had no one else to blame for her situation. She'd agreed to this scenario. Had offered herself up.

Her ridiculous morals and values. Her ridiculous Joan of Arc complex!

One day she'd wise up. One day she'd put herself first, protect herself first.

"Headache?" a deep voice murmured at her elbow. Lifting her head, Jesslyn looked up into Sharif's face.

The lashes fringing his silver eyes were thick and black. Strong cheekbones jutted above an equally strong jaw.

"Terrible," she admitted, but unwilling to tell him that he was the source of her tension.

"Food will help and they have our table waiting."

Sharif signaled to the maître d' that they were ready, and immediately the host showed them to a prime window table with a view of the entire city where skyscrapers glittered in every direction.

Sharif ordered several appetizers to be brought right away as well as platters for dinner. "Eat," Sharif said when the first of the appetizers arrived, pushing the small plates of seasoned meat, fish and assorted flat breads toward her. "You'll feel better."

But eating in front of Sharif was almost impossible. Even though the dishes were superbly prepared, chewing and swallowing required a Herculean effort, and after a few more bites of food Jesslyn gave up.

Sharif had watched her attempt to eat and now observed her pushing her food around her plate. "Have you developed one of those eating disorders? You never had a problem with food before."

Jesslyn was grateful to drop the pretense. "It's been a long day and a hard day. I thought I'd be on a plane right now and instead…" Her voice drifted off and, looking across the table at Sharif, she gave her head a slight, bemused shake. "It's hard to take in, hard to accept."

Just saying the words filled her with fury and resentment. Sharif could have helped her without insisting she give up her holiday. He could have helped her just because he was in a position to be able to help.

"You're upset because I won," he said, his tone deceptively mild.

She turned her head, gave him a long, level look. "Is that what this is to you? A competition? Or better yet, a battle where one person must win and the other loses?"

The edge of his generous mouth curved, and yet his gaze was hard, hot, sharp, and he looked at her so intensely that she felt bolts of electricity shoot through her.

"You haven't yet learned that everything in life is a competition?" he drawled, his deep voice pitched low, his tone lazy, almost indulgent. "Life is just one endless battle after another. It's all about power. It's nothing but a quest for control."

The chemistry between them had always been strong, and even though nearly a decade had passed since she'd last seen him, Jesslyn felt wildly, painfully aware of Sharif.

"Is that what being a king has taught you?"

He suddenly leaned forward, close enough that she could see the sparks of fire and ice in his eyes. "It's what being a man has taught me."

She didn't know if it was his tone or his words but she shifted nervously, strangely self-conscious. Sharif had never made her feel this way before. Anxious. Unsettled. Undone. But then, he'd never been an adversary before and yet somehow it's what he'd become.

Winners and losers, she silently repeated as she crossed her legs beneath the table and accidentally touched his knee with her own. Abruptly she drew back, but not before heat washed through her, heat and embarrassment and a painful awareness.

Their table was too small.

The dining room was too dark.

The atmosphere too charged.

Fortunately just then more food arrived, plates and platters and bowls. Jesslyn thought the food would be a distraction and Sharif would now eat and she'd have a moment to gather her composure. But Sharif threw her all over again with his command.

"You'll serve," he said with such authority that she immediately gritted her teeth.

"Has something happened to your hands?" she flashed, unable to control her burst of temper and defiance.

"You know it's the custom for the woman to serve the man."

"If she has a relationship with or to him. But I am not yours. I don't belong to you—"

"But you do work for me," he interjected softly. "And as one that is now in my employ, it would be proper for you to serve me."

Her chin jerked up and she stared at him in mute fury. He was enjoying this, she thought. He enjoyed having power over her. "Why exactly did you come looking for me today?"

"I needed your help."

But it wasn't just that. It was more than that. She knew it was more because this wasn't the Sharif she'd known. This wasn't a man she'd want to know. "For what?"

He sighed. "You already know this. My children need a tutor. I want you to be their tutor—"

"Then don't treat me like a second-class citizen," she interrupted. "I agreed to teach your children this summer but that doesn't make me your servant or part of the royal staff, and it doesn't mean I'll wait on you or any other member of the royal family."

He held her gaze, his own silver eyes glittering with heat and an emotion she couldn't discern. "Did I upset you by not saying please?"

It was all she could do not to dump her glass of water over his arrogant head as she bit back one angry retort after another. Battling to control her temper, she looked away, out the window to the sparkling lights of the city as it curved to meet the dark sea. A helicopter buzzed past the window on its way to the hotel's landing pad.

"You upset me," she said at length, "by asking me to do something you would have never asked me to do ten years ago." She drew an unsteady breath. "Ten years ago you would have served me."

"We were in London then," he answered.

Her lips lifted in a hard bitter smile. "And you weren't the sheikh." Her head turned and she met his gaze once more. "Isn't that right? This is back to your new philosophy on winning and losing and everything in life being a battle for control."

Sharif reached for the tongs on one of the platters and served himself a generous portion of the lamb and then a scoop of the seafood-laced rice. "There," he said, pushing the bowl of rice toward her. "Consider that a victory. You've won that round."

Jesslyn blinked, her chest hot with bitter emotion. Where had the old Sharif gone, the one who'd once been so kind, so relaxed, so thoughtful?

Shifting in her seat, she accidentally bumped into his leg again beneath the table, his body big, hard, warm, and she nearly ran. She couldn't do this. Couldn't sit here and play nice, not when she remembered how it'd been between them, how he'd once been with her.

She realized that for her the attraction hadn't gone. The old desire hadn't died, and Sharif of ten years ago flashed through her mind—long hair, faded tattered jeans, beach flip-flops on his feet.

As if he knew what she was thinking he said, "I'm not a heartless ogre. I'm not cruel. I care very much about duty, family, responsibility."

Words he would never have used ten years before, at least not like that. From the first time she'd met him, he'd been concerned about his family, concerned about peoples' feelings. He would never have run roughshod over anyone.

Painful memories returned, memories of them as they'd once been—arm in arm walking through Hyde Park, laughing, talking, oblivious to the prince's security detail tailing them everywhere.

Back then Sharif had lived as though he wasn't royal, as though he had only himself to answer to.

He was wrong. And they both knew that. But they could pretend, and they did. For the two and a half years they were together, they pretended….

With an effort she swallowed around the funny lump in her throat. "Now tell me about your girls, their school, everything. Why are you so concerned about them? What is it you want me to do?"

He made a rough sound. "Give me a miracle."

She frowned, not understanding. "What does that mean?"

Sharif didn't immediately answer. Instead he toyed with his spoon, his gaze fixed on a distant point across the restaurant. "I don't actually know what the problem is," he said after a moment. "The girls apparently had considerable problems this year at school, problems I wasn't aware of until they returned home for the summer. The headmistress sent word that it had been a difficult year and she wasn't sure she could have them back, at least, not all of them."

He set the spoon down, pushed it away, his eyes shadowed. "I don't want the girls split up. They've already lost their mother. They shouldn't lose each other."

Jesslyn nodded slightly. She totally agreed with him on that. "Did the headmistress give any specifics about the 'difficult' year? Were the girls struggling academically or was it something else?"

"I've looked at their end-of-year marks and they are down across the board, but it's their conduct marks that trouble me. My daughters aren't spoiled princesses. They're good girls. Polite children. And yet it seems the school…the teachers… have come to view them as troubled."

"Troubled?"

He took a quick rough breath, as though the entire subject was so painful he could barely endure it. "The youngest had the worst marks. She essentially failed everything. She's the one the school isn't sure should return."

Jesslyn waved off the waiter who was trying to refill her water. "Perhaps it isn't the right school for the girls."

"They've been there for nearly two years."

"Not every school is right for every child."

"My wife attended the same school. It was her desire they go there."

"How old are your children?"

"Takia is five, Saba is six and Jinan, the eldest, is seven," Sharif answered.

"They're babies!"

"My wife went away to boarding school early, too."

Jesslyn had also gone to boarding school in England, but she'd never enjoyed it, never felt happy about the long school term and the all-too-brief summer and winter holidays. She'd also been terribly homesick at first, but she'd adapted. But then again, she'd been quite a bit older, almost nine when she'd first gone away. And she hadn't been grieving the loss of a mother, either.

"Maybe they're too young," she said carefully. "Or maybe it's too much, too soon after the loss of their mother."

Sharif nodded, jaw flexing. "If that were the case they would be happy now that they're home. But they're not. They're still quite withdrawn. It's as if they've become someone else's children."

"Maybe it's not an academic issue at all."

"I wondered the same thing myself, so I invited a doctor, a specialist in children's mental health issues, to come meet them, spend the day with them, and the doctor said that children go through different adjustment periods and that eventually they'll be fine."

Jesslyn heard the tension and frustration in Sharif's voice. He genuinely cared about his girls. He wanted to help them. He just didn't know how.

He said as much when he continued speaking. "That's why I've come to you. You were always so good with children, even back when you'd just started your teacher training in London. I thought that if anyone could help them, it'd be you."

"Sharif, you know I'm not a therapist, I'm a teacher."

"Yes, and I need you to teach them. Takia can't return with her sisters if she doesn't make up missed and failed coursework, and the other two are struggling in several subjects. You're to teach all of them. They will attend lessons with you every day. I've converted the palace library into a classroom and purchased all the necessary textbooks."

"I haven't taught children as young as yours in years," she reminded him. "My specialty is older children, middle schoolers and high school students, and the curriculum is American based, not UK—"

"That's fine. I've bought teacher's editions, and should you find you require something else, materials, computers, an assistant to help you, just let me know and it's yours."

Why did his reassurance not make her feel better? Why did

that niggle of doubt within her just grow? Was it because elementary education wasn't her area, or because she was afraid of failing when it came to teaching Sharif's children?

"Sharif, I just want to make sure you understand that in this instance, I am not the best teacher for the job. I spend my days teaching literature, grammar, social studies to eleven-through-fourteen-year-olds. I don't teach how to read but how to interpret literary themes, how to deconstruct plot structure, character and conflict." Swallowing quickly she looked up into his eyes. "There are a thousand teachers in Europe more qualified than me—"

"But none more suitable," he answered, leaning forward to touch the back of her hand.

It was a light touch and yet the brush of his fingers across her skin made her breath catch and her belly knot. His touch was still familiar, achingly familiar. For years he had no place in her heart, her mind or her life, and yet in less than twelve hours he'd changed all that.

"What makes me so suitable?" she asked, her voice suddenly husky, colored with emotions and desire she hadn't even known she still could feel. Immediately she fought back, reminding herself, he isn't yours anymore. And you're not his.

But that didn't seem to matter right now, not when she was awash in emotions, stirred by desire. It'd been so easy to be his. It'd felt absolutely natural. And she hadn't known then that what they had was rare and magical. She hadn't known she would never feel that way about anyone again.

Sharif stared across the room, off into the distance, his eyes so striking, his silver-gray irises framed by the densest black lashes with black winged eyebrows beneath a strong forehead. He was her Valentino of the desert.

"There are advantages to being king," he said at last,

speaking slowly, thoughtfully. "It didn't take me long to appreciate those advantages—everyone bows to you, acquiescing to keep you happy. I'm surrounded by people desperate to please me."

He paused, frowned, before continuing. "It's taken me longer to understand the disadvantages. No one wants to earn my disapproval. No one wants to lose a job, a connection, a reward. So people are afraid to tell me unpleasant things and bad news, even if it happens to be the truth."

He turned now to look at her. "Maybe once I wanted that blind obedience, the adoration of my people, but it was a mistake. What I really needed were people who'd give me the truth." His expression shifted, growing troubled and remote. "*Truth*. Whatever it is."

Truth, she repeated silently, mesmerized by the shadows in his gaze. Those shadows hadn't been there when she knew him. When they'd been together, he'd been so bold, so confident, so…free.

But that wasn't the Sharif sitting before her now. No, this man had the weight of the world on his shoulders, weight and worry and a hundred different concerns.

"It hasn't been easy, I take it," she said, remembering how she and Sharif had once loved their evenings and weekends, time for just the two of them, time for long walks and talks followed by a stop at the corner video store and then Chinese or curry take-out. They used to hole up in her apartment and sit on her bed and eat Kung Pao chicken with chopsticks and kiss and laugh.

And laugh.

Looking at Sharif she wondered when he'd last laughed. For that matter, when had she?

But maybe that was all part of growing up. Maybe one

became a full-fledged adult and let all those romantic dreams go....

"I'm not complaining," he answered. "I love my country. I love my children. But nothing is easy, no. There are always compromises. Sacrifices. But you've had those, too, I'm sure." His head turned and he looked at her. "Haven't you?"

CHAPTER FOUR

DESPITE her sumptuous room with the most amazing Egyptian-cotton linens on the bed, Jesslyn couldn't sleep.

Every time she closed her eyes, she could feel that fleeting brush of Sharif's fingers against the back of her hand, a touch that had scorched her then, a touch that burned her still. But it wasn't just his touch that stayed with her, it was his low voice, a voice that hummed inside her head.

In the dark of her room she felt caught in a time warp, suspended in a moment where they were still together and still very much in love.

After such a fitful night's sleep, the alarm came too early, jarring Jesslyn awake. For a long moment she sat on the edge of her bed, struggling to get her bearings, and then she remembered she was in a hotel room in Dubai waiting for her morning flight to Sarq.

She was going to Sarq to take care of Sharif's children.

Jesslyn very nearly crawled back under the covers to hide but knew it wasn't really an option. Instead she dragged herself into the shower where she turned the faucets on full force.

Drying her hair, she styled it into loose waves to take advantage of her hair's natural curl. Hair done, Jesslyn chose a simple amethyst sheath dress to wear for the flight. The dress had a matching travel coat which she'd carry over her arm.

She was slipping her feet into bone-colored heels when two of Sharif's men arrived at her hotel door. They'd come to take her luggage and escort her to the car. Sharif however wasn't in the car.

"His Highness had an unexpected meeting come up this morning. He'll meet you at the terminal in time for your flight," one of the men said, holding the door for her while the other tucked her luggage into the trunk.

Jesslyn wasn't surprised that Sharif had a meeting come up, and she wasn't surprised that she was traveling to the airport alone, as he was an exceptionally powerful man, but that didn't stop her intense whoosh of disappointment.

The fact that she even felt a whoosh of disappointment scared her. The whoosh meant she still had strong feelings for him. The whoosh meant she cared about his opinion, which made her fear her motivations for taking this job.

The truth was she couldn't afford to get involved with Sharif, not when there was so much history between them.

The truth was she'd gotten involved. There was no backing out of the deal now, not after Sharif had done his part sorting out Aaron's and Will's problems.

The closer the car got to the airport, the more her stomach did crazy flips. Nervously she ran her hands along the slim-fitting skirt of her dress. She'd dressed with such care this morning, had even put on her favorite dress. And yet, wanting to be attractive, wanting him to find her attractive was just asking for trouble.

It was like cutting open an old wound.

She wasn't his girlfriend. She wasn't his equal. She wasn't his colleague. She was just a teacher. The schoolteacher Sharif had hired to mind his royal children for the summer.

The limousine turned through the airport gates, and her stomach did another nosedive. She was here. Her bags were here. Soon she'd be on her way to Sarq, a place she'd wanted to visit for as long as she could remember, and now she was on her way. As Sharif's employee.

Jesslyn swallowed the bitter taste in her mouth as she stepped out of the Mercedes. Sharif's security detail was already there. They ushered her into the beautiful marble-and-glass executive terminal. The very rich and famous used the private terminal, and various sheikhs and businessmen mingled in groups, even as private jets carrying celebrities landed one after the other.

It was a busy terminal, and Jesslyn stood aside just people watching, fascinated by the parade of wealth, glamour and beauty. She was still taking it all in when the exterior doors opened again and another group entered, this group predominantly male with one tall, robed man commanding the most attention.

The atmosphere in the terminal almost instantly changed, charged with a tangible energy, an electric awareness. Heads through the terminal turned, and even Jesslyn felt the frisson of excitement.

Sharif.

She pursed her lips, checking her smile. Wouldn't you know that Sharif could bring a bustling terminal like the Dubai Executive Airport to a standstill.

Even before he was King Fehr he commanded attention. Ever since she'd known him he'd managed to combine physical beauty with easy grace, an innate elegance and a brilliant mind.

She'd loved his mind, and she wasn't going to think about his body—that had already kept her awake far too late last night.

Now she watched as he walked swiftly through the airport, shaking hands with several people he knew along the way. He was beautiful—ridiculous, movie star beautiful—with his thick onyx hair and incredible bone structure, and again whispers of conversation reached her, murmurs about news and weddings, and Jesslyn listened to the bits of gossip swirling through the terminal.

Was Sharif really thinking about getting married again? Was he close to taking a new bride? Had that decision already been made? And is that why he wanted her to work with his children this summer? To manage any problems the children might have before their problems became public?

Puzzled, she watched him reach the exit on the far side of the terminal. He hadn't once looked at her or for her, and she felt strangely numb, like a piece of office furniture.

But then he turned at the glass door, pushed up his sunglasses and looked straight at her with his startling eyes and that half smile of his that made her suck in air, dazzled despite herself.

So he'd known all along she was there, had been aware of her as he made his way through the terminal. Her heart did a painful little jump, an embarrassing little jump.

His eyes crinkled further, his mouth quirking higher, and he gestured to her, two fingers bending, calling her. *Come.*

Come.

If only he'd done that when she'd broken up with him. If only he'd called her, come after her, asked for her to return.

Sharif's men walked her to him now, and together she and Sharif stepped onto the tarmac, the June sun blisteringly hot despite it still being early in the morning.

"How are you?" he asked, as they climbed the stairs to the jet.

"Good," she answered, ducking her head as she entered the sleek jet. "How are you?"

He gave her a quick look, catching her tone. "Sounds like a loaded question."

She shrugged as they stepped into the jet. "People are talking about you."

"They always talk about me," he answered flatly, walking her to a chair in a cluster of four seats, two on each side of an aisle. Behind the seating area was a paneled wall with a handsome paneled door. "Which reminds me, I've a few calls to make. I'll be back out when we're airborne."

"Of course."

With a nod in her direction he disappeared through the paneled door. Jesslyn couldn't see what lay behind the door other than a room with pale plush carpet, the corner of a buttery leather couch or chair and lots of open space.

As the door closed, the flight attendant appeared at Jesslyn's side, checking to see if she needed anything. And then the door to the jet closed and within minutes they were taxiing down the long runway and lifting off.

Once at cruising altitude, the flight attendant returned, offering Jesslyn a choice of refreshments. "Tea, please," she answered, as Sharif reappeared, taking a seat opposite hers.

"Coffee, Your Highness?" the flight attendant asked.

"Yes, thank you," he said before looking at Jesslyn. "So what did you hear? What are the gossips saying about me today?"

She listened to the flight attendant's footsteps recede and looked at Sharif, really looked at him, seeing the fine lines fan from his eyes and the deeper grooves shaping his mouth. He looked pensive, even tired. Silently she debated whether she should even repeat the talk, if it was worth mentioning, but she'd heard the same talk twice now and it was better to know something like this than just wonder. "I heard you're to be married again."

His eyebrows lifted but he said nothing.

She watched his face. "Is it true?"

He hesitated a long moment. "There would be advantages to remarrying," he said at last. "And there are those who feel it would be advantageous for me to marry their daughter, but is there a bride? A wedding date?" He shrugged. "No. Nothing is set."

"But you will eventually marry?"

"I'm young. I'm a widower. It makes sense."

"It's just business, then."

He made a low, rough sound. "What would you prefer me to say? That I've met the most wonderful woman and I can't wait to marry my one true love?" He made the rough sound again. "I don't have time for love. I'm too busy running my country."

"How long have you been king now?"

Sharif frowned, trying to remember. "Five years? Six? Hard to recall. It's been long enough that it's starting to blur together."

"Your father had a heart attack."

"Died in his sleep."

"I remember reading it was a shock to the family. No one had expected it."

"That's what the media reported but it wasn't true. Father had problems several years before that, but his personal physician thought things were better. Mother hoped things were better. But I sensed that Father wasn't the same, but then, he hadn't been, not since my sisters' death."

Since the fourth form Jesslyn had loved his sisters, fraternal twins who had been completely different in every way and yet were still best friends, and over the years they'd become her best friends, too. Whatever Jamila and Aman did, wherever they went, Jesslyn could be found there, too.

After graduating from university Jamila and Aman had insisted Jesslyn come to live with them in London at the home of Sharif's aunt in Mayfair. Together they had dived into work, building their careers during the day and enjoying each other's company in the evenings. To celebrate finishing their first year as career girls, they planned a summer holiday in Greece.

They were on their last night on Crete when their car was broadsided by a drunk driver. Jamila died instantly, Aman was rushed to the emergency room, and Jesslyn, who'd been on the opposite side of the car, was hospitalized with injuries that hadn't appeared life threatening.

The hospital in Athens had been a nightmare. Jesslyn was desperate to see Aman but no one would let her into the intensive care ward since Jesslyn wasn't family.

Jesslyn remembered standing in her gown, leaning on her walker, sobbing for someone to let her in. She knew Jamila was gone. She was desperate to see Aman. It was then Sharif appeared and, learning what the commotion was about, he opened the door to Aman's room himself, firmly telling the hospital staff that Jesslyn was family, too.

That was how they met. In the hospital, the day before Aman died.

"I'm not surprised it affected your father so much," Jesslyn said, fingers knotting together. "I still can't believe they're gone. I think about Jamila and Aman all the time."

"The three of you practically grew up together."

She dug her nails into her palms, her throat aching with suppressed emotion. "Your parents blamed me for the accident, though."

"My father never did. He knew you weren't even at the wheel."

"But your mother…"

"My mother has found it difficult to accept that her only daughters are gone. But that's not your responsibility."

Jesslyn nodded and yet his words did little to ease her pain. The day of the funeral she wrote a long letter to King and Queen Fehr telling them how much she'd loved their daughters and how much she would miss them. The letter was never acknowledged.

A week after the funeral Jesslyn received a call from one of the queen's staff telling her she had to be out of the Mayfair house by the weekend because the house was being sold.

It was a scramble finding a new place to live on such short notice, but she did find a tiny studio flat in Notting Hill. Just days after moving into the new flat she collapsed. Apparently, she'd been bleeding internally ever since the accident.

The upside was they stopped the bleeding and did what they could to repair the damage.

The downside was that they warned her the scar tissue would probably make it impossible for her to ever have kids.

And then in the middle of so much sadness and darkness and loss, flowers appeared on her Notting Hill doorstep, white tulips and delicate purple orchids, with a card that said, "You can call me anytime. Sharif."

Sharif had scribbled his number on the card. She tried not to call. He was Prince Fehr, the eldest of the beautiful royal Fehr clan, the one Jamila and Aman had said would eventually inherit the throne.

But he'd also been kind to her, and he'd been the one to break the news to her that Aman had died.

Jesslyn called him. They talked for hours. Two days later he called her, inviting her out to dinner.

Sharif took her to a little Italian restaurant, one of those rustic hole-in-the-wall places with great food and friendly service. Jesslyn thought it was fantastic. Dinner was fantastic because it was so normal, so comfortable, with Sharif putting her immediately at ease. That night they talked about Jamila and Aman, they talked about Greece, they talked about the unseasonably cold weather they were having for late August, and at the end of the evening when he dropped her off, she knew she'd see him again.

She did see him again, she saw lots of him despite the fact that he was this famous rich gorgeous prince and she was, well, she was very much a nice, middle-class girl. But they enjoyed each other too much to think about their differences, so they just kept seeing each, never looking back, never looking forward. Not for two and a half years. Not until his mother found him a more suitable woman, a princess from Dubai.

"There are few people in this world like your sisters," Jesslyn said, her voice husky. "They were just so much fun, and so good humored." She tried to smile, but tears filled her eyes. "They knew how to live. They embraced it, you know?"

"I do know," he said as the hum of the jet changed and the nose dipped down. "Check your seat belt," he added gruffly. "We'll be on the ground soon."

A fleet of black Mercedeses waited at the airport, all in a line on the tarmac, not far from where the jet had parked.

In less than three minutes they disembarked, settled into the cars and were off, exiting the small private terminal reserved for the royal family's use and heading through the city streets to the palace.

Jesslyn already knew that Sarq was ninety percent Muslim and yet as they drove through the streets Jesslyn saw relatively few women wearing the veil, apart from a few still wrapped in white robes, and although she'd lived in the Emirates for the past six years, she was still surprised by how relaxed everything seemed, the people on the streets appearing open and friendly.

"It feels like everyone's on holiday here," she said, as the car idled at a traffic light waiting for it to turn.

"People say Sarq is becoming the southern Mediterranean's Costa del Sol."

"Is that good or bad?" she asked, watching a cluster of girls cross the street linked arm in arm.

"It depends on who you talk to. In the past ten years a rather staggering number of beach resorts—inexpensive as well as deluxe properties—have opened along the coast. Some welcome the growth with open arms—my brother Zayed—for one, while others, like my nomadic brother Khalid, want to ban further development."

"What do you think?"

"I'm in between. Economic stability enables Sarq to remain free and independent of any other country, and yet growth has a price. While the developing tourism industry has strengthened our economy, the environment's paid a stiff price with the destruction of sand dunes and the troubling disappearance of wildlife."

"You sound like you lean toward wildlife conservation," she said.

"I have to. My father didn't consider the impact development would have on our country's natural resources, and now I'm forced to deal with the consequences."

The car turned down a long drive marked by high stuccoed walls, lush, towering palm trees and flowering citrus trees beneath.

"We are here," Sharif added as the Mercedes sedan slowed

before immense wood and iron gates and the ten-foot-tall gates smoothly swung open.

Jesslyn craned her head to get her first look at the palace, a place she'd heard so much about from Jamila and Aman.

The girls had called the palace "heaven" and "paradise." They'd said it was like a jewel in the most beautiful garden ever, and indeed, as the car turned round a corner, she spotted a sprawling pink building, the palace a compound of one-story stuccoed villas draped with trailing purple, pink and peach bougainvillea.

Elaborately carved columns and miniature domes marked the entrance, and Jesslyn knew from her friends' description that inside were elaborate courtyards filled with fountains, dwarf palms and date palms and flowers.

White-robed and uniformed staff appeared in the entrance, greeting Sharif and welcoming the king home.

Sharif introduced Jesslyn, explaining that the teacher would be with them for the summer and he wanted everyone to make sure she lacked for nothing.

While Sharif communicated his wishes, Jesslyn surreptitiously glanced around. The palace's cool, crisp interior contrasted with the soft pastel hues of the exterior. The walls inside were white, the high ceilings painted blue and gold, huge carved wood columns soared up to support the elaborate ceilings forming cool narrow columned corridors and intimate seating areas.

Introductions finished, the staff dispersed and Sharif offered to take her on a minitour while they waited for his children to return.

"Where are they now?"

"Out for an afternoon excursion," he answered, "but they'll be back soon for tea."

Sharif's pride was tangible as he pointed out some of the rare works of art housed within the palace walls—paintings, sculptures, armor, weapons and more. Jesslyn was awed by the history of the collection, sculptures dating back to Greco-Roman civilization, a flawless mosaic from the tomb of a Byzantine king, an enormous scarlet rug that could be traced to the Ottoman Empire.

"And this has always been here?" she asked.

"For generations." He smiled faintly. "Some people go to museums to see priceless artifacts. I grew up with them, am still surrounded by them."

They'd reached the end of a long arched corridor, the stone floor patterned with sunlight shining through the dozen square windows high on the wall. The ceiling, painted shades of cream and gold, reflected the brilliant late-morning light and cast sparkly starbursts and circles on the whitewashed walls.

Before they'd even turned the corner, Jesslyn could hear the tinkling notes of a fountain, and indeed, as they walked through an arched doorway, they came to stone stairs that led to a sunken living room from which she could see the fountain in a picture-perfect courtyard.

"This must be where you entertain," she said, dazzled beyond words. The living room exuded elegance and beauty and calm, every detail exquisitely thought out, from the sweet spicy perfume of antique roses, to the huge glass doors drenched in sunlight, to the low cream couches that formed comfortable conversation areas.

"It's actually where you'll entertain," he said, an enigmatic smile lighting his eyes. "This is part of your room, the most public of your quarters."

She walked behind one of the sofas heaped with beaded and embroidered silk cushions in mouthwatering orange, lime and dusky rose. Impulsively she leaned over to touch one tangerine-colored pillow, and it gave beneath her hand, the down-filled insert deliciously soft.

"Oh, lovely," she whispered, unable to hide her delight. She'd lived such a Spartan existence these past six years, and the luxury here was beyond her comprehension. "This room is fit for a princess!"

"This was Jamila and Aman's room."

Straightening, Jesslyn turned to face him. "Really?"

He nodded.

Pain splintered inside her as she looked at the beautiful room and the fantasy courtyard with fresh eyes. "Maybe I shouldn't stay here."

"It'd be wrong for you not to stay here. My sisters loved you dearly. They'd want you here."

Blinking back tears, she drew a quick breath and ran a light hand over the tangerine pillow. "As long as it won't offend anyone. I don't want to offend anyone—"

"No one will be offended."

"If you're sure…?"

"You doubt me?"

She didn't know if she should laugh or cry and she did both, smiling unsteadily as she dashed away a tear. "I'm not normally this emotional and yet ever since yesterday I've been a disaster."

"It's a shock seeing each other," he answered.

Her head tilted and she looked up at him, her gaze searching his face. "You feel it, too?"

"How could I not? We were once very close. You knew me better than anyone."

A shiver coursed through her, a shiver of remembrance and hurt and pain. But she hadn't known him better than anyone.

His mother had known him better. His mother had known he'd choose his future, and his throne, over her.

Over love.

And he did.

Chilled, she turned, rubbed her arms. "Show me where the books are. I'm ready to look at everything, plan the afternoon's lessons."

"There won't be any teaching today. Use today to meet the children and settle in."

A knock sounded up the stairs on the outer door. "Ah, the children," Sharif said. "I believe they've arrived."

Instead Sharif's personal butler stepped into view at the top of the stairs. "Your Highness, an urgent call."

Sharif frowned. "The children aren't here?"

"No, Your Highness."

"They should have been here over an hour ago."

The butler paused, head bowing further. "I believe that is the nature of the phone call."

Sharif's expression didn't outwardly change, but Jesslyn felt a whisper of tension enter the room. "If you'll excuse me a moment," he said to her.

"Of course."

"This shouldn't take long," he added.

"Don't worry. Take as much time as you need. I can unpack."

"I'm sure that has already been done for you, but if you'd like to see your bedroom and ensuite bath, they are just through that door. In the meantime, I'll send for refreshment," he said as he started toward the stairs.

"I'm fine, Sharif. I can wait."

He turned in midstep, powerful shoulders shifting, robes swirling, his brilliant gaze locking on her face. "That's where we disagree," he said, his voice so rich, so beautifully pitched it pierced her chest, burying deep to beat in time with her heart. "I think we've waited long enough."

She didn't know if it was his expression or his tone of voice, but suddenly she couldn't breathe. "For tea?"

He paused, considered her, one eyebrow lifting. "If that makes you feel better."

CHAPTER FIVE

As HE LEFT to take the call, Sharif's thoughts lingered on Jesslyn.

She'd always been beautiful in that haunting English-beauty sort of way. A heart-shaped face framed by loose, dark curls. Flawless skin. Warm brown eyes. Perfectly arched eyebrows.

But there was something else different, something that he couldn't quite put his finger on but made him look and look again.

Beautiful yes, but more so.

Changed.

More reserved. Distant. Closed.

He'd watched her face, these past few days, as they'd spoken, and she'd treated him the way everyone now treated him—supremely politely. With deference, if not respect. And it didn't exactly bother him, but he missed the easiness between them. She'd always been the one person who had treated him like a man not a prince.

She'd teased him, laughed at him, loved him.

She'd loved him.

She didn't anymore. She hadn't when she'd left him nine years ago. And she hadn't when she'd begun accepting bribes from his mother.

But that was to come later. He'd get his answers later. In

the meantime he was determined to enjoy her beauty and revel in her softness and take what he could. Just as she'd once taken so freely from him.

After Sharif left to take the call Jesslyn anxiously paced the sunny living room with Sharif's parting words played endlessly in her head.

I think we've waited long enough.

What did he mean by that? What had they waited long enough for? And waited too long for what?

Was he referring to the girls? Was he wishing he'd taken action to help them sooner? Or…

Or…

She gulped a panicked breath, fingers squeezing into nervous fists. Was he referring to something far more personal, something that had to do with *them?*

Almost immediately she squelched the thought. Sharif had brought her here for his children. He wanted her for his children.

But still her heart raced and her body felt too warm and her veins full of fear and hope and adrenaline.

A soft musical sound in the doorway interrupted Jesslyn's pacing and turning. She watched a young, robed woman, a woman she guessed to be in her early twenties, descend the stairs carrying a heavy tray.

"Something for you, Teacher," the woman said in halting English as she carried the tray laden with food and flowers and a pot of tea into the living room.

Jesslyn felt some of her tension ease. "Thank you, that's lovely."

The woman smiled shyly as she placed the heavy silver tray on one corner of the low tables next to the cream-covered sofa. "I pour?" she asked, indicating the pot of tea.

There was something infinitely endearing about this young woman, and Jesslyn sat down on the couch. "What is your name?"

"Mehta, Teacher," she answered, kneeling and patting her chest and smiling again, this time revealing two deep dimples in her cheeks.

Jesslyn couldn't help smiling back. "Mehta, I am Jesslyn."

Her head bobbed. "Teacher Jesslyn."

"No, Jesslyn's fine."

She bobbed even more earnestly. "Teacher Jesslyn Fine."

Jesslyn liked Mehta, liked her a great deal. It couldn't be so bad here, not if she could see Mehta now and then. "Will I see you much, Mehta?"

"Yes, Teacher. I help you every day. With your clothes and bath and tea." She leaned forward, pointed to the tea. "I pour now?"

Jesslyn's cheeks ached from smiling. "Yes, please."

Along with the tea there were crescents of honey-soaked pastry stuffed with walnuts and pistachios, and the ever-popular *makroudi,* ground dates wrapped in semolina.

Jesslyn was shamelessly licking the sweet sticky honey from her fingers when Sharif reappeared. Mehta, spying Sharif, bowed and slipped soundlessly from the room.

In the meantime Jesslyn watched Sharif descend the pale stone stairs, and she could tell from his expression that he wasn't happy. His brow was dark and his jaw looked as though it'd been hammered from stone.

Sitting upright, she watched his progress across the floor of her lovely living room, troubled by the anger and frustration in his face.

It struck her that there was something else going on,

something he wasn't telling her, something he didn't want her to know.

She cocked her head, looked at him, trying to see past his striking good looks to what lay beneath. What was he really worried about? The girls failing academically, or the girls having emotional issues?

"It's the children, isn't it?" she asked

He nodded distractedly, his gray eyes burning with fire and frustration. "Yes."

"Are they hurt?"

"No. They're safe." He dropped onto the couch opposite hers, covered his face briefly with his palms and for a long moment said nothing, tension rippling through him in waves. He took a deep breath and then another before finally looking at her. "They're just not here."

"When will they be here?"

He didn't answer but she saw one hand curl, fingers forming a fist.

Did this happen often, she wondered, or was there something else troubling him, something more he hadn't told her?

"In time for dinner?" she persisted when he didn't answer.

He shook his head. "Hopefully tonight by bedtime, but realistically, it'll be tomorrow morning."

"Hopefully? Realistically? You're talking about your kids, right?"

Again his eyes flashed with frustration, but he didn't answer her directly, and his silence troubled her as much as the information he was telling her.

"Sharif, where *are* they?"

"With their grandmother."

"Zulima's mother?"

"Until recently Zulima's mother lived here, but she's returned to her family in Dubai. She lives with her second son now."

"So the children are with your mother."

He nodded.

Jesslyn was watching his face closely, trying to put the various puzzle pieces together. Sharif was leaving far more unsaid than said. "Why did Zulima's mother leave? Was there a problem?"

Sharif made a low mocking sound. "Is there ever not a problem here? The two mothers-in-law never did get along. It was always a battle of wills, and my mother tended to win."

His mother usually won, Jesslyn thought, more than a little concerned about what he was telling her.

Jesslyn knew Sharif's mother well enough to know that the queen had always been in charge. Sharif's late father might have been king, but Sharif's mother was the ruler of the palace.

Sharif's mother had never liked her. Not as Jamila and Aman's close friend. And definitely not as Sharif's girlfriend.

"So where are your mother and the children right now?" she persisted.

"She has a small house on the coast, about an hour and fifteen minutes north from here. It used to be the summer house where we'd go for holidays, but my mother has claimed it for herself." He reached across to the table, checked to see if she had any hot water left in the pot. There was none and he let the lid fall. Meanwhile his expression grew blacker. "She took the girls there this morning and they're with her now."

"Did she not know you'd be returning today?" she asked, thinking that it was going to be hard enough living in the palace without having to contend with Her Highness, Queen Reyna Fehr. Her Highness had actually grown up as a commoner in the Emirates but had made up for her lack of royal connections with stunning cheekbones, a perfect nose and best of all, a very rich father.

"She knew," he answered tautly. "We talked last night and again this morning. But she does what she wants when she wants and everyone else can be damned."

Jesslyn bunched an iridescent pillow and held it to her chest. "You and the girls see her often then?"

"Every day. She might have claimed the summer house but this is where she still lives, this is home. She just goes to the summer house when she wants to make a point."

Jesslyn was having a hard time taking in everything Sharif was telling her. Queen Reyna had never wanted Jesslyn to be friends with her daughters and she'd made that clear in a hundred different ways over the years, but this, this was a relationship between a doting mother and her eldest son. "And what is the point your mother is trying to make?"

Sharif made a rough, mocking sound. "That she's in charge."

Things were starting to become clearer. "Does Her Highness know I am going to be working with the girls for the summer?" she asked.

He paused, and that hesitation alone gave Jesslyn her answer.

Sighing, Jesslyn sank back against the low couch and clutching the pillow even tighter, closed her eyes. "She doesn't know."

"She knows I was bringing back a tutor."

She opened her eyes and gave him a pained look. Sharif was in fine denial mode today, wasn't he?

And maybe, just maybe, this denial mode wasn't helping the children adjust to their school or their life without their mother.

But before she could find a delicate way to say any of this, Mehta returned with another tray. "Tea, Your Highness," she said bowing low before Sharif and placing the tray on a table in front of him.

"Mehta, I can pour for His Highness," Jesslyn said, drawing the tray closer to her so it wouldn't be in Sharif's way.

"Yes, Teacher Jesslyn Fine," Mehta answered with yet another bob of her head before hurrying away.

Sharif glanced at Jesslyn. "Teacher Jesslyn Fine?"

Jesslyn grimaced. "I think she believes Fine is my last name."

Sharif just looked at her a long moment before shaking his head. "You're an interesting woman."

"A euphemism for an odd, peculiar spinster?"

"We know you're not a spinster," he flashed, watching her fill his cup. "You've had boyfriends."

"I have," she said after a moment. "And it seems you have your mother."

Sharif's head jerked up and he nearly spilled his tea. "What?"

"You said your mother wants to think she's in charge, and I'm curious to know, is she?"

Sharif gave her a withering look. "No."

He might say no, she thought, but if Queen Reyna thought she was, or could be, you had the makings of a classic power struggle, the kind she'd seen between parents many times before, but in this case, the struggle was between father and grandmother. "Are you and your mother disagreeing on how to raise the girls?"

He barked a laugh, ran his hand through his dark hair, his expression tortured. "Not that I know of."

"Then what?"

He lifted his hands in mute frustration. "There's something wrong here, but I don't understand it. I don't see the children enough to know how they really are. When we are together, they hardly look at me or speak to me. When I ask them a question they do answer, but they stare at the floor the entire time and—" He sighed. "I've never known children to behave this way. My sisters certainly didn't behave this way. I'm confused."

"So what is it that you really want me to do, Sharif? Teach the children? Be a companion to them? Observe their behavior? What?"

He looked up at her, gray eyes shot with bright silver, and yet there was no light in his eyes right now. "All of the above."

"So essentially you want a nanny."

"No, they have a nanny. I need…" His voice drifted off and his forehead creased. "I need you."

She wasn't sure what he meant by that, but there was something in his eyes, something in his expression that made her heart ache. Impulsively she reached out toward him. She'd meant it to be a friendly touch, warm and reassuring, but instead of touching the loose sleeve of his robe, her fingers grazed his forearm, his bronzed skin warm like the sun, and she shuddered, stunned by the electric heat.

Abruptly she pulled back, pressing her hand to her breastbone. She'd imagined that fire, she told herself, she'd imagined that wild streak of sensation that had raced up her arm, into her shoulder, into her chest. But looking into Sharif's eyes she suddenly wasn't so sure.

There was the same fire in his eyes, a fire that made her remember how it'd been in his arms, beneath his body, in his bed.

"Something wrong?" he asked, his gaze traveling slowly over her hot face.

Fresh heat surged through her cheeks making her skin sensitive and her lips tingly. "No," she breathed, nervously pressing her hands to her lap. "I just think it'll be good when your daughters get here. It sounds as though there is much work to do."

"You will be very busy," he agreed, his gaze now resting

on her mouth as if fascinated by the curve and color of her lips. "Perhaps you should welcome having the rest of the afternoon and night free. Once the girls return you won't have much time to yourself."

She felt her lower lip begin to throb as though it had taken on a life of its own. It was all she could do not to cover her mouth. "I just wish it was sooner rather than later. It's still early in the day and I know you have work to do—"

"I'm sure Mehta would be delighted to show you the library. It's where you'll be teaching tomorrow. Feel free to have a look around and examine some of the books I've bought."

"That's an excellent suggestion. I'll use the afternoon to begin preparing tomorrow's lessons. Thank you."

Rising to his feet he smiled vaguely, amused by her enthusiasm. "So you'll be fine on your own this afternoon?"

"Yes. Definitely."

"Great. I'll see you at dinner—"

"Maybe we should pass on dinner," she suggested hurriedly, unintentionally interrupting him. "I'll have tons of reading to do tonight and I know you've a great deal of work."

He stared down at her, and she had to tilt her head back to see him.

"We'll talk about the children during dinner," he said blandly. "That should make you feel better." He started to leave but paused on the stairs. "And dinner, Jesslyn, is always at seven."

The afternoon passed far too quickly for Jesslyn. She'd discovered the library and had immediately fallen in love. The room was huge and airy, a beautiful gold dome topping high walls lined with floor-to-ceiling shelves. The library reminded Jesslyn of some people's ballrooms, large enough to comfortably hold two couches, two wooden desks, four armchairs and a long antique table with impressively carved legs.

She found the stack of teacher's editions right away, but before sitting down with those, she looked at the books the children were using. She was familiar with the publisher, and had taught the middle school version of the literature and language books. The material she'd be teaching was simple enough. Her concern was the quantity. There were stacks of books for each child. Math, science, social studies, literature, grammar, foreign language, and then music and art books, too.

Jesslyn carried the stack of children's books to one of the armchairs and sitting down with notepad and pen, she looked at the number of chapters in each book, and then the number of days between now and school starting, and mapped out a plan of how much could be comfortably covered in each subject.

She was still hard at work four hours later when Mehta lightly knocked on the door. "Ready for a bath, Teacher Fine?" she asked with her dimpled smile.

Jesslyn glanced up quizzically. "A bath?"

"Before dinner."

"Ah. Right." Closing the science textbook she wondered how to explain to Mehta that she didn't feel it necessary to take a bath before dinner. She'd taken a shower that morning and it was just a business dinner. "I have so much to do before tomorrow that I might just wash my face and touch up my hair for dinner."

Mehta looked at her uncomprehendingly. "No bath?"

"I took one earlier."

"No bath before dinner?"

Jesslyn set the book down. "I don't take a bath before every meal, Mehta."

"No bath."

"No."

Mehta's dark brows pulled. "No dinner?"

"No, I will have dinner. I'm meeting Sheikh Fehr for dinner at seven. We are meeting to discuss business—"

"Dinner with His Highness."

"Right." Jesslyn smiled with relief. Finally. They were both on the same page. "Dinner," she said. "At seven."

Mehta held up her wrist, tapped her wrist as though there was a watch there. "Half past five. Dinner seven. Bath now."

Jesslyn sighed heavily. She really didn't want to argue about a bath with a young member of Sharif's palace staff. She'd only just arrived and she was going to be here all summer. And from the sound of things she was going to need someone on her side.

"A bath sounds lovely," she answered with forced cheer as she reluctantly moved all the books off her lap and chair so she could stand. "But I'm not finished with these," she added. "I'll want to read them later."

Mehta was delighted. "Yes, Teacher Fine. Now come."

Jesslyn hadn't seen the bedroom before, but following Mehta down the columned hall into the bedroom, she discovered that the bedroom with its spacious antique bed was just as lovely, and even more feminine, than the sunken living room.

The antique bed reminded Jesslyn of a Russian ballet with dramatic floor-to-ceiling pink and rose silk and satin curtains that could be untied and draped around the bed to provide intimacy and seclusion. The bed, built like an oversize daybed, had neither headboard nor footboard but high sides softened with pillows to match the silk panels.

A short silver vase teeming with fragrant pink rosebuds sat on a side table, and Jesslyn bent over to breathe in the heady sweet perfume. It wasn't easy to grow roses in the blistering heat of the desert, which made these all the more precious.

"Your bath," Mehta said, standing in yet another doorway gesturing to a room beyond.

The bath was a Roman bath with sunken tub and endless white marble. A delicately painted dome arched over the airy room, capping high walls with high narrow windows that drew in early-morning and late-afternoon sun but didn't sacrifice privacy.

"I will help you?" Mehta asked, gesturing to Jesslyn.

The huge sunken tub had already been filled, and steam rose from the surface. "I can manage," Jesslyn answered, thinking the whole help thing had gone far enough. Turning, she spotted a white robe on a small iron stool, and she picked it up, held it against her. "I'll take the bath and then put this on and then I'll come out, okay?"

Mehta smiled. "Okay."

Once the bathroom door was shut, Jesslyn dropped her clothes and slid into the tub's hot water with an appreciative sigh. She hadn't wanted to take the bath, but now that she was here, chin-deep in water scented with a tantalizing vanilla and spice oil, she couldn't imagine not bathing.

The little bathroom in her apartment had a tiny tub, but the water never got properly hot and then turned cold halfway before the tub was even filled. Soaking in this deep tub was pure decadence. Closing her eyes, Jesslyn just floated, content, absolutely content—

"Massage now, Teacher Fine. Okay?"

Mehta's voice suddenly pierced Jesslyn's dream state and her eyes flew open. Mehta was leaning over the tub smiling at her. "Okay?"

Jesslyn sat up abruptly, drawing her knees to her chest. "I don't need a massage."

"Nice massage before dinner."

Spotting a large woman, Jesslyn shook her head. "The bath is perfect. The bath is lovely. I'll just get dressed."

"Dinner with His Highness," Mehta said.

"Yes, yes, I know, but—"

"Massage before dinner with His Highness."

Oh, for Pete's sake! Enough with this dinner-with-His-Highness. It was just Sharif. She'd had hundreds of meals with Sharif. It was ridiculous to go through all of this just because she'd be joining him to eat.

"No." Jesslyn hugged her knees tighter. "I really—" she broke off as the masseuse behind Mehta scooped up the robe and came marching toward her.

Mehta and the masseuse waited expectantly.

Jesslyn looked up at them, water trickling down her chest and back. She honestly didn't know if she should laugh or cry. Coming here, she thought Sharif would be the problem, but Sharif was no problem, not compared to her baby-faced attendant with the biggest dimpled smile in the world.

"Anything for the king," she said from between gritted teeth as she stood up in the bath and was wrapped in the robe.

Mehta smiled, her deep dimples growing bigger, deeper.

But of course Mehta smiled. Mehta was having a great time. She'd managed in less than a day to turn Jesslyn into a living Barbie doll.

CHAPTER SIX

JESSLYN'S heart thudded as she stood in the doorway of the royal courtyard. She couldn't take another step, painfully self-conscious in the open-shoulder silk blouse Mehta had insisted she wear after going through all of Jesslyn's clothes. The black silk was sheer and heavily embroidered with silver, the top draping off her shoulders and then dipping low.

It was a splurge top she'd bought for the Australia trip, a dressy fun top she'd imagined wearing in Cairns or Port Douglas for a special dinner out. Instead she wore it tonight for dinner with Sharif, the top paired with slim black satin trousers and high heels.

"Where did Miss Heaton go?" Sharif's deep voice sounded from the opposite end of the courtyard, and Jesslyn searched the shadowy walled garden lit only by moonlight and the odd torch.

"I'm not sure," she answered nervously, taking another step into the courtyard, feeling the chunky, black wood bead necklace sliding across her bare skin. "This wasn't my idea," she added defensively, pressing the big glossy wood beads to her sternum, wishing the beads covered more of her as her top left far too much bare. She shouldn't have allowed Mehta to dress her. She should have finally, firmly, put her foot down.

Sharif moved from the shadows into the light. "I've never seen you like this."

Instead of his traditional robes, he wore Western clothes, tailored black trousers and a long-sleeved white dress shirt open at the throat.

She'd never seen him like this, either. In London they'd never dressed up, never gone to very expensive or trendy restaurants. Instead their lives were simple and low-key and yet so full of happiness.

"This isn't my idea of business attire," she added nervously, shoulders lifting at the warm caress of the evening breeze. "But Mehta doesn't listen to me. Not about anything."

"Ah, yes, Teacher Fine," he remarked moving leisurely toward her as the torches jumped and flickered in the breeze. "And you do look very fine."

She touched one bare shoulder, aware that her top's black silk was so sheer her skin and the curve of her breast could be seen. The fact that the silk had been bordered in silver ribbon and embroidered with fanciful silver designs did little to comfort her. The top had merely seemed playful when she'd planned to wear it on holiday. Now it felt far too daring, provocative and sexual and it mortified her.

She wasn't trying to seduce Sharif. She wasn't trying to do anything but fulfill her promise to him. All she wanted to do was help his children and then return to Sharjah in eight weeks for the new school year.

"Would you like a cocktail, a glass of wine or champagne?" he asked.

She fidgeted with the black beads. "No, thank you. I don't really drink. I know a lot of the expats in the Emirates do, but since most people don't drink…" Her voice trailed off as she looked up into his face, her train of thought disappearing as she got lost in his eyes, eyes that tonight looked like the pewter gray of the precious Tahitian pearl.

"How is life in Sharjah as an expat?" he asked, his head tilting to one side, his lips curving lazily, and yet the cool, sardonic smile only made the spark in his eyes hotter.

"Good. I'm happy there. It's become my home." She tried to smile, but found it impossible when Sharif was looking at her like that.

Looking at her as though she was the most interesting thing in the world.

But she knew what she was and she knew what she wasn't, and this—all of this—was a huge mistake. She should never have come to dinner dressed this way.

A lock of her dark hair fell forward, and reaching up, she shyly pushed it back from her brow. Mehta had done her hair, as well, brushing and backcombing the crown, before sweeping most of it away from her face and pinning it at the back of her head with small jeweled hairpins that left some hair loose in soft dark curls.

Looking in the mirror at her reflection earlier, Jesslyn had nearly fainted. It wasn't that she didn't look beautiful, but the hairstyle and the blouse and the dark eyeliner and pale glossy lips all whispered sex. Seduction. Pleasure.

She'd tried to take the jeweled hairpins out, but Mehta had shocked her by bursting into tears. "No Teacher Fine, no," she'd wept and Jesslyn had been so stunned and so uncomfortable she'd left her hair and makeup alone.

Jesslyn tried to smile but couldn't quite pull it off. "Sharif, I really feel awkward. This outfit, this hair—" She lifted a hand, gesturing to her head, hating how her hand shook like a nervous schoolgirl's. "This isn't me. It isn't right. I'm sorry."

"Don't apologize, that's really not necessary. But I do agree with you. Something's not right." Sharif folded his arms across his chest, his features firming in lines of concentration as he slowly walked around her, studying her from head to toe.

Then, turning away, he called a quiet command and one of Sharif's uniformed butlers appeared. Sharif spoke quickly, two or three abrupt sentences that Jesslyn couldn't follow. She spoke basic Arabic, but he wasn't speaking a dialect she understood.

She looked at Sharif questioningly as the butler disappeared. Sharif simply looked at her, his expression unreadable. "This shall be an interesting evening," he said at length, allowing himself the smallest hint of a smile.

His smile filled her with fresh trepidation. She didn't want an interesting evening. She wanted a safe evening, a predictable evening, an evening that was courteous, professional, routine. The Sharif standing before her at the moment represented none of those things.

"I spent the afternoon reading through the children's textbooks," she said with unintentional force. She was nervous, so nervous, and already she felt wound too tight. "I'm quite familiar with the publisher as I've taught the middle school editions of the literature and language books, and as textbooks go, they're very good."

His silver gaze gleamed. Deep grooves bracketed his sensual mouth. "I'm glad you approve."

She had to look away, unnerved by the intensity of his gaze. He was looking at her far too intently, looking at her as though he could strip her bare at any moment, as though he would strip her bare at any moment....

"The science and math textbooks are of course new to me. I'm not credentialed in those subjects, but it's not difficult material to teach." She was babbling, knew she was, but couldn't help it. Anything to keep from thinking about his eyes, his mouth, his lips. Anything to keep from looking at the width of his chest and the beautiful bronze skin revealed by his open shirt. A shirt like that wouldn't be acceptable in his culture, but he didn't seem to care about rules.

Regulations.

Propriety.

"I'll work with them on handwriting, too," she added breathlessly. "I imagine Takia is still just learning to print."

He didn't answer and she glanced up, looking at him from beneath her mascara-coated lashes. His jaw flexed. He was fighting a smile. She knew because she saw the briefest flash of his white teeth.

"Are you afraid to be alone with me?" he asked, an eyebrow half rising.

"No." She laughed and it came out high and thin, more like a hysterical bleat. "No," she repeated more firmly. "I'm just thinking about the children. Our first day of school."

"You're a most dedicated teacher."

She refused to meet his gaze and she stared at her fingers and the ring on her right hand. "I try."

"I like that about you." He paused expectantly as the butler returned with a stack of medium to large jeweler's boxes. "Let me see what we have."

Jesslyn watched as the butler opened one box after the other for Sharif. A priceless necklace nestled inside each box's black velvet and satin lining, thick diamond clusters, long strands of large black and white pearls, a glittering sapphire, diamond and South Sea pearl necklace.

She'd never seen jewelry like this, never in her life. She'd seen photographs in magazines of exquisite jewels, had watched a famous actress claim an award with borrowed

Harry Winston diamonds, but that was on TV and everyone knew television wasn't real life.

As each box opened Sharif glanced at Jesslyn, his gaze narrowed consideringly. After the third and final box opened he turned to her, "Which do you prefer?"

Heat stormed her cheeks. "Don't tease."

He shrugged. "I'll pick the necklace for you, then." And after perusing the selection for another minute, he lifted the dazzling, thick, diamond necklace, an entire strand of diamond starburst after diamond starburst, and moved behind her.

"Lift your hair," he said.

"This is absurd, Sharif."

"Your hair."

A shiver raced down her back as she hesitantly reached up to take off her wood bead necklace and to pull her heavy hair off her neck, revealing her bare nape and nearly naked back.

She closed her eyes as she felt him settle the heavy necklace around her neck, his fingers brushing her skin as he deftly fastened the small hook. The necklace was cold against her chest, hitting four inches below her throat.

"Turn. Let me see," he said.

Slowly she turned to face him and he took a step back to give her a critical once-over. "Pretty," he said, but he didn't sound very convincing, and yet with so many huge diamonds she knew the necklace had to be worth hundreds of thousands of dollars. If not more.

"Please take it off," she urged, looking down and catching sight of the diamonds' white fire.

Instead he turned to another jewelry box, the one with the decadently long strand of flawless South Sea and Tahitian pearls, each pewter and cream-colored pearl the size of her knuckle. Unhooking the clasp, he lifted the pearls from its box and, again moving behind her, he draped these around her neck. The pearls fell between her breasts, hung so low that the luxurious strand brushed the full swell of her breast before settling low against her breastbone.

"Turn," Sharif commanded.

She gave him a fierce look over her shoulder. "Remember our conversation from last night? I am your employee, not your servant."

He met her angry gaze and he smiled slowly, a provocative gleam that quickened her pulse and turned her belly inside out. He was playing a game, a game she didn't understand, a game where he made the rules and she was to follow.

"What do you want?" she whispered, her voice failing her.

"I want to see you covered in jewels, the way you could have been." His lashes dropped, concealing the pearl gray of his eyes. "The way you would have been."

Goose bumps covered her arms. The fine hair at her neck stood on end.

"You could have been my queen," he repeated.

She looked at him, seeing him as the world must see him, that noble face both beautiful and severe, and then there were those eyes of his, those silver eyes that had haunted her in her sleep for years.

She'd told herself after leaving him that she'd never regretted ending their relationship, told herself she was better off without his controlling mother and foreign culture and far-off palace, but at night her dreams told her differently.

At night, even years later, she still dreamed of him, and in her dreams she tried to cling to him, tried to make the differences go away. Tried to redeem herself.

Now she reached up to try to remove one of the necklaces, but before she could unfasten a clasp Sharif gently batted her fingers away and, taking the diamond, sapphire and pearl strand from his butler, he told her to lift her hair.

She shook her head. "I can't do this anymore."

"But you still have one more."

"No. I don't want it, I don't want any of these."

"But you like jewelry. You love fine jewelry. And best of all, you look stunning in exquisite jewels like these. Now lift your hair because dinner is being served and we don't want it cold."

She looked up at him, bemused. She'd never owned fine jewelry, only trinkets and hand-me-down bracelets and necklaces and rings from her mother. An antique cameo. A silver Art Deco brooch. Wooden bangles. A jade pendant.

"I don't feel comfortable, Sharif."

"But you look beautiful. You're absolutely gorgeous. Like a living treasure."

He was paying her compliments and yet there was an edge to his voice, an unspoken anger.

"Maybe we should just eat," she whispered.

"One last gift," he said. "Please move your hair."

Eyes burning, she gathered her heavy hair into her hands and lifted it high to give him access to the back of her neck. His fingers brushed her skin, his fingertips so light, so teasing she arched helplessly at his touch.

She didn't want him.

But she did want him.

She didn't love him anymore.

But she loved the way his skin felt on hers, loved the heat and how he made her feel so hot, so electric.

She wanted more heat, more hot, more electric. Closing her eyes she could imagine his hands on her hips, his hard body against the back of her thighs, his palms sliding up her ribs to cup her breasts.

Then suddenly his lips were there at the back of her neck, planting a fleeting kiss where his fingers had been.

"There," he said, his voice deep, warm reminding her of honey and sun. "Perfection."

Turning her around, he extended her a hand. "Dinner, *laeela*."

They were eating outside at the opposite end of the court-yard, dinner served in a beautiful pale-ivory tent lit by a delicate crystal chandelier hanging above the linen-covered table. Three more white candles flickered on the table, making the porcelain china shimmer. Tuberoses and white lilies floated in water, their fragrance so sweet it nearly made her dizzy.

Or maybe she was dizzy because Sharif watched her so intently she felt as though she couldn't breathe properly.

Dinner started with a variety of appetizers, ranging from roasted peppers with feta and capers to artichoke hearts with ginger, honey and lemon, followed by chilled almond and garlic soup with roasted chili and grapes, then course after course including spiced *kefta*, lamb meatballs, poached in a buttery ginger and lemon sauce, beef *tagine* with sweet potatoes, spicy beef *koftas* with chickpea puree.

The parade of dishes didn't stop until the very end when they were presented with a choice of desserts, figs and pears in honey or Sharif's favorite, *m'hanncha*, crisp buttery filo filled with an almond paste, spiced with cinnamon and scented with orange flower water.

Jesslyn refused dessert, too full, too nervous, and too anxious to leave. She wanted the meal to end, but Sharif ordered one of each dessert and strong coffee.

After the steward left, Sharif leaned back in his chair. "You said Sharjah feels like home. But how did you end up living in the Emirates? It seems like a most unlikely place for you to settle."

Jesslyn shifted in her chair and as she did, the low pearl necklace unexpectedly swung between her breasts, brushing one breast and then the other, and the touch of warm pearls on her skin felt strangely erotic.

She squeezed her thighs tighter, not wanting to be distracted by sex, and yet the pressure only made her more conscious that she was aroused.

"When I was teaching in London at the American School I heard there was an opening at the American School in Dubai. The pay was very good and I was getting bored in London, felt restless. I thought I'd go to Dubai for a year, teach, have a bit of adventure and then return." She shrugged. "I never returned."

"How long did you teach in Dubai before taking the job in Sharjah?"

"I was there only a year, but the private school in Sharjah suited me better. Smaller school, more hands on, I could help decide the curriculum. I like that."

What she wasn't telling him was that Germany and France both had faculty openings in their American schools but she chose Dubai because she missed her friends, she missed Jamila, Aman, and…Sharif.

How could she tell him that living and teaching in the Emirates made her feel as though she were still somehow close to all of them? That living as an expat in the UAE felt more comfortable than living anywhere else?

"But you'd never even visited the Emirates before," he persisted.

"I know. But I've never stopped missing your sisters," she said. "Living in the Emirates I can almost imagine that I'll run into them again. You know, turn a corner, and there Jamila will be, her eyes sparkling with laughter, a huge shopping bag on her arm.

"Jamila loved to shop," Jesslyn continued, feeling the words rush through her nearly as intense as the emotions. "And of course Aman liked nice things but not like Jamila. I remember one time Aman shouting she'd never ever go out with Jamila again because all Jamila ever did was shop, shop, shop…" Her voice faded and she lifted her shoulders.

"I know you're getting tired of hearing this, but I really do miss them. They were both so fiery and fun, so full of life. I've never been able to replace them. But then, I've never wanted to."

"I could never get tired of hearing you talk about them. No one else speaks about them." His brow furrowed, and he looked at her for a moment as though puzzled. "You really did love them."

"Of course I did. They were my best friends. But you know that." Looking at his face, she suddenly wasn't sure that he did. "Sharif, you've always known your sisters were my closest friends."

"It's hard to know sometimes what's real. What's true. And what's fiction." His gaze narrowed and he stared past her, his expression inscrutable. "I've learned in the past nine years that things aren't always what they seem."

She clasped her hands in her lap. "Like what?"

It seemed as though he was going to answer, and then he shook his head. "But it's good to hear you talk about my sisters. My mother doesn't mention them anymore. I don't think anyone does."

"You don't, either?"

"I should, but I haven't. So many years have passed, and their deaths created so much pain that I suppose we've all tried to move on, forget."

The back of her eyes burned hot and gritty, and she blinked

to keep the salty sting from blinding her. "I don't want to forget them. I like thinking about them. They were so loving, so warm."

He glanced from one of the flickering torches back to her. "They were loving, and protective of those they loved. And especially protective of you."

Jesslyn heard that hint of anger in his voice again, as though there was something he very much wanted to say but couldn't or wouldn't. And yet it made no sense. Why would Sharif be upset with her all these years? He was the one that married quickly. He was the one that had a family and children. She was still single, still trying to come to grips with love in all its different forms.

They were still sitting in silence when their attendant returned with coffee and dessert. Jesslyn took her coffee and added several teaspoons of sugar.

"Your brother, Khalid," she said awkwardly, trying to move the conversation along, "he doesn't speak of the girls, either? If I recall, he was quite close to them. I know he took their deaths very hard."

"I don't know who took it worse—Khalid, my father or my mother—but it has been very difficult for Khalid. He was three years younger than the girls, and my sisters absolutely doted on him. Khalid worries us sometimes, he's quite the loner. We don't see much of him. I haven't seen him in at least a year."

"Where does he live?"

"The middle of the Great Sarq Desert." He exhaled wearily, rubbed his brow. "He's our nomad. A scholar, a gentleman and a recluse, but also unreachable—" He broke off, shrugged impatiently. "But what's the expression, 'We can't save everyone?' I suppose we're lucky if we can even save ourselves."

"Sharif, are you angry with me?"

"Why would you think that?"

She didn't know, couldn't imagine. He'd married the woman he'd wanted to marry. He'd had the life he wanted to have.

Hadn't he?

Reaching out he touched the diamond necklace glittering against her skin and then trailed his finger to the second strand, the pearl and diamond and sapphire one, and then down lower to the warm pearls nestled between her breasts.

She inhaled hard, a quick silent protest as the back of his fingers brushed her breast slowly, so slowly she knew he was aware of what he was doing.

"I never could see you here," he said, stroking beneath the heavy pearls, caressing the vee between her breasts and then over to the other side to brush the full swell, her nipples now erect, pressing brazenly against the sheer fabric of her silk blouse. "You were always so smart and kind and sweet. You were open and sunny and fun. But you were a bit scruffy in your jumpers and corduroy skirts and jeans. You're not scruffy anymore. You're stunning. Other-worldly."

The entire time he talked, he touched her, fingers tracing maddening circles on the sides of her breasts, and she did nothing to stop him. Nothing. Because she wanted that touch, as improper as it was. She wanted him to run his hands along her rib cage beneath her breasts. She wanted him to take her aching nipples in his fingers, in his teeth and suck and lick and kiss and bite.

She wanted his hands on her body, on her belly, on her hips and between her legs.

She wanted him poised between her thighs and she wanted to feel him again, feel him press into her, his shaft hard, thick, hot.

And she never thought this, wanted this, with her previous

boyfriend, Robert. She never thought this, wanted this, with anyone but Sharif.

But Sharif wasn't interested in her. He was just toying with her, punishing her.

With effort she pulled away. "You made the right woman your queen," she said, reaching up to remove the first necklace, the diamond starbursts, and drop it in his hand, the brilliant stones catching the candlelight and casting long glittering rays in every direction. "Your mother approved. Your father approved. You made everyone happy."

His fingers closed around the diamonds. "Even you?"

Ah, that one hurts, she thought, taking a short, sharp breath as she worked at the clasp holding the sapphire and diamond necklace around her neck.

Did he know that too late she realized she'd martyred herself, rejecting him in a fit of childishness and then too proud to go to him and say she was wrong, she'd been wrong, she'd just been acting out.

Looking back at how she'd been, she realized now she'd been not merely young, but naive. She'd actually thought Sharif would come after her, she'd thought he'd declare his undying love and devotion and they'd marry and live happily ever after.

Ouch. Talk about living in a fantasy world. Finally the clasp opened, and drawing the diamond and sapphire necklace from her neck she draped it across his wrist.

"Were you happy with my decision?" he persisted.

"I don't know how to answer that," she answered trying to smile, because truly, she wouldn't have been a proper wife for him, she wouldn't have served him or the country, not the way she was. But she had loved him, as passionately and completely as she could love anyone.

Leaning forward, he wiped a finger beneath her lower lashes. "A tear," he said, holding his finger up for her to see and a small opalescent tear trembled there.

"There are always regrets, Sharif." And she smiled harder, smiling against the tears as she began to unhook the clasp of the pearl necklace. "But here we are, nine years later, and so life is full of surprises, little twists and turns we never see coming." And then she sniffed, battling to hold back the tears. "I can't undo the necklace. Would you please unfasten it for me? I never thought we'd speak again."

"Keep it," he said, his gaze holding hers, the silver depths enigmatic. "Another souvenir for your collection." And then abruptly he leaned forward, covered her mouth with his and kissed her.

It wasn't a tentative kiss, no shyness involved. He kissed her hard, parting her lips beneath his and plundering her mouth with his tongue. It was almost as though he was taking her mouth the way he would take her. Hard, fierce, mercilessly.

Just as abruptly he broke the kiss off. "Consider this necklace paid for."

He was gone, walking away before she understood he was finished and leaving.

Confused, she sat and watched him go, and it wasn't until he was gone she numbly realized he'd never touched the desserts, nor his coffee, and she'd only had that one sip of hers.

He was angry with her. Very angry. And she didn't understand why, how or what. But she just realized that what he wanted from her might have nothing to do with the children.

CHAPTER SEVEN

ON HIS roof terrace, Sharif leaned against the cool wall, robe hanging open over his trousers, and stared up into the moonlit, star-drenched sky.

He knew better than any that two wrongs don't make a right and yet he'd intentionally seduced Jesslyn tonight, starting with the bath and then the massage with the scented oil. He'd told Mehta he wanted Jesslyn to wear beautiful clothes, and Mehta had answered that Jesslyn had no beautiful clothes, just ugly teacher things.

However, in the end, Mehta had found something sexy, far sexier than anything he could have imagined Jesslyn wearing, and things had progressed from there.

But he wouldn't call tonight a success.

He didn't know who he'd upset more tonight—her, or him. Because he was upset. He was troubled. Angry. Guilty. Obsessed.

Obsessed with kissing her. Touching her. Feeling her body against his.

Digging his knuckles into the wall, Sharif knew he wasn't just obsessed with possessing her. He was obsessed with the need to come to grips with his life, including the past he'd lost, the present that tormented him, the future he couldn't have.

By bringing her here he'd thought he'd finally get some answers, find some peace, but her presence was having just the opposite effect.

She'd thrown him straight back into hell.

So much for killing two birds with one stone. Jesslyn might be able to sort his children out, but she was torturing him.

All these years he'd been angry with her for betraying him. All these years he'd imagined her living it up in Dubai, living a lavish lifestyle supported by his mother, and yet on visiting her school and then her apartment he found she lived like a pauper.

So where was all the money his mother had given her?

What had she done with the treasured family jewels?

Had she spent all the money?

Or had she needed the money for something he didn't know about? Had she been pregnant? *What?*

The what was driving him half mad.

But he'd get the truth, he told himself, forcing a deep breath, struggling to relax. And the best way to get the truth was to stay with the plan. Perhaps the plan was cruel, but as he'd told her last night in Dubai, he needed the truth.

After all these years, after a painful marriage, after his wife's tragic death, Sharif wanted—craved—truth.

He didn't even have to like it. He just had to know it.

But that kiss tonight…that kiss had nearly dismantled him. How could the kiss of a woman break you?

Again he clenched the wall, his heart blistered all over again.

He'd loved her endlessly once. He couldn't have imagined life without her. How much would he have sacrificed for her? What would he have risked?

Everything.

Everything.

* * *

Jesslyn was up early, before it was fully light. Dressing quietly, she washed her face, pulled her hair into a ponytail and headed to the library.

The palace was dark in places while in other areas she saw lights and could hear voices as the palace staff prepared for another day.

Nodding to various security staff, she entered the library, gently closed the door and turned on the light. Her books were where she'd left them and, returning to the armchair, she curled up and set out to finish what she'd started yesterday— a schedule for the summer.

There was no way to cover everything, but she'd spend the first week doing informal assessments, discovering what the girls knew and didn't know, before diving into half-day lessons followed by afternoons free for play.

She was still hunched over the books, taking notes, scribbling plans when the door opened. She'd expected Mehta and coffee, but it was Sharif, and immediately her insides buzzed with butterflies. He'd changed so, he wasn't even the Sharif she knew anymore, and she wasn't sure how to cope.

"Good morning," she said, hiding her unease.

"I was told you've been in here working since five-thirty," he said.

"I couldn't sleep. Wanted to get the rest of the lessons mapped out."

"You're very dedicated."

"You're a concerned father and I've promised to do what I can."

He nodded, glanced around the room and then back to her. "Have you had coffee or breakfast yet?"

"No, but I'll get some coffee soon. I'm beginning to drag a bit."

Sharif reached for the door. "I'll have them send some to you. And toast?"

"Toast would be lovely. Thank you."

He paused. "I heard from my staff that you're having difficulty reaching Robert on your wireless phone. If you'd like to use the house phone, you're more than welcome."

"Thank you," she answered awkwardly. The truth was, she hadn't tried very hard to reach Robert. She'd pulled her phone out twice, and left him a message once, but he'd never called her back and she'd given up. Temporarily, of course.

Fortunately, toast and coffee arrived. Unfortunately, it arrived with Sharif. He didn't take a seat, though, just stood inside the doorway while the breakfast tray was set up near her armchair. "Is there anything else you need? Fruit? Water?"

She clutched Jinan's science book to her chest. "No, this is great. I'm set."

She'd thought he'd leave then, but he didn't. Instead he watched her, his brow furrowed, creases fanning from his eyes. He seemed perplexed by her, which was perplexing in and of itself. They'd never had a complicated relationship. Having met under such horrible circumstances, they'd been open from the start.

"I was thinking about something you asked me yesterday," he said unexpectedly. "You wanted to know if my daughters took after my sisters, and this morning it hit me that Saba, my middle daughter, is the most like them. Saba's my feisty one. I thought middle children were supposed to be the peacemakers but she has some of Jamila's boldness."

"So she'll be my little fighter," Jesslyn said, smiling.

Sharif suddenly smiled back. "Takia would be the lover."

"And she's the youngest."

He nodded. "My little one."

"And your eldest daughter?" she asked.

"She's a typical firstborn. Smart, responsible, hardworking. A perfectionist, and a little mother to Takia."

"But aren't Jinan and Takia just a couple of years apart?"

"Two and a half."

"Amazing." Jesslyn shook her head, unable to imagine having three children in as many years. "Your wife was amazing. I couldn't do that, have so many children so close together."

Sharif tipped his head against the wall. "Neither could she," he hesitated, remembering. "She died after complications from an emergency C-section."

"After Takia's birth?"

"No. After the fourth baby. The baby was stillborn."

Jesslyn shuddered inwardly. What a terrible loss for the entire family, both mother and baby dying and then leaving three small children behind. "I'm sorry."

"She didn't give her body a chance to recover between pregnancies. After each baby she wanted to try again. And again." His jaw jutted grimly. "It was madness. It—" He broke off, swallowed hard. "It killed her."

Jesslyn had always felt such jealousy whenever she'd thought of Sharif's beautiful noble wife. Just seeing Princess Zulima's photograph in a magazine used to fill her with the worst sort of pain. But that jealousy changed now into something else entirely. Sorrow. Pity. "But why did she rush so? You were both young. You had time, and it's not as if you didn't have children. You had those little girls."

But the moment the words were spoken she knew. Lifting her head, she looked into Sharif's eyes.

Little girls.

And what was it that Queen Reyna had said to her all those years ago?

Sharif needs sons if he is to be king. Sharif needs heirs who will inherit the throne from him.

And you, Queen Reyna Fehr had said, *looking straight into Jesslyn's troubled gaze, can't have children. Can you?*

"Despite all that, you were happy with Princess Zulima, weren't you?" she asked quietly, her fingers gripping the book tightly. "You never regretted marrying her."

His dark brows pulled. "Is that a question or a statement?"

She grinned. "I'm not sure. Maybe both." She looked at him, and then as she stared at him, taking him in, her smile slowly faded.

The years had changed his face so much, adding deep lines and worry and shadows to his beautiful eyes. She missed his easy laugh. She missed his warmth. She'd once loved him so much it grieved her to see him this way.

"If I have regrets," he said carefully, "it's that we came here to the palace to live after we married. We would have been better off living abroad, or getting our own home."

"It was difficult for her here?"

He shrugged almost tiredly. "It was difficult for both of us, but she never complained."

Just like his children, she thought, biting her lower lip. "She sounds like a lovely person. Incredibly brave. I would like to have known her."

Sharif laughed roughly and ran a hand through his dark hair, combing it back from his face. "No, you wouldn't. Zulima was beautiful, well educated and royal. But she wasn't very friendly. She didn't have time for people who weren't…"

"Royal?" she supplied when he seemed to struggle to find the right word.

"Important," he corrected mockingly. "In that respect she and my mother were cut from the same cloth."

"So your mother and Princess Zulima were friends?"

Sharif barked a laugh. "Zulima hated my mother."

"Was your mother meddlesome?"

"My mother wasn't a real royal." His expression turned sardonic, and he folded his arms over his chest, the simplicity of his white robe a perfect contrast to his chiseled features. "Living here was like walking on eggshells. Someone was always upset. Lots of drama, lots of tension." His voice dropped low, so low that his next words were all but inaudible. "I hated living here. Everyone did."

Jesslyn wasn't sure she'd heard him correctly and she didn't know what to say. Platitudes at this point were just that, platitudes, and pointless. "Perhaps your children still feel sadness here. Perhaps this palace reminds them too much of what they lost?"

"Then wouldn't they be happy in England? Wouldn't they want to stay at school?" His head shook, his expression dark, brooding. "You'll see once the children arrive what I'm talking about. The girls don't laugh or giggle. They barely talk, and when they do, it's just with each other."

No, not normal, Jesslyn thought, not for three girls that age. "What about affection?" she asked. "Where do they go for hugs? Comfort? When they have nightmares or scrape a knee?"

"Their nanny tries," he answered flatly.

"What about you? Don't they want to come to you?"

Again that odd haunted look came into his eyes. "No."

"Why not? You're not an ogre. You talk about them with such love—"

"Talk's cheap though, right?" Abruptly he pushed off the wall, glanced behind him, down the column-lined corridor. "They're here," he said, the shadows deepening in his eyes. "They've arrived."

* * *

Introductions were even more strained and painful than
Jesslyn had imagined. The girls stood before their father in
the palace's soaring entrance, with shoulders straight and
heads bowed. They never once looked up at him. For his part,
his voice was without warmth or emotion.

"My daughters," he said, pointing to each child in turn. "Jinan,
the eldest. Saba, the middle daughter. And Takia, the youngest."

Each child bobbed a head, but none looked up and none
greeted her with words or even a curious glance.

Jesslyn knew Sharif was watching her face, trying to read
her reaction. Thank God she could hide her emotion behind
professional detachment because frankly, she was shocked.
These children resembled beautiful wooden dolls. He'd been
right when he said there was no life in them, no sparkling eyes
or quick smile.

If children had come to her classroom like this, she would
have immediately suspected abuse. Whether it was hunger,
deprivation, emotional neglect or physical abuse she wouldn't
have known right away. Just as she didn't know the source of
their misery yet. But she would.

Looking down on their small dark heads, she vowed she
would. If not for Sharif's sake, then the children, because
Jamila and Aman would never have stood for this. Never.
Jamila and Aman's nieces deserved better.

A half hour later Jesslyn ushered the girls into her
sunken living room, which now streamed with warm white-
gold sunlight.

She had her small charges sit on the floor in a circle among
the big silk pillows, and she took a seat with them. Sitting like
this, on the floor, eye to eye, she could see their faces better,
and the children were absolutely beautiful, perfect oval faces
with high regal brows, elegant winged eyebrows, large eyes,

small straight noses and little rosebud mouths. With beauty like this, they'd be models or child actresses in any other culture.

"We're going to play a game," Jesslyn said cheerfully, knowing that all she'd be doing the next few days was trying to crack that wall they kept around them, and trust didn't come overnight. It'd take time, but it'd be worth it. These children needed to laugh. They needed to smile.

"Do you have a favorite game?"

The girls just stared at her.

"Well, I play lots of games," she continued brightly, "and I wanted to teach you one of my favorites. It's called Duck, Duck, Goose."

The girls' expressions turned even more wooden if such a thing were possible.

"I'll go first and I'll show you how to play." Jesslyn got to her feet. "I'm going to go around behind you and I will tap each of your heads and say duck, duck, duck, until I finally say goose and when I say goose, whoever gets 'goose' jumps up and chases me."

"Why would we want to chase you?" Saba blurted, and all three girls stared at Jesslyn, waiting for an answer.

Jesslyn shrugged. "Because it's fun to jump up and down and run around." She could see from their cloudy eyes she hadn't convinced them of anything. "You'll see once we get going."

Little Takia's brow furrowed. "And why is it goose? Why isn't it chicken?"

"Excuse me," Jinan cut in imperiously, "but *Jaddah*, Grandmother, said we were to be studying. Why aren't we doing maths and reading books?"

Jesslyn had to fight to keep a straight face as she gazed into their pensive little faces. "You'd rather do maths than run around and play?"

"Playing is for children," said Saba.

Jesslyn bit down on the inside of her lip to keep her smile from showing. "I believe your father told me you're five, six and seven years old."

"Actually, Jinan turned eight last week, and I'll be seven in two months," Saba said, a flicker of disdain in her eyes.

"How lovely, did you have a party?" Jesslyn asked, turning toward Jinan, the most grown-up eight-year-old Jesslyn had ever come across in her life.

Jinan shook her head.

"Why not?" Jesslyn asked.

"Parties are for little children," Jinan informed Jesslyn.

"Ah, I see," Jesslyn said, thinking that there were already quite a few things she'd like to say to Sharif, but knowing she'd have to wait until later when the girls returned to their nanny for free time.

"What do you see?" Takia asked, sounding confused.

"I just see the bigger picture now," Jesslyn explained. "I see why you don't want to do games and run around and play. You're all older now and you're thinking about university, and where you're going to go and what you're going to do—"

"I don't want to go to university," Takia interrupted with a wail. "I hate school."

"We all hate it," Saba chimed. "And we hate going to England but we have to do it."

"But sometimes England is better than here," Jinan said meaningfully, looking at her two sisters.

Interesting, Jesslyn thought, sitting back down on the floor and rejoining the circle. "When is boarding school ever better than home?"

But suddenly the girls were all tight-lipped again, and they just looked at her with their big serious eyes and their small pinched lips, lips that looked as though they were hiding some very heavy secrets and stories.

"Well," Jesslyn said. "I guess we're going to play some games. I'll go first. And the game is played like this," and she launched into a demonstration that soon had at least Takia in a fit of giggles.

Outside the living room Sharif stood in the hall listening to Jesslyn convince the girls that her game was fun, and he wasn't sure she could succeed until he heard Takia's peal of laughter.

Her laughter made his chest ache.

He hadn't heard that sound in so long.

What had happened to them all? What had happened to his children? What had happened to him?

He didn't know, although he'd tried talking to the children's headmistress. He'd even switched the girls' nanny here. But nothing had made a difference. The girls wouldn't speak to him unless it was a formal good-morning or good-night.

But Jesslyn would help. Jesslyn had already helped, he told himself, heading toward the entrance where his limousine waited.

He was stepping into the limousine when his mother appeared. "You're leaving without saying hello or goodbye?" she asked coldly, standing so stiffly before him that her veils slid over her shoulder revealing her dark hair without a hint of gray

Sharif's jaw flexed. "You don't take my children out of the city without my permission."

"I just took them to the summer house."

"Listen closely. If you ever take my children from the palace without permission again you'll not be allowed back here. Is that clear?"

His mother's eyes glittered with humiliation. "You've no right to speak to me that way!"

Sharif smiled thinly. "I've every right when you publicly shame me—"

"I've never."

"Every one of my staff knows you were not to have taken the children for the day. Every one of my staff knows you were to have been here for tea yesterday, and instead you spend the night at the summer house."

"The traffic—"

"We have our own helicopter, remember?"

She gestured impatiently. "If you're so upset, why leave now?"

He didn't immediately answer, battling to keep his temper in check. "You knew I had to fly out to Paris this morning. You knew I only had yesterday with the children."

"It's impossible to keep track of your travel schedule."

"I'll have a calendar made for you." And putting his hand on the door he stepped into the back of the car.

She walked closer. "Make one for the children, too. I'm afraid your daughters don't even know you."

He looked up at her, and a dozen protests came to mind, a dozen things he could say in his self-defense. But she was right. His children didn't know him. Today they hadn't even looked at him when he greeted them in the hall. They'd stared at the ground as though he were their worst nightmare.

Pain burst through his chest, red and hot and endless. My God, how did a life that started so promising, become a nightmare like this? "I'll be back on the weekend. Let the children know they can call me anytime."

She lifted her chin. "You can call them."

His burning gaze met hers. "Mother, I try. But someone has to locate them and then put them on the phone."

* * *

Late that afternoon Jesslyn walked the girls to their wing of the palace where their nanny, Mrs. Frishman, waited for them. Jesslyn's first impression of Mrs. Frishman wasn't that positive. The older woman, hired for the summer, seemed far too dour for such young children, but Jesslyn secretly hoped this was just a first impression and her feelings would change upon getting to know the Swiss German nanny better.

"I'll see you at dinner," Jesslyn said as Mrs. Frishman appeared in the doorway. "I'll be interested in hearing how you spent the rest of your afternoon—"

"The children have dinner with their grandmother," Mrs. Frishman interrupted sharply.

"Very nice," Jesslyn answered. The children glanced up at her, their expressions uneasy, and their unease just fed her own. What were they not telling her? she wondered. What was it the girls wanted to say, but wouldn't?

Clearly they weren't comfortable enough to speak candidly to her yet, and so she reached out, touched each child on the top of the head. "Perhaps I'll come say good-night to you once you're in bed."

"It is my job to put them to bed," Mrs. Frishman said, large hands folded in front of her. "You are the teacher. I am their nanny."

Jesslyn's outward serenity never slipped. "Excellent. Then you girls are free of me for the night. But I will see you in the morning after breakfast and be prepared for lots of work then."

"Right," Takia said. "Like Duck, Duck, Goose."

Jesslyn could feel Mrs. Frishman's disapproval and she hid her smile. "Exactly. More Duck, Duck, Goose, and other difficult endeavors." And lifting her fingers to her lips, she blew them a kiss. "Until tomorrow, then."

Turning away, Jesslyn walked back down the hall, conscious that four sets of eyes watched her go, and while she was no mind reader, she could have sworn that the children didn't want her to leave.

Returning to her own wing, Jesslyn walked through her living room and then out the large glass door to her sun-drenched courtyard. Potted lemon trees were interspersed with tree roses, and Jesslyn wandered through the fragrant garden, sniffing blossoms, admiring the vivid apricot- and coral-hued roses. Yet as much as she appreciated the beautiful garden, she couldn't shake her apprehension.

What had traumatized the children so? What was making them withdrawn and fearful in their own home?

"Teacher Fine," Mehta called to her from the doorway. "Would you like tea now?"

"Yes, please," Jesslyn answered gratefully, "and could I enjoy my tea out here? It's lovely in the garden now." And it was lovely with the high walls creating a welcome shade and the twitter of birds mingling with the sound of the splashing fountain.

Mehta returned a few minutes later and presented her with an enormous black binder.

"I'm sorry, the tea isn't ready," she said, bowing. "But His Highness said to give this to you. You are to use it."

Jesslyn watched Mehta hurry away, then glanced down at the big bulky binder in her lap.

What was this? Information from the school? Medical records? Copies of the children's transcripts and homework?

Curiously Jesslyn opened the binder and scanned the table of contents and realized with a start that the binder wasn't background information on the children, but information for her about her job.

The binder was organized in such detail that there even was a table of contents and four separate sections. As she leafed through the binder she saw that every section dictated how she was to behave here, and how she was to interact with the children.

There was to be no hugging, touching or other inappropriate interaction.

The children were to use quiet voices at all times. There was to be no laughing, no singing, no games.

No laughing? No games?

Jesslyn's brow creased and she continued reading, increasingly troubled.

The girls were not allowed to watch television unless it was educational, and even then, only proper programs celebrating their Sarq culture.

The girls were to practice restraint. Tantrums, tears, theatrics and other displays of inappropriate emotion were never permitted.

By now Jesslyn could hardly keep reading. Her chest hurt. Her heart raced. She felt absolutely sick to her stomach.

Swallowing the acid taste in her mouth, she forced herself to move on to Education & Objectives. Surely this wouldn't be so severe, and indeed, this section was relatively basic. The girls were to study every day, to cover all sections in their textbooks that they had received low marks in, and to improve their study skills tremendously. But in addition to eight hours of study a day, they were expected to take twice-weekly dance lessons and voice lessons, they were also required to get thirty minutes of "other" rigorous exercise daily, as well as practice piano and violin an hour every afternoon, and that didn't include art lessons, either.

Swiftly she added up the number of hours to be spent in the classroom, then hours in exercise, hours performing arts, hours practicing one skill or another and the children's day was endless. It began early, concluded late and, studying the list of activities, Jesslyn saw no time scheduled for just old-fashioned play. There was no free time at all, no opportunity for little girls to jump rope, play with dolls, play dress-up or play house.

Everything was regimented. Everything scheduled to the minute.

Little wonder the girls were depressed. Jesslyn felt depressed just looking at their schedule. Taking a pen from her purse, she began making notes in the margins.

She was so busy reading the pages, snorting at the ridiculous expectations and making notes in the margins that she didn't realize someone was standing at her elbow, reading over her shoulder until she heard a very cold female voice.

"You have a problem with your responsibilities already, Miss Jesslyn Heaton?"

Jesslyn startled, jerking upright, hating the shiver that raced through her. She'd know that voice anywhere. Queen Reyna Fehr. "I'm just not sure what this is," she answered, lifting the binder.

"It's obvious. It's your resource binder." Reyna leaned over and snatched the black binder with both hands. "And you're completely defacing it."

Jesslyn felt heat rush through her cheeks, but she held the elder woman's gaze. She wasn't twenty-something anymore. She wouldn't be intimidated. "Well, I won't be using that book, so you can keep it."

Reyna's stare only grew more withering. "It's for you. It explains exactly how to do your job here."

"Thank you, but I don't need to be told how to do my job." Jesslyn stood up so she could be eye level with the queen. "I've already mapped out a course of action for the summer—"

"But this is what we've been using all summer, and this is what you will also follow."

"No," she said quietly.

Reyna's jaw dropped. "Pardon me?"

"No, Your Highness." Jesslyn saw the astonishment on the other woman's face and she felt a tiny prick of pleasure before squashing it. She wasn't here to pick fights or even win them. She was here to help Sharif's children. "The children are seriously depressed. I've rarely met such unhappy little girls, and that binder is partially to blame."

"How can you say that? The children are floundering academically—"

"Only Takia is floundering. I looked at the headmistress's letter. And Takia's floundering because she's homesick. She's far too young to start school—"

"Enough," Queen Reyna snapped, cutting her short. "You don't even know them. You've only just met them. You're in no position to take that tone with me."

Years ago this would have crushed Jesslyn, but nine years ago she didn't know how ruthless or manipulative Sharif's mother could be. "Maybe I don't know them yet, Your Highness, but I make my living working with children and I know how to teach them. And I will teach them, but I shall do it my way."

"I will speak to Sharif!"

"I wish you would," Jesslyn answered evenly. "And while you're at it, do let him know I'll be speaking with him, too."

CHAPTER EIGHT

JESSLYN waited all evening to be summoned to Sharif's chambers. She remained dressed so she'd be ready to go the moment he was free. She'd sent two messages with Mehta, and then one with Sharif's personal butler.

But Sharif didn't call for her, and at midnight, her stomach in knots, Jesslyn finally went to bed.

The next morning she discovered why she'd never heard from Sharif. He was gone, away to Paris, and wouldn't be home for five days.

It would have been nice for him to tell her.

She spent the next few days busy assessing the children's strengths and skills, while introducing the first of the lessons. The children were very bright and enjoyed learning, and as she praised them for their excellent reading and writing, they positively blossomed, somber faces beginning to offer shy smiles.

Counting the days, Jesslyn knew Sharif should be home tomorrow. There were so many things she needed to discuss with him. But the next morning she was informed by Queen Reyna that Sharif would only be home for a brief visit before flying out early the next morning and wouldn't have time to see her.

"He'll see the children," Jesslyn said, trying to hide her disappointment.

"Of course. But they're his family."

Jesslyn sent word to Sharif's butler, anyway, that she needed to see the sheikh when he returned home. She told him it was about the sheikh's children, and the butler assured her he'd pass the message on.

But once again she didn't hear from Sharif, not that night nor the next morning.

Not about to give up, Jesslyn sent another message later in the day that she had to see His Highness, that it was absolutely essential and urgent that they meet. She had concerns about the girls, questions to ask, things only he as the children's father could answer.

This time he sent word back that he'd very much like to meet with her but he'd already left for Jordan, and from there he'd head to New York. However, once he was back in Sarq he'd definitely sit down with her and listen to her concerns.

Her concerns, she thought, sitting at the library table with the children and looking at their bent heads as they labored over their math problems.

Her concerns were his concerns. Her concerns were his children.

A half hour later when the girls had finished their math, Jesslyn casually asked the children if they'd seen their father. "Were you able to see your father while he was home?"

Jinan stacked her books. "He came to say good-night to us last night."

"Did he read you a story?" Jesslyn asked.

Saba's lips pursed. "He doesn't read."

Jinan frowned at her sister. "He reads," she corrected, "but he doesn't read to us."

Jesslyn leaned on the table, arms folded. "But it was a nice visit, right? You talked. You told him about your day and your studies…?"

The girls just shook their heads.

"Why not?" Jesslyn persisted.

"We can't bother him," Takia said.

Jesslyn looked from one to the other. "Why not?"

The girls struggled to answer but finally Saba just shrugged. "*Jaddah,* Grandmother, says he has many worries and we must not trouble him."

Jesslyn reached out and covered Saba's hand with her own. "But it's not a trouble for him to hear about your day. Your father wants to hear about your day."

The girls looked at each other and then Jinan shook her head. "We can't bother him," she repeated stubbornly. "He's the king."

Jesslyn swallowed hard, forced a smile and vowed to speak to Sharif the moment he returned, no matter the cost. She would see him and she would make him understand that it was Sharif who had to change. It was Sharif who had to fix things.

Fortunately, the next five days passed with surprising speed, and by the end of the second week the little girls' shy smiles had turned into giggles and bright eyes. The girls had taken to holding her hand as they walked through the palace gardens. Takia was skipping. Jinan and Saba were telling her jokes. Thirteen days and the girls were finally acting the way little girls should.

Friday arrived, the Friday when Sharif was to return again. She knew he was to return between ten o'clock and midnight.

All evening Jesslyn kept an eye on the clock, and when ten o'clock arrived, she left her room and, ignoring Mehta's anxious enquiries about where she was going, headed to the wing that housed Sharif's personal chambers.

Sharif's butler must have been informed she was coming

as he met her midway down the hall to tell her that His Highness had not yet returned.

Jesslyn looked at the butler for a long moment. "I must see him."

"But he is not yet here."

"He is coming home tonight though."

The butler inclined his head. "Yes, but he could arrive very late. I will tell His Highness that you wish to speak to him and tomorrow you can—"

"I'm not waiting for tomorrow," she said, interrupting him as politely as possible. "I will stay up and wait for him here."

The butler looked aghast. "You cannot wait here."

"Why not?"

He glanced around. "There's nowhere to sit."

"I'll stand."

"But you can't. It's not proper."

"Why not?

The butler was completely flummoxed. He looked over his shoulder, to the left and then the right before throwing up his hands in a helpless gesture. Jesslyn actually felt rather sorry for him.

"I must see His Highness." She smiled apologetically. "And I'm going to stay here until he comes home."

The poor man gave her a rigid half bow before stalking off only to return minutes later with a small stool and pillow.

"Here," he said gruffly. "You must at least be more comfortable."

Jesslyn smiled her thanks and sat down on the stool next to the wall. She wasn't sure how long she'd wait, but suspected it could take a while.

And it did. Fifteen minutes became thirty, thirty minutes became an hour.

An hour.

Jesslyn sighed and tried not to fidget, but she was getting numb from sitting on the small stool even with the pillow. There were plenty of things she wanted to do, needed to do, but right now nothing seemed more important than speaking with Sharif about his children. So she'd wait.

Leaning back against the wall, she bent her legs and tried to relax, telling herself it couldn't be long now. It was nearing midnight. Surely Sharif would arrive soon.

Another half hour passed, creeping by with exhausting slowness. Her head felt heavy, her eyes gritty. She'd close her eyes just for a moment, just to relax for a moment.

"What are you doing here?"

It was Sharif's deep voice speaking from very far away. Jesslyn sleepily opened her eyes and as she opened them she realized where she was, and how she was right now sitting on the marble floor at Sharif's feet.

"Waiting for you," she answered, blinking up at him as she unsuccessfully hid a yawn. "They said you were coming home tonight and I had to talk to you."

"It's nearly three in the morning."

"Oh. It is late." Jesslyn tried to get up, discovered one foot was asleep and with a yelp, sat back down. "Just a minute. It's got that pins-and-needles feeling."

"You've been here since when?" he asked, gazing down at her, his expression somewhere between pity and shock.

She yawned again, finding it very hard to wake up. "Um, ten, tenish."

"Five hours," he muttered. "Unbelievable."

"I insisted," she answered. "You never called me this week and I left you so many messages."

His hands were on his hips and he just shook his head at

her. "Unbelievable," he repeated before crouching next to her and scooping her into his arms.

She stiffened instinctively. "What are you doing?"

He stood easily, lifting her as though she were a child Takia's size instead of a woman. "Taking you back to your room."

He'd already set off for her room, walking swiftly through the halls, his stride long. Her heart beat hard and fast. She felt silly, vulnerable, shy. This was an intimacy she couldn't handle. "Put me down, Sharif," she whispered into his neck as they passed members of Sharif's security detail, "this is embarrassing."

He grimaced. "Imagine how I felt finding you sleeping on the floor outside my chambers."

"I wasn't on the floor. I had a small stool," she protested, wiggling her legs and trying to slide free. "I can walk now. My foot is awake."

He didn't let her go. "We're almost there."

He was right. They'd reached the stairs to her living room and he carried her down those, across the spacious room to the adjoining bedroom.

"All right, I'm here," she said, as he entered the bedroom. "You can put me down now."

Sharif lowered her onto the bed and then took a step back. "No more waiting up half the night to see me."

She looked up at him. "I wouldn't have to wait up if you'd just return my calls."

He stared down into her eyes, his own gaze troubled. "I'm sorry. I never got the messages."

"I asked on four different occasions, spoke to three different household members and palace staff letting them know I needed to speak to you."

Deep furrows etched across his brow while fine lines

deepened at his eyes. He seemed to struggle to find the right words. "Things here at the palace are not what they should be."

"That's a fact."

She got up onto her knees to better see his face. "Things are absurd here, Sharif. You say you want what's best for your daughters and yet—" She broke off, her courage suddenly flagging.

It was one thing to understand a problem; it was another to voice it. In Sarq, men were responsible for taking care of their women, including their mothers. Mothers returned to their sons' homes after their husbands died. Mothers were protected, cherished and supported by their sons. Sharif was the eldest of the Fehr brothers. It was his duty, his responsibility, to provide for Reyna, but in this case the personal cost was too high.

"Yet what?" he pressed.

"It's nearly four in the morning. This isn't the time."

"It's nearly four in the morning. We're running out of time." He put a finger beneath her chin, tilted her face up to his. "So tell me, you've been here nearly two weeks on your own. What's wrong with my children?"

She scanned his face, searched his eyes. How was she to say this? How could she put it without stepping on his toes? "That binder you left for me, the one full of a hundred horrible rules—"

"What binder?"

"The black one, the one that says your children can't be hugged, touched or kissed. The one that says they can't laugh or tease. The one that insists they must study ten to twelve hours a day. That binder."

"I don't know what you're talking about. I never left you a binder. I would never make up, or enforce, rules like that.

Surely, you know me better than that. It must have come from my mother."

If he thought this would soothe her, he was wrong. She reared back, balled her hands on her thighs. "That doesn't strike you as wrong? As deeply, morally offensive? Your mother has created a virtual prison for your children and you shrug it off with an 'Oh, that's my mom.'"

"That's not what I said!"

"No, but it's damn close." She was breathing hard, her pulse racing. "The problem isn't your children. It's your mother."

"I get your point," he said flatly.

"You don't. You've no idea. Your mother is filling the children's heads with fears and phobias that have no bearing in reality."

He sighed wearily. "I know you've never liked her—"

"That's not what this is about! It's about protecting your children!"

"From my mother?" He gave her an incredulous look. "Jesslyn, you forget I am her son and this is her home, too."

"I know you're her son, and I'm aware this is her home, too, but maybe you need a home of your own." She reached out to tug on his robe, wanting him to listen, really listen and not just give lip service to her words. "A home where *you* are the head of the household, and the father to your children, a home where you can make the decisions without constantly being challenged."

He pushed one of her dark curls back from her cheek. "And you wonder why my mother didn't take to you all those years ago."

"I was always nice to her. Too nice," she added faintly, closing her eyes at the feel of his fingers. Every time he touched her she thought her heart would burst. Every time he came near she wanted that past they'd shared, they'd lost.

"Can we just forget about my mother for a moment?" he asked, thumbs sliding beneath her jaw to clasp her face.

"But we can't forget her. We—you—have to do something about her."

"I will." And then his head dipped and his mouth covered hers in a kiss so slow, so sensual she had to grasp his robe with both hands for support.

Part of her brain was telling her there was no way she should be doing this again. Part of her brain was telling her she had to stop, had to pull away, but another part of her brain was drugged, seduced by the hot, sweet pleasure of his mouth on hers and his warm strong hands on her skin.

He nipped at her lower lip with his teeth before exploring the same tender lip with his tongue. Shivering, she leaned against him, and Sharif wrapped an arm around her, drawing her even closer to his muscular frame, holding her so firmly against his powerful body that every breath he took teased her nipples, every flick of his tongue made her more aware of his erection pressing urgently against her hips.

The pressure was a bittersweet pleasure, stirring fresh desire, a purely wanton need.

She'd forgotten that a man's body could feel like this, had forgotten the sinewy pressure of a man's thighs and the width of a real chest. She'd forgotten that bodies could feel so good so close together, and while she'd had several other relationships in the past nine years, it'd never been like this. Never this heady, dizzy seduction of memory and emotion and the senses. And until now she hadn't realized how closely desire was tied to emotion, because she didn't just want him physically, she wanted him the way she'd once wanted him—mind, body and soul. She didn't just want his fingers and lips and skin, she wanted his heart, too.

They were both nearly out of control, a fact she registered in the dimmest part of her brain, but instead of putting a stop to the passionate frenzy, the thought had the opposite effect, driving her to frantically slide her hand beneath his robe, wanting his bare chest, wanting to find that heart she'd lost years ago.

Kissing her even more deeply, he lifted her off her knees and onto her back, before stretching out over her.

She shuddered as he lay on her, his body so warm and powerful and hard, and it hit her yet again how much she'd missed him, how much she'd missed this. Almost whimpering, she tried to drag his robe off so she could feel him properly against her. Skin to skin. Chest to breast.

As she pushed at his robe, struggling to get it off his thickly muscled shoulders, he unfastened the buttons of her navy knit blouse until the blouse lay open in a puddle of fabric at her sides.

Lifting his head, he gazed down at her, gray eyes dark with passion, and he looked at her as though he'd never seen her before, looked at her as though he might never see her again. The expression in his eyes was enough to make her chest constrict and to cut off the air in her throat.

Eyes burning, she slid her fingers through his dark hair, fingers twining tightly in the crisp, silken strands, dragging his head down, dragging his mouth back to hers.

This time she kissed him, this time she kissed him hard, fiercely, opening her mouth to him, playing with his tongue, sucking on the tip to try to drive him wild, wanting him to feel what he was doing to her.

What he'd always done to her.

She loved him. She hated him. She was half-dead without him.

Tears slid from beneath her lashes as she gave herself to him, overwhelmed by the hunger and the need and the knowledge that this, what they were doing now, would never happen again.

Sharif's hands were everywhere, on her belly, on the cleft between her thighs. He was touching, stroking, making her soft and wet, so wet that she had to have him, with her, in her.

She helped push his trousers over his hips and then leaned over his body to kiss the flat hard muscles of his abdomen and the smooth arc of hipbone and the lean line of muscle of his thighs.

As she kissed down his thigh, her lips and tongue alternating soft kisses with flicks of her tongue, she felt his hands bury in her hair, tugging at her head with the urgency of his passion.

She knew what he wanted, and felt his hands on her breasts, cupping the fullness of her breasts as she bent over him, her mouth now so close to his rigid shaft but still not giving him the satisfaction he ached for.

Sharif massaged then pinched her nipples between his fingers, his body straining, his skin hot, glowing golden. She blew warm air across the tip of his erection, heard him groan deep in his throat and then lightly, so lightly she took the head of him into her mouth.

He was huge in her mouth, and yet so beautifully firm and warm and satin smooth, his thickness perfect for his length and with her hands and mouth she stroked him until, panting, he abruptly pulled her off.

"I don't want to know who taught you that," he growled, voice raspy, his eyes burning with hunger, fire.

She stared into his eyes, wanting to remember this, wanting to remember him, wanting to have all the passion she'd gone without for the past nine years.

"You did," she whispered, lightly raking her nails down his chest, savoring the texture of his skin over hard muscle.

"We never did that before."

"I always wanted to. So tonight I did."

He lifted her off her bottom and onto his thighs, forcing her to straddle him. "Why?" he asked huskily.

Her shoulders lifted and fell. "I wanted to see what it'd be like if you were mine."

She heard his swift intake of breath, felt his hand bunch tightly in her hair, and after staring up at her for long, silent minutes he released her hair and his hands slid down over her shoulders to the fullness of her bare breasts.

"Has it always been this way with us?" he asked, a strange note in his voice.

She had to swallow against the tears. "I don't know. I don't remember." *I just remember how much I loved you.*

"I want you. Heaven knows I want you, even though I don't know what that means—"

She cut him off by leaning forward and covering his mouth with hers, kissing him slowly, softly, kissing him with her eyes closed so that he couldn't see how much she needed this, wanted this, wanted him. She wasn't experienced in bed, the only time she'd ever enjoyed making love had been with Sharif, but after all these years she knew what their bodies were for and she knew what making love meant.

And kissing him, she took away all the words, all the thoughts, all reason. Kissing him, she took away everything but the moment because that's all she wanted. She never asked for anything for herself. She never wanted anything for herself, but right now she wanted this. She wanted him.

One night. Right now.

But Sharif wasn't going to let her dictate the kiss. Instead he took the kiss and made it hot, desperate, fierce. He kissed her with a savage hunger that left her trembling in his arms, against his chest.

Lifting her against him he rolled her onto her back and parted her knees with his. She felt him shift over her, the sinewy pressure of his thighs against her own, his shaft rigid against her, pressing against her most delicate flesh. She was ready for him, and yet when he finally entered her it took her breath away. Helplessly she pressed her fingers into his chest, overwhelmed by the size and strength of him. He was bigger, thicker than she'd remembered, and the sensation of silk and heat entering her, opening her, filling her made thought impossible.

Instead she clung to him, arms wrapping around his neck, her mouth turned to his warm scented chest, as he withdraw a little and then thrust again, deeper this time, harder.

Again he withdrew before driving into her, and with each thrust it felt as though he were marking her, branding her, making her his. Indeed it was a taking, a claiming, a ravishment of body and senses.

Sharif filled her, plunging deeply into her, she ground her hips to match each of his thrusts, wanting to satisfy the wildness of her own need, her desire for him insatiable. She wanted as much of him as he'd give her, and she groaned against his chest, craving the power of his sleek body, the hard contours of his back, the lean force of his hips.

She was beginning to lose control and, eyes tightly closed, Jesslyn clung to him, her body tightening convulsively. She felt the tension within her building, the pressure rising swiftly, too swiftly, making her feel as though she'd soon explode.

Sharif's hands covered hers, palm to palm, and as he drove again into her, his fingers laced with hers. And that last thrust pushed her over the edge, sending her shooting into nothingness, just darkness, oblivion.

For an endless moment she felt lost between worlds, no longer attached to her body, her mind spinning away, and then Sharif was kissing her and with one final thrust, he climaxed, his orgasm following right after hers.

Jesslyn felt his body tighten and release and, wrapping her arms around his back, she held him, held him as though she had eternity instead of a night of stolen minutes.

This was, she realized, struggling to catch her breath, the beginning of the end, of the end…of a life as she knew it. No matter what happened now, life as she knew it was changed. Dubai would be different. Dubai was too close to Sarq.

Heart still hammering, body still warm, she held her breath trying to remember this feeling. It was a good feeling. A very good feeling. Being in Sharif's arms wasn't about sex. It was about making things right, making things fit, making her belong.

With Sharif she always felt as if she'd come home.

With Sharif she wasn't that poor little orphaned girl, or that scholarship girl. She wasn't Aunt Maddie's poor niece. With Sharif she was perfect. With Sharif she was whole.

Acid tears filled her eyes, and she closed her eyes, kept them closed, to keep any tears from falling.

Maybe this wasn't such a good idea after all. Maybe making love had just broken her heart all over again.

Suddenly Sharif shifted and the mattress sagged beneath his weight as he moved off her and then climbed from bed. "It's nearly six," he said, standing up and stepping into his trousers.

Opening her eyes, she looked at him. He was reaching for his robe, pulling it over his head and shoulders.

"The staff are already up," he added. "I hear voices down the hall. Mehta will be here soon."

Slowly she sat up, pulled the pale-pink silk coverlet over her to hide her nakedness and only then realized she was shivering. She was cold, freezing cold, her teeth nearly chattering and it was shock that was making her cold, shock that it had ended so abruptly, ended without a kiss or tender word.

But what was he supposed to say? What did she want from him?

And just like that she remembered he'd hired her for the summer. To take care of the children. To teach his heirs.

Eyes gritty, she bit down on her lip and tried to smile, because if he was going to walk out on her she wasn't going to let him see her cry. No more tears, she told herself, not for him, not for her. She got exactly what she wanted—sex. Hot sex. A great big orgasm, and wasn't that fantastic? Wasn't that just what she needed?

Her throat was sealing closed. Her eyes burned like mad but she kept her head up, kept her lips curved.

Smile, she told herself, smile like there's no tomorrow. Smile like you do this kind of thing all the time.

"Are there lessons scheduled for today?" Sharif asked, barely glancing at her as he combed his fingers through his thick dark hair, taming the inky strands.

That's right, Jesslyn thought, chilled to the bone. She wasn't his girlfriend or his lover.

She was the teacher. Hired help. Cheap summer labor.

CHAPTER NINE

"LESSONS?" Jesslyn repeated incredulously, clutching the coverlet to her chest. "On Saturday?"

He shot her a quick look. "What does that mean? You don't work on Saturdays?"

She heard the criticism in his voice and chose to ignore it. "Children benefit from breaks. This is also their summer holiday."

"You know they must get caught up with school."

"And by summer's end, they will be, but what they need most is time to relax, time to play, time to see you and be a family."

"Later today," he answered. "First, lessons with you this morning, and then let them know I'll come during their afternoon tea."

"Oh, lovely, King Fehr. I'll be sure to pass the message on."

He spun on his heel. "What was that?"

She held his gaze, her eyes hot and bright. "You haven't seen the children in nearly a week and you'll make them wait until tea to see you?" She made a soft sound of disgust. What the hell had happened to Sharif, her Sharif, the one she'd dated and practically lived with? Now he was like a stranger again, a king.

That man had been the consummate lover—warm, patient,

considerate—a man who instinctively seemed to know what a woman wanted, felt, and Jesslyn had been so sure he'd be the same kind of parent someday. Warm, patient, loving, kind. But that wasn't who he was at all.

As a father he was far too distracted, which made him too distant with his children. Maybe he wanted to be involved, maybe he even imagined himself involved, but the truth was the girls saw more of their grandmother and nanny than they did of him.

"What has happened to you?" she added roughly, wrapping the coverlet more tightly around her and sliding off the bed. "Where did you go?"

He groaned impatiently. "I don't have time for this."

"No, of course you don't, but then, you're not the Sharif Fehr I knew. That man took care of his friends and family. That man wasn't cold and preoccupied."

"I have a job now."

"You had a job then, and you were successful, and people liked you, people admired you. *I* admired you."

"My people here are happy. My people are content. There is no war, no plague, no devastating disease. The economy is strong. People have jobs. People have lives."

"You don't," she choked. "You have a job, and you work, but you don't have a life. At least, you don't have a life that includes your children."

"I see them."

"Once a week!" Heat rushed through her, warmth burning her cheeks. She was heartsick and disappointed. Disappointed in him. "You see your children for moments in hallways, between meetings and appointments and fights with your mother."

"Why do you think I brought you here? I know they needed help—"

"But I'm not you, and what they need is you." How could he not see that? How could he not understand that he was not just their father but their family? He was all that kept his children from being lost, orphaned like her.

He clenched his jaw. "I'm sorry you don't approve of my parenting skills, but I am trying. I am doing my best. I never saw my parents. And, yes, it was difficult. And, yes, I'd get lonely, but I understood they had important jobs and I understood they cared even if they didn't see me as often as I would have liked."

"Cared?" she repeated. "Is that the same as love?"

"Jesslyn."

"If your children had been sons, would you have been more involved?" She pressed on, a massive lump in her throat. "Would you have had more time for them?"

He took a furious step toward her. "How dare you? How dare you take such liberties with me?"

She pressed her lips together, misery mingling with the brutal disillusionment. "I dare because you came to me a couple of weeks ago and told me your children were in trouble. I dare because you insisted your children needed me, and you needed someone to tell you the truth. So here I stand, telling you the truth." She looked at him levelly. "The girls don't need another paid babysitter or kind stranger. They need you. You, their father, the only parent they still have left."

"And what of my people?" he demanded. "What do I do with the millions who live in this country and look to me for help? What do I do about them? Tell them I can't help them? Tell them I don't have time because I have three daughters who require all my attention instead?"

"Why must you make a joke of it? The girls don't need you all day, but they do need time, each day, every day. If you set some routines, made a point of having dinner with them every night, or some nights, read to them before putting them to bed—"

"Shall I invite my cabinet to story time, too?" he said, mocking her.

She looked at him a long moment before shaking her head in sorrow. "You might be king now, but I liked you better when you were a man."

She wasn't surprised when Sharif walked out without a word or backward glance. After what she'd said, she hadn't expected anything less.

Now with Sharif gone, Jesslyn sat back on her bed and drew the coverlet around her and tried not to think, because thinking at this point wouldn't help. Thinking would just lead to recriminations and she didn't want to feel bad or guilty or anything else.

She had a good life, and when she went back to Sharjah, she'd still have a good life. She had a career she loved and students she adored. Her colleagues weren't just people she worked with, but close friends. She didn't need Sharif or the palace or this complicated life in Sarq. She didn't need his children, either, although she was beginning to think they very much needed her.

In his ensuite bath, Sharif's jaw clenched tight as he stripped his clothes off and stepped into the shower.

What had she thrown at him just before he'd walked out? She liked him better when he was a man?

He bit down harder, knowing she'd hit below the belt on that one. Violently he turned the water on, stepping beneath the spray before it'd even warmed up. It was cold but he didn't shiver. Instead he stood there, icy water pounding down on his head.

Fool, he was such a fool. What had he done, making love to Jesslyn? How could he possibly have thought that would help matters?

No, making love hadn't satisfied him. It'd hurt. Leaving her had hurt. Being with her had hurt.

She felt so good in his arms, so good against his chest where he could almost imagine she was his one true love, Jesslyn, the only one he'd ever loved.

Closing his eyes, he turned around, leaned against the wall, letting the water sluice down.

Zulima had hated him for not loving her better. Zulima had hated him for once calling her Jesslyn while making love. After that she just withdrew from him, completely shutting down and withdrawing to a place he couldn't reach her. But he tried. For years he tried. Yet she wouldn't forgive and he couldn't make it up to her.

And then she died.

Talk about the ultimate punishment—leaving him with a lifetime of guilt.

He felt guilty for ruining his marriage, guilty for depriving his daughters of their mother, guilty for not being a better husband and father.

Turning the water off, Sharif stood in the shower, hearing the water drip.

Who would have thought that an English teacher could level a king?

Finally grabbing a towel, Sharif headed to his room and forced himself to action. After dressing and shaving he headed for his office to start the day.

Sharif's butler was at the door to Sharif's office before Sharif was even there, opening the door for him and turning on the lights.

"Coffee, Your Highness?" the butler asked as Sharif took a seat behind his desk.

Sharif's eyes burned and his body ached as he sat down, but exhaustion wasn't an excuse. It didn't excuse him from work. While he was in Paris and New York problems still arose in Sarq.

"And something to eat. Bread and yogurt. Or some fruit."

"Yes, Your Highness." The butler bowed and disappeared, quietly closing the office door shut behind him.

Almost immediately the door opened again and his mother marched in, the dark silks of her gown swirling with every step.

"You should knock," he said wearily, knowing that his mother fully intended to treat the palace as though it were still hers…forever. That is, if he didn't stop her. And it was time to stop her.

"I want her gone," his mother replied.

"This isn't the time," he answered, not at all prepared to discuss Jesslyn with his mother, much less an hour after leaving Jesslyn's bed.

"Sharif, I'm not in the mood for games."

He smiled. He couldn't help it. It was that or take her head off with his teeth.

His mother wasn't just skating on thin ice, she was jumping on cracked ice. She was going under and she didn't even know. *Yet.*

"I want her—the one you've put in your sisters' room—gone," she added forcefully.

He looked up at her, expression bland. "My sisters have been gone for a long time, and you know others use that room. Just three weeks ago Sheikh al-Buremi's wife slept there."

"How could you bring her here in the first place? She betrayed you. Betrayed all of us by taking that money!"

As if his mother had had no part in the betrayal. As if his mother hadn't baited Jesslyn, tempted her and paid her off.

Sharif tapped a pen on his blotter. Thank God marriage had taught him life-changing lessons like: never show emotion; never show love; never show need. By the second year of marriage Zulima hated all displays of emotion, particularly his. She told him she'd sleep with him but wouldn't kiss him. She'd procreate to produce a child as long as he did it quickly and then rolled off and left.

And is that why he'd made love to Jesslyn and then walked away?

Was he punishing Jesslyn for Zulima's pain, or was he punishing himself?

It'd been hell this morning leaving Jesslyn so quickly and he didn't understand why he left that way. He'd wanted to stay with her but he'd been overwhelmed by his emotion, his passion, his need. It'd been nine years since he'd felt that right with a woman. Nine years since it hadn't been sex but truly making love.

"Sharif." His mother's voice turned shrill.

"I need her," he said simply. "Now if you'll excuse me, I've other things to focus on, things more pressing than worrying about you not wanting an American in the east wing."

"What do you mean, you need her?"

"I mean the children and I need her."

"No, no, absolutely not. Now, listen to me, Sharif. She was wrong for your sisters, wrong for you, and she's definitely wrong for your daughters."

"That's where we disagree," he answered, rising slowly from behind his desk. "She was fantastic for my sisters, she was wonderful with me, and she's perfect for my daughters. Now, it's been a long day, Mother, and I'm not about to start my day by arguing with you. If you were wise, you'd leave, now."

"I know you left her room this morning."

Sharif stared his mother down. "How do you get this kind of information out of people, Mother? Do you threaten them or just offer money?"

Two bright spots of color appeared in Reyna's pale cheeks, but she held his gaze. "At least I care about the future of this country! At least I know what is right."

"Do you?" He demanded softly, leaning on his desk, his palms pressed flat to the surface, the muscles in his shoulders flexing, tightening. "Then I'd suggest you take your leave before I have you thrown out."

"Sharif, it is your duty—"

"To provide for you and protect you, yes, I know. But if my brothers knew the truth about you, if they knew you bribe and blackmail and intimidate to get your way, they'd have you on the streets, too."

In the library Jesslyn sat at one of the long tables working with the children. It was late morning with lunch still an hour away and the girls were drooping with fatigue.

"Is our father really home?" Jinan suddenly asked, looking up from her notebook, her dark eyes huge in her face. "Or were you just teasing us?"

Saba and Takia were both looking at Jesslyn now, too, and the longing in their eyes took her breath away. They weren't scared of him, she realized, they were desperate to know him.

Jesslyn swallowed, her heart hurting for the children. "He's promised to have tea with you."

"When is tea?" Takia asked, the tip of her tongue showing through the gaps in her bottom teeth.

Jesslyn had spent the day trying not to think about Sharif and tea. She'd fought to forget last night and the painful way

Sharif had left her this morning. "After lunch, after several more hours studying, and then it'll be tea."

"Four hours," Jinan said.

"Four hours?" Saba groaned, putting her head on the table in despair. "That's so long."

"Forever," Takia agreed.

Jesslyn took in their distressed faces and she wanted to scoop them all into her arms and give them the biggest hug. She loved spending the day with them, it wasn't a chore and it didn't feel like a job. It felt right. The girls needed love and she needed to be needed. It's why she'd become a teacher in the first place.

"How about we do something different for a while?" she suggested, leaning on the table. "What if we do something...fun?"

Jinan shook her head. "We can't have fun. Remember?"

Jesslyn hadn't heard the library door open but suddenly Sharif was there in the doorway. "Why can't you have fun?" he asked, his deep voice surprising everyone so much that the children jumped.

The girls immediately all stood and bowed their head. "Welcome home, Father," they chorused obediently, and yet they were staring at the table, their faces blank.

"Thank you," he answered, walking toward them. "It's good to be home."

He paused, looked at each of them and then at Jesslyn, his expression perplexed. Jesslyn wasn't sure what to do, but it seemed far too awkward to have the children still standing with their heads bowed as if waiting the executioner.

"Girls, perhaps you could sit and show your father what you're working on," she suggested, hoping to sound matter-of-fact and yet horrified that her own heart was beating so fast. Moments ago they'd all been so comfortable, and now tension threatened to slice the room into shreds.

The girls sat down and drew their textbooks back in front of them, but no one spoke or volunteered to go first.

"Jinan," Jesslyn said, "why don't you tell your father about the story you're reading."

Jinan glanced up at Jesslyn, her eyes enormous, expression stricken.

Jesslyn heard Sharif's sigh. He was disappointed. She was, too. She really wanted the children to relax better around him, but he didn't help. He didn't seem to know how to talk to them.

Looking at Sharif she managed a smile. "This morning has been a reading morning. We're all reading short stories and then this afternoon we're going to paint something that could have happened in the story." Pausing, she looked at them, praying they'd jump in, praying they'd try to reach for their father. "Your daughters are excellent readers. All of them."

"I'm not that good." It was Takia and she was worriedly looking up at Sharif, her tongue poking out between the gaps in her bottom baby teeth. "I don't read very good."

Jinan's head jerked up. "She does, too. She's very good for a five-year-old."

Saba nodded and reached out to pat Takia on the back. "That's true. She's a very good five-year-old."

Jesslyn crossed her arms over her chest, hands balling to hide the rush of pride. She loved these girls. Somehow they were becoming her girls.

"Takia, I knew you'd be a good reader," Sharif answered gravely. The girls looked up at him, their foreheads creasing faintly.

"How did you know?" Takia asked.

The corner of his mouth lifted. "Because you loved to chew on books when you were a baby."

Saba giggled. Takia smiled, and Jinan looked at her father with something between bewilderment and wonder.

"Do you remember me as a baby?" Saba asked.

He nodded, and sat down on the edge of the bench not far from Jinan. "Your favorite thing to do was scream."

This elicited more giggles from Saba and Takia while Jinan continued to look at her father from beneath her lashes as though she couldn't decide if it was okay to smile yet.

"And Jinan?" Saba asked, pointing to her big sister. "What about Jinan? What was she like as a baby?"

Sharif looked at his eldest daughter for a long searching moment. "Just like that," he said nodding at her. "So serious. So wise. So determined to do everything perfectly."

"Did she?" Takia glanced back and forth from her sister to her father.

"Yes." He nodded and reached out gently to place his hand on top of her head. "She has always done everything perfectly."

Jinan's head suddenly tipped back and she looked at her father, tears filling her eyes. "I don't do everything perfectly. I don't do anything perfectly." Her small mouth compressed, trying to hide the trembling. "If I did, Mother wouldn't have died and we wouldn't have had to go away to England."

For a moment there was only silence, the deafening kind of silence that follows a lethal blow, and Jesslyn dug her nails into her palms to keep from speaking, to keep from moving forward and filling the awful stillness.

Jaw clamped tight, Sharif let his hand slide from the top of Jinan's head down over her beautiful long, dark hair. "You went to England," he said quietly, "because your mother had gone to school there and it was her dream for you to attend the same school. It wasn't supposed to be a punishment."

"We hate it," Saba said bluntly.

Takia nodded soberly. "We hate it, too," she agreed.

Jesslyn saw Sharif's throat work. He was battling with himself, battling with his emotions. "Maybe you won't go back at the end of summer," he said carefully. "Maybe you can stay here."

"And Miss Heaton can teach us!" Saba cried, turning to grab Jesslyn's hand. "You could stay with us and be our teacher forever."

Jesslyn avoided Sharif's gaze. "I love being with you," she answered, trying to keep things light. "But it's still early in the summer. You might hate me soon—"

"Never." It was Jinan, and her voice was pitched low and fierce. "You're the only good thing that's happened to us since Mother died."

And that, Jesslyn thought holding her breath, said it all.

Queen Reyna rapped on the library door and stepped inside the room. "What's this? No studying? Miss Heaton, I'm surprised at you. I should have thought the children would be working right now."

"I'm giving them the rest of the day off," Sharif said, interrupting her, getting to his feet.

"Oh. Sharif." Reyna took a hasty step backward. "I'm sorry. I didn't realize you were here. Of course you're entitled to visit with the children. I just thought you might have waited until their lunch break—"

"We're going to have lunch now. We'll eat together and then do something fun this afternoon."

"Fun?" Reyna squeaked.

"Fun," Sharif answered, smiling down at the children. "Whatever that happens to be."

After Queen Reyna left, Sharif asked Jesslyn to join them for lunch. During the meal in the formal dining room Jesslyn took in the children's small faces as they talked to their father about what they were studying.

Sharif, she knew, was making a huge effort to ask questions they could answer comfortably. When he didn't seem to know what to say, Saba or Takia leaped in to carry the conversation along, and Jesslyn was touched all over again by the way the children worked together, to help each other, and to even help Sharif.

You couldn't ask for sweeter children, or sadly, more vulnerable children. They'd made some progress in the past two weeks but it wasn't enough. The girls needed stability, security, love, and with ample love they'd thrive. Without it…she shook her head, unwilling to even contemplate a future where the children weren't properly nurtured.

But looking at them now, feeling their excitement, knowing they were thrilled just to be with their father gave her hope. Growing up without a proper family of her own made her appreciate families, made her understand how important it was for children to feel as though they belonged.

"So, what are we going to do later?" Saba asked, ever the brave one.

Sharif surveyed the children and then looked at Jesslyn. He hesitated a moment and then spoke slowly. "I was thinking we haven't used the pool in a long time and maybe you'd enjoy going for a swim."

His words were greeted by silence and then Jinan leaned forward. "In the baby pool?"

He turned to his eldest, his expression every bit as serious as hers. "Do you prefer the baby pool?"

"No, but that's the only pool Jaddah said we can use. She said the other pool is for adults only."

Sharif frowned and appeared to be thinking this over. Then

he stretched out his hands and sighed heavily. "I'm sorry, children, I hate to say this—" he paused and Jesslyn could feel the children's collective sigh of disappointment, "—but your grandmother is wrong."

And then the unthinkable happened.

Jinan giggled. Saba laughed. And Takia cheered.

Sharif looked across the table to Jesslyn and his gaze met hers and held. He was smiling, one of those warm, crooked smiles of his, and it was a smile that reached his eyes, that made the gray irises glow like precious silver. "Thank you," he mouthed.

She nodded, and swallowed around the huge lump filling her throat. It was her pleasure.

CHAPTER TEN

AFTER lunch Jesslyn changed into her practical navy swim suit, which she topped with an equally conservative white terry cloth beach cover-up.

Hesitating before the mirror in her room, Jesslyn tugged at the cover-up and found herself wishing she had something more beautiful to wear. It wasn't until she'd arrived here that she saw her life in a different light, saw the spareness and plainness of not just her wardrobe, but her inner life.

Just two weeks here and her world felt full of color and energy and complexity. Just two weeks here and she felt full of life, along with a dazzling range of emotion. Emotion she hadn't felt in nearly ten years.

It wasn't just Sharif, either, that made her feel so much. It was the children. Their need for love and the love they gave her made her feel valuable. Made her want to ensure the children had the best of everything, including the time and attention from their father.

Leaving her room, Jesslyn walked in her flat sandals through the back of the palace to the pool she hadn't even known existed until today.

Waiting outside the pool gate, she peered through the

fanciful wrought iron trying to see all of the pool, which could only be described as a desert extravagance.

The pool had been constructed to look like an island paradise. It had rope bridges and was lushly landscaped with scarlet bougainvillea and palms with a dramatic waterfall as the centerpiece. The towering rock waterfall flowed into one of three enchanting lagoons, and at closer inspection Jesslyn could see that each of the lagoons were really separate pools but with different water features—slides, tunnels and currents. The pool closest appeared quite shallow and even had its own beach where gentle waves lapped onto endless golden sand.

Why hadn't the children begged her to bring them here? This was paradise!

She was still taking it all in when Sharif emerged from the palace. "You could have gone in," he said. "You didn't have to wait out here."

"It looks like Fiji," she laughed, turning to face him. "It's amazing!"

"It was completed just a couple of months ago. I had it built for the children."

She glanced over her shoulder at the waterfall and slides, the little tunnels and coves as though it were a miniature tropical island instead of the backyard of someone's home. "Why haven't the girls told me about it? I would think they'd be here all the time."

Sharif grimaced. "They don't know about it."

"What?"

He nodded, shamefaced. "My mother was very upset about the construction project. She thought it an extravagance, or something one would find in Dubai, not Sarq, so she will only permit the girls to swim in the baby, blow-up pool she keeps for 'special occasions.'"

Jesslyn laughed. She couldn't help it. "A plastic blow-up pool is for special occasions? Wow."

"Mother doesn't believe in spoiling them," he said, opening the gate and leading them into the new tropical oasis.

"It's more than spoiling, Sharif. I'm concerned that she's telling them things that aren't true."

"Such as?" he asked, closing the gate behind her.

She stepped out of her sandals and onto the hot soft sand. "They don't talk to you because they're afraid to—"

"I don't hurt them, Jesslyn. I'd never hurt them."

"But they've been told by Jaddah that they can't bother you."
"What?"

She nodded, grimacing. "The girls told me that your mother has forbidden them from telling you things because you're busy."

"But that's ridiculous. I would want them to talk to me."

"Do they know that though? Have you told them? Made time for them?"

He stared at her, genuinely bemused. "But of course."

"Recently? Since they returned home from school?"

He turned away, walked across the crescent beach, and she followed, the gentle waves from the beach pool lapping at her feet. "Sharif, they're young children and they were gone a long time. They need extra time with you, extra reassurance. Unfortunately, instead of being told how Daddy loves them very much, they're getting the opposite—"

"That Daddy can't be bothered," he concluded, his back to her.

"More or less," she agreed.

"And I thought they hated me," he said half under his breath.

She heard whispers of pain and yet also relief in his voice and, closing the distance between them, Jesslyn put a gentle hand on his back. "You didn't know."

"But I'm their father. I *should* know these things." He turned to face her, his fingers tipping her chin up so that he could look into her eyes. "And I will know these things."

She couldn't hide her smile. "Good."

"It's going to be different from now on. Everything will be different."

"Even better. You have the most lovely children. I absolutely adore them. Speaking of which, where are they? I can't wait to see their reactions when they discover the pool."

He stepped away, looked toward the house, his brow furrowing. "I think their nanny is making them take short naps. She said they needed to wait awhile after eating before swimming."

"But it's already been an hour."

"Probably my mother's involvement," he answered, tossing his beach towel down onto the sand in a spot shaded by a towering palm and then taking a seat on it. "Anything to keep everyone from being happy."

Jesslyn sighed. That was it, wasn't it? Queen Reyna wasn't happy, and so she couldn't bear for anyone else to feel good. And yet what a crime to inflict pain just to keep those around you from feeling peace or pleasure. "Sharif, I'm concerned about her. She seems angrier than I remembered her, and she wasn't happy back then."

"I know. My brothers have noticed it, too. Zayed refuses to have anything to do with her and Khalid's gone to the desert."

"Leaving you to manage her."

Sharif didn't immediately answer. Instead he looked away toward the waterfall dancing over dramatic rocks.

"I know it's not easy, Sharif."

He made a rough sound. "And I don't do it well. The truth is, she makes me so angry, which just makes me feel guiltier. I don't like her here, I don't want her here, but I can't seem to kick her out. From the time I was very small it was drummed into me—protect your mother and sisters, protect and defend them." He looked up at her, his brow furrowed. "I do try, Jesslyn, even though you think I don't. But talking, sharing, all these things that come naturally to you, are very difficult for me."

"Yet you talk to me," she answered, crossing the beach to sit down next to him in the sand.

"You're different."

Puzzled, she tucked a curl behind her ear. "How?"

"It just feels different with you. From the time I met you, I've been able to be myself with you. Not Prince Sharif this, or King Fehr that, but me, the person. The man."

She watched him scoop up a handful of sand, the grains clenched in his fist, delicate rivers of sand sliding between his fingers. "But surely with Zulima—"

"No." He shook his head, opened his hand, let the rest of the sand fall.

Jesslyn leaned forward, arms hugging her knees. "But how could she not adore you? You're smart, very kind, absolutely gorgeous, and you have a body to die for." She blushed, embarrassed she'd said the last part and quickly added, "You've also a wicked sense of humor. How could she not love you?"

His dark head was bent, and she couldn't see his face, just the thick hair at his nape and the sleek muscle that ran along the top of his shoulder. "I made a mistake early in our marriage," he said, his voice low, so low she had to strain to hear him. "Zulima never forgave me for it. Not even on the day she died."

"I can't believe that, Sharif."

He looked up at her, eyes deeply shadowed. "The day she died I was with here in the emergency room. I was holding her hand, telling her we were going to save her, telling her she'd be okay, and she said she didn't want to be saved. She said she'd rather die."

Jesslyn pressed her chest to her knees, struggling to process what he was telling her. "What had you done?"

He made a smothered sound and shook his head.

"Sharif." She touched his arm. "Tell me."

He lifted her hand, turned it over, looked at her palm and her slender fingers and then he kissed her palm before setting it on the sand. "I called her by your name while we were… together."

The kiss on her hand sent darts of red-hot feeling everywhere. "But it was an accident," she said, burying her tingling hand in the sand.

"Of course it was an accident but she knew how I felt about you. She knew I wasn't over you."

Jesslyn looked at his beautiful masculine profile with the black brows, strong nose, firm mouth and hard chin and she didn't think she'd ever loved a face as much as she loved his. And looking at him, she could feel how it'd been with them last night, when they were making love. He was everything she'd ever loved, and she couldn't even explain it, other than it felt right with him, he felt like hers, like the one who'd been made for her.

Impulsively she leaned forward and kissed him, and what was meant to comfort became something else entirely, something blistering and hot.

Clasping her face between his hands, Sharif kissed her with a hunger he didn't even try to disguise. He parted her lips, searched the inside of her mouth with his tongue, tracing the shape of her mouth, the delicate skin inside her lip, but not giving her too much, not giving her enough to satisfy.

Blindly she reached for him, hands settling on his chest, fingers twining in his robe as she struggled to meet her need for more contact, more pleasure.

This was too much, she thought wildly, too fierce, too fiery, too explosive. She felt as if she had a fever and it was consuming her and she needed him to strip her clothes off and drag her into the pool. She needed his body in hers, now, but this need wasn't physical. It came from something deeper, from a part of her that had been so closed, so shut down.

She wanted him, wanted him with a savage thirst and hunger. After trying to live a quiet orderly life all these years she wanted to break free.

His hand slipped down her neck, to the base of her throat where her pulse beat madly, wildly, and then his hand slid lower until he cupped her breast, the pressure of his fingers against her skin excruciating and exquisite. She wrapped her hand around his arm, her fingers digging into the thick corded muscle of his bicep, urging him closer, wanting as much as she could get.

But suddenly he was breaking the kiss off, pulling away and getting to his feet. He took several steps away, faced the waterfall that tumbled into the deepest pool. "Our lives would have been so different if you'd married me," he said roughly, his back to her.

"You wouldn't have had your girls."

He looked over his shoulder at her, expression fierce. "They would have been our girls."

"It wouldn't have worked that way." She swallowed, her heart was hammering so hard it hurt. She needed to tell him about her fertility issues, needed to make him realize he'd done the right thing all those years ago. He might have loved her, but she wasn't the sort of woman a future king could marry.

"The girls could have used a mother like you," he added

bitterly. "Zulima didn't know what to do with the girls once they were born. The children were always with a nanny or nannies, and she'd see them briefly each day, but there were plenty of days where she didn't visit them at all."

"It bothered you."

He exhaled slowly, rubbing his face. "I'd go see the girls at night when they were babies and toddlers. I'd sneak into their rooms and walk with them, carry them outside to look at the moon and stars. I'd tell myself that someday things would be different. Things would be better." His lips twisted darkly. "It never happened."

"That's not true. It's happening now. You're taking the steps you need to take. You're making the necessary changes now."

"But I don't know how to do this. I don't know what I'm doing. I have three children, but I've never really been a father."

"Sharif, it's never too late."

"Never too late," he repeated under his breath before looking at her, creases fanning from his eyes.

He was looking at her as though she was an apparition, a ghost, and it made her uneasy.

"Why did you leave me?" he asked after a long moment. "Will you finally tell me why?"

"We weren't right—"

"We were right." He cut her off ruthlessly. "Everything about us was right. Our relationship was so natural, so easy, so effortless. Why would you just walk away from what we had?"

She closed her eyes, felt the sun pound down on the top of her head. "Your mother never wanted me with you." Just saying the words brought back the awful day his mother had cornered her in her London flat whispering poisonous words that had broken her heart.

Sharif will never marry you. He'll never get our approval

to marry you. No only are you so wrong for him, but you can't have children, can you? And Sharif must have children as Sharif will soon be king.

It'd been crushing to have her injury thrown in her face. She hadn't expected it. She'd never discussed her injury with anyone. Hadn't even known that Sharif's mother knew. "Your mother told me I wasn't an acceptable bride for you."

"And that's why you left me?" Sharif drawled. "You wanted my mother's approval?"

"It wasn't about approval."

"Then what was it?"

She got to her feet and nervously glanced at the palace, knowing the children would arrive any minute. "It's personal. Hard to discuss."

"Come on, Jesslyn, you're a teacher. You can talk about anything."

Not this, she thought, amazed that it could still hurt so much. It'd never been easy to talk about. She loved kids. She'd always wanted kids. Discovering she'd never be a mother had been crushing.

"Would you like some help?" he added, strolling toward her. "Should I tell you what I heard?"

She lifted her chin. "Why not?"

"Why not," he repeated softly, laughing without humor, his features taut, his eyes lit by anger. "Why not indeed." And standing in front of her, he gazed down into her eyes. "My mother said you made a little deal. You'd go away and as a thank-you for your cooperation, you'd leave with some money."

Jesslyn's heart thumped. Was he out of his mind? "You're suggesting she paid me?"

His hands encircled her upper arms, holding her fast before him. "Did she make a deal with you that day?"

"Oh, let me guess who might have told you this," she flashed, trying to pull away but he wouldn't let her escape. "Your *mother?*"

"Just tell me the truth, was there a deal? Did you ever accept money from her?"

It felt like he was punching her, one quick brutal blow after the other. She stared at him through blurred vision. He didn't even look the same—tall, broad-shouldered, raven-haired, towering above her, fierce, furious, frightening.

And even as intimidating as he was now, she knew she'd always loved him. There was no way she could betray him. It went against everything she believed in, everything she held dear.

"No," she whispered through dry lips, her throat parched and her voice even raspier. "I never betrayed you. I never did anything but what was right, what was best." She took a quick breath, a breath that felt like it was on fire. "For you."

"Is that the truth? Look me in the eye and tell me it is the truth."

She flung her head back. "I'm looking you in the eye, King Sharif Fehr, and I am telling you the truth. I am telling you that the conversation your mother and I had that day in my apartment had nothing to do with money and nothing to do with bribes or payoffs or payouts. It had to do with Zulima, your future wife Zulima. Your mother told me that you were engaged, and had been engaged, and that within six months you'd be marrying her."

She yanked free, took a step away, her chin lifted defiantly. "And you did." Then suddenly her lower lip quivered, and all her bravado threatened to disappear. Ruthlessly she bit down into her inner lip to stop the quiver. "You did," she repeated, this time her voice firmer, her emotions once more under control. "So don't you ever talk to me that way again, because the truth is, you never planned to marry me. The truth is your mother had been planning your wedding all along."

A tinkling bell sounded at the large doors, and Mrs. Frishman appeared with the children.

"They're here," she said under her breath as she swiftly, surreptitiously reached up to make sure her eyes were dry.

"We are not finished," he answered quietly.

She was equally furious. "No, we're not."

"I shall speak to you later this evening."

"I can't wait," she seethed.

His eyes narrowed. "I don't appreciate your sarcasm—"

"Then perhaps you'd consider sending me home."

He laughed. "Not a chance. We made a deal. Your bed is made."

"Then you'll know where to find me later, won't you?" she flashed heading for the palace even as the children spied the pool and let out muffled shrieks.

"Jesslyn," he called after her. "Where are you going?"

"I've a few papers to grade," she answered, and then spying the girls she gave them all quick hugs. "You're not going to believe that pool!" she whispered to them. "It's out of this world, and guess what?"

"What, what?" the girls cried.

She tickled their tummies. "He made it for you! Just for you! Go see."

The girls were running through the gates now, laughing as they tumbled onto the sand, their excited voices carrying as Jesslyn disappeared through the palace doors.

She was on the way to her room when Queen Reyna appeared, stepping from the shadows.

"You do know why he's come to you, don't you?" Queen Reyna said, putting a hand on Jesslyn's arm to detain her.

"He's going to marry again. He has to marry again. He needs a son or his brothers will inherit. Now, I don't mind if his brothers inherit. They are my sons, too, after all, but Sharif minds. He minds very much. You must know that he's always wanted to be king. He's done everything he can to be king. Even married someone he didn't love because it was the right thing to do." Her lips curved.

"This is really none of my business, Queen Fehr," Jesslyn said, taking a step back. "If you'll excuse me."

"He's smart, you know. Very smart. He's just using you, using you to get the children whipped into shape so he can bring a new bride home."

Jesslyn wasn't about to bite. She'd known Queen Reyna too long; she knew how the older woman operated. "As I said, it's really none of my business—"

"The bride is already chosen," the queen continued ruthlessly, looking at her from beneath her long black lashes, the same lashes Sharif had inherited. "Or did my son once again forget to tell you that?"

"He told me he might remarry at some point, but there's no bride, there's no one specific in mind—"

"Oh, my, how foolish you are," she said with a little laugh. "You haven't changed. Neither of you. You and Sharif both refuse to deal in reality. He's engaged. The wedding date is set. But of course he won't tell you the truth. He didn't then. Why should he now?"

"It was a pleasure speaking with you, Queen Fehr. I always enjoy these little visits." Jesslyn smiled a blinding smile, battling to hang on to her tattered pride. "Have a nice day."

Reaching her bedroom, Jesslyn closed her door flung herself on her bed, stunned. Exhausted. Numb.

This palace was mad. Everybody, everyone, everything.

She wanted to go back to Sharjah. Needed to go back to Sharjah. Back to her small tidy apartment and her small tidy life. Nothing here was small or tidy. Nothing here let her escape or forget.

Sharif had told her he was thinking about remarrying, she knew that from their conversation during the flight over, but did he already have a new bride in the wings?

Was there one woman already selected and waiting?

She covered her eyes, trying to erase the pictures in her head, pictures of Sharif with another beautiful Arab princess, another gorgeous royal bride with money and beauty and a womb perfect for making healthy babies.

Rolling up, she sat on the side of the bed and stared across the room, past the silk and satin bed hangings, to the sheer silk panels draping the window.

Sharif might be getting married again, but she didn't blame him, couldn't blame him. She also couldn't blame him if he thought the worst of her. She'd never told him why she left. She'd never given him a say, or a choice. She'd taken matters into her own hands and made the decision for him.

No wonder he was angry.

She gripped the bedcovers, thinking she would have been so much wiser—and braver—if she'd just told him she couldn't have children and she knew he needed children.

And apparently from what his mother just said, he still needed that all-important male heir.

A light knock sounded on her door and Mehta appeared. "Teacher Fine," she said breathlessly, "His Highness needs you at the pool. Now."

"Has there been an accident?" Jesslyn asked, scrambling off the bed.

Mehta shrugged helplessly. "His Highness says for you to come now."

Jesslyn practically ran through the palace halls as nightmarish pictures popped into her head. A child missing. A child being pulled unconscious from the pool. Sharif performing CPR.

But instead when she reached the pool the children were playing in the shallow end of the beach pool, with Sharif sitting on the sand close to the water's edge. Mrs. Frishman was nowhere in sight.

She nearly turned around and returned to the palace thinking Sharif was playing games with her, but then Sharif called to her. "Please come here, Jesslyn. I need you."

I need you.

Such powerful heartbreaking words when they came from him.

She joined Sharif on the sand, and he nodded at Takia who was on her tummy floating around, using her arms to get from place to place.

The back of Takia's thighs were shadowed and Jesslyn stared, thinking it odd that the palm fronds above would make such dark reflections on the child's legs when she realized they weren't shadows at all but bruises. My God.

Jesslyn's head jerked up and she stared at Sharif trying to mask her horror.

"Do you see what I see," he said slowly, hardly able to contain the emotion in his voice.

"Yes."

"What the hell is that?"

Biting her lip, Jesslyn leaned forward, seeing more clearly the bruises and ridges on the back of Takia's legs. They were welts, she realized, shock and disgust forming a lump in her throat. "Welts and bruises," she whispered. "She's been spanked."

"That's not a spanking. That's a beating."

CHAPTER ELEVEN

"WOULD you watch my girls?" he asked, his deep voice cracking, his face creased with shock and strain and fury. "I'd like to go speak to Mrs. Frishman."

Jesslyn swallowed. "You think she did this."

"I haven't ever liked her. I should never have let her in this house."

"Go," she said, touching his arm. "The girls are safe with me."

He turned to look at her, really look at her, and Jesslyn caught a glimpse of the anguish in his eyes before his gaze shuttered. "I know they are," he said roughly. "I knew they would be."

He left and she sat down on the soft sand, the water lapping at her feet. She kept looking at Takia's back, and each time she did, shock and disgust made her want to throw up. Takia was absolutely lovely, a little girl who'd immediately stolen Jesslyn's heart, and it was beyond comprehension how anyone could physically punish her, much less hit her so hard as to leave bruises and scars.

Finally, Jesslyn summoned her courage. "Takia, did you fall?" she asked with studied casualness. "I can see some bruises on the back of your legs."

Saba sat up, water streaming from her hair and eyes. "She got punished," she said bluntly.

Takia glanced over her shoulder at Jesslyn, her eyes big, her expression fearful.

"Why did you get punished?" she asked Takia gently.

Takia stopped swimming. Her eyes grew bigger.

"Tell her," Jinan ordered imperiously. "Tell her why."

Takia's forehead wrinkled, and her eyes welled with tears. "I'm bad," she whispered.

"You're not bad," Jesslyn answered firmly, hiding the depth of her shock. What on earth had the child done? Broken something? Stolen something? Lied about something?

"I am bad," Takia whispered, slowly rising from the water to stand before Jesslyn. "I do bad things."

"What?" Jesslyn demanded, lightly holding Takia's wrist and glancing from Takia to Saba to Jinan and back to the five-year-old again. "What do you do that's wrong?"

"I…" Takia ducked her head. "I spoil my bed."

Spoil her bed?

For a moment Jesslyn couldn't understand. And then it hit her. Oh, God. She means she *wets* her bed. A chill went through Jesslyn at the thought of a five-year-old being beaten for wetting her bed.

"Who does this to you?" she asked quietly, her voice nearly breaking with pain.

"Jaddah," Jinan answered matter-of-factly.

Their grandmother? Sharif's mother?

Jesslyn's mind raced. She knew the matriarch was stern, old-school, but to punish a child so severely that welts covered the backs of her thighs? "Not Mrs. Frishman?" Jesslyn persisted.

The girls all shook their heads. "If Takia doesn't stop having accidents she can't go back to England," Saba explained, "and Jaddah says we have to go."

Jesslyn frowned. "Why do you have to go?"

Saba shrugged miserably. "Father's getting married in September."

So even the children had heard about the wedding. Then it must be true. And Sharif hadn't been honest with her. He'd even made love to her despite the fact that he would be married in just months.

Once again she felt shocked—the same shock and denial she'd felt before when Queen Reyna had cornered her in her London flat. She felt cornered now.

Taking a deep breath for calm as well as control, Jesslyn suggested the girls swim for another half hour and then go in, saying she didn't want them to get sunburned.

They nodded obediently and returned to playing and splashing, but Jesslyn couldn't focus, not when her heart was in her throat and her thoughts spun wildly this way and then the other.

The next thirty minutes passed with agonizing slowness. Grandmothers didn't beat their children. Grandmothers didn't threaten young granddaughters. And grandmothers didn't tell their grandchildren their father was getting married before he did.

Mehta was waiting for Jesslyn and the children the moment they returned. "His Highness wants to see you now, Teacher Fine."

"I've the children," Jesslyn answered, "and they're wet and need baths and their hair shampooed."

Mehta nodded and smiled. "I give them their baths. His Highness says I can do that. You go see him."

"No, I want to—"

"Teacher Jesslyn Fine, I have two daughters, two sons. I can give baths. Yes?"

Jesslyn tugged on the belt on her cover-up as Mehta steered the children into their rooms.

She knew Sharif was waiting, but there was no way she could go to his office dressed this way. The cover-up might be fine at a pool but was too short for the palace, much less Sharif's official chambers.

In her room she quickly changed into a straight white skirt with a black-and-white-striped top and scooped her hair into a smooth ponytail low on her neck.

Heading to Sharif's office, she was almost afraid to enter, afraid to tell him what she'd discovered, afraid to confront him about his September nuptials, but she'd do both. She was determined to do both. No more secrets and lies, she vowed. No more hiding the truth.

She rapped firmly on his door. Sharif opened it personally. "Come in," he said, stepping aside.

He was dressed in faded jeans and a casual black polo shirt he'd left untucked. The faded denim fabric clung to the hard outline of his thighs, and his polo shirt, open at the collar, showed the strong tanned column of his throat.

It was the first time she'd seen him in jeans since she'd arrived, and it surprised her and unnerved her more than a little bit. He looked like her Sharif. He looked like the one she'd been so happy, so comfortable, with.

"Mrs. Frishman's gone," he said by way of greeting as Jesslyn entered the room.

"Mrs. Frishman didn't do it."

"I know." He dragged a hand through his dark hair and dropped into one of the armchairs at the opposite end of the room from his desk. "It's my mother."

"So why is Mrs. Frishman gone?"

"She had a responsibility to tell me—or you—what was going on. Instead she covered for my mother."

"How did you find out it was your mother?"

Sharif pressed two fingers to the bridge of his nose. "Mrs. Frishman."

"Did you know Takia had a problem wetting her bed?"

He sat still, his brow furrowed, deep lines etched at his mouth. "I knew Takia had some…accidents…at school. The headmistress wrote to me about it, suggesting Takia would be better off staying home until she outgrew the…behavior." He glanced down at the carpet before lifting his head to look at Jesslyn. "I asked my mother to work with her. My mother said she was."

Jesslyn slowly sat down in one of the chairs opposite his. "You left discipline to your mother?"

He closed his eyes. "I had no idea she'd take her responsibilities so seriously. When we were small, my mother used to hit us with a cane but it never crossed my mind she'd cane my children. Never."

"Oh, Sharif."

His eyes opened, the gray depths dark against the ashen pallor of his face. "This is my fault, too. I blame only myself. I've failed to protect my own children, in their own home."

"You trusted her," she said softly.

"Yes, I did. At least I wanted to. She's my mother, and it's my duty to respect her—" He was cut short by the sound of raised voices in the hall and then a pounding on his office door.

Before Sharif could speak, the door opened and Queen Reyna marched in.

"I guess I can't say she didn't knock," Sharif muttered as he watched Reyna's progress.

"I've just heard about Mrs. Frishman," the queen said, bearing down on them. "She was an excellent nanny and she came with impeccable references—"

"Sit, Mother." Sharif rose and pointed to a chair.

"No, thank you."

"Sit," he said more quietly, his tone harder, less tolerant.

"I will not have you speak to me that way." Queen Reyna cast Jesslyn a disparaging glance. "Furthermore, I will not discuss anything with you until she is gone."

"She's staying," Sharif answered, his voice implacable, like velvet covered steel. "And you're sitting, or I'll have my security detail escort you to the car now."

Reyna sat and this time she did not look at Jesslyn.

"I've seen Takia's bruises," Sharif said without preamble. "I know what you did. You caned her. You've been caning her since she returned home."

"It's just discipline," his mother answered coldly. "Children must be disciplined or they grow up thoughtless, selfish and wild."

Sharif stepped in front of her, stared down at her, his expression bemused. "But you punished her for something she couldn't control."

Her lips tightened. "I was trying to teach her. And yes, I did use the cane on Takia, but it's better to bruise her pride now than to lose her forever." Reyna rose imperiously, smoothing her gown. "Now I'm done here, I won't be interrogated like a common criminal. Sharif, I've packed my things and my driver is out front waiting to take me to the summer house. I won't be back either, at least, not until she's gone," she concluded, nodding at Jesslyn.

Sharif's eyes darkened. "In that case, you won't ever be back."

Queen Reyna glanced from one to the other, smiling a thin hard smile as if she knew something he didn't. "Sharif, it didn't work the first time around. It won't work this time. Your Miss Heaton is cheap, common and completely unsuitable. And yes, we've both already agreed you need a wife, but for God's sake, Sharif, get a proper wife."

An eerie silence descended, and Jesslyn pressed her hands together. She watched Sharif walk to his desk, pull open a drawer and retrieve an envelope. He returned with the envelope, extending it toward his mother.

"I knew it," he said. "I knew all these years you were lying. I knew she would never have taken your money. But I know you'll take mine. Here," he said, thrusting the envelope at her. "A check for a half million dollars. The same amount of money you offered her. A half million. It's yours. Take it. I never want to see you again."

Reyna opened the envelope and looked inside. "What are you doing, Sharif? What is this about?"

"You knew I wanted to marry, Jesslyn," he said, "all those years ago you knew I loved her and I intended to ask her to marry me. But then you went in and whispered little poisonous words, and you ruined everything."

His mother closed the envelope and handed it back to him. "All I did was protect you. I did what any good mother would do. I made sure you didn't throw your future away." She shook the envelope. "Take this back. I can't take your money. It's ridiculous."

"You're right." Sharif took the envelope and, holding it up, tore up the envelope with the check in it in a half-dozen pieces. "I'm not giving you any more money. You're done. You're leaving here and you've gotten all you'll get from me. You can have the summer house. Consider it home."

Reyna stood frozen, her gaze fixed on Sharif's face, the features set in harsh, unforgiving lines. "I wasn't going to let her ruin your life."

"Far better you ruin my life, right?"

"You needed a wife, you needed a male heir and Zulima gave you that heir—"

"He was stillborn, Mother, and Zulima died."

"But at least she could have children." Queen Reyna turned to look at Jesslyn, her gaze almost pitying. "Your dear Miss Heaton, despite all her charms, can't. Her tubes were crushed in that accident in Greece. She's completely infertile." She paused. "Or has she still not told you?"

Jesslyn felt Sharif's gaze as well as his tension. He hated this, all of this, and she didn't blame him. No one liked emotional dramas. But then he looked toward the door and called for his security detail, who had been standing just outside. "Please see Her Highness to her car. I believe her driver is waiting."

Sharif then turned away. He was leaving the room, walking away before he had to watch his mother forced out. Jesslyn couldn't move, though. She felt frozen, rooted to the spot.

"Sharif." Queen Reyna screamed, a piercing heart-rending scream, the sort one might scream on hearing a loved one had died.

Queen Reyna was screaming his name again, but Sharif kept walking.

Jesslyn put her fists to her mouth, horrified, terrified. It couldn't all end like this. He couldn't walk away from his mother like this. Yes, his mother was wrong but this…this…

Reyna was still screaming his name while she was half escorted, half dragged from the room. Jesslyn couldn't bear it. She ran after him, caught Sharif by the arm, held fast. "Please, wait. You don't have to send her away like this."

He tried to shake her off. "She gets what she deserves."

"But I can't bear it. She's wrong. She is. But don't do this. The children can probably hear her. The children have been through enough, too. Please talk to her. Calm her down. Let her leave with some dignity."

Sharif stopped, looked down at her, his expression harsh and unyielding. "But don't you hear her? Don't you hear her lies? She can't stop. Even now, she can't stop. The things she says, the things about you not being able to have children—"

"It's true." She had to cut him off, had to stop him now. "That's true. And it's why I left you. I knew you needed children and I knew I couldn't give them to you."

Sharif's eyes narrowed on her face, but he wasn't listening. He didn't seem to be listening, instead he seemed to be somewhere else, somewhere in his head. "That's what she said to you in the apartment that day. Those were the magic words, weren't they?"

She clung to him tighter, her fingers hanging on to him as though he were a lifeline. "I didn't want you to be the one to tell me to go. I didn't want you to tell me I wasn't enough. I thought it was better for me to leave before it came to that." She exhaled in a soft short gasp. "I thought I was being mature."

"Mature?" he repeated numbly, blinking and refocusing on her.

"I'm sorry. I'm so sorry, Sharif. I didn't want to go, I didn't want to leave you. I loved you so much I felt like it was killing me—"

"Stop," he said hoarsely, turning away.

Jesslyn's hand dropped from his sleeve and she watched him walk away.

"What has she done?" he demanded, his voice low and rough. "What has she done to all of us? What has she done to you? Why does she have such a personal vendetta against you?"

"Because I'm alive," Jesslyn answered softly. She saw Sharif turn toward her and she tried to smile but failed. "I'm here, living, breathing, and your sisters aren't."

Sharif stared at her in disbelief. "No. She can't be so petty."

"She's a mother who lost her only daughters, and in her mind it's not petty. Both her daughters die and I walk away, almost unscathed."

"But you were hurt." He stared at her, his gaze searching her face.

"Yes."

"Yet you came to Aman's funeral."

"No one knew I'd been injured so severely."

He groaned and closed his eyes for a moment as if unable to believe what he was hearing. Then he opened his eyes and extended a hand to her. "Come," he said, "let's go somewhere else. We need to talk, and I don't want to do it here."

They went to her suite as it was far from the palace entrance. Sharif paced the living room floor, and Jesslyn sat on one of the low white couches, a brilliant ruby-hued pillow clutched to her middle.

One of Sharif's butlers appeared with an enormous silver tray laden with coffee, warm fresh bread, small meat pies and pastry snacks, and a smaller plate of dried figs and stuffed apricots. With a bow he placed the tray on the low sofa opposite Jesslyn, then left.

Neither Jesslyn nor Sharif even looked at the food.

Sharif finally stopped pacing. "How do you know you can't have children?"

She stood, and lifting her striped top, and hiking down the waist band of her skirt, she showed him the scar on her abdomen. "Remember this? From the accident?"

He crossed the room, sat down on the edge of the couch and studied the scar on her abdomen. Gently he traced the scar. "You broke your pelvic girdle."

She shivered at the light touch of his finger on her skin. "There ended up being more damage than we realized. I had a lot of bleeding and we discovered belatedly that I'd hurt myself more than we thought. I lost one tube, the other had so much scarring it'd be impossible to conceive, and then the rest wasn't in great shape, either."

He looked up at her, his hands moving to hold her securely by her hips. "But you never told me."

Her heart ached and reaching out she smoothed the deep crease in Sharif's forehead. "I was twenty-two," she answered simply. "I didn't want to believe it was true. So I ignored it, pretended it'd never happened." She gazed down at him, her expression tortured. "Until your mother came to me and reminded me that you needed children and I couldn't give you an heir. Fortunately, she had a solution."

His grip tightened on her hips. "Zulima."

She smoothed the angry furrow between his eyebrows. "I should have come to you myself. I should have told you myself."

"Yes." He tugged her down onto his lap, exhaustion in the deep lines at his mouth and the fine creases at his eyes. "You should have. The only way I know what you need, the only way I know what you want, is if you tell me."

She nodded as she felt his arm curve around her, holding her fast. "I used to hope you'd come after me. I used to pray you'd not forget me."

"And I did." He kissed her on the forehead, and then on her nose and finally her mouth. "I did. And maybe it took nine years, but I wasn't going to give up. I had to find you. Had to see you. Had to bring you to my palace and make you mine."

"I thought you just wanted a teacher," she teased, sliding her arms around his neck.

With one hand he reached up to tug the elastic from her ponytail allowing her dark hair to spill over her shoulders. "A teacher for my children, but a bride for me."

She suddenly wasn't sure what he was saying, and her chest grew hot and tight. "A bride?"

"I need a wife, don't you think?"

She stared into his face, her gaze locked with his. "Sharif, you know—"

"I know," he answered, dropping his head to cover her mouth with his. "I know," he murmured lifting his head long minutes later. "And I don't care. I love you. I want you. I want you to marry me and be my wife, my love, my queen."

He did get married, but it wasn't a September wedding. It was a July wedding at the peak of the summer heat.

Dressing for the ceremony, Jesslyn couldn't believe it was happening, couldn't believe she was the bride this time. A lifetime ago she'd dreamed of being Sharif's wife, and now, after a decade of hurt and heartbreak, her dreams were coming true.

Bathed, massaged with oils, smoothed with scented lotions, Jesslyn was finally dressed, and as she stood before her mirror she couldn't believe the woman she saw.

Even Mehta was awed.

It was the most beautiful gown, Jesslyn thought, reverently touching the white satin embroidered in gold and encrusted with pearls and diamonds. More pearls and diamonds hung from her neck, and a long delicate veil floated down her back, pinned to the small gold crown on her head.

"Teacher Fine is so pretty," Mehta said, hands clasped together. "Now Teacher Fine is a pretty princess."

Jesslyn blushed, blood rushing to her cheeks, and, catching the veil in her hand, she turned away from the mirror, dazzled, overwhelmed.

She did feel like a princess from a fairy tale, and now all she wanted was her prince, her very own Sheikh Fehr.

Less than an hour later Jesslyn stood before Sharif, reciting vows in both English and Arabic. Sharif had incorporated elements from both their faiths in the service, and the ceremony was both intimate and spectacular, beyond anything she could have ever imagined.

Things like this didn't happen to ordinary girls.

Things like this didn't happen to schoolteachers.

The little girls were part of the wedding, too. Jesslyn had insisted they be her junior bridesmaids, and in their beautiful matching pale-gold gowns with darker gold sashes, they looked not just stunning, they looked happy, and they smiled and laughed like little girls should.

After the ceremony Jesslyn caught the children in a hug, not caring that her flowers were smashed, not caring that the hug knocked her crown and veil crooked.

"You're our mother now," Jinan said shyly, touching the pearl and diamond necklace roped around Jesslyn's neck.

"Yes," Jesslyn answered with a kiss.

"Does that mean you're not going to be our teacher anymore?" The little girl persisted.

Sharif overheard and reached out to touch his oldest daughter on the shoulder. "Why do you ask?"

Jinan flushed guiltily. "Because Jaddah said when you got married we'd have to go to boarding school, and we don't want to go back to boarding school—"

"You don't have to go back," he interrupted firmly but kindly. "You can study here at home with a tutor, or perhaps attend one of the small private academies in Sarq that are based on the UK or American curriculum like the American school in Dubai."

Jesslyn lifted her head, looked at Sharif. "Is there an American School in Sarq?"

"No, but there should be something similar. Perhaps that's something I could put you in charge of. Perhaps that's your first job as Sarq's first lady."

"You'd let me start a school?" she asked, trying to contain her delight because she'd loved being a teacher, and education was one of the best ways to touch and improve the world.

"If it was something you'd enjoy doing."

"I'd love it, and I'd love the girls to be our first pupils."

Takia had been listening, and she started jumping up and down. "No more boarding school!"

Jesslyn grinned. "That's right, my darling. No more boarding school. You're home, and you're staying home, right, Sharif?"

He leaned over and kissed each of the girls. "Right."

Later that night, the first night of the rest of their lives, Sharif made love to her as though it was the only night of their lives.

He kissed her and loved her with tenderness and pride and passion. When he took her to the peak of pleasure, he came with her, his body perfectly in tune, and afterward as she lay shuddering in his arms, he held her for hours.

"I didn't even know how lost I was until I found you," he said much later, his deep voice low and husky in the dark. "I was so angry for so many years. I hated myself, hated who I was and what I'd done—"

"Sharif, I can't bear it when you say those things. You are such a good man. You've always been a good man."

"It didn't change my hatred or guilt. But you have. Just having you here, back with me, changes everything."

"Good." She curled closer to him, her cheek resting on his warm chest, her hand on his thigh. "Only happiness now."

"And I can feel happiness now. I knew I loved my daughters, I knew I loved my country, but on the inside I was numb. Dead. And now I know what I was missing. I was missing you."

Jesslyn buried her face against his shoulder, breathing in his warm fragrant skin that smelled of spice and musk and sun. He was beautiful to her, beautiful in a way that was wordless, timeless. It was just him. It was the way he held her and touched her and made her feel.

"I'm so glad you didn't forget me," she whispered, her lips brushing the smooth thick muscle that wrapped from chest to shoulder. "Otherwise by now I might be another man's bride."

Sharif choked on a smothered laugh. "You are all mine, you always were in my heart, *laeela.*"

Her smile faded as she thought about Sharif's late wife. "You did care for Zulima, didn't you? You did try to make your marriage work."

He slid his hands through her hair. "I did, and I wanted to be a good husband. I tried my best to be a good husband. It's a terrible thing when a marriage fails, and I never want that to happen again." He lifted her face, looked at her in the dark. "Ours won't fail. I won't let it."

"I won't let it, either," she answered, sliding forward on his body to kiss him. "I love you so much, Sharif."

"I love you more, my queen."

"We're finally together."

He kissed her slowly, parting her lips with his and using his tongue to tease her into shivers of delight. "It's a miracle," he murmured, between kisses that melted her all the way through. "And you are," he said against her mouth, "the greatest miracle of my life."

EPILOGUE

SHARIF was wrong.

The greatest miracle of his life arrived twenty-two months later when Jesslyn gave birth at Sarq's royal hospital.

"The wonders of modern medicine," Jesslyn whispered, cradling the infant against her chest, his small newborn body swaddled in a pale-blue blanket.

"You are a miracle woman," Sharif said, leaning over to kiss her brow, her nose, her lips. "You make miracles look easy."

She laughed softly, exhausted by the long labor and yet euphoric, too. "Easy? Ha!" Six failed in vitro attempts. Six different cycles of drugs, injections, blood draws, egg retrievals…but none of that mattered now. All of that was behind her. They had a beautiful baby, a baby they made together. A baby the doctors said couldn't be made.

Suddenly tears were filling her eyes, tears of joy and gratitude. "Is he really here?" she whispered, stroking his tiny cheek.

"He is."

"And this is real?" she asked, taking the still-unnamed infant prince's hand in hers and examining his tiny fingers and even tinier knuckles.

Sharif leaned over the bed, watching them. "Yes, my darling. This is as real as it gets."

"We have a baby." She shook her head. "A son. A *son*." Abruptly she looked up at Sharif, worry in her eyes. "Do you think the girls will mind a brother?"

Sharif laughed. "Not at all. I think they're going to love a baby brother. Shall I get them?"

"Please. I know they can't wait to meet their new baby."

"Their baby?" Sharif asked, hesitating.

"You know how brothers and sisters are. He'll end up theirs as much as ours." She smiled reassuringly at him. "But that's what we want, isn't it? A family? A real family?"

He stared down at her for an endless moment before cupping her face and kissing her once, twice and again. "I love you, Jesslyn. I owe everything to you. My home, my happiness, my heart. Whatever can I ever do to pay you back?"

She reached up to touch his beautiful firm mouth. "All I want is forever," she said, her voice suddenly husky. "That's not asking for much, is it?"

"Not at all."

She tried to smile. "Just live a long life with me. Be my best friend until we're old."

"I will be with you forever. I will be there when the children go to school and get married and start families of their own. I will be with you here on earth and someday in heaven."

She caught his hand in hers and held it tight. "Do you think that could really happen?"

"Yes."

"How do you know?"

He kissed her fingers. "Miracles are virtually guaranteed with you."

* * * * *

The Desert King's Pregnant Bride

ANNIE
WEST

Annie West spent her childhood with her nose between the covers of a book—a habit she retains. After years preparing government reports and official correspondence she decided to write something she *really* enjoys. And there's nothing she loves more than a great romance. Despite her office-bound past she has managed a few interesting moments—including a marriage offer with the promise of a herd of camels to sweeten the contract. She is happily married to her ever-patient husband (who has never owned a dromedary). They live with their two children amongst the tall eucalypts at beautiful Lake Macquarie, on Australia's east coast. You can e-mail Annie at www.annie-west.com or write to her at PO Box 1041, Warners Bay, NSW 2282, Australia.

With warmest gratitude to:

Leanne McMahon, equine expert extraordinaire;

Anna Campbell, the best friend a girl could have;

and my very own hero, Geoff.

Thank you.

This book wouldn't have been
possible without you!

CHAPTER ONE

MAGGIE bowed her head against the sheets of icy rain as she plodded along the muddy road.

Slick fabric stuck to her where she'd forgotten to do up her raincoat. Water sluiced down her legs, into her wellington boots. Her hair, so carefully washed and dried, now hung in saturated rat-tails against her neck. Vaguely she was aware of the chill numbing her body. After running, stumbling, then trudging so far in the lashing darkness, her steps slowed, became unsteady.

If she'd been thinking clearly, she'd have taken her battered Jeep. That hadn't occurred to her. One look between the carelessly drawn curtains of Marcus's sitting room and coherent thought had fled.

She'd stood, rooted to the spot, heedless of the drenching rain. When her brain had finally caught up with the message her eyes had conveyed, she'd simply run. She must have raced past her car into the welcoming blackness.

Pain tore at her throat as she sobbed in a deep racking breath. She had to get home, before the emotions churning inside overcame her.

Yet she couldn't escape the memory of what she'd seen: Marcus, naked in the arms of his lover.

Now she understood why he'd blown hot and cold, sometimes too busy to see her and at others attentive and loving. His affection had been a sham. He'd only wanted her to conceal his affair with the trophy wife of a jealous horse breeder.

Maggie's stomach churned. She'd been so gullible.

She'd believed him when he'd spoken of respecting her, not rushing her after her recent loss. He'd said she needed to be sure before they took their relationship further.

In her innocence Maggie *had* been sure. She'd decided to show him she was a desirable woman, mature and ready for a deeper relationship. She'd read every magazine she could lay her hands on, aiming to transform herself into the sort of woman she thought he wanted. She'd overcome her fears and thrust aside self-doubt. She'd even taken the long trip to town and bought herself a *dress*!

Her bitter laughter was swallowed by the rushing wind.

He'd never wanted her. She'd been too inexperienced and starved of affection to see he was using her. Nausea welled in her throat and she bent over to dry-retch again.

Strangely, this time as she looked down she could see her boots and her legs, wet and muddy below the raincoat. She frowned muzzily, trying to focus on the present, not the scene of contorting naked bodies replaying in her head.

Where was the light coming from?

'Do you need help?' A deep voice curled out of the roaring darkness to reach her.

Blindly, she raised her head and found herself blinking in the headlights of a massive off-road vehicle. A man stood silhouetted before it. He was tall, lean and unfamiliar. Something about the set of his broad shoulders and his wide-planted feet intimated he was a man prepared for anything, a man able to deal with trouble of any kind.

Maggie knew an instant's insane craving to lean forward into his strong body, rest against those more-than-capable shoulders and slump into oblivion.

Then sense overcame instinct. She had no idea who he was. Besides, she'd just learned her judgement was fatally flawed.

She'd believed Marcus to be everything she wanted in a man, a lover, a mate. She'd thought…

The shadow moved closer, near enough to make her stunningly aware of his superior height and power.

'You're not well. How can I assist?' This time Maggie caught the faintest trace of an accent.

'Who are you?' she said, barely recognising the reedy whisper as her own voice.

Silence for a moment as the wind stirred the collar of her coat and drove the rain almost horizontal.

'I'm a guest at the Tallawanta Stud. Staying up at the homestead.'

Now she recognised the latest top-of-the-range vehicle. Only the best for those at the big house. And there was a special guest this week. The Sheikh of Shajehar, who owned the whole enormous horse stud, had sent an envoy on an inspection tour.

That explained his accent. The precise, clipped English, as if he'd attended a top British public school. It was overlaid with a slight softening of consonants that hinted at something far more exotic.

'Or do you intend that we both stand out here till we're saturated to the skin?'

There was no impatience in that voice, but nor was there any mistaking its steely undertone. Maggie jumped, reining in her wandering thoughts. What was wrong with her? She couldn't seem to concentrate properly.

Only now did she realise the stranger wore no overcoat. He must be even wetter than she.

'I'm sorry.' She shook her head dazedly. 'I'm not…'

'Have you been in an accident?' Again that easy, calm voice with just a hint of iron in its depths.

'No. No accident. I… Could you give me a lift, please?' Maggie had no qualms now about cadging a ride from him. He was the visiting dignitary she'd heard about. They were on the estate's private road and no one would be out in this weather unless they belonged here.

'Of course.' He bowed his head, then preceded her to the four-wheel drive. His stride was long, purposeful and easy, as if pacing down a carpeted corridor instead of a muddy, uneven gravel road. Maggie stumbled after him as best she could, her limbs horribly uncoordinated.

He opened the door and stood back for her to get in.

'Thank you,' she murmured as a firm hand cupped her elbow and helped her into the high cabin. Without his support she wouldn't have made it.

Maggie subsided onto the cushioned seat. Slowly she loosened her cramped fingers and let go of the straps of her high-heeled sandals from one hand, her frivolous new purse from the other. They tumbled to the floor. She'd barely been aware she still held them.

The door closed and she sank back, stunned by the warm comfort of the cabin after the howling wind and teeming rain that had drummed incessantly in her ears.

This was…luxury. Heaven.

Maggie shut her eyes, overcome by the quiet peace.

'Here,' a deep voice filtered into her consciousness, 'take this.'

Slowly she turned towards the velvet-soft voice, fighting the intense dragging weariness that consumed her. She didn't want to rouse herself, but he was insistent.

Reluctantly, she opened her eyes. He sat in the driver's seat and she looked up into the blackest eyes she'd ever seen. Deep-set, hooded eyes that surveyed her closely, taking in every nuance of her appearance.

Maggie's eyes widened at the sight of her rescuer in the cabin's pale overhead light.

His jet-black hair was slicked back from a face tanned almost to bronze. Her breath snagged at the strong, spare beauty of his features, each plane emphasised by the sheen of rain on burnished flesh. Lean cheeks with slanted cheekbones that mirrored the stark angle of his brows. A strong, aristocratic nose with just a hint of the aquiline. Narrow, well-shaped lips that she could imagine tipping into a smile or turning down in displeasure. A jaw that spoke of solid power and bone-deep assurance.

The combination took her breath away. It was as if someone had opened a precious old book and conjured a warrior prince straight from the *Arabian Nights*.

But nothing in her juvenile reading matched this man for pure magnetism. He looked exotic and masterful.

Maggie had never known any man could look so…

'Here,' he repeated, thrusting a soft woollen blanket into her hands. His brows angled down in a frown as he surveyed her. 'Are you sure you're not injured?'

She nodded, then hid her face in the folds of wool, holding the blanket with hands that trembled. Embarrassment washed through her, whether because he'd caught her staring, or because of her strange wayward thoughts, she didn't know.

She must be in shock. That would explain her heedless flight and the muzzy feeling that everything was distant, unreal. Yes, that was it. Shock.

Any woman would be shocked to discover what she had tonight. And no doubt she looked a sight: workaday raingear over her beaded dress—

'Stop it.' A firm hand curved around her jaw and swung her face towards him. His fingers were hard and warm and comfortingly real against her numb flesh.

Maggie blinked, amazed to discover the water spiking her lashes wasn't rain, but tears. They burned her eyes.

'Stop what?' she whispered on a hiccough, staring into liquid dark eyes that held hers mesmerised.

Gradually her galloping heartbeat slowed. The breath shuddered out of her constricted lungs. She dragged in air, conscious of a tight ache around her chest.

'You were becoming hysterical.'

His clasp of her chin shifted, fingers splaying wide to tilt her head higher as if he needed to see her better in the dim light. The heat of his touch burned life back into her frozen skin and she was content to let him hold her so. She felt strangely lethargic.

'S-s-sorry.' She frowned. She'd never stuttered in her life. And as for being hysterical… 'I've had a bit of a sh-shock.' There, she finally got it out. She had trouble coordinating her lips and tongue. 'I'll be all r-right.'

'You've been out in this storm too long.' He took the wool from her white-knuckled grasp and lifted the blanket around her shoulders, pulling the edges together. The enveloping comfort relaxed her into a boneless huddle and the movement drew him close. She caught his scent, faint yet intriguing. Heat and sandalwood, spice and damp male skin. Her nostrils flared as she slumped forward.

Large hands on her shoulders propped her away from him.

'Where did you come from? How long have you been out?'

Maggie's lips curved up in a dreamy smile as her eyelids drifted lower. She really did love that accent. The softening consonants and lilting rhythm almost hidden behind the crisp intonation sounded quite…seductive. She could imagine going to sleep to the sound of that voice.

Her eyes popped open as fingers curled hard into her shoulders.

'Did someone hurt you?' His voice sounded different. She shivered anew at the hint of anger in his tone.

'No! No, I'm fine. Just…' The words petered out and she blinked, confused. She really did feel odd. 'I need to g-g-get back. Please.'

Abruptly, he nodded, pushing her back into the moulded seat and reaching for her seat belt. The heat of his torso as he leant near was warmer by far than any blanket.

'Where to?'

He straightened and immediately the chill invaded her body again. When he switched on the ignition the cabin was plunged into darkness but for the light from the control panel. Her gaze strayed to his shadowy profile: powerful yet elegant in a toughly masculine way.

Instinct told her she could trust him absolutely.

'Another s-s-six k-kilometres. Then r-right. I'll direct you f-from there.'

He eased the vehicle forward. Rain pounded on the roof and the four-wheel drive slid in the thick mud.

Mud. Her boots. Her gaze spanned the interior of the luxury vehicle.

'I'm sorry,' she whispered. 'My b-boots are f-filthy.'

'This is a farm vehicle,' he responded. 'I'm sure it collects its fair share of mud.'

Spoken like a man who never had to clean said vehicle, Maggie realised. This was no work vehicle. It was reserved for important guests, used when only the best would do.

'Who are you?'

For a moment she thought he hadn't heard her question over the sound of the rain.

'My name is Khalid. And yours?'

'Maggie.' She hugged the blanket closer, 'Maggie Lewis.' Thank goodness her teeth had stopped chattering.

'I'm pleased to meet you, Maggie.' His voice was grave, almost formal. Suddenly she wondered how this man spent his time when he wasn't visiting Australian horse studs or rescuing stranded women from deserted roads.

Khalid concentrated on the road as driving conditions deteriorated. He had to get her warm and dry quickly. She was in shock and might be on the verge of hypothermia.

Six kilometres and then how far to reach her destination? He couldn't take that risk. Instead he'd drive her to Tallawanta till she recovered.

She was an enigma. There was no abandoned car and those weren't work clothes beneath her oilskin. The glimpse of long slender legs below her coat had instantly caught his interest. And the high heels she'd dangled from her hand were for dancing the night away or seducing a man.

Was that what had happened? Had some man hurt her?

Despite her height, tall enough to top his shoulder, there was a fragile air about this woman. Her shadowed eyes were huge in that milky pale face. Her bowed neck as she'd hunched over in the road was long and slender and delicate.

She hadn't been at tonight's dinner of luminaries who'd turned out to meet the heir to the throne of Shajehar. Khalid would have noticed.

He flicked a glance at her, huddled beneath the tartan rug, her eyes closed and her head lolling against the seat. She looked weak and defenceless, but she must have a core of gritty strength to head out in this weather on foot. The woman was an intriguing mix that triggered his curiosity. That hadn't happened in a long time.

He felt a spurt of satisfaction that tonight, for once, he was without his entourage of security aides and obsequious hosts. He could indulge his curiosity, follow his instincts. Given the tight perimeter security on the vast estate, he'd won the argument that he was safe alone within its boundaries. Perhaps his security chief had realised too that it would be wise to give him space.

For six weeks Khalid had dutifully toured his half-brother's royal holdings in Europe, the Americas and Australia. But he didn't share Faruq's enjoyment of pomp and luxury. As heir to his terminally ill half-brother, Khalid had recently acquired a huge security retinue. Its size was due to Faruq's love of ostentation rather than any threat. Plus he had a schedule full of social engagements.

Social engagements! His time would be better spent supervising his latest project, a fresh water pipeline from the mountains in remote Shajehar. At least that would bring tangible benefits to his people.

Lights shone ahead in the streaming darkness and the tension eased across his shoulders and arms. Once he got her inside, in the light and warmth, he could assess her injuries, call a doctor if need be.

He bypassed the garages and drove round to the private owner's wing of the sprawling homestead.

'Here we are.' He leaned across to shake her awake. She was limp beneath his hand. Frowning, he paused only a moment before touching her pale cheek. It was icy.

'Maggie! Wake up.'

That voice again. The crisp warm voice with its tantalising hint of a lilt. She smiled to herself as she pictured an exotic prince in flowing robes, a gleaming scimitar in his hand.

'Maggie!'

She shrugged off a hand that threatened to interrupt her lovely dream. In her mind her prince smiled and tugged her to him. Eyes brighter than gems gleamed down at her and her breath caught. He slipped his hand beneath her legs and lifted her in his embrace, his arms like cushioned steel.

She'd never felt so safe, so secure, so full of anticipation. Those black eyes were shadowed with the promise of unknown delight, his narrow lips curving in a knowing, sensuous smile that made her long for his kiss.

The steady drum of his heartbeat pulsed against her and his arms rocked her close as he strode over the warm sand. Soon now they'd—

Maggie's brows pleated as hard drops of water beat against her face. Did it rain in the desert?

Instinctively, she turned her head, snuggling closer to his warm, solid body, filling her nostrils with the evocative scent of man. But her frown grew as she discovered he was wet, his clothes sodden.

She opened her eyes and found herself in a man's arms as he strode through a howling rainstorm. Her startled gasp was torn away by the wind.

Carriage lights shone along the veranda of a classic-style colonial homestead. Warm light gleamed through a massive fanlight window above the door. Suddenly everything clicked into place. Marcus, the long walk home, the exotic stranger. They were at Tallawanta House.

'You can put me down.' Maggie tried to lever herself up and out of his hold but she could get no purchase.

'We're almost there.' He stepped under cover and the needling rain on her skin ceased abruptly.

Wordlessly he pushed open the front door, pulling her closer. Muffled against his chest, she was assailed again by that yearning. To stay here against him, his body warming hers. To discover more about the inexplicable excitement that shivered through her blood when he held her like this.

She squeezed her eyes shut. This was no fantasy. This was real. Yet she felt oddly relaxed, almost floating. A yawn seized her and her head lolled against his shoulder.

Khalid. That was his name. She loved the sound of it. Her lips moved as she traced its syllables.

A moment later his grip changed, strong arms holding her flush against him as he lowered her legs. She slid down a hard torso till her feet reached the floor. Yet it was his unyielding embrace that kept her upright.

'Now,' murmured that seductively low voice, 'it's time to get your clothes off.'

'What?' Her eyes snapped open, instantly arresting him. In the bright light he found they were the colour of rich honey sprinkled with green fire. *Mesmerising.*

Unsteady hands shoved at his chest, fending him off.

Khalid's lips firmed as he watched her battle to remain upright. Had someone taken advantage of her tonight? The idea sent heat roaring through his blood.

'You need to get your wet clothes off.'

'Not with you watching!' Pink tinted her cheeks, fascinating him, highlighting a spattering of light freckles. A woman who still knew how to blush. When was the last time he'd come across one of that rare breed?

'I simply want to make sure you don't get hypothermia. I'm not interested in your body.'

The blush intensified to a deep rose hue and her gaze slanted swiftly away from his. Her teeth sank into her pale bottom lip. She was embarrassed.

'I can look after myself. I don't need your help,' she mumbled.

Didn't she? His curiosity was roused, and his concern. And, damn it, his time was his own, for tonight at least.

Khalid had always believed in two things. Following his instinct and his duty. Years ago, in the darkest days of grief after Shahina's death, only duty had kept him going. Embracing his responsibility to his people had given him purpose and strength when he'd wanted to shun the world and mourn his wife, the only woman he'd ever love.

Now both instinct and duty dictated he remain.

And something else. Something about Maggie Lewis that reached out to him in a way he hadn't experienced in a long time. The realisation fascinated and appalled him.

'So I should have left you out in the storm?'

'I didn't mean that. I appreciate the lift.' Her widening gaze roved the massive bathroom as if she'd never seen marble tiles before. 'It would have been easier to take me home.'

Her words were still slurred. But her eyes were clear and bright, the pupils normal. He guessed it was hypothermia, not drugs or drink, affecting her speech.

He released his hold slowly, looking to ensure she could

stand alone. Then he shrugged out of his dinner jacket and draped it over the edge of the spa bath.

Maggie watched his swift, economical movements as he turned and took off his jacket. The frame of his spectacular shoulders, the impressive V of his torso, the classic male form of powerful chest and narrow waist. The wet shirt clung lovingly to every inch of his skin, and her mouth dried, absorbing all that physical perfection.

Fiery heat burned her face as embarrassment sizzled under her skin. Of course he wasn't interested in seeing her naked! She'd always been gawky and unattractive. A wave of anger and humiliation broke over her, threatening to tug her down into a tide of self-pity.

Rapidly she blinked. She'd known for years she wasn't the sort of girl men desired. Tonight had only just confirmed…no, she refused to go there. The memory was too raw, too mortifying.

There was a whoosh of water and she dragged her focus back to the present. He'd leaned in to turn on the shower. His black trousers were sodden, shaping long, powerful legs and a tightly curved backside.

Maggie's eyes widened. Even Marcus, with his laughing blue eyes and his tall chunky build, couldn't hold a candle to this man for sheer physical perfection.

'Let me help you with your coat.' He didn't wait for an answer. Clearly he was used to being obeyed.

Wordlessly she stood while he deftly slipped it from her shoulders. It dropped in a puddle at her feet.

Maggie fixed her gaze on his black silk bow tie rather than on that vast expanse of wet male torso. But, perversely, the longer she stared, the greater her desire to reach out and tug the tie undone, to part the collar and see whether the flesh over his collarbone was the same burnished gold as his face.

Horrified at the wayward thought, she shut her eyes against

temptation. She'd never felt quite so…abandoned. Had to-night short-circuited something in her brain?

She was shocked to realise she hadn't felt anything like this for Marcus. She'd cared for him, respected him and believed intimacy was the next logical step in their relationship. But she'd never felt this charged awareness of him as a man.

Now she felt edgy, as if her skin had grown too tight.

Was this desire?

Her experience was so limited. She'd spent her life on the farm, isolated by her domineering father and long work hours. That was why her fledgling relationship with Marcus had seemed so precious.

'Next your dress, then we'll see if you can manage alone.' Khalid's voice was matter-of-fact. Yet he could have been re-citing entries in the telephone directory and she'd have lis-tened, enthralled, to his sexy smooth voice.

No! This had to stop. The sooner he left, the better. Then she'd become herself again: ordinary, pragmatic Maggie Lewis. No more flights of fantasy, no more…melting at the mere sound of a voice. This responsiveness to a com-plete stranger was due to shock and tiredness.

Maggie bit her lip on an instinctive protest as he reached round to the back of her dress. Her hands were so unsteady she knew she'd never manage the zip herself. So she com-plied, holding herself still as he tugged the zip.

Its downward slide took for ever. Blood pounded in her ears, blocking the sound of the shower. The sensation of the fastening lowering, centimetre by slow centimetre, drew her skin tight in goose flesh. He didn't touch her but he stood close, arms encircling her, his heat enfolding her.

She swayed then, horrified, caught herself and stood straighter, her spine ramrod stiff.

'There. Almost done.' His voice was expressionless, his eyes on the dress as he peeled it gently down.

He might have been undressing a store dummy for all the

interest he showed. And that, for some reason, was worse than anything that had gone before.

A shimmer of furious tears blurred Maggie's vision.

Here she stood, naked but for her brand-new ultra-feminine underwear, and he didn't even spare her a glance. It was as if she weren't a flesh-and-blood woman. Not a real one, capable of snaring a man's interest.

Who did she think she was kidding with her new clothes? Her body was too long, with too few curves. She had none of the sensuality other women took for granted.

The only time men noticed her was at work, for she was good at her job. In the stables she was one of the guys. Didn't that say it all? Something deep inside shrivelled up. An ache cramped her belly and she hunched over.

'Maggie? Are you in pain?' Eyes of fathomless black met hers. His hard, callused hands bit into her shoulders.

'No.' It emerged as a desperate gasp. 'But I need to be alone. Go. Please.'

His gaze raked hers. His mouth firmed into a grim line. Then slowly his fingers loosed their grip and his arms swung to his sides.

'As you wish.' Abruptly he was gone, leaving her in solitary possession of the magnificent bathroom.

For a bereft moment she wanted to call him back, ask him to hold her, to protect her from the hurt that welled up inside and the marrow-deep cold that gripped her body.

Then pride reasserted itself. He'd been only too thankful to escape. Besides, she was used to managing alone. That was the way it had always been.

She turned towards the shower, her steps as slow as an old woman's. She didn't bother to lock the door to ensure her privacy. There was no need.

Why did the knowledge hurt so much?

CHAPTER TWO

MAGGIE emerged from the bathroom swathed in soft white towelling, an oversized robe that swamped her. She hadn't even noticed Khalid take her discarded dress. The plush robe was warm against her damp skin. She hiked up the collar and dug her hands into the deep pockets.

For a heartbeat she hesitated in the doorway, then swung round at the sound of his voice.

'Feel better now?' Khalid halted a few paces away, legs planted wide in a stance that was intrinsically male. He surveyed her from top to toe. Her pulse hammered hard and loud. 'You look better. There's colour in your cheeks.'

And no wonder! Maggie felt the heat sizzle under her skin. She was uncomfortable wearing his robe, but it was all she had to hide her nakedness.

Under his survey the brush of fabric against her bare flesh suddenly took on a new dimension. Tingles rayed out from her sensitive breasts, her stomach, thighs and buttocks as she shifted her weight uneasily.

Or maybe it was reaction to the sight of him, clad in black trousers and black shirt that emphasised his spare, powerful frame. Her glance dropped all the way down past his muscled thighs to his bare feet. Her breath stopped. He even had sexy feet. She hadn't known that was possible.

Maggie snagged a desperate breath and jerked her gaze up to his, praying he hadn't noticed her ogling him.

'Thank you. I feel a lot better. Hot water works wonders, doesn't it?' Was she gabbling? For the first time since he found her, she felt truly nervous. She slicked her tongue over her bottom lip as her mouth dried.

'Come.' He held out his hand imperiously, and to her surprise, she reached out unhesitatingly. The hard heat of his palm and fingers enfolding hers was strangely comforting. If she could ignore the tendrils of shivery pleasure snaking up from their clasped hands.

He led her into a large sitting room. It should have been overpowering with its gilt-edged mirrors and elegant antique furniture. But it was lit by a fire in the grate and the mellow glow of lamps. The long sofa drawn up before the fire looked cosy with its many cushions and rich red throw rug.

'Sit.' He gestured to the sofa. 'It will be a while before your clothes dry and we can get you home. In the meantime you need to keep warm.'

As she subsided into the soft luxurious cushions Maggie knew there wasn't any danger of her growing cold. The hot shower, the fire, but most of all the way her blood heated at his touch, made her glow with warmth.

Wordlessly he covered her knees, then passed her a delicate glass in a filigree metal holder.

Maggie inhaled the steam rising from the glass. It smelt wonderful.

'What is it?'

'Sweet tea, Shajehani style. The perfect remedy for shock and exposure to the elements.' He stood before her, his back to the fire. Maggie drank in the sight of him, his imposing frame, his obvious strength, the stance of a man utterly confident and in control. Something squeezed the pit of her stomach. Hurriedly she bent her head to drink.

'It's delicious!'

'Surprising, isn't it?'

'No, I didn't mean—'

'It's all right. Drink up and relax. I'll be back soon.' He moved away and her breathing eased.

This was what she needed, to be alone to collect her thoughts and overcome these unfamiliar emotions that tonight ran so close to the surface.

She stared at the blazing fire, sipped her tea and wondered at the intensity of her reaction to Khalid. He was a stranger. A breathtakingly gorgeous one. Yet it wasn't just his looks she responded to. It was his easy kindness, that sense of rock-solid dependability, the way he took charge and looked after her as if it was the most natural thing in the world. She wasn't used to it.

Maggie blinked. She'd forgotten what it was like to feel cared for. To lean on someone else. No one had ever taken care of her like this. Not since she was eight and she'd arrived home from school to find her mother had walked out, taking Maggie's little sister, but not Maggie.

There'd been no warmth at home after that day. Her father hadn't been one for creature comforts, let alone a hug or a sympathetic smile. He'd been a hard man, dour and demanding. Even in those last months as she'd nursed him he hadn't softened.

'Is there anything else you need?' Khalid's deep voice came from beside her. She hadn't heard him return.

To her horror, the hint of concern lacing his words opened a floodgate of raw emotion. Painful emotion that ignited a terrible weakness in her. She wasn't accustomed to sympathy.

Her lips quivered. What was wrong with her? She'd discovered Marcus's betrayal and she'd got a soaking. It wasn't the end of the world.

She was made of sterner stuff than this. Maggie Lewis

never cried. It was one of the reasons she'd been accepted so quickly into the male realm of the horse stud.

'No.' The word emerged as a raw croak and she tried again. 'No, thank you.' She relinquished her stiff-knuckled grip on the glass as a large, tanned hand took it from her.

'In that case let's get your hair dry.'

Maggie opened her mouth to object, but already he'd draped a towel over her head and shoulders. Long, strong fingers massaged her scalp through the thick towelling and her demurral dissolved on her tongue.

Whorls of sensation spread from his supple hands, sensation that made the last of her resistance melt like chocolate on a hot summer day.

Her head lolled back and forward, following the easy rhythm of his hands, till she forgot what it was she objected to. Ripples of delight spread out, down her spine, across her shoulders and lower, deep inside her.

She had to stifle a sigh of regret when he lifted the towel away. It felt so good, the warmth, the company, the comfort of his presence.

She squeezed her eyes shut against the awful sensation of loss and loneliness welling inside her. The aching void of emptiness that stretched all around her.

Quickly she shook her head, hoping to dislodge the ache, the unfamiliar need. Tonight *had* been a shock, a blow to her self-esteem and her hopes, but she'd get over it. This curious sense of frailty was a passing thing. She'd always been strong. Always coped.

'Don't cry, little one.' His voice was so low it was a mere thread of sound, weaving into her consciousness. His touch was tender as he wiped moisture from her cheeks.

Maggie kept her eyes tight shut. For the second time tonight she had tears in her eyes. The second time in fifteen years. She hadn't cried since her mother had deserted her all those years ago. Maggie had sobbed herself sick then and hadn't cried since. Now in one night the dam had broken. A shudder of anxiety racked her.

'Please,' she whispered. 'I don't want to be alone.'

Khalid stared into the flames, legs outstretched in a casual pose that belied his inner turmoil. Tension pulled his shoulders tight and a charged sense of expectancy weighted his limbs.

Beside him Maggie sat with her feet curled beneath her. She was close enough for him to be aware of her every move and feel her beckoning warmth.

Yet he didn't touch her.

He fought his instinctive reaction to reach out and hold her, comfort her. He had more sense than that.

Just sitting here was a test of his willpower, and his honour. His desire to pull her into his embrace wasn't as altruistic as it should have been. Maybe bringing her here hadn't been wise after all.

Instead of leaping flames the picture filling his brain was Maggie Lewis, standing in his *en suite*, wearing nothing but lace underwear and pride. She'd been brave, beautiful and hurting, unable to hide the raw anguish in her remarkable eyes.

But it wasn't her eyes that had riveted his attention. Her lithe body was all elegant lines, pale skin that dipped and curved in exactly the right places. His hands had itched to reach out and take the weight of her high, proud breasts, to smooth over her narrow waist to the gentle curve of her hips. Hunger had surged in him so strongly that he'd been forced to leave the room, lest he do something unforgivable.

She'd looked so perfect, so pure, he could almost have believed her untouched.

Why was he imagining his hands, dark and hard, on her pristine flesh? He'd never fantasised about taking a virgin. His experience in that area was a lifetime ago.

His mind slammed shut on the old memory. There'd been

women since Shahina. Beautiful, clever, accommodating women who gave him the satisfaction his body craved. But never had his mind or his emotions been engaged. That was exactly how he wanted it. Short, easy relationships built on physical pleasure were no threat to his heart. That was how he'd lived his life since the death of his wife and it was precisely how he intended to continue.

He frowned, recognising that tonight, with Maggie Lewis, something was different. Sexual need was there, a scorching spike in his bloodstream. But something else too, more complex than physical desire. A shadow, a hint of something *more*. Something that stirred his emotions, as well as his libido. Something he had no wish to feel.

He dragged in a deep breath, trying not to notice the way her clean, feminine scent stirred his senses.

'Do you want to talk about it?' So much for his determination not to get involved.

He couldn't contain his curiosity about the intriguing woman so innocently sharing his couch.

He rubbed his jaw. He couldn't remember sharing anything innocently with a woman since Shahina.

'Did someone hurt you?' He'd make it his business to find the man and bring him to account.

'It was my fault,' she muttered, eyes downcast.

A chill iced his veins. 'Don't say that.'

'It's true. I was the one with expectations.'

'If some man forced himself on you after you'd changed your mind, it's not your fault.'

In the fire-lit shadows huge eyes met his. Her hands clenched tight together.

'No. You've got it all wrong.' Her words ended on a hiccough of unsteady laughter. 'No one forced himself on me.' Her voice was stronger, her mouth firm. 'I wasn't assaulted, if that's what you think.'

On a surge of movement she wriggled higher, squaring her slumped shoulders. Unfortunately the movement made the collar of the robe gape to reveal a sliver of pale, enticing flesh. Khalid moved restlessly and shifted his gaze. But despite the thick towelling he could easily visualise her pert breasts and smooth, silken skin.

He turned to the fire, trying to ignore the rapid thump of his pulse and the heat igniting in his loins.

'You don't need to worry. Untouched by the hand of man. That's me.' Her voice was bitter and hard.

'Pardon?' For a moment he was startled, remembering his fantasy of her as virginal, awaking to his caress. He realised how unlikely that was. She must be talking about tonight. He swung around, unable to resist temptation.

She looked different, more alive, more vibrant. A flush of colour tinted her cheeks and her eyes were bright.

His belly contracted hard as desire stabbed him. She'd got under his skin when she'd been pale and fragile. Now her features were animated, renewed energy evident in her taut body. She was far too alluring.

'Nothing happened tonight.' She lifted a dismissive hand. 'Nothing momentous, that is.' Her lips twisted in a tight grimace that belied her words.

Taking in the determined jut of her chin, he knew she lied. He gave her full marks for her valiant effort. But something *had* happened, even if it hadn't been rape.

'You said you'd had a shock.'

She shrugged, pursing her lips. 'Have you ever made an error of judgement?' she asked at last.

'Of course. Everyone has.'

'There's a comfort.' She paused. 'Well, I just made a mistake. A huge one.' She drew in a deep breath. Khalid fought to stop his gaze straying to the shadow of her cleavage. 'Tonight I found out just how stupid I'd been.'

Her words were defiant, her profile proud, yet Khalid had

seen her at rock-bottom just an hour ago. He knew she must still be hurting badly.

Over the past eight years countless women had tried to snare him with guile, seduction and emotional appeals. He'd remained unmoved. His heart had died with his wife and he had no intention of laying himself open to the raw pain of loss again. But his experience had taught him to distinguish female wiles at a glance. As a result he knew Maggie Lewis was the genuine article. No hidden agenda other than concealing her own weakness.

That stubborn pride was something he knew all about. Hadn't his father accused him of being too proud when Khalid had refused to live in indolent luxury? When instead he'd forged a life of hard work that brought its own rewards?

'At least you won't make the same mistake again.'

Solemn eyes met his before a shadow of a smile curved the corners of her mouth.

'Absolutely not! I'll *never* be that gullible again. I've learned my lesson.'

Intrigued, Khalid watched her rueful expression morph into one of determination. But even that was attractive…too attractive.

Her intelligence and character intrigued him as much as her vulnerability and her unvarnished beauty. She wasn't conventionally pretty, but there was something about the spare elegance of her features that drew the eye again and again. He wished she'd sat beside him at tonight's tedious dinner. Instead he'd been sandwiched between a yawning bore and a flirtatious airhead.

'He's a fool, whoever he is.'

'He?' She arched her eyebrows.

'The man tonight. The one who's caused you such grief.'

'How did you know there was a man?' She looked genuinely shocked.

He smiled at her naïvety. 'It's relationships between the sexes that cause most pain.'

'I can't imagine you having any such trouble,' she riposted instantly. A moment later her expression changed to one of dawning horror, as if she couldn't believe she'd just uttered the words. 'I'm sorry,' she whispered. 'I—'

'You'd be surprised,' he murmured as memories crowded in. 'Wealth is no guarantee of happiness.'

Maggie watched with a pang of regret as the vertical lines reformed at his brow and bracketed his mouth. For a little while there the grimness had lifted from Khalid's features. Now it was as if a storm cloud loomed, shadowing his face and blocking the hint of light she'd glimpsed.

She knew a crazy impulse to reach out and touch him, soothe away the pain she saw. But that wasn't an option. Instead she changed the subject.

'You're from Shajehar, aren't you?'

He nodded. 'I am.'

'Could you tell me about it? I've never travelled and it sounds so exotic.'

Dark eyes seared hers as if searching for an ulterior motive. Maggie shivered and rolled her collar higher against her throat. Perhaps she should go. It didn't matter if her clothes weren't dry, she'd been here long enough and that look made her nervous. But the raging storm and the long trip to her cold, empty house held no appeal.

'It's a country of contrasts and great beauty. Some parts are not unlike your Hunter Valley, though much is arid. There are wonderful riches if you care to look, and I'm not talking about oil revenue.' His expression told her he loved his homeland.

'The people are strong and proud of their traditions. But they're struggling now to meld their old ways with the best the modern world has to offer.' He paused, focused on her. 'You've never travelled overseas?'

'I've never been anywhere much.' At his curious look she

continued. 'I grew up on a small farm. Making ends meet was always a struggle. Travel was a luxury.'

'And when you left home?'

She ducked her head, watching her hands fold the thick fabric in her lap.

'I never left. I had plans to go to the city and study, but there was a drought and my father couldn't spare me.' He'd reminded her time and again that it was her duty to stand by him as he'd done his duty and kept her with him all those years. A pity his concept of duty didn't include even a skerrick of warmth or love.

'And now?'

'Now? I work here.'

'Helping your family?'

Maggie thought of the empty front bedroom in the old house, the echoing loneliness of the place she called home.

'There was only my father.' Maggie hadn't had any contact from her mother or sister since the day they'd left. 'He died a few months ago.'

'You must miss him.'

Must she? Miss the stern lectures, the disapproving attitude, the dour temperament?

'I… He wasn't an easy man to live with.' That had to be the understatement of the century. Nothing Maggie ever did had been good enough, even when her extra income had been all that kept the old farm afloat. 'He should have had a son. A daughter is a disappointment to a man like that.'

'I'm sorry, Maggie.' The words were filled with understanding. She darted a glance at Khalid. Was that compassion in his liquid dark eyes? 'Some of us aren't blessed with the best of parents.'

'You too?'

He paused, as if taken aback by the personal question.

'My father had no time for his family,' he said eventually. 'No time for children. He had…other interests.' Khalid's tone made it clear those interests weren't anything he approved of. 'He was an absentee parent, rarely home. And when he was, let's just say he had little patience with small boys.'

Reading between the lines, Maggie felt a sharp stab of fellow feeling, a sympathy for the suffering Khalid had skated over. For the stoic endurance not to collapse under the weight of a parent's cruel neglect.

'I'm sorry.' Her voice was husky. 'Little boys need a dad.'

'And so do little girls.'

To her horror, his ready sympathy cracked the brittle wall she'd built around her feelings. For years she'd struggled against the belief that she was unlovable, ever since her mum had rejected her, taking Cassie instead. Tonight her fears and pain had coalesced into an aching void of anguish that filled her very being. The force of it clogged her throat and fractured her breathing.

'Maggie.' Khalid must have seen the stricken expression on her face. He reached out and pulled her close, tucking her head into his shoulder. He rubbed her back with small, circular, soothing movements.

'You've done this before,' she murmured, trying to regain her composure and downplay her reaction to his touch. 'Do you have sisters?'

'No sisters.'

'A wife?'

She was dimly aware of his pause before he said, 'No wife.'

A heartbeat of silence and then he urged, 'Hold me, Maggie.'

She needed no second urging. Maggie slid her arms around him and burrowed close to his heat. She knew later she'd be horribly embarrased but for now her need for comfort drove her beyond her usual diffidence.

His arms tightened around her and a shiver rippled through Maggie as his warmth seeped into her bones. The rock-solid strength of him, the tangible, living power of muscle and bone and sinew, were more real than anything else in the world. His unique spicy scent invaded her nostrils, making her nerves tingle into an awareness that had nothing to do with solace.

The scent, the feel, even the sound of him, the powerful throb of his heart beneath her ear, were all wondrous. She pressed her face to the fine silk of his shirt. Through the fabric his skin was hot, taut and inviting. She breathed deep, drawing in the heady aroma of warm, healthy male.

That was when she registered his quickening heartbeat, the changed tempo of his breathing. Tentatively she lifted a hand to splay over his chest.

The tiniest of tremors rippled across his skin. The hand palming her back ceased its movement and his other hand clamped down on her arm, as if to drag it away.

Thunder echoed in her ears as her pulse raced. Suddenly this innocent embrace had transformed into something charged with unspoken danger.

With excitement. And longing. It bubbled up inside her like a newfound spring—the need for more. The need for *him*. This was nothing like what she'd felt with Marcus. This was... elemental, as sudden as a thunderclap and just as unmistakable, even to someone of her limited experience.

Heat blossomed deep within as her breath caught, stilled by the stunning realisation of how much more she wanted from this man.

'It's time you moved.' His voice sounded stretched.

Heat flamed her cheeks. What was she thinking? He'd offered her comfort, not a sexual invitation. Just because she felt that sunburst of white-hot desire didn't mean it was reciprocated. Hadn't she learned anything tonight?

'Maggie, you need to sit up. You don't want to do something you'll regret later.'

She frowned. Something *she'd* regret?

'What do you mean?' she whispered at last.

Strong hands pried her away, gently pushing her back to her corner of the sofa. Ebony eyes met hers. His face was grim, his mouth a tight line.

'You're upset. You're not yourself. It's time to end this. You don't want to play with fire.'

'Fire?' She wasn't normally obtuse, but surely he didn't mean what she thought he meant. Was it even remotely possible that he felt it too? The sudden overwhelming need for intimacy that ousted everything else? The consuming hunger? A need for *her*, for plain, no-frills Maggie Lewis?

His gaze narrowed, flicking down to her mouth, and lower to the V-neck of the robe she wore. Flames licked her skin beneath his trailing gaze and tension coiled tight in her belly as her breathing shortened.

'I'm a man, Maggie. If we don't stop now it won't be comfort I'll be giving you. It will be something much more intimate.'

The words echoed on and on in the silence between them. They should have shocked her, made her draw back. But instead the blatant weight of sensuality in his bald statement had the opposite effect. Excitement tingled down her spine and drew her stomach muscles tight.

Maggie strove to be sensible, careful, reserved, all the things she'd been before tonight.

But something vital had changed. Now, for the first time, she knew what it was to want a man. *Really* want, with every fibre of her body. It was an urgent, unstoppable force. A compulsion shuddering through her very bones.

She had two choices. She could pretend this wasn't real. Shrug on her usual self-effacing persona and try to hide from this surge of powerful desire. Or she could welcome it; give in to the strongest need she'd ever felt.

She could be bold or she could be sensible.

She'd spent a lifetime being sensible and self-sacrificing. Where had that got her?

'And you don't want to do that?'

She didn't recognise her hoarse voice. Excitement and anxiety closed her throat. She couldn't believe she'd just invited another rebuff, but the new sensations heating her blood were too compelling to ignore. She had to know.

Hooded eyes surveyed her and she felt the distance grow between them. He was going to reject her. Something dimmed inside her.

Finally he spoke. 'I shouldn't.' He raised his hand and thrust it back through his hair in a jerky gesture. 'I shouldn't but…yes, God help me, I want to.'

CHAPTER THREE

HE COULDN'T. He mustn't.

This woman was exhausted, not thinking clearly. He mustn't take advantage, no matter that his need for her was visceral, all-consuming. She deserved his protection.

Her eyes glowed a shimmering green-gold. She looked pale but beautiful, her fine-boned features pure, alluring and incredibly sexy with that hopeful pout.

'You're hurt. This is your pain speaking.' Khalid forced the words out. 'But this isn't the answer. You want someone who can give you more. More than a few snatched hours.'

More than a man who could only promise physical pleasure. Who had given up on emotional commitment years before.

For one absurd moment he felt a piercing jealousy for the man who'd one day give Maggie Lewis everything she wanted.

Her chin tilted fractionally in a way that spoke of pride and pain together.

'What if I said a few snatched hours are exactly what I want? That I'm not in the market for anything more? Not any longer?'

Tension held Khalid rigid as desire spiralled and his groin tightened. Each muscle was rock-hard at the effort of remaining still when he wanted to lean over and imprison her beneath his hungry body.

Desire he understood. He had a healthy male appreciation

of a sexy woman. But this craving was something else entirely. It shook him to the core. Unbelievably this felt far more significant than the simple sexual urge he'd assuaged through the recent years with beautiful, willing women.

This felt…different. More real, more vital than anything he'd experienced in years.

A shadowed vision of velvet-soft brown eyes filled his mind and pain lanced his chest.

'No. I can't.' He forced the words out over a constricting throat.

'Yes, of course.' Her whisper drew his sensitised flesh to prickling alert. 'I understand.'

Khalid drew a shuddering breath. He'd done the right thing, the honourable thing. Now he just had to—

The sight of her bowed head, her white teeth cutting deep into her bottom lip, brought him up short.

'Thank you for helping me tonight,' she said stiffly, looking away. 'I'm sorry I embarrassed you with my…with my…' She shook her head and soft hair the colour of toffee swirled round her neck, catching the light.

'I apologise,' she murmured, wrapping her arms around herself. 'You must have women coming on to you all the time.'

Apologise?

Her profile was taut, her lips pinched. His chest hollowed as he realised he'd caused her more distress. Instinct overcame caution as he cupped her chin in his hand and turned her face around. She resisted, even grabbed his wrist as if to tug his arm away.

'You don't owe me an apology.'

Bright eyes met his, startled and disbelieving. He wished the texture of her soft skin weren't so enticing.

Khalid hoped fate would repay him one day for his superhuman restraint. It was killing him by degrees, inhaling her tantalising scent, sexier than any bottled fragrance. The feel of her, the sight of her, seduced him, more real than any shadowy memories of the past. That scared him, yet he ached to learn the taste of her.

She reared back, away from his touch. Her chest rose and fell rapidly beneath the oversized robe.

'I understand.' She spoke too quickly, her words tripping over each other. 'It's all right.'

But it wasn't. She thought he lied about wanting her. Could she really be so blind? What had happened tonight to make her so unsure of her attractiveness?

'I think I should leave.' Her voice wobbled on the last word. Automatically she angled her chin higher as if to counteract any sign of weakness.

She was a fighter, this woman who played havoc with his good intentions, who'd got under his skin from the moment he'd seen her. Who had to be one of the most alluring women he'd ever met. Even without make-up, drenched and shivering in her underwear, she'd exerted a terrible fascination.

The hot tide rose in him, welling and cresting, and his resolve crumbled, his caution disintegrated.

One kiss. He'd permit himself a single kiss to alleviate the compulsive need to touch her again. To reassure her that she *was* desirable.

'Maggie.' Once more he lifted her chin, this time bending close. Her eyes widened, her mouth slackened just a little as she realised what he intended. Perfect.

Her lips trembled beneath his and he wrapped his arms around her, sweeping her close. The brush of her slender, feminine form and her fresh, sweet taste on his tongue sent a roaring wave of need juddering through him. Khalid breathed deep, summoning control. He had to concentrate, to keep this a gentle, exploratory kiss.

The feel of her lips shaping to his and the sound of her soft sigh were poignant. She fitted his arms as if made for him. It was as perfect as any lover's kiss he'd known.

He reeled as the discovery slammed into his astonished brain.

Her tongue slid tentatively against his as he entered her mouth and a dart of pure pleasure shafted through him.

Just another minute…

Maggie clung to his shoulders as the world spun and she closed her eyes, dizzy with delight. The feelings he evoked with the touch of his mouth and his arms holding her close swept her into a new world.

She felt desire, daring, a thrill of excitement as his tongue stroked her mouth. Shivers ran down her spine, along her arms where the skin pulled tight and down to her nipples. She gasped as he delved deeper.

Their hearts pulsed in unison, their mouths fused as need exploded. She clamped her hands desperately to the back of his skull, pulling herself higher, closer.

Still, it wasn't enough.

Her need for him was a twisting, hungry sensation in the pit of her stomach, and lower, where a curious ache filled her. Maggie squirmed, trying to ease the hollow feeling deep within.

Recklessly she kissed him back, the fever in her blood urging her on. For now, for tonight, this was what she craved, the sweet headiness of shared passion. All Khalid's magnificent power concentrated on her.

When he cupped her breast she gasped against his mouth, unprepared for the electric charge his touch evoked. Blue-white fire flickered behind her eyelids as he brushed his thumb over her nipple. Incendiary sparks exploded through her, drawing her body tight and expectant.

Maggie pressed forward into his hand and was rewarded as he firmed his hold. She arched her back in a spasm of pleasure. Yes!

'Please,' she mouthed, not even knowing what it was she pleaded for.

Devastation hit when he removed his hand, but a moment later he slipped it into the neckline of her robe. Her skin contracted, sensitised to his touch. His hand closed again around her breast, only this time there was nothing between him and her. No barrier. The feeling of him slowly massaging, then gently squeezing her there was indescribable. Perfect.

She sagged back against his embracing arm, breaking their devastating kiss as she gulped oxygen into her air-starved lungs. She gazed up at him.

Eyes like glittering dark pools shone down at her, unreadable. His shoulders rose and fell as he breathed quick and deep. His heavy-lidded eyelids spoke of passion, tightly leashed. So powerfully controlled.

Would he go now? Would he slide his hand away? Could he possibly leave her alone and so desperately wanting?

She couldn't bear it. He'd given her a taste of something special, miraculous, something only he could give. And she wanted more. Was it so bad to seek, just this once, the intimate pleasure she'd never had?

Maggie covered his hand with her own, pressing into his hold. His fingers tightened and delicious ripples spread through her.

'Please, Khalid.' She knew what she asked this time. She wanted him to show her more, let her experience the intimate joy of truly being with a man.

His face looked grim, the flickering firelight emphasising the sharp cut of his cheekbones, the hard, aristocratic line of his nose and his set jaw.

He was going to do it, she realised. He was going to leave her. Pride warred with need. Already tonight she'd cast aside any pretence of dignity.

Wordlessly she pulled the other side of the robe open to reveal her bare breast.

Cool air shivered across her skin.

Her heart pounded fast in trepidation and anticipation. She watched the muscles work in his throat as he swallowed. Then his chest expanded on a mighty breath.

She waited, trembling, but his next move was to slip his hand away.

Maggie knew defeat then. He didn't like what he saw. Why was she surprised? She'd always known she wasn't feminine enough with her underdeveloped curves. She dragged the robe back, covering herself, even though it was too late for modesty.

The touch of his hands made her jump. Before she could gather her wits she was hauled off the couch and up into steel-hard arms. His eyes were molten hot as they clashed with hers.

'Are you sure you want this?' His voice was a low burr that reverberated deep in that hollow place within her.

She nodded, her mouth too dry to speak as excitement effervesced in her bloodstream. There was silence but for the crackle of the fire. Maggie held her breath, waiting.

'Then so be it.'

He turned so fast the room blurred. A moment later they were in a massive, shadowed bedroom. Maggie had an impression of sumptuous furnishings, of a vast royal-blue and gold bedspread, before he ripped the covers back in a single ruthless tug and tumbled her down onto the sheets.

Their eyes met and held and her blood pumped harder, faster. It was a thunderous buzz in her ears as his hands went to his shirt and he tugged it off, not bothering with buttons. Seconds later the rest of his clothing dropped to the floor.

He stood before her, magnificent and more beautiful than anything she'd seen in her life. The warm glow of the bedroom fire gilded his skin and cast shadows across his body. Each plane and curved muscle was thrown into relief. He was long-limbed, strong and virile. She'd never imagined a man could look so potent, so perfect.

Maggie pushed back a moment's doubt, wondering if she should tell him she was a virgin. He wouldn't have taken seriously her crack about being untouched.

But she didn't want him having second thoughts now. A man such as this must have had many lovers. Would he be disappointed? Maggie quashed the worry as soon as it entered her brain.

For this one night she'd live for the moment, thrust caution aside and take what life had to offer.

Heat washed her as he reached into a bedside drawer to retrieve a foil packet and put it on the table.

She was grateful he'd thought of protection, but somehow this reminder of real-world responsibility made her feel awkward and nervous.

'You have too many clothes on.' His words short-circuited her thoughts. The sound of his voice drew her skin tight over her bones. Then his hands were on her, drawing the belt from her robe, slowly opening it, laying the sides wide so she lay virtually naked. He stood there, not saying a word as his gaze travelled the length of her body. She had time to feel anxious again, wondering what he thought of it.

He drew in a deep breath and Maggie watched, mesmerised, the movement of muscle and tendon tightening across his torso. He had the superb body of an athlete.

Then there was no chance for further thought as he bent and stripped the robe away, flinging it to the floor. A moment later he was crowding her back on the bed. His body was as hot as a furnace. Everywhere they touched she registered unfamiliar, exciting sensations. The brush of wiry hair as his legs tangled with hers. The impossibly erotic slide of his chest against her heated skin; hard-packed muscle and a drift of silky hair against her own sensitised breasts. And, lower, his heavy erection on her thigh.

Her breath shuddered as sensory overload hit.

But there was more to come. He lowered his head to her breast and ecstasy consumed her.

'Khalid!' Her hoarse cry was barely audible as she fought to catch her breath. The sensations coursing through her as he suckled, at first gently, then hard, stiffened her body in shocked delight. Then his hand was on her other breast, circling and teasing. She wondered if it was possible to die from pleasure. His body heat against hers was exquisitely exciting.

Her fingers speared through his thick hair, holding him close. Liquid heat throbbed through her bloodstream and pooled between her legs. An urgent longing filled her. She wanted him. Now.

But Khalid was in no hurry.

'Patience, little one.' He turned his attention to discovering her body with a single-minded intensity that made her head spin and her blood sing.

From her shoulder to her fingertips, from the sensitive place just behind her ear to her collarbone and her breasts, he took his time caressing, kissing, learning her. Arousing her. She sighed as he moved lower, to her navel, her hipbone, her thigh, even the back of her knee.

Pleasure rippled through her as sensation after sensation bombarded her. She grew alternately limp and stiff with excitement at his touch. The one constant was the ever-building need that grew stronger by the minute. Soon it was a throbbing ache.

Hours might have passed by the time he paused to reach out a hand to the bedside table. Then he was back, his hard hands tender, his breath hot on her sensitive inner thighs and higher, on the place where the heat scorched brightest and hottest.

She cried out as he caressed her there, at the very apex of her need, and she almost jolted off the bed as jagged lightning shot through.

She was burning up; she couldn't breathe. Her pounding heart must surely suffocate her.

'Khalid.' Her fingers dug into his shoulders as she tried to drag him higher. Her legs twisted wide as instinctively she offered herself.

There was no doubt in her mind now. This was right. *He* was right. It was almost as if he was the one she'd been waiting for all this time.

The burgeoning realisation fractured into nothingness as he covered her body with his and she ceased to think.

He was heat and power, hard muscle and surprisingly silky skin. Maggie slipped her hands around his neck, her breath faltering as her breasts rubbed his chest.

Dark, fathomless eyes held hers and amidst the maelstrom of desire she felt…safe.

She hung on tight as he propped himself up on one arm and she felt the muscles in his shoulders ripple. His other hand moved down to touch her between her legs. His fingers glided through slick folds, over the throbbing nub and inexorably lower. Wildfire blazed in her bloodstream at his touch. Her body convulsed as he pushed inwards and her breath tore away.

For a long quivering moment she waited, eyes wide, fingers clenching tight in his hair as her body tugged at him. She saw his pulse jerk heavily in his throat and felt the throb of his erection against her.

She shifted against him, not sure how to proceed but knowing she'd die if he stopped now.

Clumsily she unwound an arm from around his neck and slid it down till her fingers curled around him. He came to life at her touch, pushing into her palm: hot, heavy and powerfully strong. Tentatively she squeezed.

A guttural rumble of Arabic near her ear might have been encouragement or an oath.

'Stop!'

Instantly she loosened her hold.

Khalid's lips were drawn back in a grimace of pain. Or pleasure? His eyes glittered febrile-bright as he stared down at her.

Then he moved and there were no more doubts. He braced himself over her as his palm spread her thighs wider. Her legs shook as she complied. He nudged at her entrance and instinctively she rose up to meet him.

He dipped his head to her neck, kissing and grazing her

tender skin with his teeth as he pushed in. The movement was smooth, easy and impossibly long. Maggie experienced a strange sensation of fullness, of stretching, of weight and heat. There was discomfort at first, but when he stopped she couldn't believe the feeling of oneness.

Khalid raised his head, a pinch of a frown marking the centre of his brow. He stared down at her through narrowed eyes for a long moment. Then raised a hand to her cheek in the gentlest of caresses. To her amazement Maggie registered a tiny tremor in his touch.

She turned her face into his palm, revelling in the slide of his callused fingers against her cheek.

'You are a treasure. So generous,' he murmured in a deep husky voice that curled her insides.

His mouth took hers in a sensuous kiss. His body moved away, then slid back, again and again in an easy rhythm that set incendiary sparks flying through her body. Frantically she hugged him, giving him back kiss for desperate kiss as the tension coiled tighter and tighter inside her.

Then the fire they'd built consumed her in a flare of white-hot light and the world exploded around her, blotting out everything but the perfection of that single climactic moment that went on and on and on.

It was dark when Maggie woke. Time for her early start in the stables. Yet she didn't stir. She felt lethargic, yet energised. She tingled with effervescent energy as if her bloodstream ran with champagne.

Her lips curved as she snuggled down on her pillow, enjoying the remarkable sense of well-being that filled her. She felt like a different woman. Not plain old Maggie Lewis. Then she registered the heat behind her. The living heat of another body.

Khalid.

Memory crashed upon her in a bitter-sweet tide.

She thought of last night, of Khalid's passion and the way he'd made her feel…beautiful. She'd never been given such a gift before. She hugged the memory tight to herself.

When he'd made love to her she'd even, for a moment, believed herself to be a desirable woman.

The tentative curve of her lips faded. Her mouth flattened into a grim line. Her—desirable? No, she couldn't fool herself like that. She was strong enough to face the truth.

Khalid had made love to her because she'd thrown herself at him. She'd seen the pity in his eyes. She'd read his initial unwillingness. She'd played on his sympathy and he'd read her desperation.

It didn't matter that she'd needed him so badly she'd felt she might shatter with the force of her feelings. Or that their love-making had been the most wonderful experience in all her twenty-three years.

Last night she'd told herself she should grab what she wanted. Anger had welled at Marcus's duplicity, at the dull, demanding life she'd accepted for so long, at the hurt she'd endured. She'd wanted for one night the powerful pleasure she'd known instinctively Khalid could give her.

He'd probably spent the encounter thinking of some voluptuous beauty, not the awkward emotional woman in his arms.

Mortified, Maggie felt her face burn.

She was strong, a survivor. But did she have the nerve to face him this morning? She imagined him trying to stifle his distaste.

Maggie darted a furtive look over her shoulder. He lay asleep. Even in the pre-dawn gloom the set of his shoulders and deep chest above white sheets snared her gaze. Heat built inside her. That needy ache was back again.

No! She buried her face in her pillow, only to inhale the faint spicy scent that lingered there. The evocative scent of Khalid's skin. Her resolve splintered. The temptation to stay was so strong.

But Maggie was done with fantasy. Last night had been a wonderful, once-in-a-lifetime experience, but it couldn't lead anywhere. Better to let Khalid wake alone. He deserved that. He'd be relieved to find she wasn't clinging to him still.

Slowly, her heart heavy, she pulled back the covers and slipped noiselessly from the bed.

Khalid woke at dawn. His recall of last night was instantaneous, evidenced by his early-morning erection. Despite the startling perfection of sex with Maggie Lewis it had been a frustrating night. Once was rarely enough for Khalid and last night his climax, despite its rare intensity, had barely scratched the surface of his need. He'd itched for more.

Only the knowledge that, incredibly, he was her first lover had restrained him from sating himself in her slim, sexy body again and again.

A powerful shudder ran through him.

Her first. The knowledge stirred a deeply primitive satisfaction in his belly. He didn't deflower virgins. He sought pleasure with women who were worldly, experienced and unlikely to cling. Women who knew he no longer had a heart to bestow even on the most generous lover.

Yet here he was, rampant with sexual hunger for his next taste of Maggie.

Last night's shock at her inexperience had worn off. So too had his reservations, that hint of guilt that he'd taken advantage of her vulnerability. She'd wanted him. Had eagerly welcomed him. Then afterwards had curled into him with the trusting innocence of a kitten. No, there could be no regrets.

The liaison had been unlooked-for, but now it had begun he knew no qualms about pursuing it further. He was a generous lover and she would have no regrets. He'd change his flights to extend his stay. But first… He rolled over, seeking the warm, welcoming embrace of his new lover.

The bed was empty.

He swiped his arm over the sheets. There was barely a trace of her warmth. A single movement propelled him out of bed, striding across the room. She wasn't in the bathroom. Her clothes had disappeared.

Khalid's puzzled frown accelerated into a scowl.

She'd left him without as much as a word? As if he was some sordid secret to be ashamed of! He sucked in a deep breath and willed his clenched hands to relax. But nothing could stem the surge of annoyance, of…outrage.

Never had a woman walked out on him. His pride rebelled at the very idea. Usually he was the one distancing himself from importunate lovers.

He swung round, scanning the room. No note. No explanation. Annoyance and frustration warred with curiosity. What had sent her hurtling out of bed at that ungodly hour? Fear? Guilt?

For a moment he pictured her racing off to sell her kiss-and-tell story to some slimy tabloid. The press was insatiably hungry for stories about him.

But…could he have been so wrong about her? Instinct told him not, told him she was exactly what she'd seemed last night. But he'd better make sure.

The buzz of his mobile phone caught his attention, interrupting his unwanted doubts. One glance at the caller ID had him connecting the call and sinking into a chair.

Ten minutes later he ended the call and stared across the shadowy room, his eyes fixed on a distant place.

Khalid's world had changed in those few minutes.

Faruq was dead. Khalid was Sheikh of Shajehar.

He drew a slow breath, thinking of the half-brother he'd barely known. There'd been no love between them, but regret pierced him at that life cut short.

After a while he rolled his shoulders and stood. His people needed him. He'd return immediately. He paused, his gaze settling on the wide, rumpled bed. He had no time to look for

Maggie Lewis now. Yet there was unfinished business between them.

The situation was easily remedied. He'd have her located and brought to Shajehar. His lips curled in a faint smile.

It would be his pleasure to renew their acquaintance.

CHAPTER FOUR

'COME on, Tally. Let's get this show on the road.'

Late-morning sun beat down on Maggie through her long-sleeved cotton shirt as she led Tallawanta's Pride to the ring. The dry heat reminded her of an Aussie summer and the smell of horse, hay and sawdust was comfortably familiar.

Yet everything else was different in Shajehar. The stables were infinitely more luxurious than in Australia. The sheikh obviously lavished a fortune on his horses.

Pity he didn't give as much attention to his people. In the days since she'd flown in, accompanying the Tallawanta horses, she'd seen the stark divide between rich and poor. Extravagant modern complexes beside slums.

'Almost there, Tally,' she whispered as the mare caught an unfamiliar scent and shuddered to a halt. The flight to the Middle East had been a long one for the horses. Only now, after lengthy veterinary checks, were they being paraded for the sheikh's approval.

Not that he'd deigned to come. Always the cushioned seat at the centre of the ringside stand, the gilt-covered chair set aside for the sheikh, had been empty.

She tensed as they entered the ring, scanning the crowd for the imposing figure of the man who kept her awake each night.

Khalid. The thought of him sent excitement skimming down her spine, though it was a month since they'd been together.

She hadn't seen him since the morning after they'd made love. She'd thrown herself into her work, hoping to erase the memory of her behaviour that night. But nothing could blank the recollection of Khalid holding her, loving her. No matter how she berated herself, she couldn't prevent the fillip of delight inside when she remembered.

She'd spent the next day fearful he'd visit the stables. She'd been on tenterhooks, anxious that she might come face to face with the man who'd made her discover a new Maggie. A needy, sensuous, wanton woman who responded to his touch with a total lack of control.

Yet when she'd overheard someone mention the stud's VIP guest had changed his plans and left that morning, it hadn't been relief she'd felt. It had been disappointment.

A small foolish part of her had hoped their passionate encounter had meant something to him. That he'd want to see her again. But she'd been an object of pity, nothing more.

Maggie notched her chin up as she led the mare around the ring. Khalid was probably on the other side of the world with some beautiful sophisticate in tow.

Sunlight glinted to her left and movement caught her eye—new arrivals taking their seats in the stand.

Maggie faltered as she caught a glimpse of the man at the centre of the newcomers. Tall, lean and dressed in concealing robes. But the stark white fabric couldn't hide a pair of spectacular shoulders, a physique that made him top his companions by a head.

It couldn't be.

He was obscured by a bowing usher yet Maggie was sure she'd seen a familiar profile: spare, powerful and unmistakable. Her stomach churned and fire fizzed through her bloodstream.

Khalid.

If it was him, what then? Would he acknowledge her or pretend they were strangers?

Maggie bit her lip. Would he remember her? He was a

man with a wealth of sensual experience. No doubt there were plenty of women—beautiful and glamorous—who'd captivated his attention for more than a couple of hours.

No, he'd remember that night for a while at least. It *had* been out of the ordinary—making love to a gawky, bedraggled wreck of a woman.

A shout and a loud whinny from the entry tunnel snapped her out of her reverie. She clung to the lead-rein as Tally sidled abruptly towards her. Tally plunged and it took all Maggie's strength to hold the spooked mare. Her arms felt as if they were being ripped out of their sockets. But she knew her job and her horse, and soon had it under control.

The same couldn't be said for Tallawanta Diva. Maggie caught a flash of black as the horse thundered into the ring, kicking up sand and sawdust, its head tossing wildly.

Damn it. She'd counselled against giving Diva to a new, untried groom. Diva was too skittish and unsettled and far too mettlesome for inexperienced hands. But the stable manager had insisted. Maggie wished it could be the stable manager who caught the fractious horse.

Swiftly she turned towards the ringside seating and thrust Tally's lead-rein into the hands of the local trainer who'd worked with the horses. His startled eyes met hers, then she was spinning away, striding to where the other horse ran loose.

The new groom picked himself up, looking stiff and wary. Meanwhile Diva showed every symptom of a highly strung beast who was out of routine, out of familiar surroundings and working herself into a frenzy. Maggie saw the whites of her eyes as she tossed her head and lashed out with her hindquarters at a silk banner waving on the edge of the ring. She skittered sideways at a ripple of movement in the stands as spectators rose, eager to watch.

Maggie didn't take her eyes off her for a second. She knew only too well the power of the animal. None of the grooms turned their back on this horse. Slowly she approached, keeping her voice low and soothing.

Diva listened, ears flicking back and forth at Maggie's familiar tone, but still sidling nervously, muscles twitching and head jerking at each movement in the encircling stands. Every so often she'd swing round to lash out at a shadow or at the banner snapping in the breeze.

A deep, authoritative voice called out something short and sharp in Arabic, then, thankfully, the spectators subsided in their seats. Thank goodness someone in the audience had had the sense to see the horse was spooked by the rippling movement of so many long robes.

At last Maggie was close enough. Keeping eye contact, talking all the while, she stepped forward, reaching for the lead-rein. Her fingers touched leather. She almost had it.

Suddenly the horse reared, spun round and backed towards the ringside. Maggie had an instant's grace to extricate herself from the gap between horse and stand. She almost made it. Then she was crammed back against the wooden structure and pain slammed into her.

A moment later Diva danced sideways and Maggie snatched the chance to brace herself, head bent and hands on knees, gasping in air. Then she straightened and turned to the horse. There was pin-drop silence in the ring.

Maggie circled, hand raised to grab the lead-rein. Then she discovered the job had already been done. Someone stood at Diva's head, holding her steady.

Through the smells of sawdust and horse Maggie caught another scent. Sandalwood and warm, male skin. She stopped dead. Diva moved and suddenly Maggie caught sight of the man who'd vaulted into the ring to capture the mare.

'Khalid!'

Maggie's heart revved and her throat closed on an instantaneous burst of pleasure. He looked so good.

His expression was hard, his mouth a taut straight line

bracketed by grim slashes. His ebony-dark eyes had narrowed, his nostrils flared as if he needed extra oxygen. Or as if he clamped down on anger.

He looked all male in a way that sent spurts of excitement racing through her. With his face framed by a pristine head-cloth that emphasised his dark tan, he looked the epitome of some exotic fantasy.

He held the mare with the easy competence of an experienced horseman. Already Diva was calming.

In the bright light of the open air Khalid was even more arresting than she remembered. Heat blazed deep inside as her mind strayed to the memory of him naked, his superb body gilded by flickering firelight.

'Maggie.' His tone was abrupt. 'You're on your feet? You need to sit and get your breath back.' Clearly he wasn't disturbed by memories of their night together. He was anchored firmly in the here and now. Embarrassment washed her in a hot tide and she drew herself up taller.

'I'm OK.' The response was automatic.

Dark eyes held hers while her pulse thumped in her throat. What was he thinking? Was he remembering?

'That remains to be seen.' He turned and gestured and the head groom appeared. Khalid said something in Arabic and the groom nodded before leading Diva away.

'I'm perfectly capable of...' Maggie's voice died as Khalid lifted warm hands to her face, his touch like a benediction on her skin. Slowly he dragged long fingers down her throat and across her shoulders.

Sensations sparked from his touch and rippled out across her skin. Convulsively she swallowed.

His touch was light. The brush of his fingers across her skin reignited sensations she'd discovered for the first time weeks ago. When he'd caressed her, aroused her.

'No! I'm fine.' She tried to jerk out of his grasp but his grip firmed on her upper arms.

Had he stepped closer? His body heat seared through the cotton of her shirt and his eyes were so close she felt she could lose herself in their glittering depths.

'We need to make sure.' His tone was adamant as he cast an eye over her dusty clothes.

Maggie, brought up on her father's maxim of 'no tears, no complaints, just get up and get on with it', couldn't believe how easily she subsided in the face of Khalid's determination. Obviously he was a man used to issuing orders and receiving unquestioning obedience.

She could barely believe he was here.

'Do you make a habit of rescuing strange women?' Her voice was husky.

His mouth quirked up briefly in what might have been a smile. Or a grimace. 'You're my first.' He met her gaze then. The intensity of his look dried her throat instantly. No more flippant remarks.

For a moment Maggie was back in Australia, in bed. Khalid leaned over her, his glorious naked body propped above her, his eyes warm with the promise of delight. Desire swirled like hot treacle in her abdomen.

Then she registered a buzz of sound. Belatedly she remembered they weren't alone. This time when she tried to step away he didn't prevent her. His hands dropped to his sides. For an absurd moment she felt…bereft.

Maggie turned and saw, beyond him, a cluster of strangers watching with concern and open curiosity. Blood rushed to her cheeks.

'What were you doing here?' she whispered. It was easier to focus on him than the encircling onlookers.

His brows rose. 'Viewing the horses.'

Of course. His presence had nothing to do with her. Hadn't she already guessed he'd probably prefer to be anywhere else than with her? At Tallawanta he'd accepted her departure easily, choosing to leave the estate without trying to contact her.

He met her eyes, his expression unreadable. 'We'll have a doctor examine you.'

'No, I'm OK.' She cast a look around the ring but the horses had disappeared. 'I'm needed in the stables.'

'Nevertheless, it would be sensible.'

'But—'

'Especially since you are a visitor here.' His voice brooked no argument. 'We take our responsibilities to our guests very seriously. You need to be fit to do your job.'

'Sire.' A man stepped forward from the group around them. 'The doctor is here as requested.'

Maggie frowned. *Sire?*

'I don't need a doctor!' She was horrified at the fuss they were making. 'Look, this is overkill.'

'Let him do his job,' Khalid said in a low voice that only she could hear. 'Unless you'd prefer to make a scene?'

The tilt of one sleek eyebrow dared her to argue. She shook her head. If submitting to a medical check meant she could escape these curious eyes, she'd do it.

'Good. Sensible woman.'

Watching Khalid, Maggie was struck by the knowledge that, for all they'd shared, he was a stranger. In a long robe that emphasised the lean power of his tall frame and a *keffiyeh* hiding his dark hair, he looked exotically foreign. His expression was unreadable but his stance was commanding. She noticed that the other spectators, for all their curiosity, kept back a few paces.

Then the doctor was there, distracting her thoughts. He bowed to Khalid before checking for injuries. Then he announced that she should accompany him. Good. The sooner she escaped this crowd, the better. She was mortified at this fuss. And at the impossible yearning she felt still for Khalid's touch, his tenderness.

If fate was kind, she wouldn't see him again. Then she

could pretend her reaction to him was due to shock and not, as she feared, something far stronger.

Khalid paused before the door to the first-aid room, glad he'd finally shaken his entourage. He hadn't missed the speculative glances at the ring. They were used to Faruq, who had been too lazy and self-indulgent to bestir himself for anyone else, much less an employee. He'd never have personally rescued a groom from the trampling kicks of a frightened horse.

Khalid could imagine the whispers circulating about him and the Australian stable hand. The graceful, courageous, *female* stable hand.

He'd already made a name for himself as an unconventional ruler, more serious and hardworking than either his father or half-brother. Now the courtiers would wonder if at last he exhibited a family weakness for beautiful women. Whether the slim girl with the wide eyes and luscious mouth had captured his fancy.

Let them speculate. If he'd waited to intervene...

Khalid's blood had run cold, seeing her in danger. He'd ordered the spectators to sit, to give her a chance to quieten the thoroughbred. She'd almost done it too. She'd shown no fear or doubt, just a single-minded intent and a reckless disregard for her own safety that had filled him with admiration even as it had chilled him.

He reached for the door, deliberately taking his time.

Four weeks since he'd been with this woman. Yet the impact of her in the flesh was more devastating than he'd expected. He'd told himself his memory was faulty. That he'd imagined that intense sensual spark between them.

Perhaps this compelling sense of unfinished business, this acute physical hunger, stemmed from the fact that Maggie Lewis had, uniquely among women, walked away from him.

Khalid Bin Shareef was not a man used to being denied.

For all his modern education, his forebears had been arrogant and strong leaders, who took what they wanted.

His blood sizzled in anticipation as he rapped on the door, paused and then pushed it open.

She sat primly in an upright chair. Why didn't it surprise him that she wasn't lying down after what must have been a frightening experience?

Her light toffee hair fell around her shoulders. She looked dirty, dishevelled and ridiculously alluring. Perhaps because he could so easily picture the creamy smooth skin and pert pink nipples beneath her shirt.

He didn't want to remember. It would have been so much easier if he could look at her again and feel nothing. But even that first glance at her in the ring, her profile clear and proud, her body supple and tempting, had brought his libido roaring into life, making him pause to watch before taking his seat in the centre of the stand.

A knot of desire tightened his groin as he saw her mouth slacken in surprise. He recalled her soft, astonished gasp of pleasure as he'd brought her to climax. The sound of it, the remembrance of her innocent temptation, had haunted his nights ever since.

'What are you doing here?'

Maggie could have bitten her tongue as soon as the words were out. She sounded waspish.

Last time they'd met she'd been a wreck. Was she destined always to be at a disadvantage with him? She was grimy and tired and the doctor's continued absence was making her jittery. She sat straighter, watching Khalid cross the room with his long, easy stride.

'Hello, Maggie. It's a pleasure to see you too.' There wasn't a hint of reproach in his voice, but he looked grim. She curled her fingers tight round the edge of the chair.

'Hello, Khalid.' Just the sound of his name on her lips sent excitement twisting inside her. She notched up her chin, as if to repudiate the reaction.

'What was the doctor's verdict?'

She shrugged. 'I'm fine. I'll be back to the stables soon.' At Khalid's querying look she added, 'The doctor is just running a couple of tests.'

When she'd mentioned that she'd felt a little light-headed lately the doctor had kept her longer. But surely that odd sensation had been due to the bustle and excitement of her first overseas trip. Maggie had spent the last weeks so busy she'd been more exhausted than she could ever remember.

'You walked out of the lodge without a word,' Khalid said abruptly. 'Why?'

Maggie stared at him, horrified at the change of subject, and wondering where to start. She had nothing in common with this man who was clearly a VIP. A man of power and wealth who'd taken pity on her when she'd hit rock-bottom. That night was best forgotten.

She braced her shoulders, stiffening her spine as she met his glittering eyes head-on.

'We had nothing to discuss.'

She didn't want him thinking she was some clinging vine, shown pity once and ever after seeking what she patently couldn't have. Pride came to her rescue and kept her gaze steady.

'Not even the fact that you were a virgin before you took me into your body?'

Her gasp was loud in the silent room.

'How did you know?' she blurted out, then silently cursed herself. No doubt her clumsy embraces had been eloquent testimony to her lack of experience. She didn't need him to spell it out for her.

He took a single pace towards her. That was close enough for her to feel the sizzle of his presence. The air between them almost zapped and crackled.

'You were untried. Your body told me.'

Maggie bit her lip as blood rushed to her cheeks. At least he'd spared her comparisons with his other lovers.

'So?' The single syllable sounded belligerent. Better that than pathetic.

'Don't you think I wanted to know you were all right?'

'Of course I was all right! It was just sex, after all.' The blush intensified as the words spilled out of her mouth. Inside she cringed.

'Just sex.' His lips pursed and his eyes narrowed as if he were seeing her for the first time, assessing her and finding her wanting. He shook his head. 'We both know it was far more than that, Maggie. How old are you?'

The question threw her off balance and she answered automatically.

'Twenty-three. Why?'

'Twenty-three and a virgin.' His brows tilted up as if in surprise. 'That's not so common these days.'

Of course, he was an expert on the matter! Maggie opened her mouth to say so, then snapped it shut as she realised he probably had far more knowledge of the subject than she did. With his tantalising good looks and that subtle air of command, he'd cut a swathe through women wherever he went.

His lips twisted up in a brief smile that sent a tingle of shocking pleasure through her. There was an edgy, unsettled sensation deep in her pelvis, a hollow ache she'd never known before the night they'd first met. And when he looked at her, his eyes hooded and secretive, her nipples tightened and puckered. She lifted one hand to grasp her other arm, trying to look nonchalant as she hid her pebbling nipples from his view.

'You had been saving yourself,' he murmured in a tone so deep it made her skin tingle.

She shrugged. 'Even if I was, it didn't matter. The man I'd thought was the one wasn't what I'd believed him to be.'

Her night with Khalid had achieved one thing at least: it

had shown her just how little Marcus had really meant to her. She'd been in love with the idea of love. Her night of intimacy with Khalid had blasted the illusion apart with a white-hot surge of power and the old, naïve Maggie had gone. Now she was stronger by far, unencumbered by stupid fantasies.

'You're not still in love with him?'

She shook her head and turned to stare out the window at the cloudless sky. 'No. I don't think I ever was.'

The sound of the door opening made her swing her head around. Thank goodness. The doctor. At least now the personal questions would stop. And with the doctor here she wouldn't be tempted to meet Khalid's liquid dark eyes again. Each time she did her stomach went into free fall.

'Sire.' The doctor stopped abruptly just inside the room. 'Shall I come back later?'

'No, no.' Khalid waved him forward. 'I'm sure Ms Lewis is eager to hear the results of your tests.'

Maggie's brows furrowed. It was on the tip of her tongue to ask why Khalid was addressed in such a formal way. But she didn't want to prolong his presence with questions.

'Of course.' The older man approached the bed, his serious gaze caught her attention and she sat straighter, staring. It was impossible he'd found anything wrong with her. She was as healthy as a horse. Yet the tiny frown on the doctor's face sent anxiety pulsing through her.

'Is there something wrong?'

'No, no,' he assured her. 'Nothing wrong.' Yet the look he cast over his shoulder at Khalid looming nearby was clearly unsettled.

'I'll leave you alone,' Khalid said immediately.

'No!'

Two pairs of startled eyes fixed on her and Maggie chewed her lip. She'd never been a coward, had always faced life with all its problems and disappointments head-on. But if there was bad news, she felt a fervent, unreasoning wish that

Khalid be here too. She was in a strange country and he was a familiar face, she rationalised, blindly ignoring her own desire just moments ago to escape his dominant presence.

'Please stay,' she said, curving her lips into what she hoped was a smile.

Now the doctor looked really uncomfortable, his eyes sliding to the younger man, then away. Suddenly Maggie had a very bad feeling about this. She remembered her father's cancer being diagnosed and how, at the end, it had ravaged him beyond help.

'It's all right,' she assured the doctor, eager now to get this over and done with. Whatever the news, she'd rather know it now than wait on tenterhooks. 'Please tell me.'

The doctor nodded and cleared his throat. 'You're in excellent health, Ms Lewis. Apart from some bruising you're fine. However…' He paused and Maggie felt her heart sink.

'However, are you aware that you're pregnant?'

CHAPTER FIVE

'But I... It's not possible, surely.' Maggie's voice was breathless, her face tense with shock. 'Are you positive?'

Khalid knew Aziz too well to doubt. If he said she was pregnant, then Maggie Lewis was expecting a child.

His child.

The idea scraped a hollow in his chest.

Immediately he discarded the possibility that Maggie had gone from him to another man who'd got her pregnant. The idea was ludicrous. More than that, to his consternation he discovered it was untenable. Khalid couldn't imagine her in anyone else's bed. Just his own....

The realisation froze him into physical lockdown, his mind rejecting the gut-deep certainty. Warning lights flashed across his consciousness. Such possessiveness should be absurd. *Should* be. His chest heaved as he dragged in a slow, shuddering breath.

'I assure you, Ms Lewis, the test is positive. Congratulations.' The doctor's words and Maggie's response faded, drowned by the roar of blood in Khalid's ears.

Pregnant! This was one issue he'd never expected to confront. Not since his life had ripped apart eight years ago. Since then he'd plunged himself into a gruelling schedule of demanding projects rather than face the aching void inside him. When he found solace in a woman's company, he ensured the liaison was temporary. No entanglements, no complications.

A child…that was definitely a complication. A child meant family. Emotion. Love.

Khalid's jaw tightened, pain radiating from gritted teeth. He'd vowed never to go down that path again. He'd spent years avoiding anything that might develop into an emotionally intimate relationship. He'd wanted never to lay himself open to the risk of such anguish again.

That was the only safe way. The only way to survive.

The blur of emotion cleared and he saw Maggie, clinging to the chair with a white-knuckled grip. Her hazel eyes sparkled yet her face was too pale. She looked wan and shocked. She needed support. She needed *him*.

Not pausing to think, Khalid spun round, headed to the sink and poured a glass of water.

'Here. Drink.' It took a moment to catch her attention. Her fingers trembled as she took the glass. A surge of protectiveness washed over him.

Pregnant.

Regret stabbed him. Or was it guilt? Shahina had longed for a baby. She'd borne the news that she could never have children with a stoicism that had almost broken his heart. The one thing above all that his beloved wife had wanted and it had been denied her.

Yet, despite the poignant memories, it was satisfaction he felt deep in the pit of his belly. A kernel of pleased anticipation at the idea of his seed, his child, growing inside Maggie. His blood flowed effervescent and his heart pumped stronger and faster.

'But we took precautions,' Maggie said to the doctor.

Aziz shook his head. 'No precaution is foolproof, Ms Lewis. Nature has a way of succeeding in her purpose, no matter how hard we try to thwart her.'

Khalid considered the odds against that night leading to pregnancy. They'd made love only once and he'd been scrupulously careful to use a condom. And Maggie hadn't made love before. Her untutored caresses and tight, virginal body had been a potent aphrodisiac, tempting him to completion almost before he'd ensured her climax. Only the knowledge of her inexperience had prevented him turning to her again and again in the night.

There was no doubt this child was eager to come into the world. It must share its mother's indomitable spirit.

His gaze settled on Maggie, her slim form rigid. His emotions were jumbled and confusing. Yet above all there was a sense of rightness and of acceptance.

Khalid wanted this child.

'For now, I want you to rest,' Aziz said to Maggie. 'Your baby is safe and we'll continue to monitor its progress. We can discuss antenatal care later,' he added with a smile.

'Antenatal care?' Maggie's brow pleated in confusion and Khalid found himself wanting to step forward and soothe the frown from her face. Clearly the news had stunned her.

'Of course.' Aziz nodded. 'We'll need to discuss your diet among other things.'

'But I'm only here for a short time, to settle the horses in.'

Aziz looked from her to Khalid and Khalid knew he was trying to assess the situation between them. Khalid's presence here was unprecedented. It would be obvious to the meanest intelligence that this woman was special to him.

He stepped forward. 'Dr Aziz will see you tomorrow. No doubt by then you'll have questions for him. As for your stay in Shajehar, there must have been a misunderstanding. Your presence is required in the long term.'

'But my visa—'

'A new visa will be issued. Don't fret about it.'

Maggie watched the two men walk to the door, one comfortably plump and concerned, the other enigmatic and powerful. They conversed in their own language and she felt she'd wondering what he was thinking. His fac...

could discern no expression.

...with someone, are...

'You're not…with someone. He...

the horrifying idea surfaced. He...

were other sorts of commitment...

A fiancée?'

'No.' His voice was...

one now.'

He'd had a wi...

Maggie st...

into forbi...

Ob...

Ma...

Yet, despite the difficulties, Maggie knew absolutely that she wanted this baby. Already the thrill of excitement was overtaking stunned shock. She had no idea how she'd manage but there'd be time to sort that out later. Determination and joy welled inside her.

She'd have to scrimp and save and work hard and learn as she went. Nothing new there. And at the end of her pregnancy she'd have a precious child, family of her very own to love and care for.

A smile tickled her lips as she raised the glass once more. Crazy it might be, but she was excited.

'You're happy about the baby?' Khalid broke across her thoughts as he returned.

'It's…overwhelming,' she murmured as she met his gaze. Would their baby have eyes like his? Dark as jet and beautiful? Her pulse quickened. *Their baby*. It was incredible.

His stare was so steady, so intense that Maggie shivered,

e was so still she

you?' she blurted out as
e wasn't married, but there
nts. 'Do you have a girlfriend?

curt. 'I had a wife once. But there's no

fe once…

red up at his hard-edged face, transformed now
ding lines of aristocratic hauteur and disapproval.
iously his ex-wife wasn't a subject for discussion.
ggie wondered what the woman had done to deserve
uch disfavour.

'Why?' His expression was remote. 'Are you proposing?'

'Of course not!' Maggie heaved in a shocked breath. 'I just wondered… I don't want to cause trouble.' She paused, thinking. 'But then it won't matter, no one need know.'

Instantly Khalid's brows tilted together in a thunderous frown. 'You intend to dispose of our child? Is that what you're saying?'

Maggie edged back from the ferocious anger vibrating in his voice and put her glass down, not taking her eyes off him. His large hands fisted and his jaw looked honed of solid rock. She got to her feet and braced herself.

'No.' She shook her head till her hair swirled around her neck. 'How can you even suggest that?'

He regarded her intently, his flared nostrils and the rigid tendons in his neck proclaiming his tension.

'I don't know you,' he said eventually.

'Well, believe me, nothing would make me get rid of this baby.' She slipped her hand across her abdomen in a shielding gesture, overcome by wonder at this news and by the intense protectiveness she felt already for her child. She'd do everything she could to keep it safe.

His frown didn't ease and she felt like an insect scrutinised under a microscope, about to be dissected. She jutted her chin. He had no right to judge her.

'It's true. I want this baby.'

Our baby. But she couldn't say that, not when he looked at her with the eyes of a disapproving stranger. It was impossible to reconcile him with the generous, passionate man who'd taken her to paradise in his arms.

'Why do you want it?' He sounded like an interrogator, unconvinced and ready to believe the worst.

'I…' What could she say when she didn't know the answer herself? All she knew was that this child was part of her and she'd do anything to protect it.

'I don't believe in unwanted children,' she said at last. 'Every child should be wanted…and loved, by someone.' She'd spent most of her life knowing she wasn't loved, that her father only sheltered her out of grudging duty. She wouldn't wish that on anyone.

Her child would be loved absolutely and unconditionally. It would never know an instant's doubt about its special place in the world.

'I'll make sure this baby is loved and cared for.'

'That is not your responsibility.'

'Sorry?' His words brought her head swinging round to meet his gaze, ready to do battle.

'It is ours.'

Ours? Khalid's and hers? Her shoulders slumped in relief. For a moment there she'd thought he implied she wasn't fit to raise her own child.

'You want a role in bringing up this baby?'

'I will be involved in caring for *our* child.' Each word was clipped and definite. His posture, his look, proclaimed an arrogant certainty she secretly envied.

Maggie shook her head. Surely the difficulties of long-distance parenthood must outweigh the benefits.

'You'd deny me my rightful position as its father?'

He took a step forward and suddenly he was right there in front of her. Heat radiated from him and wrapped close around her. The scent of his skin invaded her space, overwhelming her attempts at rational thought. Instantly she was in bed, the smell of sandalwood and fresh male sweat tangy in her nostrils as he caressed her and drew her to shattering climax. Once more that secret, telltale heat ignited in the pit of her belly.

She closed her eyes, trying to master the surge of memory that shattered her thought processes. How could she think when he stood so close?

'It wouldn't work,' she murmured at last. 'It would be too difficult to manage.'

Warm fingers tilted her face up. Her eyes popped open and she met his gaze. It glowed with heat and something else, some burning emotion she couldn't define. For a moment absurd hope welled that perhaps he felt something for her. Something more than sympathy. She wanted that so badly it was a physical ache.

'Nothing is impossible, Maggie.'

The air sizzled as that spark, the connection she'd experienced only once before, arced between them. When he spoke like that, looked at her like that, she almost believed everything would turn out wonderfully.

Her heart accelerated to a hammering throb as she sank into the luxury of his heated gaze. Unthinking, she relaxed in his hold, slumping closer, drawn to his hard strength.

'We will find a way to make it work,' he murmured.

For all her prized ability to stand up for herself, this one man had the unerring ability to find weakness where none had existed. He made her feel she wasn't whole without him. She melted at his touch, even questioning the precepts she'd spent a lifetime learning: independence, pride and self-reliance.

Khalid was dangerous in ways she was only beginning to understand. She had to resist him and think rationally. Too much was at stake. Not merely her pride, but an innocent new life. Maggie jerked her chin from his hold, leaning back till his hand dropped away. Instantly she missed the warmth of his touch, craved its return.

'It's not that simple,' she argued.

His eyes narrowed to glittering slits and his challenging expression froze to implacable.

'Perhaps you'd like to explain why you're insistent I not take responsibility for my child.' He crossed his arms over his chest. The movement emphasised the spare power of his taut frame and gave him a threatening air.

Maggie looked away. It was far too easy to stare in helpless fascination at him. For all the belligerence of his stance, he was utterly mesmerising.

'Is it because I'm not from your country? Because I am a foreigner to you?'

Helplessly she shook her head. 'That's got nothing to do with it. It's just…' How did she explain that they were poles apart in wealth and status, in experience and expectations, without making it sound as if she were seeking reassurance? 'You're here and I'll be in Australia and—'

'Not necessarily.'

'Pardon?'

'We needn't be separated. For our child's sake, the sensible thing would be to stay together here.'

'Together?' she squawked. He couldn't mean what she thought. 'Together' didn't mean anything personal.

Still, it took far too long for her galloping heart rate to slow back to normal.

'That's not an option. I have to return home.'

'Perhaps I could persuade you.'

One sleek eyebrow rose questioningly and his lips quirked up at one corner in the merest hint of a smile. A pulse of heat throbbed deep inside her, impinging on her ability to think clearly. How did he do that?

Heaven help her if he ever deigned to smile properly. She'd dissolve into a puddle of molten desire at his feet. Maggie scrambled to compose herself.

'I'll be in Australia.'

'Do you really think that's best for our child? One parent in Australia and one in Shajehar?'

Anger unfurled in Maggie's belly at his calm question. She'd been rocked by today's news and was still grappling with the implications. Apparently Khalid had taken it in his stride. Unreasonably she resented that.

'You think you know what's best for the baby? Is that it? You're suddenly an expert with all the answers?'

She caught a glimpse of banked heat in his eyes. Was he so accustomed to deciding, always having his way? Did he expect her to accept his decision meekly?

'I don't pretend to be an expert, Maggie.' His voice was low and calm. 'I just know our child deserves the chance to be loved by both its parents.'

She felt as if he'd punched a hole through her indignation and her fear, right down to her secret, scared inner self. A desolate, black void of long-buried hurt yawned before her, threatening to suck her under. What did she know about parental love? She'd had so little of it.

For one panicked, sickening moment she wondered if the lack of love in her own childhood meant she was fated to be a poor parent herself. Was it possible? Could that sort of thing be inherited?

She gulped in an unsteady breath. Surely not. If anything the neglect she'd suffered meant she'd try harder to be a good mother.

'Maggie! What's the matter?'

Khalid watched her, his brow knitted with concern. Suddenly she was claustrophobic. This small room and his dominating presence were too much. She was used to being outdoors, on the move, not cooped up indoors.

'Can we leave here now?' she asked abruptly. 'We can talk this through later. I have to get back to the stables.' She stepped to one side, eager to escape the confines of the sickbay and Khalid's scrutiny. Surely they could put off this conversation till she was more in control of her emotions.

But he didn't budge. The set of his jaw told her he wasn't going anywhere. His proximity was daunting. Her breath shortened, but she refused to back down.

'Look.' She angled her face up to meet his impenetrable stare, steeling herself not to flinch. 'We have lots to discuss, I know. Lots to work out. I'm not trying to avoid you. But wouldn't it make more sense to talk this through later? Somewhere private where we're not likely to be interrupted?' That would give her time to adjust to the news and marshal her thoughts.

'If I'm not back at work soon, my boss will be furious. I've already been gone for ages. It's a wonder he hasn't stormed in here demanding I get back to the stables. What we have to discuss is too important for interruption.'

Her heart thudded as Khalid watched her silently. Eventually he inclined his head.

'You're right. This isn't the most appropriate place for our conversation. As for being interrupted, you need have no fear. No one will intrude on us.'

'You don't know the stable manager. He's—'

'No one you need worry about.'

At her astonished stare Khalid's lips curved up into that delicious quirk, then slowly spread to a full-blown smile that made the pulse thunder in her ears and her nerves jangle in awareness.

He was utterly, indescribably magnetic. He was far more vibrant, more potently attractive than any man had a right to be. Her breath snared and she swayed, feeling the full impact of that attraction.

A firm hand grasped her by the elbow and turned her towards the door. The heat of his touch sizzled like summer lightning across her skin.

'I see you haven't caught up with the latest news, Maggie. You don't know who I am, do you?'

'Your name's Khalid,' she murmured, unsettled by the glint in his eyes. 'You were the sheikh's envoy.'

He nodded. 'I was. Now my position has changed. Four weeks ago I became Sheikh of Shajehar. You're an honoured guest in *my* palace. *My* country.'

Maggie sat quietly in the ornate garden pavilion as Khalid thanked the servant who'd brought refreshments. Then he conversed briefly with a man in an expensive suit who obviously had important news.

She was grateful for the respite, was still reeling from the shock of Khalid's identity. Even now she couldn't quite believe it!

Yet watching him she wondered that she hadn't guessed the truth. He had the face of a storybook prince: strong, commanding and aristocratic. More than that, his air of authority, of uncompromising power, was unmistakable.

Hadn't she seen him with her own eyes, about to sit on the gilded throne at the centre of the ringside stand? Hadn't she heard the doctor refer to him as 'sire'?

Khalid, the man who'd made tender, tempestuous love to her weeks ago, the man who'd cared for her when she was distraught, the man who'd leapt into the ring today and taken control of Diva…was the royal Sheikh of Shajehar.

'My apologies, Maggie. My chancellor had a few urgent matters that required attention.'

'That's OK.' She nodded, though she felt completely out of her depth. She didn't have a clue what a chancellor did, much less a monarch. The opulent luxury of the pavilion with its silk-covered divans, exquisite murals and breathtaking views to the indigo mountains only reinforced the fact that she didn't belong here.

She'd never seen the previous Sheikh on his visits to Australia, but his wealth and power were legend. It was rumoured he'd had a silver Rolls-Royce. Not silver-coloured but made of silver. That he bought entire luxury resorts so he could holiday in private. More than that, here in Shajehar his word was law. He'd been an absolute ruler.

As Khalid was now.

That was the sort of man who'd fathered her child. A man of wealth and power beyond her imaginings. A man who could buy anything he wanted.

Suddenly fear jolted through her. If he wanted the baby badly enough, could he take it from her?

'I won't give up my baby.' The words were out before she'd even had time to consider them.

Khalid paused in the act of passing her a glass of tea and raised his brows. 'No one is asking you to, Maggie.'

Relief swamped her. She'd grown up without her mother and she wouldn't inflict that on her baby. That permanent sense of loss, the sadness for missed intimacies and love and laughter. The lingering self-doubt, that maybe it was something she'd done that had driven her mum away. Maggie had missed so much, not having a mother to share her hopes and fears and guide her as she grew from girl to woman.

'Good.' She refused to apologise. 'I just thought it better you knew up front.'

He nodded. 'And you should know that I will not walk away from our child, either. Here.' He pressed the glass into her hand. 'Drink up. It'll do you good.'

Maggie inhaled the familiar aroma of sweet tea, Shajehani style, and remembered Khalid telling her once before that it was good for shock. She hoped he was right.

'I can recommend the pastries too.'

She looked at the perfectly presented delicacies. Could the tray really be solid gold?

'Not at the moment, thank you.' Instead she sipped her tea

gratefully. But the sensation of his eyes on her made her look up. He watched her so intently.

'You have no cause to fear me, Maggie. I'm a civilised man.'

'A civilised man who rules his own country and can buy the best lawyers in the world.' She bit her lip, willing herself to shut up before she dug herself any deeper.

'That's not how I work!' There was a flash of fury in his eyes before he looked away towards the distant view. Instantly regret filled her, but she had to be sure.

'I didn't ask to be sheikh, didn't expect it. But my half-brother died without a son so I shoulder the role.'

'I'm sorry about your brother.'

He inclined his head and she paused, searching for words.

'You don't sound as if you enjoy your new position.' Which was probably tactless, and definitely not royal protocol. But their relationship certainly wasn't normal. And she needed to understand him.

'I will never shirk my duty,' he said in a low voice. 'There is much to do here. In the past my family were true leaders and visionaries, protecting their people. But—' his expression tightened '—since the discovery of oil, our rulers devoted themselves to squandering the country's wealth. It's my task to make up for years of neglect. To rectify the damage. It will be my lifetime's work.'

Now she understood. Khalid was a man of honour, driven by duty. 'You see our baby as your responsibility. Your duty.' She slipped a hand over her abdomen.

'Together we are responsible for that new life growing inside you.' At his words she felt heat unfurl within her, a tingle of excitement and awe. Her lips curved up in a faint smile. She still found the news wondrous.

'So together we must make the best arrangements for our child's future.'

She looked up, wary at his portentous tone. His heavy-lidded eyes gleamed with a sultry, unfamiliar heat.

'There's an obvious solution,' he continued.

'There is?' Her heart pounded and her nerves stretched thin as something like fear awoke in her breast.

'Of course.' His lips curled up at the corners in a satisfied smile. 'We will marry as soon as possible.'

CHAPTER SIX

KHALID was ready for Maggie's reaction: sheer, stunned silence. He knew that in her world people usually married for love. That children were often born out of wedlock.

Hadn't he married for love himself? Then vowed never to marry again, after losing Shahina tore his soul in two?

Nevertheless, the dawning horror in Maggie's eyes irked him. She hadn't found him so repulsive when she'd offered herself to him just weeks ago. And he knew any number of women who'd do almost anything to elicit his proposal. Some had already tried.

'You're… Are you serious?' Her voice was husky.

Khalid clamped down on rising anger. 'It is the most appropriate way forward.'

'The most appropriate.' Her lush mouth twisted. What did she expect? That he'd turn his back on her and the child? That he wouldn't care about them? She could hardly expect a declaration of undying love. Besides, that was something he could never give any woman.

'Maggie, think about it. Our child will be born into a family. It will have two parents that love it. He or she will grow up in a stable environment, not hauled across continents and cultures, divided between distant parents.' He watched the green flecks darken her eyes.

'And you will have wealth, security, status.' All the things so many women desired.

'What if I'm not interested in money or status?'

Khalid pursed his lips against a smug grin. If she'd been the sort to chase him for his wealth this situation would have been different. But he knew Maggie Lewis was no gold-digger. Even the investigator who'd located her had said she was poor but hardworking, honest and reliable.

'Think of what this will mean for our baby. Isn't that most important? You said your father brought you up alone and it wasn't the happiest of situations. How much better for our child with both of us to care for him or her?'

He watched her chew her lip and felt a spurt of triumph. And a surge of sensual awareness. 'We have that in common, remember? My father wasn't a good parent, either. But we two together could provide the sort of home neither of us had ourselves.'

'But there's no guarantee it will work. What if we marry then separate? That can shatter a child.'

Khalid took her hand, smoothing his thumb over her skin. Her bones were fine, yet she was strong. He took it as a victory that she didn't pull back.

'You have my word, Maggie, that I would never drive you away or ask you to leave. You have my bond that I intend to work at building a warm, loving home for our child. And since we're not marrying for love, then our relationship won't be cluttered with emotion. We won't have the power to hurt each other as lovers can.'

The more he thought about it, the more perfect this arrangement sounded. Yet he read doubt in her eyes.

'But what if you fall in love with someone else?' She shook her head. 'No, marriage is a recipe for disaster.'

Strange, he thought, that she didn't consider the possibility she might fall for someone. Not that he had concerns in that regard. He knew how to keep a woman satisfied and happy. Maggie wouldn't be looking at other men while she had him.

'I am not the sort to lose my heart. You can be absolutely sure of that,' he murmured, determination firming his lips. His heart was well guarded now. He had no intention of ever opening it again.

Yet, still, she wasn't satisfied. 'Why do you want to marry? Is it so you have a legitimate heir?'

'You believe it's wrong to give our child the security of two parents and the protection of my name?' Khalid straightened in anger. Couldn't she see this was best? There was nothing shameful in his proposal.

'No, of course not,' she said slowly.

'Good. I have no intention of allowing our child to be born illegitimate.'

Khalid knew too well the unwanted implications of that. If his Uncle Hussein had been legitimate, instead of the fruit of a brief liaison between Khalid's grandfather and a dancer, Hussein would have been Sheikh. Honest, serious, hard-working, he would have been an excellent ruler. Instead the crown had passed to his younger, feckless, legitimate brother, Khalid's father, a shallow man, wrapped up in his own importance and with an obsession for personal gratification. As a direct result Shajehar had suffered all these years.

'So you want an heir.' Her voice was disapproving.

He shrugged. 'If I have no child the sheikhdom will pass to someone else in my family. But there *is* a child. Or there will be.' He darted a glance at her flat belly and a stab of wonderment shafted through him at the idea of her swelling as his child grew inside her.

A visceral, possessive sense of ownership filled him. This was *his* baby. And Maggie Lewis, though she didn't know it yet, was *his* woman. Already the sexual pull between them was too strong to deny. A single look was all it took to ignite roaring need inside him.

'Would you deny our baby its birthright? The chance to know its father's culture? Would you stop it from taking its rightful place here?'

'You're assuming it will be a boy.'

'No, you're the one making the assumptions.' He released her hand and surged to his feet, striding away, then spinning round to face her. 'I will love our baby if it is a boy or a girl. If it has pale skin and gold hair like yours or olive skin like mine. What matters is that it is our baby and we do the best for it.'

He looked at her as she sat, tea clasped in one tense hand. Despite her obdurate front this woman needed gentle handling. Pain, as well as strength, coloured her view of the world. Her eyes still revealed the shock of Aziz's news.

Silently he cursed his tendency to instant action. When he saw his way ahead, he never delayed. Perhaps this time he should have tempered his response and given her a chance to absorb the implications of her pregnancy.

Her pregnancy. His child.

He stepped close and took the glass from her. 'Come, Maggie. We will talk of this later. It's time you rested.'

Maggie was hot and dirty and weary. Yesterday's revelations still stunned her. She could barely believe she was going to be a mother! Yet her excitement was tempered by a morass of confused emotions.

Nor had her mood improved when she'd arrived at the stables this morning to discover she'd been ordered onto light duties. A day of menial tasks and curious stares had done nothing to rebuild her equanimity. Her every move was watched, assessed, speculated over.

'Come on, Tally.' She led the mare through the yard to the horses' swimming pool. Tally's ears flicked forward and her nostrils widened as she scented water.

'Maggie!'

She stopped mid-stride, held fast by that voice. Khalid's

tone was commanding. Her heart pump faster, knowing he was here, watching her. She felt his stare, like a hot knife blade between her shoulders.

Slowly she turned. He stood framed in the shadows of the arched gateway. The late-afternoon sun gilded his long, pale robe. It highlighted his superb breadth of shoulder, the tensile strength of his tall frame, the breath-stealing male beauty of his stern face.

The hiss of her indrawn breath was loud in her ears as she stared in helpless fascination and felt her instant response. It was as she'd feared. A flare of excitement, of anticipation, sparked deep within her at the sight of him. It didn't matter that he was angry. His scowl only emphasised his strong features and his air of authority.

She'd never liked domineering men. Had vowed never to fall into the trap of caring for a man like her father. But, despite the potent masculine power that fair sizzled off Khalid, Maggie couldn't douse her thrill of pleasure. The air between them sparked with enough energy to light his vast palace. She couldn't drag her eyes away.

'Hello, Khalid.' She hated her breathless voice. She'd been expecting another summons, not the man himself.

He paced across the sun-warmed pavement and something sank inside her as his stride ate up the distance. Her only hope had been that she wouldn't be affected by his presence as before. That hope shattered as she stood, held in thrall. Now she knew: her response was dangerously real.

'I asked you to come and see me.' His narrowed gaze trawled over her and heat blossomed under her skin in its wake. She tried to look nonchalant.

'Did you? That's odd. The message I received didn't sound like an invitation. It was more like a royal decree.'

It took every ounce of strength to meet his glinting eyes. Now she was paying for her refusal twenty minutes ago to obey his summons instantly.

After a sleepless night she was still confused and anxious, unsure what to do for the best. All day she'd expected to see him, had been taut with nerves, preparing to face him again. Yet he'd kept his distance. No doubt he had other, more important things on his mind than her pregnancy!

'And yet you chose not to come.' His voice was cool, his expression composed, but she felt anger in him as he stopped, far too close for her peace of mind.

Tally must have sensed her agitation for the horse started forward towards the ramp that led down into the pool and Maggie had to work at holding her steady.

'I'm not a subject to come at your bidding.'

His sudden stillness told her that barb had hit home.

'But you *are* my employee,' he said eventually, his voice low. 'Or doesn't that matter?'

Maggie blinked, reeling that he'd choose to use her position here to bring her to heel. What was between them was personal and private.

'My apologies, *boss*.' She almost choked on the word. 'I hadn't realised you wanted to discuss my work.'

He raised a hand and massaged the back of his neck, as if to soothe away a knot of tension. The blood thundering in her ears pounded out the passing seconds of silence.

'I'm sorry, Maggie. That was uncalled for,' he said at last. 'I apologise.'

He looked so uncomfortable that she felt a swell of sympathy for him. Was he as unsettled by this situation as she? No doubt he was used to making demands that those around him were eager to meet. Especially women. She'd guess they'd be only too happy to deal with his requests, no matter how *demanding*. The idea created a niggle of discomfort so intense it dismayed her.

'Accepted,' she said quickly. 'I was going to come to you as soon as I'd finished here.' She avoided his eyes. 'I take my work very seriously.'

'You think the matter between us isn't serious?' His tone told her he wasn't used to people refusing to comply with his wishes. That straightened her backbone.

'I assumed you didn't need to see me urgently, since you waited all day.'

'Ah.' He paused for so long she wondered if he had no reply. 'Again I must beg your pardon, Maggie. I've been with representatives of two neighbouring countries while we negotiate multilateral agreements on trade and regional infrastructure.' His voice dropped to a deep pitch that unravelled some of the tightness in her shoulders. 'I wanted to see you earlier but it was impossible. The meetings were organised months ago.'

Which made Maggie feel smaller and less significant than ever. Of course he'd had a good reason not to see her. It was stupid to be piqued at his lack of attention.

'Do you mind if I take Tally in?' she asked abruptly, nodding to the deep channel of water. 'She loves her swim.'

'And when you've done this, you'll finish for the day.' It was a statement, not a question. Maggie had the suspicion that even if she hadn't finished, Khalid would ensure she stopped. 'Please, go ahead. I'll walk with you.'

She turned and led the mare into the water. Maggie walked beside the pool as Tally hurried down the ramp and into the channel sunk below ground level. Soon the horse was swimming in the deep water, kicking out strongly.

'Marriage is the best option. You know that, Maggie.'

No preliminaries, no hesitancy. Was Khalid always so supremely sure of himself?

Didn't he see how preposterous his suggestion was? As if it were totally logical for her, a girl who worked in the stables, to marry a man who ruled his own country.

'Not from my perspective,' she murmured. She kept her head averted, watching the mare.

'My manager hasn't spoken to you yet about my plans for the stables, has he?'

She jerked her head around. He walked beside her, closer than she'd realised. His eyes were grave.

'What plans?' Anxiety shivered down her backbone.

'Your job at Tallawanta will end in the near future.'

Her mouth dried. 'What do you mean?'

'I'm disposing of the stud. While there's so much to be achieved here in Shajehar I don't have the stomach for such luxuries, even successful ones. Which means...' he paused, surveying her carefully '...that your job in Australia will no longer exist. The stud's new owners may need you or they may decide to bring in their own staff.'

Foreboding ratcheted up Maggie's pulse and she faltered. Cold sweat prickled her nape at the thought of her job disappearing.

Her arm jerked as Tally swam ahead and Maggie tried to concentrate on the mare. But her thoughts circled around Khalid's news. She needed her job to support her baby. Good positions were scarce and she had no other qualifications.

Surely he wasn't doing this to force her hand?

'I'd decided to sell it, and several of Faruq's other indulgences, well before we met.'

Had he read her mind and the doubt hovering there?

'But I need a steady job for the baby, and to save so I can train one day as a vet.' Even as she said it she realised how unlikely that dream was. Looking after her child had to be her priority now.

'There's a fine university here in Shajehar. Veterinary study is one of its specialties.'

Sure, as if she could enrol. She couldn't even speak the language. Maggie pursed her lips in a derisory grimace.

'So I should stay here because it would be easier than finding a new job?' She couldn't keep the bitterness from her tone. She felt as if he'd pulled the whole fabric of her world askew. She was adrift on a sea of uncertainty.

Maggie urged the mare on, wishing she could run ahead,

outpace Khalid and absorb this news alone. But solitude was a luxury she didn't have anymore. Whether she wanted it or not, Khalid was determined to be involved in her future.

Correction, their child's future. The two were inextricably linked. Claustrophobia encompassed her, binding round her till she could barely breathe.

Tally surged up the ramp and out of the deep swimming channel. Even the comical sight of the mare shaking herself like a dog didn't make Maggie smile. She felt overwhelmed.

'Maggie?' Khalid stepped in front of her, straight into her line of vision. 'You will have a new job whether you like it or not. Being a mother will be very demanding.'

She shook her head in amazement. 'And you think it will be easier for me if I emigrate, tie myself to a man I barely know and marry into a royal family?'

'You would not be alone. You would want for nothing.' His tone was patient, warm and reassuring.

Yet she'd run the risk of losing what little she had achieved for herself. Her independence, her plans for the future.

Though perhaps it was inevitable. Her future wasn't her own anymore. A shiver of panicked excitement shot through her as this new reality struck her again. *Pregnant.* Maggie breathed deep and calmed herself.

'I don't fit your world.' She waved a dismissive hand over herself. Her boots were dusty, her trousers splashed and liberally sprinkled with horse hair. 'I don't belong in a palace. I'm ordinary. I work for my living.'

His eyes held hers and a pulse of something unexpected beat between them. Connection.

'As do I, Maggie.'

Instantly she regretted her words. Already she'd learned how seriously Khalid took his responsibilities.

'I'm sorry, Khalid. I know you do. But our circumstances are different.' She tethered the mare, reaching for a plastic scraper and beginning to dry Tally's wet coat. It gave her the perfect excuse not to look at him. She focused on the slide of the plastic over Tally's body, sluicing the water away. If only it were as easy to remove one large, stubborn male from her vicinity.

'Surely you need to marry someone who will fit in.'

'You will fit in, Maggie.' He took a step towards her. The world narrowed to *him*. His glowing eyes, his rangy power, his presence. Her heart pounded against her ribs.

'I'll be right here with you.' His voice dropped to a soft rumble that made her insides squirm with pleasure.

She shook her head, denying the shiver of tentative delight. He didn't understand at all! How could she marry a man who saw their wedding as 'the most appropriate way forward'? Who didn't love her and never would? She'd be mad to tie herself to such an arrangement.

'I mean, you must be expected to marry someone—' she swallowed her pride '—beautiful and elegant, groomed for the position. Someone from an important family.'

As he watched she squared her shoulders and lifted her chin. It was body language he recognised, a stance he'd used himself as a child when ordered to some irksome duty.

She didn't hide behind the usual female prevarication. She was so transparent he felt a moment's qualm for her vulnerability. But that couldn't sway him. He intended to have her as his bride, by persuasion if possible.

'The sheikhs of Shajehar have a reputation for marrying to please themselves.'

He conveniently omitted to mention the tentative negotiations Faruq had instigated just months ago to cement a dynastic match between Khalid and a princess from a neighbouring kingdom. Khalid had been opposed to the idea from the start. He'd never wanted to marry again.

Until now.

This was necessary. Marriage was his duty to his unborn child. Fate had given him this opportunity for a child and he could no more turn his back on it than stop breathing. He knew exactly how precious life was and he intended to be an integral part of his child's world.

That meant having Maggie too. He felt surprisingly reconciled to the idea.

'No one will believe you want me.' Her voice was cool, but her mouth had a vulnerable slant.

Maggie stepped aside, turning to work on the horse. Her movements were smooth and rhythmic, almost but not quite concealing the tension that gripped her.

The dying sun lit her hair to old gold. It outlined her sleek curves and lissom body. Heat shot through him at the memory of those endless legs encompassing him the night he took her virginity. Of her exquisite body coming to life for the first time at his touch. Maggie was so wonderfully responsive, so endlessly enticing.

He might not be marrying for love this time, but there was no doubt he wanted this marriage. He *wanted* Maggie. All these weeks, through the turmoil of taking up his role as Sheikh, he'd missed her. More than he should have.

Missed the woman he'd known for just one night!

Marriage was his duty—obvious and unavoidable. But not entirely simple. He thought of her passion, her vitality, how she'd roused him and satisfied him, then made him hunger for her again with a desperate intensity that was entirely new.

This marriage would be about pleasure too. As Maggie would soon discover.

He stepped close and felt her heat through the fine linen of his clothes. Instantly an answering fire scorched his flesh, drawing it taut with sexual anticipation.

'No one will question my choice, Maggie. They will know as soon as they see you that I want you.'

She swung round to face him, her hazel-gold eyes wide with astonishment. And something more. A flicker of pain.

'Don't. They'd take one look and know that for a lie.'

Had she never looked in the mirror? Never recognised the heady eroticism of her own body? The bone-deep beauty, the elegance and allure? Had she truly no idea how gut-wrenchingly sexy she was in slim-fitting trousers, her face pure of artificial embellishment?

Heat pooled low in his body, his groin tightening, his arousal burgeoning heavily. It would be the work of a moment to reach out and haul her against him. Show her exactly how much he wanted her.

But that shadow of anguish in her expression stopped him. This was difficult enough for her. Pregnant, in a foreign country, still grappling with the idea of marriage. She looked ready to take flight. He had to proceed slowly.

'Clothes can be changed. They are nothing.' Instantly a vision filled his mind of her standing there, absolutely naked, for his personal delectation.

Every muscle froze at the potent image.

He drew in a sharp breath and continued before his good intentions deserted him and he resorted to a more earthy form of persuasion.

'I will treat you with respect. I will treat you as my wife. There will be no doubt in anyone's mind.'

She shook her head. 'You mean, the respect the mother of your child deserves.' Her words had a wasp-sharp sting.

'That too,' he murmured. He read Maggie's set face and changed tack. 'I can promise you respect and loyalty. Is that such a bad bargain?' Ruthlessly he tightened the net. 'What do you have to go home to? Is there so much waiting for you there you can't give it up for a new life?'

He didn't need to say more. The truth lay stark and unrelenting between them. No one waited for her. Her own country held nothing except unemployment, loneliness and the struggle of single parenthood.

'But we have nothing in common,' she said at last, her mouth a flat line, her eyes averted.

Khalid repressed a smile. He'd won, though she might not admit it yet. Spears of hot anticipation lanced him.

He steered away from mentioning their explosive sexual compatibility. Instinct told him she found that unsettling. Time enough to deal with that when they were wed. He looked forward to that day. To alleviating the heady arousal he experienced whenever he was with her.

'We will find that with time,' he assured her. 'For now we have our child and our honesty. That's a better beginning than many.'

'Here you go, sweetie.' Maggie gave the little boy a boost up into the saddle of the sturdy pony.

It didn't matter that he didn't speak English nor she Arabic. His grin told her all she needed to know. Quickly she checked his feet were in the stirrups and that he held his reins properly. She motioned for him to straighten his back and shoulders, smiling and nodding approval as he did.

When she reached for the leading-rein a torrent of outraged protest issued from his lips.

'Don't pay any attention, Maggie.' Khalid's voice came from just beside her. 'Hamed knows he's not ready to ride alone yet.'

Maggie flashed her rider a look that indicated she wouldn't brook any nonsense, then dropped the lead-rein, leaving the pony standing tethered. There was instant silence as Hamed realised he wasn't going anywhere just yet.

'He'll be OK.' She turned to Khalid. 'It's just his pride talking. I'll give him a moment.'

Khalid's smile was warm and Maggie felt the tension of the past forty-eight hours slip away. This afternoon spent with Khalid and his cousin's brood of children had been more fun than she'd expected. Not once had he mentioned marriage, though his proposal stood between them, silent and unavoidable. As always, being with children had lightened her mood.

She'd revelled in their excitement at visiting the ponies Khalid kept for them.

'You know about young boys.' Was that approval she heard?

She shrugged. 'Back home I help out with a programme for disabled riders. We meet every second Saturday and most of the riders are children. I've picked up a thing or two.'

'You enjoy being with children?'

'Of course. What's not to like?' Kids took you as they found you. They were open and honest about their feelings.

'Have you always wanted children?'

'I…suppose so.' His eyes held her so she couldn't look away. 'It wasn't something I'd planned just yet.' She grimaced. This pregnancy was anything but planned. 'But I'd always assumed I'd have children. One day, when I met…'

'The right man.'

Silently she nodded, rocked again by the vast difference between reality and her secret hopes of everlasting love. It was time to forget her dream of finding a man who'd love her for herself. She had to think now of her baby, not pie-in-the-sky romantic dreams.

'How about you? Did you want children?'

His face was still, suddenly sombre. 'It wasn't a lifetime ambition, but yes, I've wanted children.'

Maggie didn't understand the shadow of pain in his eyes. Khalid wasn't a simple man to understand.

She turned back to Hamed with an encouraging smile. Soon she was leading him round the stable yard, reminding him to sit still while he chattered nineteen to the dozen.

But as they walked it was Khalid who held her attention. Khalid standing with little Ayisha in his arms, showing her how to feed a carrot to one of the horses. There was a squeal of delight as the mare snuffled up the treat and Ayisha giggled. Alone of all the children, Ayisha had been timid with the ponies.

Maggie watched Khalid cradle the child against his strong

frame and felt something give way inside her. The big man and the tiny girl were so perfect together.

She heard his murmured encouragement, saw his swift movement to prevent Ayisha lunging recklessly at the horse's head. He was patient, gentle, caring. Khalid would be a doting parent, but no pushover. Their child would have boundaries but plenty of love too. If she married him.

That was what she wanted for their child. Not the constrained existence she'd led, always anticipating her father's disapproval, his temper. Khalid was nothing like her father. He'd encourage, not destroy youthful aspirations. For all his power and wealth, Khalid would make the sort of father she wanted for their baby.

Her breath expelled in a sigh. Could she commit to a loveless marriage when she'd craved love all her life?

She couldn't allow it to matter. She'd do whatever it took to give her baby the best.

Khalid would never love her, never regard her as anything other than the mother of his child. His 'proposal' had left it baldly obvious his emotions would never be engaged. This was about the baby. About legitimacy, honour and duty.

He kept his distance, never touched her now. Any marriage would be in name only. She'd have to find a way to stop the surge of physical longing she felt for him. She bit her lip. Maybe it was because she'd been a virgin till so recently. Perhaps this…desire that haunted even her dreams would cease with time.

'You look very serious.'

Maggie found Khalid blocking her path, Ayisha still in his arms. The sight made her think about him holding their child. Of the love and support he'd give it in abundance.

She drew to a halt and Hamed's pony nuzzled her side.

'I was thinking.'

Was that a flash of something in his dark eyes or a trick of the light?

'Thinking about us,' he murmured. 'About the baby.'

He was so sure of himself she wanted to deny it. But what was the point? Of course she'd been thinking about them. It was all she thought about, wondering what to do for the best. Scared to trust herself to a stranger, but forced to acknowledge the benefits for their baby.

'You've decided.' His stare imprisoned her. 'Tell me.'

Maggie's heart rose in her throat. She'd finally made her decision.

'Yes, Khalid. I'll marry you.'

CHAPTER SEVEN

BARELY two weeks later Maggie stood in front of the full-length mirror in her luxurious new suite of rooms. Amazement filled her at the stranger she saw there. It was incredible what a fortune in clothes and jewellery and the attentions of a small army of women could achieve.

There wasn't so much as a whiff of the stables clinging to this royal bride.

Uncertain, she walked closer, aware with every step of the unfamiliar weight and the stiff formality of the cloth-of-gold fabric embroidered with pearls. Someone with an eye for her colouring had insisted on emeralds for her jewellery. They made her eyes sparkle.

Or was that trepidation? The butterflies in her stomach were the size of giant condors and her second thoughts took up most of her time.

And yet… She stared at the woman in the mirror and wondered. Could she make this work? If she could look the part maybe, one day, she could grow into the role of sheikh's wife. And she did look—

'Magnificent!'

She spun round in a flurry of long skirts, her pulse jumping.

'Khalid! What are you doing here?'

He'd been leaning against the doorjamb. Now he straightened and paced towards her. He looked every inch the royal sheikh. More, he looked like her fantasy prince come to life: lithe, gorgeous and dangerously intense. His splendid robes emphasised the lean elegance of his masculine frame.

The look in his eyes made her blood sizzle.

'I'm admiring my bride.' He halted in front of her. His intent scrutiny made her heart pump harder.

'But are you supposed to be here?'

'Where else would I be on our wedding day?'

His gaze dropped, travelling slowly over her flushed cheeks, lingering on her mouth. She snatched a breath. Her lips throbbed and parted and his eyes narrowed. Heat flared across her skin at the intensity of that look.

He surveyed every inch of her from the ornate gossamer-thin silk veil covering her hair, down to the full-length gown. A little earlier, being dressed in all her finery, Maggie had felt like an impostor. The luxurious fabrics and the wealth of jewels weren't for the likes of her. Yet as his gaze heated her skin to a white-hot sizzle she let herself wonder, just for a moment, what he really thought of his bride. His eyes lingered on the emeralds, heavy at her ears and breast.

Slowly he smiled. If she hadn't known better, she'd have said it was a proprietorial smile. Like a man coveting a secret treasure. Yet that was impossible.

She frowned, trying to concentrate on something other than the desperate yearning she felt for this man. He wanted her only as the necessary means to obtain his child. Lust for her husband was not an option.

'Isn't it bad luck for the groom to see his bride before the wedding?'

'Luck?' he scoffed. 'We make that for ourselves. Besides, you are alone on a day when a woman looks to her family and friends for support.'

He stepped close and took her hand, his warmth enfolding her. 'You have no family and you didn't invite any friends to the wedding. So I am here to take their place. I didn't want you to be alone, Maggie.'

The timbre of his voice was low and rich and warm, sending a frisson of emotion through her.

She'd expected him to be kind, and she knew him to be generous, but she hadn't thought he really cared.

'Thank you, Khalid.' The words seemed woefully insufficient.

He squeezed her fingers and the churning in her stomach eased just a fraction.

'You're right. It's better not to be alone.' She'd spent too long today fretting over old hurts, wondering where her mother and sister were. Her attempts to trace them hadn't got far and she had no idea where they were. The stab of disappointment had been sharp. She'd always dreamed of having her mother at her wedding day. Of her sister, Cassie, standing up as her bridesmaid.

This morning, even surrounded by chattering ladies-in-waiting primping and fussing over her outfit, she'd felt horribly alone.

She forced a smile to her lips and met Khalid's eyes.

'I'm gaining a new family,' she said, her hand smoothing low over the lush fabric covering her abdomen. 'It's a new beginning.'

Khalid saw the determination in her steady gaze, the strength of purpose, as well as the shadows of pain. He slid her arm through his, drawing her close.

'You honour me, Maggie. I will make sure you never regret it.'

How different was this wedding day, this bride, compared to his first marriage.

Then there'd been festivities and family celebrations for months before. He'd felt the buzz of excitement, anticipation and heady expectancy. A sense of adventure as he and the woman he adored embarked on their life together.

This time there were no hearts involved. He and Maggie were simply making a sensible, considered commitment for the sake of their child.

That didn't stop him wanting to wipe her hurt away.

He curled a finger under her chin and lifted her face. Her eyes glowed brighter than the gems she wore and he felt a shaft of heat pierce him. He was looking forward to their wedding night. He'd ached for her for weeks.

'Trust me. Just relax and don't worry about anything.'

'So, wife, what do you think of our Shajehani wedding celebrations?'

Maggie sat straighter in her seat as Khalid's warm breath feathered her cheek, detonating a whole series of explosive sensations through her body. The way he said 'wife' in that low tone made her pulse throb and her nipples peak with secret pleasure. His voice was a rumble of sound that reminded her of the night they'd become lovers. His scent teased her, evocative and arousing.

'It's spectacular,' she said. 'Just stunning. I hadn't expected anything like this.'

Ever since she'd agreed to the wedding, Khalid had kept his distance. They'd met only in the presence of others. There'd been no private words. No chance to retract her promise. Until today when he'd prowled into her room with the casual insouciance of…she stifled shocked laughter…of a sheikh visiting his harem! But today had been about supporting her, that was all. Despite that single searing look, Khalid had been a model of decorum ever since. He'd merely been concerned for her welfare.

To her dismay she found herself regretting that this marriage was to be a formality. With Khalid so close, that skittering sensual excitement quickened her blood again. She wanted him, in every way a woman wanted a man. But she'd tied herself into a bloodless union!

'I'm glad you approve,' he murmured.

Avoiding the temptation to turn and meet his eyes, she gazed out over the throng. She'd never seen so many people in one place. The vast open-sided tent was crammed with people and the noise was a constant din. Beyond the main tent people spread as far as she could see, seated on rugs, lit by ornate braziers. The smell of roast meat and spices filled the air. The sound of music and laughter. A hubbub of conversation and goodwill.

'They don't seem to mind your choice of bride,' she said tentatively. 'Everyone has been friendly.' It had been a relief to find some familiar faces, like Khalid's uncle Hussein and his wife, Zeinab, who had taken Maggie under her wing and begun teaching her Shajehani customs.

'Of course they approve. They wouldn't question my choice.' For all his talk of progress and his desire to modernise the country, the arrogance in Khalid's tone was that of an autocrat, superbly sure of himself.

A ripple of unease feathered down her spine. How well did she know the man she'd married?

'They can see you are a woman worthy of their sheikh. You are beautiful tonight, Maggie.' His voice dropped to a deep whisper, so low it vibrated right through her.

Despite her best intentions she gave in to the need that clawed at her, to take her fill of the sight of him, to bask in his nearness. Slowly she turned. His glittering eyes, dark as midnight, met hers and her heart turned over with a thud she could almost hear.

'You don't need to say that, Khalid. I don't need to be humoured.'

'Humoured?' His sleek eyebrows arrowed down. 'You must learn to trust me, Maggie. I do not lie.'

But he exaggerated. She appreciated his kindness. He was trying to reassure her and boost her self-confidence.

He leaned close. 'Your eyes are like stars. Your mouth is sweet invitation. Your throat is as delicate as—'

'Khalid! Please!' she hissed. She tried to prevent the delight that rippled through her at his words and, more, at his heavy-lidded look. 'Don't!'

'Don't what?' His mouth twisted in a tight hard curve that she didn't understand. He looked annoyed.

'Please, don't say things like that.' She darted a glance over her shoulder, but for once everyone seemed absorbed in their meal, their conversation, and not in their prince and his bride. She could only be thankful as heat flushed her cheeks, then ebbed away.

'As you wish.' He paused, only speaking again when she turned round to face him. 'So, what shall we discuss?'

What had got into Khalid? She could almost believe he was angry. All she'd done was stop him acting the part of smitten lover. She knew it was purely for public consumption, but still it came too close to her secret yearnings to be tolerable.

She reached for the golden goblet in front of her, swallowing the cool, rich cordial in an attempt to relieve her parched throat. She was aware of his eyes on her and felt clumsy, her movements jerky, her skin uncomfortably tight. Her hand shook as she put down the goblet.

'How long does the celebration last?' Out of nowhere a wave of tiredness hit her. The wedding ceremony had been surprisingly short, but the festivities had continued all day. It had taken hours simply to welcome all the guests. Then there'd been the various entertainments, including displays of horsemanship where Khalid himself had displayed a prowess that had brought her to her feet applauding.

'A few days.'

'Days?' Maggie couldn't imagine it. 'I don't think I have the stamina for it.'

His eyes gleamed but his face was serious as he said, 'We Shajehanis pride ourselves on our stamina.'

He was talking about the ability to feast and provide hospitality for days on end, not…anything else. Nevertheless, under his unwavering gaze, heat coloured her cheeks.

'Are we really expected to party for days?'

'No. Our customs have changed. Over the next few days there will be a range of festivities. The celebration tonight will continue until much later. I'm expected to attend most of it, but—' his gaze sharpened '—if you're tired, it will be quite acceptable for you to retire.'

'Really?' Suddenly the prospect of sleep was overwhelmingly tempting. A yawn rose in her throat and she stifled it hurriedly.

'Come.' Beside her Khalid rose, tall and imposing in his fine embroidered robes.

As she looked up at him a hush fell over the crowd. He held out his hand and she had no option but to place hers in his. It closed warm and vital around her fingers, drawing her inexorably from her seat till she stood before him. She trembled as his heat reached her, inviting her to lean close to his strong, perfect body. Instead she stood ramrod straight, her gaze fixed on his broad chest, rather than meet those dark eyes that she suspected saw too much.

He turned and led her from the raised dais. As he did so pandemonium broke out. Cheers and laughter and music.

Maggie faltered and looked questioningly at him.

'What's going on?'

She couldn't read his expression. It was set in severe lines yet even with his back to the lights she sensed his intense regard. His eyes glittered like black diamonds.

'They're encouraging me.' His lips quirked up then in what should have been a smile. 'They approve of the fact that I'm finally going to bed my new bride.'

CHAPTER EIGHT

KHALID led her through the scented gardens and into the palace.

Maggie racked her brain for small talk to fill the silence but nothing came. Her mouth was dry, her breathing agitated and her mind spinning. The touch of his hand on hers did that, the awareness of him close beside her.

And the fact that this was their wedding night and her handsome husband was leading her to bed.

Tension spiralled through her and an excitement she shouldn't be feeling. It wasn't meant to be this way. This was supposed to be a marriage of convenience. Yet now, feeling his dark lustrous gaze like a caress on her skin, Maggie acknowledged how desperately she wanted more.

She wanted her husband.

Her heart hammered against her ribs and she realised she was in an unfamiliar part of the palace.

'Where are we?' Was that husky voice hers?

Khalid opened ornate double doors and gestured for her to precede him. Warily she stepped into a wide vestibule. Intricately carved arches led off it and an exquisite old mural of a garden covered one wall.

'Our apartments.' His rich voice, low and close beside her, made her jump. 'We're in the heart of the old palace.'

'*Our* apartments?' Only those two words registered. 'But

I have my own rooms. I just moved in.' On the very day she'd agreed to marry him.

Khalid ushered her forward, brushing so close as he took her arm that she hurried to move. His proximity quickened her breathing, drew her skin tingling tight.

'That was before our wedding, Maggie. It would hardly be fitting now for us to live on separate sides of the palace. Now we will share a suite.'

Her breath stalled in her throat at his words.

They passed a vast, luxurious sitting room, then a smaller, more intimate parlour, till they came to another door. Its wood was decorated with a tracery of fine metal, like decorative vines.

They stopped and shock sizzled through her as he lifted her hand to his mouth, pressing his warm lips to her skin in a kiss that struck right to the core of her. Maggie stifled a sigh as her knees turned to jelly.

'You handled the formalities beautifully.' His voice, like black velvet ribbon, slid across her senses, evoking a longing for more, more of his words, his tender strength, more of *him*.

'Thank you.' Her voice was ridiculously husky because she couldn't catch her breath. Khalid's praise warmed her heart.

'I couldn't have done it without your aunt. Zeinab steered me through the preparations and the language lessons.' Maggie was babbling but she couldn't stop. 'And I've met some of her friends these past weeks so I knew some of the guests. That made it easier.'

'And yet it was you who played the part so magnificently.'

Played the part.

The words dropped between them, a reminder that this was all a sham.

Reality slammed into her. The bubbling excitement, the eager anticipation in her blood, died. She'd let herself be caught up in make-believe. He didn't want her.

As if on cue, Khalid released his hold. Instantly she missed his heat, the rippling energy of his nearness. She felt cold despite the balmy temperature. As if an icy hand had pushed her away.

He stepped back a single, telling pace and her heart contracted. That pace confirmed the cold, pragmatic truth about their marriage. The truth she'd secretly yearned to move beyond.

They were strangers. Married strangers. It was what she'd agreed to so it shouldn't have hurt so much.

'This is your room, Maggie. I hope you will be comfortable here.' He inclined his head in a courtly bow.

Khalid's words sounded stilted in his ears. Like a steward showing a stranger hospitality. Not a man with his new wife. But only by retreating into formality did he stand a chance of retaining any distance.

Damn it. This was not how he'd envisaged his wedding night. He clasped his hands so tight behind his back the restricted blood flow pained him. Better that than let his resolve crumble. If that happened he'd probably take her here, now, against the door, with all the pent up urgency of six weeks' anticipation.

Khalid shook with the force of wanting her.

He surveyed her confused eyes, her trembling mouth, the shadows of fatigue and emotion bruising her fair skin.

All day he'd resisted the truth, intent on his need to have her. He'd brushed aside Zeinab's concerns. Of course Maggie was nervous—what bride wasn't? As for being overwrought—no. Maggie was too grounded, too sensible for that. Even the doctor's guarded comments this evening, that Maggie was on the edge of exhaustion, hadn't swayed Khalid from his intention to make her his tonight.

'You look tired, little one. You need to rest.' He forced the words out.

He'd denied the truth right up until he'd led her from the wedding tent. Then he'd looked into her face, proud and tense and shadowed with weariness. He'd held her close and felt her tremble with exhaustion and nerves. She'd stumbled as her usual athletic grace had deserted her.

Only a brute would demand intimacy now, he acknowledged. He'd forgotten how overwhelming royal celebrations were for the uninitiated. To a woman isolated in a strange land, in the early, exhausting stages of pregnancy. How emotionally draining this must all be.

The doctor had stressed the need for rest to protect mother and baby. Khalid would have to wait. For tonight at least.

'Just ring the bell if you need anything.'

Her hazel eyes looked enormous as they met his.

'You won't be here?' Her voice was uneven. More proof that he was doing right. 'Don't you have to…stay for a while?' Her gaze shifted to a point near his collarbone. Thank goodness. When she looked at him like that it pared his resolve paper-thin.

'Won't it look odd if you return immediately?'

'Don't worry, Maggie. I won't go back to the feast straight away.' A long cold dip in the pool and some strenuous laps might temper the fever in his blood.

His smile was perfunctory. 'You go straight to bed and get some sleep.' He paused, only just stopping himself from touching her velvet skin, caressing her slender neck. 'Sleep well, little one.'

Maggie's shoulders slumped as she entered her new room. She barely took in the airy space, the canopied bed, the elegant furniture. A few tottering steps took her to a wide divan. She sank down, drawing her knees up to her chest, careless of her gown's priceless fabric.

Why was she upset? She'd known this marriage was just for their baby. That she and Khalid would never be a real couple. Yet the pain of rejection tore at her heart.

What had she expected? That he'd take one look at her in her finery and decide he wanted more from their marriage? Impossible!

Khalid's grim expression had spelled out precisely how un-attractive he found her. His heated look earlier, the one that had curled her toes with sexual anticipation, had been the product of her over-eager imagination. He'd virtually told her just now that she was haggard beneath the jewels and sumptuous clothes.

Her heart shrivelled. Suddenly this marriage in name only seemed a lifetime sentence.

Maggie woke in the late afternoon after falling asleep around dawn. She threw back the embroidered coverlet, then paused. Was he here? Waiting for her to wake? Did they have official duties today or were they expected to stay here, seeking privacy like normal newly-weds?

Fire seared her lungs at the images her unruly imagination conjured. Of Khalid, naked and stunningly aroused, lowering himself over her. Of the perfection of that moment when her body surrendered to indescribable pleasure. Of the warm clasp of his arms around her as he held her close in the after-math of the conflagration.

She bit down on her lip, wishing the memories weren't so vivid. She needed to forget instead of torturing herself with thoughts of what she couldn't have.

Khalid's strength, compassion and generosity, his determi-nation to do what was right by their child, all made him de-sirable. And that was without the bone-melting physical attraction she felt for him.

Twenty minutes later her nerves had settled but there was a hollow ache in her chest. The suite was empty. *Khalid wasn't here.*

He'd chosen to leave her alone the day after their wedding. For all the luxury of her surroundings she'd been dumped like an unwanted piece of luggage.

Her scent reached Khalid as he sat at his desk. Attar of roses. Not the cheap, pungent perfume tourists bought, but the true, sensual distillation that worked magic when heated on warm female flesh. On her it was pure eroticism.

Slowly he lifted his head. Desire crashed through him, stoking the deep-seated fire that had burned in his loins so long, ever since their night together. Every part of him hardened, muscles and sinews pulling tight.

She stood in the doorway, wearing an *abaya* of bronze shot through with green. Iridescent beads on the dress caught the light as she moved. His mouth dried to desert arid as she paced towards him. In this light, wearing what must be whisper-thin silk, it looked as if she was braless. The gentle sway of her breasts as she crossed the room held him fixated.

She didn't look tired anymore. And only a little nervous. Had she come to seduce him?

He smiled. Blood pooled hot and urgent in his groin.

Maggie's steps faltered, her eyes widened.

'Hello, Maggie.' The words emerged as a deep, satisfied rumble. She looked alert, refreshed, a bloom of colour in her cheeks. Satisfaction coiled inside him. And anticipation. Obviously his wife was feeling much better. Well enough for...

She stopped in front of the massive desk, crossing her arms as if to hide her breasts. But she was too late. He'd already spied the delectable points of her nipples pressing against the silk *abaya*. So she felt it too, the surge of hunger as their eyes met. The knowledge fuelled his need.

'Hello, Khalid.' Her voice was cool. 'I didn't hear you come in.'

'I just got back. You're feeling well?' he asked, needing to be sure. 'You've recovered from yesterday?'

'Yes.' Her brows knitted. 'I'm perfectly fine. I was just tired, that's all.'

'I'm glad to hear it.' The understatement of the year. 'Please—' he gestured to a chair '—take a seat.'

'No, thank you.' Her gaze darted around the room. 'But we need to talk. This pretence that we're married—'

He sat up bolt upright, instantly alert. 'It's no pretence.' His voice was rough with warning. 'The marriage is valid, Maggie. There's no going back.'

'I didn't mean it like that.' She pursed her lips and he read embarrassment there. But her eyes flashed defiantly and a jagged lightning strike of desire slammed into him.

'We need to discuss the ground rules,' she said, spreading her hands.

'Ground rules?'

'What you expect. How this is supposed to work on a day-to-day basis. We never talked about that.' She straightened her shoulders in a movement that thrust her small, perfect breasts towards him. He almost groaned aloud.

'Like today,' she continued, pacing restlessly. 'What was I supposed to do? Can I go out alone? I wasn't sure if you wanted me to keep the pretence that we were here…together.' She swallowed, her gaze sliding quickly away. 'But then you left me here alone so I assume it doesn't matter if people realise our marriage isn't normal.'

'Not normal?' Was that anger sizzling in his belly?

Her eyes met his and a blast of molten fire scorched him.

'Usually a bridegroom wants to spend time with his wife.' No mistaking the cutting edge to her words.

He stared. Did she truly believe he'd wanted to stay away?

'I did come to see you this afternoon. But you were still asleep. I thought it best not to wake you.'

He'd looked down at her curled in the centre of her vast bed and his libido had clawed like a wild thing, clamouring for release. Urging him to take what was his.

But he had an obligation to care for her. She had no one else. The fact that she'd slept so late only highlighted her fragility. Reluctantly, cursing his scruples, he'd returned to today's wedding celebrations, barely overcoming his frustration as he'd parried well-intentioned congratulations.

He'd only just returned to his rooms and tried to settle to

work, believing Maggie needed the rest of the day to recuperate. It seemed he'd been wrong.

Good. He'd waited long enough.

'If I'd known you were awake I'd have come back sooner.'

The shimmer of heat in his eyes disconcerted Maggie. It was like looking into the face of someone she knew and finding a stranger. A tremulous whisper of unease raced through her.

'Why did you come to see me?'

'Why does any man want to see his bride the day after their wedding?' His voice was a dangerous caress that warmed her blood and drew her breasts tight and full. His lips curved into a smile that seemed almost hungry. Her eyes widened and she backed a step, suddenly uncertain.

'Don't play games. Please.'

'You wanted to talk about ground rules.' Khalid's voice was a rich drawl. 'I agree. It's well past time for that.' The intensity of his stare held her taut and breathless as her heartbeat thudded, loud in her ears. Something had changed. Treacherous undercurrents swirled between them.

Deliberately his gaze moved, skating over her face, her bare neck, the rise and fall of her breasts. Silently she cursed the fact she hadn't bothered with a bra after her long soak in the bath. The rhythm of her breathing altered, now fast and shallow. A frisson of anxiety skated down her spine even as desire spiked in her bloodstream. She gasped and stepped back from the desk.

'Perhaps we could work the details out tomorrow. It's getting late.' Her words tumbled out in a rush. Maggie felt strangely vulnerable in this highly charged atmosphere.

'There's no need to wait until tomorrow,' he murmured.

In one lithe movement Khalid rose from his chair. At once the spacious room seemed to shrink, as if the walls pressed closer. Or maybe that was because her heart thudded so hard she couldn't catch her breath.

'There isn't?' Maggie watched him stride around the desk,

each movement slow and purposeful. She found herself turning so her back was to the desk and Khalid stood between her and the door.

The atavistic impulse to run and hide tensed her limbs. For the first time ever Khalid looked…dangerous. His easy, loose-limbed stance morphed into something much more aggressive. The expression in his eyes looked hungry, that baring of his teeth feral. She hardly recognised him. No sign now of the urbane, compassionate man she thought she knew.

Maggie blinked but the image of Khalid as a large, threatening, predatory male didn't shift.

Tremors of shock vibrated through her. And something else. A tiny thrill of excitement. She must be mad!

'No,' he said, his voice a deep rumble. 'We'll sort this out tonight.'

Her eyes were lustrous gold in the lamplight, shot with emerald fire. Khalid had never known any like them. Her chest rose and fell rapidly, her breasts thrusting in wanton invitation against the fabric. Her lips parted as her breaths shortened.

His body tensed to the point of pain as he prolonged the suspense of anticipation a moment more. He'd never been one to rush his pleasure.

And Maggie would be pure pleasure.

Tonight there was a fire in her, a vibrant energy that stoked his desire to smoking hot. The blaze in her eyes, that proud stance, her utterly sexy body were all magnificent.

He'd seen her brave, both in the horse ring and defying her physical weakness the night they'd met. Her stoicism, honesty and wry humour had instantly appealed. As had the way she'd battled an unhappy childhood and emerged strong yet still vulnerable and feminine.

'There's only one rule between us, Maggie. I am your husband and you are my wife.' Strange how satisfying the words were on his lips.

He closed in, backing her up against the desk till she had nowhere to go. Her eyes were stunned though she jutted her chin up. Was she fighting the force of need so powerful between them?

Her spirit, as much as her delectable body, made him hard with wanting.

'Really?' She was breathless. He liked that. The sound reminded him of her gasping out her pleasure the first time he'd taken his fill of her. It was a heady, erotic memory.

'Yes.' His voice was a growl. 'I will treat you as a man treats his wife.'

Her eyes grew huge and he watched her swallow convulsively.

He lowered his head, compelled to taste her again. She stiffened as his lips brushed the skin at the base of her neck. It was like rose-scented velvet, impossibly soft, decadently delicious.

For an instant her breasts slid against him before two feminine palms pushed at his chest. He nipped at her neck, a graze of teeth on sensitive flesh, and her hands faltered. He smiled as he inhaled her perfume and kissed his way up to the lobe of her ear.

'Khalid! What are you doing?'

'You don't like it?' He paused for a moment, lifting his mouth. She swayed a telltale fraction towards him in wordless protest at his withdrawal. Maggie's body knew what it wanted, even if she didn't.

'But this is surely what a bride expects of her husband.' He took pity on her, and himself, and kissed her neck, the angle of her jaw, the corner of her mouth. She groaned and shuddered against him as he drew her close.

He covered her mouth with his and plunged deep. The honeysweet taste of her, the potent intimacy of that hungry kiss, sent spirals of heat exploding through his ravenous body. The feel of her slim curves pressing against him sent him into meltdown.

He needed to slow down. Quickly.

He slid his hands round her waist, feeling a kick of primitive satisfaction at the way they almost spanned her slim body. Then he lifted her up onto the desk, at the same time stepping in against her.

Urgently he reached higher, discovering to his delight he'd been right. No bra. He cupped her perfect breasts. They were warm, high and firm like delicious sun-ripened fruit. Her moan of delight vibrated inside his mouth as he squeezed. She spasmed in his hold.

He pulled back just enough to murmur against her lips, 'Sensitive?'

Wordlessly she nodded, her head falling back to leave her arched neck exposed. He slid his tongue along it, tasting musk. Ripples of pleasure coursed through her as he caressed her breasts through the thin fabric. The blood drew downwards in his body to pool heavily in his loins.

He bent his knees and took one breast in an open-mouthed kiss. The silk was no barrier to pleasure, becoming a slick second skin as he suckled hard, and she jerked in his arms, her whole body taut with ecstasy.

She was so responsive, so needy, so sensuous. He couldn't get enough of her. He wanted her *now*, and at the same time wanted to draw out the pleasure for both of them.

He wrapped an arm tight round her, pulling her hard against him. His mouth worked her soft flesh through the wet silk as he caressed her other breast. Gently he grazed his teeth across her breast in the tiniest nip.

She jolted in his arms. He could almost hear her heart pounding a frantic rhythm.

'Khalid. Please.' It was a choked gasp.

'Shh,' he soothed her as he straightened, his hands fastening on the fabric covering her thighs.

'We can't!' She shook her head, her eyes still closed.

Already the silk was bunched in his fists, her legs bare beneath his seeking hands.

'Of course we can.' He shoved her skirts up to the top of her legs. Her pale satiny thighs quivered beneath his palms. His need was urgent.

'You are my wife.' He hooked his fingers in her demure white lace underwear and tugged until she shimmied her hips, shifting her weight so that he could drag the fabric away.

'You're carrying my child.' His fingers probed the dark blonde triangle of hair at the juncture of her thighs, finding her satisfyingly slick and eager. This was what he wanted, the heady, physical pleasure she'd given him weeks ago then denied him all this time.

With one hand at her back he slid her towards him so she perched right on the edge of the desk, her legs falling further open as he insinuated his thighs between them. She was exactly where he wanted her.

His gaze roved her as he reached for the fastening of his trousers. Her eyes were slitted half closed against the pleasure that plumped her parted lips and drew her breath in short, hard pants. Her *abaya* bore the marks of his mouth, one nipple surrounded by an aureole of wet silk plastered to her breast. She looked glorious, wanton, ready.

His questing fingers probed her entrance, feeling the wet heat of her pleasure.

This time there'd be no need for protection, no barrier, since his seed was already securely planted inside her. The knowledge was supremely satisfying. And arousing. Possessiveness swept through him, so strong his knees trembled.

'Open your eyes, Maggie.'

Emerald light dazzled him from those golden depths. She reached up and curved her hands round his shoulders, tight, as if she was afraid to let go.

She looked bewildered by the force of their passion. Yet there was no shadow of protest from her. She felt it too, this prodigious, urgent need.

He positioned himself against her and slipped his hands beneath her legs. Her brow creased and belatedly he remembered this was new to her.

'Lift your legs.' It was a husky command, barely audible. His mouth dried when he felt her encircle him. He'd dreamed of this sweet ecstasy so often.

He splayed his hands over her hips, anchoring her as slowly, deliberately, he pushed inside.

She was just as he remembered, slick and hot and impossibly tight against his over-sensitive flesh. And the look of wonder on her face was sweet balm to his masculine ego. He rotated his hips just a little, watching the expressions of delight and astonishment flit across her face. Her fingers tightened, clawing through the fine linen at his shoulders. Pinpricks scored his flesh as her short nails dug in. Her breath was audible now, shallow pants that matched the rhythm of his pulse.

Carefully he withdrew, then abruptly surged forward, this time rewarded by a twitch of her pelvis as she lifted a fraction to meet him.

He smiled, though it was probably a rictus-hard grimace. Even that small effort to meet his thrust was enough to send him spinning almost out of control.

His wife was pure dynamite!

He'd never reached such a fever pitch of need so fast. Desperately he hung on to the remnants of his control. But it was no good. There'd be time for long, languorous lovemaking later, he assured himself. Right now it felt as if someone had lit a trail of gunpowder through his belly.

He shut his eyes, hoping to last just a few moments longer if he couldn't see her, so open and ready and generous. But in the darkness every sense concentrated on the feel of her all around him, delicious torture he couldn't withstand. The scent of her was in his nostrils, rose and earthy, feminine musk. The taste of her filled his mouth. The sound of her gasps of pleasure was all he heard over the rush of blood in his ears.

He thrust again and again. Felt her clench hard around him as her fingers clawed tighter.

Khalid opened his eyes as the darkness began to explode. He held her shocked gaze with his, watching the flush of sexual excitement flare across her throat, her cheeks.

His rhythm was steady now, smooth and deep, until she seemed to choke on a keening cry. Her muscles spasmed out of control and her desperate hands tugged him close.

He went willingly, nuzzling her warm silk hair, gathering her to him as the fiery heat rose and filled him. Flames exploded in his bloodstream and he was lost, juddering in violent completion that rocked them both.

When it was over he smiled wearily.

His plan for a convenient marriage had one definite benefit. Sex with his new wife was phenomenal.

Ruthlessly he squashed a niggle of unease in his subconscious. A sense that it was more than simple physical release that had made this coming together so powerful.

What more could there be?

CHAPTER NINE

KHALID slid the *abaya* off Maggie in one swift movement, then carried her to his bed. She felt perfect in his arms, a luscious bundle of warm femininity.

He didn't bother with lights for the moon lit the bedroom to a pale glow. Soon she was lying spread before him, naked and gloriously enticing. Her long legs and gentle curves were pure temptation.

His hunger rose again, unquenched. He frowned. He'd expected an easing of this urgency after their frantic coupling, but there'd been precious little respite. His climax had been a white-hot catharsis that should have left him sated. Yet the sight of her naked, like a delicacy offered for his personal enjoyment, had him ready for more.

His craving for her was marrow-deep. If he paused to consider the implications, he knew he wouldn't like them. He'd signed on for a convenient marriage, not one that stirred him to the very core.

She reached out a hand for the sheet as if to cover herself.

'No!' His voice was rough. Too rough. He saw her freeze, her eyes wide and luminous in the grey light.

'Leave it.'

Her breath shuddered out in a long sigh. Fascinated, he watched her breasts rise and fall, the nipples thrusting up at him. His hands itched to possess them.

Wordlessly he stripped off the rest of his clothes and let them fall. Then he climbed into the bed. Hastily she wriggled aside, thwarting his intention to blanket her body with his own. He'd revelled in the sensation of her impossibly soft skin, her yielding curves against him. He wanted that again. Now. But she was barely experienced, might even be tender. He swallowed his impatience.

Yet the reminder of her innocence merely fuelled his possessive hunger. There was undeniable satisfaction in realising all she knew of physical intimacy he'd taught her. His body clamoured at the prospect of initiating her into new pleasures.

Swallowing his frustration, Khalid propped himself up on one elbow and clamped his thigh over her restless legs. Immediately she stilled.

She needed time. Fine. He'd allow her that. But he had no intention of letting her hide herself from him. He let his hand settle on her collarbone and was rewarded with the rapid thud at her pulse-point, throbbing against his palm.

'You don't have to do that.' Her voice was so low he could barely hear it.

'Do what?' he said absently. He focused on the delicious curve of her flesh as he trawled the pads of his fingers down towards her breast.

Her hand closed hard over his, halting the movement. 'Touch me like that.' He heard her swallow. 'I didn't come to you for sex.'

'But it was good, wasn't it?' Satisfaction filled him. He turned over his hand and grasped hers, preventing her attempt to break his hold. He raised his eyes to her face. Even in the gloom he could read her pinched lips and shadowed eyes. Then she turned away, her mouth a flat line.

She was proud. Yet she was vulnerable too, unsure of herself. That made her prickly. She'd even had the temerity to turn down some of the gifts he'd planned to give her on their betrothal, saying they were too lavish, too expensive for her.

Most women he'd met had been fascinated by his family's legendary wealth. He'd forgotten there might be some who valued things other than money.

Shahina had been the same. Though born to a wealthy family, it wasn't luxury that had made her smile. It had been the things money couldn't purchase—friendship, shared joy, a mountain sunset, a baby's smile.

Khalid frowned. Despite their differing backgrounds, Maggie and Shahina had much in common. Not least their indomitable spirit. Shahina had lived with life-threatening illness, not letting it constrain her till the very end. Maggie had triumphed over the sort of childhood that, from the little he'd discovered, bordered on cruelty and neglect. Yet she faced the world with unique courage.

Strangely the comparison brought no guilt, no sense that he betrayed Shahina with this new marriage. To his surprise, Khalid felt instead a spreading glow of satisfaction. Of contentment.

Yes. He'd done the right thing. Marrying Maggie, bringing up their baby together, was best for them all.

He released her hand and slid his palm down to her proud, ripe breast. Instantly heat shot to his belly, his groin, and his fingers tightened possessively.

'I'll have your belongings moved in here tomorrow.'

There seemed little point in Maggie using the next room, even if there was a connecting door. They weren't in love, so it had seemed sensible to give them both a little space. But now she was here, her flesh warming his, he realised with a pang of surprise that he felt no desire at all for distance. He couldn't get enough of her.

He slid his leg higher across her thighs till he reached the heat of her most feminine place. She moved beneath him and a bolt of anticipation shot through him, pulling every muscle and tendon tight.

'No! Don't!' Her cry startled him.

She shoved his hand away from her breast with a force

that astounded him. 'There's no need to pretend with me, Khalid. Please.'

He scowled. 'What are you talking about?'

'I enjoyed making love with you.' The words tumbled out in a rush. 'It was…very nice. But now you've consummated the marriage and it's all legal. You don't have to…'

She stopped and chewed her lip. 'Could you move, please? I'd like to get up.'

'Not so fast.' Khalid couldn't believe what he was hearing. Very nice! His loving was *very nice*! Next she'd be giving him a score out of ten!

His head reeled as he stared down at her averted face, wishing now he'd turned on the lights so he could read her expression properly.

He pressed his leg down harder so she couldn't slide out from beneath him. After a few moments she subsided, lying still but for the agitated rise and fall of her breasts. She didn't look at him.

'You think what just happened, the sex we just shared—' he watched her flinch '—was a legal formality?' He didn't believe it. Couldn't believe it. Hadn't she been as moved as he'd been, by the stunning perfection of their love-making?

'Khalid, please—'

'No! It doesn't please me to release you.' His voice was harsh with anger but he couldn't prevent it. Anger with himself for having held back from her earlier? Or with her for being so blind?

Guilt clenched his innards. He'd taken no time tonight to reassure or persuade or even seduce her. He'd simply seen her, stalked her like a predator intent on its prey and taken what he'd wanted. Assumed she'd wanted it too.

'What happened between us has nothing to do with the law, Maggie.'

'Don't lie, Khalid.' Her head whipped around and he saw the bright glitter in her eyes. 'It has everything to do with it.

I know you don't want me. Not really. That first time you only stayed with me because I pleaded with you. You had no desire to see me again.'

He shook his head. He'd known Maggie hid emotional scars. He'd seen the evidence that first night. But he'd had no idea how deep they were.

'I was *there*! Remember?' Her voice rose, raw and throbbing with emotion. 'I saw the pity in your eyes, the reluctance. Well—' she put both hands on his imprisoning thigh and tried to shove him away '—we don't have to pretend anymore. There's no one but us here to see.'

'You think we had sex because I felt sorry for you? And then because I had to legitimise our marriage?' Even now he couldn't credit she was serious. Yet the evidence was there in her increasingly frantic attempts to free herself and the pain in her face.

'Do you really think we needed to consummate our marriage to make it legal when you're already pregnant with my baby?'

'I…I don't know.' She sounded confused.

'As for not wanting to see you again—it was you who left me, remember?' That still rankled. 'When I learned of Faruq's death I had to leave immediately. Otherwise you wouldn't have walked away so easily. As it was I had to wait for weeks till you could come to Shajehar.'

'Wait? You weren't waiting.' She shook her head, but her voice was less certain.

'Who do you think insisted on your coming here to work, Maggie?' His voice dropped low. 'We had unfinished business between us.'

'No!' It was a mere whisper of sound.

He took her chin in his hand and swung her round to face him fully. Lowered lids veiled her eyes but she was watching. He felt her gaze like hot ice on his flesh.

'No? Then how do you explain this?' He shifted closer,

pressing his burning hard shaft against her. The friction of soft feminine flesh against his rampant need was a taste of paradise.

Shock froze her features and her eyes bulged.

'I assumed…' She paused for the longest time, then swallowed convulsively. Her gaze slid from his. 'I thought you must have been thinking of someone else while we had sex.'

If it weren't so tragic this would be laughable. But right now Khalid felt more like breaking something. Fury swirled in his gut, edging his voice with a rough burr.

'Believe me, Maggie, I wasn't thinking of anyone but you. The reason I hesitated that first time was because I didn't want to take advantage of you when you'd been through some sort of trauma.'

'Oh.'

That was all she could say?

'Yes, oh. Believe it or not I have scruples about who I take to bed. Injured women who can't think straight aren't high on my list.'

The knowledge had haunted him ever since, that he'd taken advantage of her. He'd told himself she'd known what she was doing. But he'd never been able to shake that seed of doubt, especially when she'd run away.

'I slept with you because I desired you, Maggie. I still desire you.' He grasped her hand and pulled it down between their bodies, till she touched his turgid flesh. The sensation of those slender feminine fingers closing around him was sweet torment. A shudder vibrated through him and hot spears of flame danced behind his eyes.

'One thing you must learn to do, wife, is trust my word. I have already told you that I do not lie. Ever.'

The shocking reality of his arousal, hard, heavy and unbelievably exciting, stopped her thinking straight. The feel of his silky soft skin, his steely strength in her palm, was the most erotic sensation. Trembling, she snatched her hand away.

'But I…' *I what? I'm too gawky and angular, too unfeminine to be desirable? Too…unlovable?* Maggie bit her lip, her mind whirling.

'But nothing. You are my wife and I want you. Those are the facts.' He looked down at her, his breath warm on her already burning face. 'Do you want me, Maggie?'

Her breath stalled in her throat. How could he even ask? Hadn't she just melted in his arms, given herself up to the heady pleasure of his embrace out there, on his desk of all places? She'd been so needy, so abandoned, she'd been unable to pull back, even believing it wasn't *her* he really wanted in his arms. Her desperate hunger had swamped even her pride.

'I…' She swallowed the knot of emotion in her throat. 'I want you, Khalid. You must know that.' She had no pride left now. Nothing to protect herself.

Yet, even as the thought formed in her brain he lowered his face to hers, brushing her lips in the sweetest, most tender kiss imaginable. She sighed, feeling herself fall under his spell, uncaring of her surrender.

'I want you, Maggie. I desire you.' He pressed kisses to the corner of her mouth, her cheek, her jaw. 'You are sexy.' His teeth grazed the lobe of her ear. 'And beautiful.' He licked her neck and she shuddered. 'And every man at our wedding was jealous of my good fortune yesterday.'

His words melded into a deep husky purr as he rained kisses down her throat. Helplessly she arched against him, revelling in the whirlpool of sensations he created in her body and the glorious haze of well-being in her mind.

The words didn't stop. They flowed unceasing from his clever lips as he mouthed her flesh, slid down her body, caressing her. She was on overload, stunned by the sound of his husky, persuasive voice telling her again and again how beautiful she was, how desirable and how much he craved her. And all the while his mouth, his hands, his body touched her in ways that drowned out her doubts and fears and tugged her down, deeper into ecstasy.

'Khalid! Please, I…'

'Yes, Maggie. Don't hold back.' His words were muffled against her flesh, his breath hot, inciting flames of urgent sensation as he slid lower, to the place where heat pooled and swirled.

The press of his lips, the pulse of his tongue on that hyper-sensitive point was all it took to ignite her whole body in a roaring conflagration. It was instantaneous and indescribable.

When her mind returned to her body jolts of shivery delight still racked her, delicious aftershocks of pleasure. He slid higher, the heat of his body sheer erotic torture against her exquisitely sensitised flesh. Desire burgeoned anew.

'I love watching you come,' he murmured against her navel, his tongue flicking out to caress the spot. Maggie's breath seized at the edgy hunger hollowing her insides again. Her eyes widened as he tipped up his head and snared her with his glittering gaze.

'You're so beautiful. I want to watch you again.' His hand inched lower to her damp curls.

'No! Please, Khalid.' Desperate as she was for his touch, she needed more, far more. She ached for him.

His eyes held hers as the seconds stretched. The only sound was their breathing and the pound of blood in her ears. He was waiting.

'I want you, Khalid,' she whispered at last.

'And I want you, Maggie, my beautiful wife.'

He surged forward, positioning himself between her legs, and propped himself on muscled arms above her. The air was electric with anticipation as his heat surrounded her.

Heaven was in the deliberate glide of his erection against her slick folds. He was hard and heavy and potently virile. Even the brush of tickling hair on his legs against her sensitive inner thighs excited her.

'I need you, Maggie. Now.'

She looked up into the obsidian glint of his eyes and knew she wanted this, wanted him, more than anything. What she felt for her husband was stronger than pride, more potent than a lifetime's self-doubt, headier than anything that had gone before.

'Yes,' she gasped.

A second later he took her, fast and quick and urgent, with a breathless rhythm that confounded her lungs. But she didn't care. He wanted her, desired her. Just as she craved Khalid with every particle of her being.

The connection between them was so strong. Even when the climax broke upon her, he held her with his gaze and when the world splintered around her she wasn't alone. He was there too.

Together, beyond words, they shuddered out their release, their hoarse cries of ecstasy mingling in the darkness. And still that bond was unbroken between them.

At last, as the trembling eased and she dragged in a deep unfettered breath, Khalid pulled her over to lie sprawled across him, her cheek on his chest where she could hear the rapid tattoo of his heart.

'Never doubt that I desire you, Maggie.' His voice was rich and slow and deep, like the warm eddies of contentment swirling through her body.

His hand palmed her hair and her eyes fluttered closed. She gave herself up to sleep with a feeling of utter well-being such as she'd never known in all her life.

When Maggie woke the sun was high. Her lips curled in a secret smile as she remembered the pleasure, the intimacy, the tenderness she and Khalid had shared last night.

Her husband had given her such a gift. Not just the physical pleasure of his body, though that had been magnificent. A coil of desire twisted anew inside her at the recollection.

More than that, Khalid had looked at her and really seen. He'd somehow understood the uncertainty that plagued her, a girl who'd grown up without female role models. Whose tentative steps towards femininity had been ruthlessly crushed by a disapproving father who'd treated her like the son he'd wanted. A girl who had earned acceptance only by eschewing her femininity in a male realm.

The echo of Khalid's urgent voice, husky with need, telling her again and again how beautiful she was, how he desired her, filled her like warm sunshine. The way he'd looked at her, the unsteady rumble in his voice as she'd touched him, the way he'd loved her again and again through the night and above all his words, mellifluous then urgent then gasping, had convinced her as nothing else could.

Khalid found her desirable. He'd wanted her.

She'd been resigned to a marriage on paper only, for the sake of their child. She'd never expected the sort of caring he'd shown last night.

Surely he cared for her. He desired her. That in itself was miraculous. More than that, he'd taken the time to convince her, thoroughly and unequivocally, that he found her beautiful. He'd made her feel like a woman, precious, treasured and appreciated.

She breathed out on an unsteady sigh as she recalled his infinite patience and care last night.

There was desire, respect, tenderness. Was it possible that one day, perhaps, there might be even more?

Instantly she pushed the idea aside. She'd be happy with her new life here. She wouldn't chase after rainbows.

'A surprise? For me?' Maggie looked into Khalid's dark eyes and hoped he couldn't read her emotions.

After last night's loving she felt strangely vulnerable, as if in opening her body to her new husband she'd also let him into her mind and her heart. She'd never before trusted anyone enough for that.

'Yes, a surprise. Come on.' He ushered her out of the pavilion and through the palace grounds.

She kept up easily as he matched his long-legged stride to hers. This morning he wore traditional clothes again, the long robe and headscarf plain yet elegant, emphasising the lean, hard muscle of his powerful body. Maggie fought to keep her eyes on the path and not watch him avidly.

They skirted a courtyard, heady with the scent of blossom, through an archway tiled in turquoise and gilt, and into a familiar yard. The aromas of horse and hay filled the air and she frowned. She'd thought Khalid preferred her not to visit the stables now they were married.

'In here.' He gestured to a building she'd never entered. Smaller but no less luxurious than the racing stables where she'd worked.

He nodded to a stable hand and led the way to a roomy stall. Maggie looked in to find a pair of huge liquid dark eyes staring back at her. The Arab mare was gorgeous, alert and exquisite. She whickered into Maggie's outstretched hand and moved closer. Automatically Maggie smoothed her hand over her silky milk-pale coat, sizing her up.

'She's a honey,' Maggie murmured as she sidestepped to get a better view. 'May I go in?'

'Of course.'

'Was she bred here?' she asked as she ran her hand over the mare. 'She really is a beauty.'

'No, up in the mountains,' Khalid responded. 'She's only been here a few days.'

'You must be very proud of her.'

'You approve, then?'

'What's not to approve?' The mare was a dream, and, if her affectionate nuzzling was a true indication, good-tempered too. Maggie wished she could take her through her paces.

'You have a good eye,' she murmured. But that was expected. On their wedding day she'd seen him in a crowd of horsemen, all outstanding riders, yet Khalid had stood out among the throng. The sight of him—proud, capable and handsome—had set her heart singing. Of course he knew his horseflesh.

'I'm pleased you think so.' His voice was a warm caress. 'She's yours.'

'Sorry?' Maggie jerked round to meet his eyes. They gleamed with a heat that set her limbs quivering. Thoughts of last night and Khalid's passion, her own uninhibited responses, swamped her with edgy remembrance.

'Afraa is yours. My wedding gift to you.'

'Mine?' Maggie couldn't believe her ears. He was giving her the mare? This perfect horse was hers?

Her eyes widened as he nodded. 'Did I not say so?'

Maggie stared, dumbfounded. To be given any gift at all…but to be given such a precious thing. She blinked, opened her mouth to say something, then shut it. She had no words. The mare gently butted her with its head and she faltered back a step towards the wall, overcome by his generosity and by the way her heart filled at the gesture.

'Maggie?' Khalid was frowning, those sleek dark brows plunging down in a V. His voice sounded rough with concern. 'What's wrong?'

She shook her head, biting her lip as emotion twisted hard and sharp inside her. She couldn't remember ever receiving a present. Her father had treated birthdays and Christmas as ordinary work days on the farm. Perhaps there'd been gifts when she was younger, but those years were a shadowy blur.

She couldn't tell Khalid that. It sounded too pathetic.

'Nothing's wrong.' The words came out as a croak and she tried again. 'Thank you, Khalid. She's gorgeous.'

Maggie wished she could throw herself into his arms and kiss him, show him how much his generosity meant to her. But he made no move to approach and she hesitated, a lifetime's training holding her back.

'Afraa, did you say?'

He nodded, his gaze still fixed on her. 'Named for her white coat.'

'It's a lovely name,' she murmured, and took a step closer, wishing she could express adequately how much this meant to her. How he filled her heart with joy. 'A lovely horse. Thank you.'

She saw a flicker of expression on his face. A shadow of the heat that had flared in his eyes last night as he'd made love to her time and again, till she'd felt wanted and desirable. Instantly her insides melted.

'We will need to consult your doctor about riding while pregnant. But even if you need to wait until after the birth, she will be here, waiting for you.' He paused. 'I know it's difficult for you, Maggie, giving up your job, your home. Adapting to a new life. I want you to be happy here.'

Maggie rubbed her hand over Afraa's silky coat, emotion choking her at his words. He really did *care*. She was awed at the thought Afraa was hers. No gift could have meant more.

'I'm afraid I don't have a present for you,' she said, regretting that it hadn't even occurred to her.

Khalid held out his hand. When she placed her palm in his he drew her close. His heat, his warm scent, surrounded her and instantly her body responded, awaking into tremulous awareness.

'There's no need for a gift,' he murmured as he stroked his other hand lightly over her abdomen, his fingers splayed. It was a purely possessive gesture, like the kindling look she read in his eyes.

'You're carrying my child. What more could I want from you?' His words were smug with satisfaction. Male pride and ownership echoed in his tone and in the proprietorial glide of his hand over her body.

Maggie froze. There was no room for equivocation or misunderstanding. He made it abundantly clear there was nothing else she could give her husband. Nothing that he would want from her. Except sex, of course.

All that mattered to him was the baby.

It was like stepping out of summer sunshine into a glacial cave. Out of dazzling brightness into wintry darkness. A cold, hard knot of pain formed in her abdomen. So cold it iced her veins in a ripple of frost that sent a shiver across her skin.

She told herself it didn't matter. Their marriage was for the baby. If sex between them was passionate and exquisitely tender, that was a bonus. It was far more than she'd expected from their union.

Then why did it hurt so to be reminded that their marriage was simply pragmatic and convenient?

CHAPTER TEN

'TELL me about the school you went to, Maggie.'

Khalid watched her head shoot up from the page she was reading.

'Pardon?'

'Your school. I want you to tell me about it.'

He'd failed all evening to concentrate on the new plans for outreach education. His mind kept slipping to the woman on the other side of the sitting room and the change in her since she'd accepted his gift.

The mare had been a perfect wedding present, or so he'd thought. Maggie's eyes had glowed with delight, her face transformed by her rare beautiful smile. The impact had struck him deep in his chest, for a moment depriving him of oxygen.

Then inexplicably the light inside her had been extinguished.

It irked him that he had no idea why. One minute she'd been ecstatic. The next the shutters of reserve had slammed down, closing her off from him. And she'd stayed like that.

'Why do you want to hear about my school?' Her eyes were golden in the lamplight. They shimmered with doubt.

He got up from his desk, stretching. His eyes narrowed as he saw her furtive glance slip over him. He suppressed a satisfied smile. That was one area where he and Maggie connected—in their physical passion.

Her sexual response to him was deliciously enticing. A

mixture of innocence and erotic abandon that he found increasingly addictive.

He wanted to make love to her right there on the sofa. Make her come alive in his arms. His body throbbed with hungry anticipation.

Yet it wasn't Maggie's body he needed to win right now, but her mind, her guarded self.

He paced across to the sofa and sat beside her. Close enough to be conscious of her scent, her warmth, hear her soft, quick breathing.

'You were educated in the country, weren't you?' He gave her an easy smile. 'I'm working on a scheme to educate children in isolated areas. I'm interested to hear about the system where you grew up.'

Maggie shrugged and closed her equestrian magazine. 'It wasn't anything special. Just a small rural school.'

'How small? I've got options for building premises and for teachers who travel from place to place, going to the students.'

He saw a glint of interest in her expression and congratulated himself for hitting on the right topic. If he could get her talking, relaxing, he'd find a way to break through her reserve.

'I've never heard of travelling teachers before,' she said slowly. 'In the outback they have long-distance schooling, where students talk to their teachers on the radio and use the internet.'

Khalid nodded. 'That could be an option when we get proper internet coverage for the whole country.' He paused. 'What was your school like?'

He genuinely wanted to know. His curiosity about her grew by the day. Even after the physical intimacy they'd shared, there was so much he didn't know. For the first time in years he genuinely wanted to learn more about a woman. To understand her. The realisation intrigued him.

'Tiny, one classroom. A single teacher taught all the grades until students left for high school.'

'And it worked?'

'It was terrific.' She nodded and he caught a trace of enthusiasm in her expression. It lit her face.

'Ah, I suspect you were an A-grade pupil.'

She shook her head. 'Unfortunately not.'

'You surprise me.' He'd already discovered Maggie to be intelligent and eager to learn. The dedication with which she'd pursued her language lessons impressed him.

She shrugged and looked down at the magazine in her hands. 'It was a long trek to school and sometimes I was needed on the farm instead.'

'Your father kept you home to work?' That surprised him, even though it wasn't uncommon in his country. 'I thought school was compulsory in Australia.'

'It is.' Her mouth twisted in a grim smile. 'My father made sure I went often enough that the authorities didn't have an excuse to intervene.'

'They might have thought you were playing truant by choice. It's not uncommon among teenagers.' But even as he spoke he responded to the pain in her voice.

Her head lifted abruptly and he read tension in her eyes. 'Oh, this started well before that. It began when I was eight.'

Eight! He tried to imagine Maggie at that age. Her delicate features, her slim frame. She'd have been a will-o'-the-wisp, a dainty creature. Fury sizzled in his blood that there'd been no one to stand up for her when she was so young and vulnerable.

'He should have been looking after you.' Outrage spilled the words from his lips. Her situation wasn't unique but that didn't stop the slow throb of anger. The intensity of his fury sideswiped him.

Again that tiny shrug of her stiff shoulders. 'He thought my duty was to him and to the property. He never understood that I wanted to do anything else.'

'Like train as a vet.' He remembered her saying that when they'd discussed her moving to Shajehar.

She nodded. 'It wouldn't have worked anyway. I didn't have time to study. Nor the money to go away to university.'

'You do now,' he murmured, reaching out and taking her hand. It was a gesture of compassion, intended to comfort her. Strange how the feel of her slender fingers in his sparked such pleasure, such satisfaction in him. Something about Maggie made him feel more…grounded, more complete than he had in a long time. Perhaps because it was so long since he'd felt personally responsible for anyone else.

Her eyes, wide and wondering, met his and a jolt of electricity sheared through him. What was this connection he felt with Maggie? It was more than just physical. He was unnerved by its potency, wary of this inexplicable force. But it was there, real and undeniable.

'You were serious? I really could study here?' Excitement coloured her voice. 'I didn't think you meant it. I assumed as your wife I couldn't have a career.'

'You couldn't take on a full-time load,' he said slowly, considering. 'You'd still have official duties.' And, in time, more children. He felt a burn of pleasurable anticipation at the idea of making more babies with his wife. 'But I don't see why you shouldn't train to be a vet if you really want to.'

'Khalid.' Her eyes shone bright and excited. 'That's wonderful. Thank you.' Her other hand closed round his, enveloping him with her warmth. His chest swelled at the sight of her smile, the awareness of her happiness.

So much pleasure at such a simple thing. Maggie was a unique woman. No wonder he'd come to…care for her. He lifted one hand to her cheek, slid it along the delicate beauty of her face.

'I'm glad to make you happy, little one. You deserve happiness.' He paused, the information she'd revealed still weighing on him. 'Perhaps it would have been better if your father hadn't raised you after your mother died. Weren't there other relatives to take you into their family?'

The smile froze on her face. 'Maggie?' He kept his voice mellow, not sharp. But a spike of anxiety shot through him.

'My mother didn't die,' she murmured at last. 'At least as far as I know.'

He palmed her cheek again and felt a tremor shake her as she drew in a jerky breath. He cursed the fact that he hadn't thought to question her earlier when she'd said there'd only been her father. He'd jumped to conclusions.

'What happened?'

Her gaze dipped, her shoulders rising in a shrug that was neither easy nor convincing. 'She left. Just walked out. When I was eight I came home one day and she'd gone.'

She'd left Maggie with that brute of a father.

Raw, aching emotion lay behind her staccato words. He could sense it welling inside her; taste its bitterness on his own tongue. Khalid felt helpless, faced with this anguish he could do nothing to assuage. An anguish that must have gnawed at her for years.

'I'm sorry, Maggie.' The words were inadequate, too little and too late. But he had to say them. It was doubtful she heard; she seemed focused on a distant place.

'I haven't heard from them since,' she whispered.

'Them?' What had he missed? 'Maggie? Who are you talking about?'

She looked up. There were no tears in her eyes. Yet the weary acceptance of pain he read there was more confronting than the sight of weeping. Instinctively he realised it was an acceptance she'd worked too long and hard to achieve. Tension knotted his stomach. He wished he could wipe away the hurt.

'When she left us my mother didn't go alone. She took Cassie, my little sister.' Maggie drew a deep, shuddering breath. 'But she didn't wait to take me too.'

'Maggie.' Khalid dragged her onto his lap, tucking her head beneath his chin. He hugged her close, as if he could protect her from the pain of the past. Slowly he rocked her, comforting her as he would a child, hoping the motion and the flow of husky words would help her find peace.

What this woman had been through. Rejected by her mother, neglected and used by her father. Forced to be strong and independent far too young. Khalid recalled her intriguing mix of forthrightness and self-doubt the night they'd met.

No wonder she'd agreed to marry him when she'd realised the security he could provide their child. The sort of security she'd never had.

He tugged her tighter against his thudding heart, inhaling the scent he'd become addicted to: roses and Maggie.

It was his duty to care for her.

But this didn't feel like duty. This was far more. Something gut-deep, something he couldn't put a name to. He couldn't bear to see her suffer.

'We will find them,' he vowed.

She shook her head. 'I don't think that's possible. I tried but they must have changed their name. I even hired an investigator when I could afford it.'

'Then we will hire a better one. No matter how long it takes we'll find them eventually.' He caressed her petal-soft cheek.

'Thank you, Khalid.' Her sigh was a shudder of pent-up pain that arrowed straight to his heart.

Maggie knew Khalid well enough to understand that his word was his bond. One day he'd find her lost family. She had no doubt about that. And the realisation brought an unexpected sense of peace.

He'd given her back her hope.

No matter how long the search took, she had faith now that it wouldn't be in vain, even if it took years.

Theirs might be only a marriage of convenience, but her new husband had just given her a precious commitment. One that had nothing to do with their child. His promise meant more than anything she'd ever received in her life.

Her throat tightened.

'Maggie? It will be all right.' His voice soothed.

'I know.' She pulled back in his arms and offered a shaky smile. 'I believe you.'

Dark eyes held hers and something powerful pulsed between them, warming her right through. 'Family is important,' he murmured. 'It's part of what makes us who we are.'

She nodded. 'You do understand.'

For most of her life she'd felt adrift, alone, despite being shackled by family obligation. If she could hear her mother's side of things, perhaps she could put the past behind her.

Though, here in Khalid's arms, she felt as if she'd already moved on with her life. As if she was ready for the future, whatever it held.

'What about you, Khalid? How did your family influence you?' She'd never broached any such personal issues before. But she'd just stripped her emotions bare. Surely she had a right to know him a little better.

Gently he stroked her cheek, brushed the hair from her face, and she almost purred aloud at the frisson of delight vibrating from his touch.

'I learned independence from my family.' His words, when they came, dragged her abruptly from a dreamy stupor.

'My father was supremely self-indulgent. More interested in his mistresses than his home life.'

Her heart contracted at the image he painted. Yet the proud tilt of Khalid's head told her he didn't seek sympathy.

'In a way that was fortunate. I was brought up by my mother who loved me unconditionally, and by my uncle Hussein, who taught me responsibility and duty, as well as a passion for Shajehar. When I was old enough, I went to boarding-school. I wasn't the heir, so my father had no expectations of me. He left me to my own devices.'

'It doesn't sound as if you minded.' Maggie wished her

father had been less controlling. She'd learned self-sufficiency but had rarely experienced the luxury of true independence.

Khalid shrugged. 'My older half-brother was the apple of my father's eye. He was indulged and spoiled. Never expected to work or take responsibility for his actions.'

Khalid's mouth curved into a smile that made her heart somersault. 'Instead of sitting here waiting to inherit, I was free to take my own path. An engineering degree in Britain. Business masters in the US, then development projects around the globe till I was ready to create a place for myself here.'

Maggie watched his face light with pleasure and enthusiasm. Clearly those years carving his own way had been a challenge, not a chore. 'Being left to your own devices hasn't held you back.'

He shook his head. 'We create our own future.'

His hand slipped down to rest possessively over her stomach, his warmth branding her. Yet this time, for reasons she didn't understand, Maggie wasn't upset by his proprietorial touch.

She stared into his heated gaze and felt a thrill of anticipation ripple through her. Her husband wanted her with a passion that never failed to amaze her.

She pressed her hand over his, enjoying the sensation of silky hair and sinewed strength under her palm and the heat of his hand imprinting on her belly.

Maybe, just maybe, over time they could build something far stronger than a merely convenient marriage.

CHAPTER ELEVEN

'IF YOU stand there, Your Highness, you'll be able to see the monitor.'

Instead of moving away, Khalid gave Maggie a reassuring smile and leaned close.

'All ready?' he murmured.

She nodded. 'I'm fine.'

She'd been on edge all morning, waiting for the ultrasound. Inevitably Khalid had picked up on her nervousness. She'd been touched by his decision not to leave and tackle the paperwork and petitioners and negotiations that usually filled his days. Instead he'd spent hours with her, showing her parts of the palace she'd never seen, exotic historic treasures, as well as places he'd haunted as a boy.

His tales of mischief and adventure and of long-ago Shajehani history had been a deliberate ploy to stop her dwelling on the nagging, irrational fear that the ultrasound might reveal something wrong with the baby.

'You'd better move so the poor woman can do her job,' she whispered.

He squeezed her hand. His reassurance warmed her and she smiled.

'I'm glad you're here.'

'I wouldn't miss it.'

She didn't doubt it. Their baby meant as much to him as it did to her. It was what bound them together.

The technician took her place beside Maggie as Khalid moved away.

'Now, I'll put this on ready for the ultrasound.' The technician smoothed gel over Maggie's abdomen and she flinched.

'Are you all right?'

'I'm fine.' Her lips curved up at Khalid's concern. 'It's just cold.' She could almost believe he was as nervous and excited as she.

'Here we are.' The technician ran the ultrasound device over Maggie's belly and she held her breath. For what seemed ages the screen showed shadowy images. Then...*there*. She stared, unable to believe her eyes as the screen showed the baby—real, alive, wonderful!

Her baby. Hers and Khalid's, alive inside her.

It was a miracle. Her body had confirmed in so many ways that she was carrying a child. But nothing, not even the couple of bouts of morning sickness, had made her pregnancy seem so real.

Tenderness filled her. Wonder, and a joy so profound it had to be shared.

'Khalid! Isn't it the most amazing thing you've ever seen?' Impulsively she turned to her husband, her hand stretched out instinctively towards him.

He didn't notice. His face was frozen as he stared at the screen. Tension vibrated off him in waves. What was he thinking?

'Khalid?' Her voice was a cracked whisper as anxiety coiled tight inside her. This time he heard. Slowly he blinked and turned his head, meeting her gaze with a look of such burning intensity that she trembled. He looked...different. Not like the man she'd got to know these past weeks.

His mouth curled in what ought to have been a smile. Yet somehow it lacked the reassurance of a few moments ago. He stepped close, his hand curving tightly round hers. As if he never intended to let go.

'Does the baby seem all right?' he asked abruptly. 'Is everything normal?'

'Yes, Your Highness. So far everything looks as it should.'

Khalid stared at monitor in awe, struck dumb by what he saw.

A baby. *His* baby. The breath sucked out from his lungs as shock held him rigid. Nothing had prepared him for the reality of seeing his child on the screen. Avidly his gaze traced the outline of its head, the curled body with knees up. The rapid throb of that little heart.

Emotion held Khalid's chest in a vice as he gazed at the miracle before him. The whispered conversation between Maggie and the technician was muted by the roar of blood in his ears.

Once he'd thought he'd never have a child. It had almost been a relief, knowing he wouldn't pass on any family traits. There was precious little from his father's family he'd want the next generation to inherit.

Shahina had been so eager for a baby. For *their* baby. It had been a cruel blow, learning she'd never be able to bear a child. His heart hammered as guilt speared him. The one thing he'd never been able to give the woman he loved. Now here he stood watching his unborn babe kicking in the womb. A child created by a single act of intimacy. A child who, statistically, shouldn't even have been conceived, given the precautions he'd taken.

A child he wanted with every fibre of his being.

Khalid's mouth stretched in a grimace of pain as emotions, confused, painful and exciting, swept him.

Automatically he tried to clamp a lid on them. He'd told himself for so long that there was no place for emotion in his life. After his initial white-hot grief eight years ago he'd survived by not having feelings. Not intimate, soul-deep feelings that threatened to unman him.

Not feelings like those evoked by the sight of his innocent, unborn child in Maggie's womb. By the sight of Maggie, tears of excitement in her eyes, as she shared the thrill of this new life they'd created.

Something squeezed painfully hard inside him. An unfamiliar sensation that scared the hell out of him.

His breath hissed between clenched teeth as he realised that with this child, this marriage, he'd inadvertently opened himself up to the sort of emotional commitment he'd eschewed for most of his adult life.

But there was no going back.

He wanted this child. He would cherish it, keep it and its mother safe. A fierce surge of possessiveness roared through him.

His hand tightened on Maggie's. He'd look after them both. Whatever it took. They were his.

Khalid's face was a stiff mask as he escorted Maggie back to their apartments. He looked like a man facing an unwanted reality.

A hollow feeling yawned in the pit of Maggie's belly. This morning's smiling companion had disappeared, replaced by a man she didn't know. A man of controlled, punctilious courtesy.

The memory of his searing look back at the clinic still made her heart race. That stare had ravaged her soul, filled her with doubt and confusion. She hadn't been able to read his thoughts, only his spiralling tension, the fact that he hadn't grinned in spontaneous delight at seeing their baby. He hadn't smiled at all. Something was wrong.

Was he regretting the baby? Resenting her?

She pursed her mouth to hide the ragged hurt tearing through her. She clasped her hands tight, holding the envelope with the ultrasound photo carefully between them.

It would be all right. Of course it would.

After seeing Khalid with children, Maggie knew he'd love their baby once it was born. He had a warm, caring nature. A man like that wouldn't be able to resist loving his own flesh and blood.

Maggie wasn't foolhardy enough to expect him to extend that love to include her. It was enough that he was kind and generous. An ardent lover. He'd be a wonderful father.

'After you.' He held open the door to their sitting room and stood aside, waiting for her to enter.

'Thank you.' She grimaced, hearing her stilted tone.

Silently she crossed the room, pausing before the antique silk-covered settees grouped cosily together.

'Do you need to lie down? You look tired.'

Maggie shrugged, thankful that was all he'd read in her face. Not the confusion or the pain that lay so close to the surface. 'I'm a little weary, but no more than usual.' She'd been lucky so far with an uneventful pregnancy.

'I'll leave you to rest in that case.' He sounded relieved. He stood several paces away, as if reluctant to get close. Cold shivered along her arms.

How different from this morning when he'd touched her so readily as he'd guided her through the old palace. That easy camaraderie had vanished. Did he regret their marriage? Regret their child? No, not that. He wanted their baby at least.

Suddenly Maggie realised how desperately she needed his strong arms about her. The reassurance of his embrace. She'd come to rely on that more and more. She'd taken comfort and strength from his generous warmth and physical tenderness. She rubbed her hands over her arms as a chill invaded her body.

'Are you all right?' His voice was sharp and she averted her face, not wanting to reveal the pain that held her taut.

She didn't know what had happened back there at the clinic. She just knew that something had changed. That once more she felt adrift and alone.

'Yes, of course.' She stepped away hurriedly, towards the book-lined end of the room where Khalid sometimes worked. 'I'll just put this picture somewhere safe.'

She found herself in front of the floor-to-ceiling bookshelves. She'd walked here at random, needing to get away from his acute gaze. Now she stood, staring blankly at the fine collection of books in English, Arabic and French. The rustle of paper reminded her of the envelope she clutched in her hands. The photo of their baby.

A shaft of pain lanced her chest. Suddenly she wanted nothing more than to be completely alone, away from the bitter-sweet temptation of Khalid's presence. She swung round towards the desk.

'Do you mind if I put it here for now?' She didn't look up or wait for his agreement. She gabbled on, needing to fill the silence. 'I'll get an album, a nice big one to put lots of baby photos in. But for now it'll be safe here where it can be kept flat.'

She dragged open the top drawer filled with pens, rulers, a calculator and various stationery equipment.

'Do you think I could find one at the souk? Zeinab said she'd take me there one day soon. Or would I need to go to a department store?' She pushed the drawer in and reached for the next one. This was better. Notepads and soft leather-bound books. The photo would be safe here.

Maggie lifted a book and placed the precious envelope beneath it. 'There, that's perfect. Tomorrow I'll buy an album.' She lifted her head and flashed a brief smile in his direction, vaguely noticing that he'd stopped on the other side of the desk.

At the same time she realised it wasn't a book she held but a large leather photo frame. Her fingers traced the padded outline of the frame and the glass protecting the picture. Automatically she turned it over in her hands. Khalid's abrupt movement, hurriedly stilled, snared her attention. She took in his hands, knotted in fists at his sides, and the heavy throb of his pulse at the base of his neck, visible even from here. His dark eyes were blank.

That non-expression scared her. Suddenly she knew she'd
trespassed into private territory.

Anxiety whispered through her.

Slowly she lowered the frame into the open drawer, her
eyes fixed on his. He didn't even blink. Maggie's pulse sped
up. She felt as if she held something living, breathing and
taboo in her hands. Or was her imagination working overtime?
Khalid hadn't said anything. He just stood there…waiting.

Her hands went to the handle of the drawer and she began
to slide it in. Still no reaction from Khalid.

See, she was imagining things. Maybe he was right and she
was overtired. She'd been putting in so many extra hours on
her language lessons and her visits with Zeinab to community
centres. Maybe she'd been overdoing it, trying so hard to fit
into this strange new world and find a place for herself here.

The thought died abruptly as her gaze lowered and she
knew in an instant that she hadn't imagined a thing.

There was an audible hiss as she sucked in her breath.

Khalid looked so young. Impossibly young and handsome,
like some glowing prince in a fairy tale. And that smile. It
stopped the breath in her throat. She'd never seen him smile
like that, with utter joy, as if he held the world in his hands.

Absently she reached down and stroked her fingertips over
his face in the photo. The glass was cold beneath her touch.

He took a step towards her as she spoke.

'What was her name?'

Khalid halted abruptly an arm's length from her. She didn't
look up. Instead her eyes were fixed on the face of the woman
smiling up at him in the picture. Maggie had a sinking feeling
that she knew exactly who the woman was. With her henna-
decorated hands, her rich costume and familiar jewels, it
wasn't hard to guess.

Maggie snatched her hand from the photo as if it might
bite, bracing her arm instead on the edge of the desk.

'Her name was Shahina.' His tone was coolly blank. Instinctively Maggie understood it hid emotions too strong to share.

She looked down into the radiant faces, into the love that shone unmistakably in their eyes. It was there in the way they leaned together, in the shared intimacy captured in that moment even though they did no more than hold hands.

They looked beautiful, glorious.

Suddenly she felt worse than a fool for the stupid secret hopes she'd been unable to repress completely. The hopes of a real marriage one day. A fulfilling relationship. She felt a fraud, an imposter.

'She was a beautiful bride.' A raw ache filled Maggie.

'That photo was taken on our wedding day. Ten years ago.' His voice was clipped and unemotional, but he couldn't hide the pain that tinted his words.

Maggie heard a noise like the echo of a heavy metal door clanging shut, leaving her once more alone on the outside. Was it the thud of her heart? Had she imagined it?

It didn't matter. The truth was there, clear to see. Khalid had been utterly, vibrantly, unselfconsciously in love with his bride.

Maggie tasted the salt tang of blood as her teeth sank into her bottom lip. At least it stifled the burble of inappropriate laughter that threatened to spill out. How different her own wedding had been. She wondered if the guests had seen the difference, had known that their sheikh had married this time, not for love, but out of duty.

Of course they had. It must have been blatantly obvious.

How wrong she'd been, assuming it was disapproval she'd read in his expression when he'd said he no longer had a wife. He'd looked so furious she'd jumped to the conclusion there'd been a divorce. Now she realised his rigid control had been because she'd touched a raw nerve. The mention of his wife had evoked too many memories.

Finally she found her voice, though it was shaky. 'You must have been very young.'

'I was twenty. She was eighteen. But we'd known each other all our lives. We grew up together.'

They'd shared so much.

'She was very, very beautiful,' she whispered.

His first wife had been everything Maggie wasn't. Tiny, vivacious, lusciously curved, with sloe-dark eyes that sparkled, abundant black hair and perfect features. She was like a pretty doll, yet it was the utter happiness in her smile that made her so impossibly gorgeous.

Any woman would feel inferior to the lovely Shahina.

Jealousy stabbed her. Not for Shahina's exquisite looks, but because she had the one thing Maggie knew now she could never win for herself. Khalid's love.

Maggie had basked in the ecstasy of Khalid's solicitude, his easy companionship, his urgent passion. Only now did she acknowledge that wasn't enough. That, greedily, she wanted more.

Because she'd discovered she felt far too much for him. Because respect and companionship and sizzling sex showed her a glimpse of how life could be. If only Khalid's relationship with her were driven by his heart and not duty.

She slid the drawer completely closed and leaned forward, her grip on the desk white-knuckled. She'd seen enough. Her heart thudded painfully against her ribcage, so hard it must surely bruise.

'She was always full of life.' His words gave nothing away, but Maggie could feel the pain behind the words.

'What happened?' She didn't look up. Didn't want to meet his eyes and see the memories there.

Abruptly he moved, pacing in front of the desk, then stopping to stare out the window.

'She was asthmatic. Severely asthmatic. Her parents were told she might not survive into adulthood.'

Maggie's heart squeezed, knowing what was coming.

'Medication and a treatment plan kept the condition under

control. But she had an attack one day when we were far from the capital.' He paused and she heard him suck in a deep breath.

'It was so sudden. The medication did no good. She needed a hospital but we couldn't get her there in time. My father was entertaining VIPs and had commandeered even the medical emergency helicopters to take his guests on a desert picnic. By the time we diverted one to pick her up, it was too late.'

'I'm so sorry,' Maggie whispered, feeling the inadequacy of those words as she raised her head and took in the taut outline of Khalid's frame.

'It was a long time ago. Eight years.'

But not long enough to ease his grief. Now she understood why, despite his attentiveness, his consideration, Khalid had always seemed to hold a vital part of himself back.

Maggie swallowed down the salty, bitter taste of pain. Pain for the lovely Shahina, dead so early. Pain for Khalid who clearly had never got over the loss of his first wife. Pain for herself, the woman who could never fill Shahina's shoes. The woman who was destined always to be an inadequate surrogate in Khalid's life.

Despite his assurances, it must be incredibly difficult for him to take Maggie in his arms. To have her in his bed, his life, instead of the woman he'd loved.

When they were together, did he think of Shahina? Did the night-time darkness blanket the truth just enough so he could pretend it was Shahina he held, not Maggie?

A sob rocketed up in Maggie's throat and she clung to the desk, needing all her willpower to stifle it.

He never promised love. He's giving you all he can. You should be thankful for what you've got.

But this time it was too hard to accept. She didn't want to be his duty wife, she realised on a surge of defiant emotion. She wanted to fight for what she wanted, for Khalid. She wanted to win him for herself.

She loved him. Had fallen for the proud, honourable man

who'd given her tenderness, introduced her to pleasure, promised her security. Who'd married her because he'd felt he had to but who had made her happier than she'd ever been.

'Where are you going?' His voice was abrupt, jerking her out of her thoughts.

She paused in mid-step and turned just enough to send a vague glance in his direction, not daring to meet his gaze. Her feelings were too raw. She feared he'd read her as easily as a book.

'To the stables. I haven't seen Afraa all day. Besides, the children are due to visit.'

'I'd forgotten. I'll come with you.'

'But what about your work? You've already taken the whole morning off.' She was startled enough to meet his gaze head-on. It was like being sucked deep into a swirling tide. The blankness was gone from his eyes, replaced by a look she couldn't interpret. A look that scalded the blood beneath her skin and snagged her breath.

'The kingdom won't fall apart if I spend a day with my family.'

His family… Of course, he meant his cousin's children.

Maggie lifted her chin, hiding her hurt, as well as the inevitable, traitorous thrill of pleasure as he took her hand and drew her towards the door.

CHAPTER TWELVE

KHALID left his office and turned into a corridor, his steps slowing at the surprising sound of feminine laughter.

A door was ajar and he paused to look in. The room was full of women, like brightly coloured birds in their traditional finery. He knew from their costume that they'd travelled far from their home in the mountains.

He took in the group, clustered around vast trays of syrup pastries and steaming tea. His gaze came to rest on a figure in amber silk. Tendrils of desire snaked through him as he remembered clasping her swelling curves close last night while they shuddered through another mind-blowing climax together.

Maggie spoke in Arabic, careful but fluent.

'It's lucky for me you are so patient with my poor attempts to speak your language.'

There was another ripple of giggles, interspersed with praise for how quickly Her Highness had learned.

Khalid stared. He'd known Maggie's language skills had come on remarkably. The hours practising with her tutor were paying off. But he'd never heard her so confident.

'It's important for me to speak your language,' Maggie said. 'This is my home now. Besides, one day I want to go to university and I need to understand the lessons.'

The women's questions came thick and fast. Could a woman really study at university? Could anyone attend?

Maggie answered their questions with the help of the official at her side. She even mentioned the new scholarships for students from distant localities. The scholarships that she herself had suggested to Khalid only weeks before.

'So,' she went on, 'one day your children might study at university. But first they need to attend the school being built for them.'

There was a babble of conversation as the women discussed the reluctance of some of their menfolk to let their daughters attend classes.

Just then Maggie looked across the room and saw him. Colour rose in her cheeks and her lips formed a tempting pout of surprise that instantly ignited a lick of flame inside him. Other heads swivelled and the conversation died. Hastily he stepped away out of sight, knowing the women wouldn't be comfortable in his presence.

It was a shame to end the session. Maggie's informal chats had achieved far more than his official efforts to persuade remote villagers to support the new schools.

But what preoccupied him was the way Maggie's face had closed as soon as she'd seen him. That mask of reserve she'd perfected lately blanked out all trace of the vivacity he'd witnessed moments before.

With others she smiled and laughed. Never with him.

Khalid felt a surge of impatience. He was sick of being excluded, treated as a polite stranger except in bed. There she came alive, an uninhibited seductress in his arms. Though recently even there he'd had to persuade her into intimacy. Her earlier spontaneity had gone.

Nowadays she seemed absorbed in her work for his reforms. The reforms he'd thrown himself into more and more as their relationship grew increasingly strained, their conversation stilted and too careful.

Once he would have welcomed her restraint. The fact that

Maggie didn't cling. He'd been a loner so long, shunning emotional entanglements since Shahina.

But now…something had changed.

Since the day he'd seen the photo of himself and Shahina and realised the love they'd shared, though still real, was a faded memory.

Realised he was greedy enough, selfish enough, to want more than a memory to sustain him.

'Khalid.' Maggie sounded breathless as she joined him.

The rich fabric of her *abaya* skimmed burgeoning curves. Each day she grew more desirable. The muscles in his belly tightened. He couldn't get enough of her. The faint scent of roses and warm woman reached him. He took her hand before she could hide it away.

'Khalid?' She sounded nervous. Not pleased to see him.

Frowning, he led her along the wide hallway, back towards his offices.

'I didn't expect to see you in this part of the palace,' he murmured as he ushered her into his private suite and snicked the lock behind them.

Her glorious hazel-gold gaze widened, then darted away.

'Weren't you supposed to be resting?' he asked.

'I don't need to rest. Not that much, anyway.'

'You didn't get much sleep last night.'

To his delight a blush rose from her throat and tinted her cheekbones. Maggie's physical response to him was a perpetual pleasure.

She moved a few paces away, as if uncomfortable. By night she was his every erotic fantasy. But by day it was another story. Increasingly she was cool, composed, distant. Always busy, with her language lessons or the cultural and social activities devised by his aunt Zeinab.

Too busy for his liking, he realised. More and more he found himself wanting to share news with Maggie, see her reaction or simply have her close. It was disconcerting to discover how much he wanted to share with her. But always he held back. Ingrained habit acquired over eight long years had made him keep his distance and each day Maggie's formidable reserve grew more rigid. One seemed to feed off the other.

He watched her rub a palm down her lower back and stretch. The movement pulled the fabric of her dress taut over her proud breasts and ripe belly and instantly Khalid felt desire coil like a spring in his lower body. He'd always found Maggie's lissom body gorgeous, but there was something decadently luscious about her now she was so obviously pregnant. Carrying his growing baby.

Khalid's pulse quickened.

'Come.' He held out his hand. 'I have something to show you.' The feel of her hand resting in his pleased him. Such a little thing, but so right.

'What are you smiling about?' she asked warily.

'I was just thinking I could have saved a fortune by leaving all the consultation for the schools project to you and Zeinab. The input from your meetings has been invaluable.'

'Really? The women respond so well to Zeinab. They respect her and trust her.' A smile brightened Maggie's face before she hastily looked away. It bothered him that she could light up with enthusiasm for a public works project but not for her own husband.

'But my aunt wasn't there today.' Maggie had run the session alone and she'd done it brilliantly.

She shrugged, not meeting his eyes. 'The women were very polite.'

'Or perhaps they were thrilled to spend time alone with you,' he murmured. 'Did you consider that?'

She shook her head. 'What thrilled them is the chance to send their children to school.'

Khalid wished his wife would smile at him with even half the enthusiasm she felt for the welfare of strangers.

He was annoyed with himself. Could he possibly be jealous of his people? His own scheme?

'Here,' he said abruptly. 'I want you to see the latest plans. They just arrived.' Without waiting for an answer he tugged her to the meeting table, selecting a roll of plans he'd pored over earlier. He felt the resistance in her stiff body and kept her hand shackled in his.

'Look.' He spread them out. 'See how the architect has adapted the design for extra space? A nurse will attend a couple of days a week to trial a mother and baby clinic.'

'Really?' Avidly she leaned forward, planting her palms on the mahogany table. 'That was one of the suggestions we put forward. The women will be so excited. Where will this be built?'

Khalid answered her questions, pointing out the locations on a map of the provinces, torn between pleasure at her enthusiasm and chagrin that it was for a set of blueprints. He shut his eyes, revelling in the warm press of her body close to his and the rich earthy scent of woman that made his blood tingle.

He wanted his wife. Here. Now.

Khalid let his hands skim down her sides, circling back to rest on the taut, erotic curve of her *derrière*.

She froze, her body bent forward, arms braced on the vast table. 'Khalid?' Her voice was sharp. 'What are you doing?'

'I want you.' His voice betrayed the extremity of his need. He stepped close behind her, his body blanketing hers. He licked the sensitive spot behind her ear, then nuzzled her neck in an open-mouthed kiss.

'No! Not now.' Her voice ended on a gasp of sensual pleasure even as her body stiffened against his touch.

'Yes, now.'

'And you always get what you want, don't you?' The bitterness in her tone was new, pulling him up short. Was it possible she truly didn't want this? Disbelief slammed into him.

Surely she couldn't pretend this spark between them was one-sided. She'd never faked her desire for him!

He skimmed his hands over her breasts and felt her nipples pucker. Instantly his erection throbbed in response. He laved the sensitive spot behind her ear and felt her shake.

'Are you saying you don't want it too?'

'I…'

Shudders racked her as he bunched the silk of her dress in his fists, drawing it higher until he could slip one hand down, under the stretchy lace of her underwear, to follow the delicious contours of her backside.

'You…what, Maggie?' She tried to step to one side. Implacably he stopped her, simply by widening his stance so his legs surrounded hers. There was no way out.

'Tell me you don't want this, wife, and I will stop.'

He was hard with need. Harder, more aroused than he could ever remember being. He ached for her with a throbbing hunger that threatened his self-possession.

'Khalid, please, I…' Her words ended on a sigh as his hand slid possessively over the swollen curves that cradled their child and delved again beneath lace. He arrowed in on the pleasure point between her legs. A tremor shook her and he smiled as he nipped at her earlobe. Yes! In this at least she couldn't hold back from him.

With a groan of surrender she pushed her pelvis against his touch, just as he nudged her legs wider with his knee and let his erection surge up against her buttocks.

'Say it,' he demanded, his voice hoarse. 'Say you want me.'

'I…yes, Khalid. I want you.' It was a husky sigh of need.

He rewarded her with a gentle bite on that erotic zone below her ear, and the deliberately slow glide of his fingers against her clitoris.

'Someone could come in,' she gasped, but her hips were already rocking in an age old rhythm that told him all he needed to know about her arousal. The liquid heat sliding over his hand signalled a desire that matched his own. His pulse ratcheted up another notch.

She was his, all his. His wife, his lover. *His woman.*

He was determined to have all of her.

Khalid wrenched at his clothing, freeing himself so he could slip his erection against her soft, inviting curves as he tugged her underwear down, out of the way. His body shuddered in anticipation.

'No one will come in.' His voice was a stranger's, a strangled burr of lust.

He wanted Maggie so badly. So completely. It was more, even, than sex. This hunger for her was something primal, something he didn't understand. And it was growing more, not less, as time passed. He wanted to brand his possession of her in the most primitive way possible.

'It's broad daylight.' The words were a reedy thread of sound, a half-hearted protest. Even as she said it Maggie spread her legs, allowing him better access.

Khalid's smile of satisfaction was a grimace of tension. He positioned himself then slid slowly, forcefully, into her slick centre. With one hand he caressed her between her legs. The other he slid up, over her taut, round belly to the ripe swell of her breasts.

She cried out when he cupped her, rolling her nipple between his finger and thumb. Her whole body jerked with pleasure and he took advantage to thrust deeper inside.

'Why shouldn't I make love to my wife during the daytime?' He thrust aside the unspoken question at the back of his mind, the inexplicable matter of why he wanted her insatiably, why she was so important to him. For now it was enough to know he'd never desired a woman as he did Maggie.

He withdrew a fraction, then thrust again, further this time, each glorious centimetre a revelation in need and desire and ecstasy.

'Let me take you to paradise, Maggie.'

This time their loving was stronger, surer, deeper than anything he could remember. She'd got into his blood, his very soul and he was helpless to resist.

He didn't want to resist.

'Once more, my felicitations on your marriage. You've chosen well, my friend.'

Khalid followed King Osman's stare and spied Maggie chatting on the other side of the room with an executive of an international oil company. The company currently drilling on Shajehar's border with Osman's kingdom.

In the months since she'd come to Shajehar, Maggie had bloomed. She'd settled into her new role amazingly well, overcoming her diffidence as she grew in confidence. It had been like watching a beautiful rose open and blossom.

'Thank you, Osman. I appreciate your good wishes.'

Khalid's body tightened as he watched her. Maggie looked superb. At seven months pregnant she was more luscious than ever. The drape of shimmering fabric emphasised her perfect posture. She was elegant, eye-catching and far too sexy to be out in public.

He didn't miss the oil man's body language. He too was aware of Maggie as a desirable woman, though he was deferential.

Khalid had to stifle the primitive urge to pull her close or, better yet, immure her in the women's quarters of the old palace, as his ancestors would have done.

Maggie smiled with genuine warmth at something her companion said and jealousy bit into Khalid, bone-deep. How long since she'd smiled at him like that? He didn't want a stranger basking in those smiles she denied him. With each passing week the gulf between them yawned wider. She was slipping further from him each day, despite the intimacies they shared.

'No wonder you weren't interested in marrying my daughter,' Osman continued. 'Not when you'd discovered this lovely pearl.'

'Your daughter is a fine woman,' Khalid responded through gritted teeth. He hadn't missed the avaricious glitter in his companion's gaze, the knowing appreciation of a man who considered himself a connoisseur of women. 'I was honoured you should consider my brother's suggestion of a possible link between our families.'

And relieved when Osman had accepted with equanimity the news that Khalid had committed himself elsewhere.

'Ah, but my Fatin wouldn't have done for you. I see that now.'

Khalid repressed an impulse to steer Osman to the next room where he couldn't ogle Maggie. He didn't want any man looking at his wife like that. Especially not a lascivious old reprobate like Osman.

'I enjoyed a chat with your wife earlier,' Osman said. 'I found her to be a woman of sense. Very refreshing. She knows how to listen and when to speak up.' He cast a serious look at Khalid from under shaggy brows. 'You are a lucky man, my friend. Perhaps more than you know.'

The comment, at odds with Osman's usual preoccupation with physical beauty, surprised Khalid. He hadn't thought Osman so perceptive.

The other man was right. Khalid valued Maggie's common sense and quick mind. When it came to his reforms, her enthusiasm had overcome her diffidence. She'd helped him find perspective when barriers to change had seemed overwhelming.

'I couldn't agree more,' he said, watching her intently. 'I couldn't have chosen a better wife.'

Yet dissatisfaction gnawed at his belly. She was his helpmeet, the seductress in his bed and soon to be the mother of his child. But it wasn't enough. He wanted…more. He didn't want this distance between them.

Memories of the happiness, the closeness, he'd shared with

Shahina surfaced. To his amazement he realised *that* was what he wanted. A real marriage. A genuine relationship, not a convenient arrangement, hemmed in by the unspoken boundaries they'd both set.

Not a pale imitation of his first marriage, but something unique and special in its own right.

He thought of himself and Maggie, truly together. Man and wife in every sense of the word. For years he'd shied from anything that smacked of emotional commitment. Yet now, watching her move on to charm his aunt and uncle and a cluster of diplomats on the other side of the room, he understood that the little he had of her now would never satisfy him.

What would happen if he smashed through those no-go zones they'd erected? What if he opened himself totally to his wife? Would she, in turn, trust him with her innermost self, the woman she was at heart?

Suddenly he knew an overwhelming need to find out.

I can't do this anymore. I just can't.

Maggie's face ached from an evening of polite smiles. But that was nothing to the pain cramping her chest, the anguish of knowing she couldn't go on like this.

She listened to King Osman make his farewells to Khalid, the sound of their conversation washing over her.

She'd felt Khalid's gaze on her all through the reception, like a stroke of flame on her vulnerable skin. She'd seen the speculative look in his eye, the flare of heat, and felt a traitorous answering spark deep inside.

But sex wasn't enough anymore.

For months she'd done her best. She'd accepted what fate had handed her—a loveless marriage. She'd tried so hard to fit in even though she'd finally understood that Khalid could never reciprocate her feelings. He was still in love with Shahina.

Maggie couldn't compete with a ghost. She was too weary

to keep trying. Second-best wasn't enough for her anymore. Desire without love was, she'd learned, an empty sham.

'Come, Maggie.' Khalid's voice was rich and warm in her ear. He slid her arm through his and pulled her close. 'Time for bed.'

Instantly her treacherous body leapt at the promise in his tone, in the heat of his powerful body against hers. She looked around to see the elegant reception room deserted but for the servants. Osman had left for his guest suite.

It wasn't far to their apartments, but every step was torment. The heaven of being held close by the man she loved, the man who woke her senses to shivering awareness just with his proximity. The hell of knowing she couldn't bear this farce of intimacy any longer.

Each caress, each tender word tore her apart, for they meant nothing. Nothing more than that he found her a convenient companion. He'd never *love* her.

She shuddered to a halt just inside their sitting room and reefed her arm from his, barely noticing his look of surprise.

She deserved more from marriage. If she couldn't have a real marriage, surely she had the right to protect her sanity and her self-respect. She needed to get out of this dead-end relationship.

'Maggie? What's wrong?'

She looked up at the man who'd held himself carefully aloof from her all evening as protocol required. No matter how she pleased him in bed, no matter how hard she worked to fit into his world, he would always be just that. Aloof.

Was that how it had been between her parents? Love on one side and not on the other? Was that what had driven them apart?

Memories of the intimacies she and Khalid had shared made her insides churn. She'd sold herself to him. For security and support for her baby. For the vain hope that love might grow from physical desire.

No more. It was time she stood on her own two feet. For as long as she put up with this arrangement she doomed herself to unhappiness.

'I'm going to bed.' Her voice sounded incredibly calm. But then, now her decision was made, she felt strangely free of the emotions that had racked her for so long.

'Precisely what I had in mind, *habibti*.'

He reached for her and she stepped back a pace. That casual endearment stung like a slap to the face. No doubt he'd used it with the countless women who'd satisfied his physical needs since Shahina. Maggie was no one special.

A gaping hollow opened inside her. A cold, cruel vacuum where once there'd been excitement and hope.

How could a woman so big with a baby feel suddenly so empty inside?

'No, not that.' She saw his expression change, settling into one of cool query. He wasn't used to being denied. Yet she found no pleasure in denying him, just a weary resolution. 'I want to sleep.'

'It's been a long evening.' Even now the deep timbre of his voice made her yearn for what she shouldn't want. 'Perhaps you'd like a bath first?'

And perhaps a little seduction in the scented, soapy water?

'No.' How often had Khalid seduced her in that decadently large bath? She drew in a deep breath and faced him squarely. 'I want to go straight to sleep. I'll use the second bedroom.'

Khalid's eyebrows shot up. 'There's no need for that.' Haughty reproach laced his tone. 'I respect your need for rest. I won't bother you tonight.'

Maggie traced his proud, forbidding features with her gaze and felt the inevitable kick of desire deep inside. It would always be the same, she feared.

Quickly she shook her head. 'I want to sleep alone. Permanently.'

Khalid loomed before her, a force larger than life, his features hewn into a look of arrogant disbelief. The only signs of life were the burning intensity of his jet-dark eyes as they roved her and his flaring nostrils. Then she looked down and saw the way his hands bunched into fists, white-knuckled with sinewed tension.

Once she might have been daunted by the sight. But it didn't faze her. She felt walled off from emotion in a bubble of nothingness.

'If my love-making causes you discomfort now the baby's so big you should have told me.' Outrage vibrated in his voice. 'I won't force myself on you. I'm not a selfish ogre.'

No, Khalid was a decent man. But their relationship destroyed her, sucking her soul from her till she felt hollow.

'It's not the baby, Khalid. It's me. I don't want sex with you.' *Liar*, screamed a voice inside her. *You'll always crave him*!

Yet having only that small part of him was killing her. Their bodies so attuned but their hearts…

His eyes narrowed as if he'd heard it too, the telltale voice of her needier self.

'I don't want *you*,' she blurted out before she could change her mind. 'I can't continue on with this marriage.'

'You want to leave me?' The words erupted as a barely muted roar. But at least he hadn't closed the yawning chasm between them and yanked her into his arms.

Khalid stared, dumbfounded. He'd sensed her slipping away from him but he'd never guessed it could go this far! Nothing had prepared him. It was impossible she no longer wanted him. He knew in his bones that she lied about that.

'You can't be serious!' She belonged to him. He would never release her.

'I've never been more serious about anything in my life.' Her calm, colourless tone, those almost-blank eyes, convinced him as nothing else could. Maggie wasn't speaking in the heat of the moment. She was in deadly earnest.

A blade of pain sliced through his chest. He braced his feet wider, rocked unsteady by the force of the blow.

Pride and anger surged to the surface.

'You forget, *my wife*, that we're married.' He took a pace forward, bringing him up against her. Part of him urged action: to haul her into his embrace and seduce her with his kisses, his body, her own need for him, till she recanted this nonsense. But pride, or perhaps sense, warned that seduction wasn't the answer.

'No one divorces in the royal house of Shajehar. You are mine and you will stay mine.' His heart thumped a racing, heavy beat that muted his words. 'I will not let you leave.'

Her eyes widened as she stared up at him, but not by so much as a quiver did her body reveal any weakening. She stood strong, determined and quietly defiant. Her composure was eerie, especially given the adrenalin pumping through his bloodstream, the shock tightening every nerve ready for action.

'I don't intend to leave Shajehar. I know what I signed on for and I know there's no easy escape.'

Outrage scorched his soul at her words. And something more. Something that felt like hurt.

Signed on for!

She made their marriage sound like a burdensome duty. Hadn't he given her a place in his world, a place where she was respected and valued, able to contribute? Hadn't he given her wealth, jewels and consequence? A secure future for her and her baby? Hadn't he pleasured her and satisfied her times beyond count?

He couldn't believe she didn't want him. Sometimes he'd even fancied that she felt far more for him than she wanted him to know. Or was that male pride talking?

'So tell me. What is it you do want?'

Her eyelids flickered, then she met his gaze steadily. 'I want space. Distance. I'll still be your wife as far as the world is concerned. But I don't want us to live as man and wife. We'll bring up our child together as agreed. I'll fulfil my duties as a member of the royal family, but…'

'Not in the marriage bed.' The bitterness in Khalid's mouth made him grimace.

She said nothing, just stared up at him with those enormous eyes. Her face was pale and lovely and strained. For the first time he noticed she'd used more make-up than usual. Were those shadows under her eyes? Lines of strain bracketing her mouth?

He looked down to her hands splayed over her belly.

Did she think she needed to protect their child from her husband's fury? The sickening thought made him step back a pace, his chest heaving at the impossible idea.

'Why, Maggie?'

She was silent for so long his nerves stretched to snapping point. Finally she opened her mouth.

'It was never a real marriage, Khalid. Ours is simply a convenient marriage. I want us to stick to that.' She paused and swallowed. 'It's taken a long time but I've discovered I don't want to be intimate with a man when there's no love involved.'

CHAPTER THIRTEEN

'How far till we get there?'

Khalid darted a look at Maggie, checking for signs of fatigue before turning back to the road. She sat straight, hands clasped in her lap. The rough mountain road didn't seem to bother her.

'Not far as the crow flies, but another twenty minutes by road.'

Silence. Their conversation, as usual these days, was brief and stilted.

Was he doing right, acquiescing even briefly to her demand for distance? He wished he knew for sure.

Two days ago when he'd looked into her preternaturally calm face as she'd announced she didn't want him or their marriage, she'd been devoid of emotion. Like a lifeless doll. Or a woman under such incredible strain that she'd shut down emotionally.

That scared Khalid more than anything she'd said. Scared him so much he'd ignored his instinctive need to shatter her sangfroid and prove she lied when she said she no longer wanted him.

I don't want to be intimate with a man when there's no love involved. The words had seared themselves into his brain cells to be replayed again and again.

Love hadn't been part of the bargain. But now, knowing she didn't love him, he felt an ache deep inside. An emptiness.

Only her vulnerability kept strong his resolve to allow her time to adjust.

Maggie had enough to cope with. Was it any wonder she'd been overwrought? Pregnancy hormones. The stress of adjusting to a new life in a new country. The onerous pressures of royal duty and protocol. Physical exhaustion at the strain the baby placed on her body. Fear of the unknown. Grief for the past she'd left behind. The demands he'd put on her, with his incessant hunger for her touch and her warm, luscious body.

He had to give her time. By the time the baby was born things would be different. He'd make sure of it.

'What did you think of the village school?'

'Marvellous!' He heard the thread of excitement in the single word and suppressed annoyance that she was so enthusiastic about a temporary tent school yet dismissive of him.

'You were a hit,' he murmured. 'The children loved you and the parents all approved.'

Khalid had watched the little ones clustering around her as she rocked a toddler on her lap and listened to the juvenile chatter. He'd wanted to be with her, not talking to the village head man.

Primal heat had shot through him at the sight of Maggie cradling a child. Soon she'd have their child to nurse. Satisfaction filled him. And trepidation.

No! By then their marriage would be on track. Everything would be settled. He just needed to curb his impatience.

'Tell me what the women thought of the new school,' he prompted.

He wanted to hear her voice, especially now, he realised as the treacherous road turned into a series of hairpin bends and grim memory surfaced. Tension knotted his stomach and his hands grew clammy on the wheel.

He remembered bringing another woman this way years ago. Driving her up this road as they laughed together.

But Shahina hadn't come down alive.

The sun shone high as they crossed the narrow bridge spanning a chasm that separated the castle from the rest of the mountain spur. It was a grim fortress, squat and foreboding, rising out of sheer rock to command the valley far below and the route over the mountains above.

Maggie barely took in the massive metal-studded wooden doors, the walls, thicker than a man's shoulders, and the iron grille-work in the few windows facing the mountain.

Her thoughts focused on the man beside her, whose gentle support—an arm around her back and another at her elbow—was the most exquisite torture. His tone was solicitous, his pace shortening to her pregnant gait.

Anyone seeing them would believe their prince really cared for his wife. But they'd be wrong. The knowledge was a fathomless black well of despair inside her.

He cared, all right, cared that his precious baby was protected. But as for her, she was a necessary burden, an incubator to carry the child till it entered the world.

Unfortunately the emotionless limbo that had given her strength and cushioned her from pain had faded. Even the fact that Khalid had reluctantly respected her wishes to sleep in separate rooms brought no comfort.

She shivered and his arm tightened.

'Her Highness needs tea, in the small salon,' he said.

The steward who welcomed them bowed and turned to do his master's bidding. Maggie moved mechanically, letting Khalid lead her.

'Here. You'll feel better when you have your tea and something to eat.'

Maggie's lips pulled tight in a grimace. She doubted anything would make her feel better ever again. She subsided into the cushioned chair he held out for her, letting her weary, heavy body sink back. Every bone ached. She felt old beyond her years and tired, so very tired.

'Maggie?' She turned her head slightly at the sound of his voice, deeper, more resonant than usual. But she didn't meet his gaze as he hunkered down before her, pulling her limp hand into his. 'Are you all right?'

She blinked; her stupid imagination tinted his voice with a husky concern she knew wasn't real.

She sat up straighter. 'Yes, thank you. But that tea will be nice,' she lied. The idea of anything on her stomach, even liquid, made bile rise in her throat.

Silence stretched. With each second the distance between them drew wider and more impassable.

Deliberately she turned her head to the huge windows looking out across the network of valleys below. 'The view is spectacular.'

He said nothing for a moment then, abruptly, he stood and tucked her hand in her lap. 'On a fine day you can see for hundreds of kilometres.'

Cloud had curtained the horizon since they'd arrived on their provincial visit. She wondered if he'd ever bring her here again to see it on a fine day.

'I have some business to attend to,' he murmured. 'In the meantime enjoy your refreshments. I'll be back in time to take you to visit the next village.'

Then he was gone and she was left in the empty luxury of the enormous sitting room, its divans covered in massed silk cushions, its floor bright with jewel-coloured antique rugs. Their entourage was no doubt filling the old fortress to bursting point and yet she could easily imagine she was the only one here.

An hour later she was still alone. The castle steward himself brought a second tray of tea, steaming, sweet and fragrant. The aroma curdled her stomach and she rose from her chair on a surge of sudden energy. It was time to go.

It didn't matter that she was heartsick and listless. Or that Khalid insisted on driving her and she didn't want to be cooped up in a vehicle with him. The villagers were expecting her and she wouldn't let them down.

Besides, if she sat here any longer, dwelling on the emotional stalemate her marriage had become, she'd go mad.

'Where is my husband?' She turned to the steward who looked surprised at the simple question.

'His Highness is conferring with Lord Hussein.'

Good. Khalid's uncle was a reasonable man; he wouldn't mind being interrupted.

'Where are they? I need to speak with my husband,' she added when the steward hesitated.

His eyes slid from hers and he pursed his lips.

'It is an urgent matter.'

'They are in Lady Shahina's garden,' he said quickly.

The chill that had been confined to her heart crackled now through her whole body, like icy frost settling on a winter's morning. Shahina's garden. That was where her husband chose to conduct his important business?

Maggie nodded briskly. 'You can show me the way.' She headed for the door and he was forced to accompany her. As they made their way along a vaulted stone corridor she asked casually, 'Did Lady Shahina plant this garden?'

'No, Highness.' She heard the discomfort in his voice and almost felt sorry for him. 'Your Lord had it made after she…'

'I see. After she died.' A memorial garden, then.

Her husband had taken refuge in the place dedicated to the memory of his lost love.

See? She'd been right to stand up for herself. He'd never love her while Shahina held his heart. Far better to distance herself from Khalid than pine for what could never be. But that didn't stop the pain winding round her heart like a constricting vine.

She faltered in an arched doorway, her hand going protectively to her belly where their baby stretched and kicked.

'Highness? Are you all right?'

She straightened. 'Yes, thank you. Is it much further?'

He shook his head. 'Straight ahead, through the door into the first courtyard, then right at the next doorway.'

'Thank you.' Maggie glued a perfunctory smile on her face. 'I'll find my own way from here. I'm sure you have a lot to organise with so many guests.'

She waited till he left, till the corridor was whisper-quiet, before continuing.

The flagstones were warm beneath her feet when the scent assailed her. Damask roses and jasmine and a bounteous mix of other perfumes. In her pregnant state, the voluptuous riot of scents cloyed. Maggie paused at the arched doorway into the walled garden, one hand outstretched to the stone wall as she tried to stifle the queasiness in her stomach.

It was a moment before she realised there were voices. At the sound of Khalid's low tones she stole a step closer to the doorway. She stared at the two men on the other side of the garden.

'Don't you think you should talk to Maggie?' said Khalid's uncle.

'I know what's best, Hussein. You don't understand—'

'I understand, Khalid. Remember I saw you and Shahina together. I see you now with Maggie. I know how you feel.'

'That's not the point. I know what I'm doing.'

Maggie sagged against the doorway as her knees buckled. Khalid sounded so savage, so desperate.

'She isn't Shahina,' Hussein said in a low voice. 'You need to remember that.'

'Don't you think I know that?' Khalid's tone was brusque, rising on harsh emotion. 'Every time I see her, touch her, I know the difference.' There was intrinsic violence in his gesture as he flung out his arm, in the abrupt way he turned and

paced, that spoke more loudly of his feelings than even his
terse words.

'I feel it *here*.' He thumped his chest so hard it was a wonder Maggie couldn't hear it resonate. Maybe her gasp of
anguish drowned out the sound. She reeled back as if he'd
slammed his fist against her, robbing her of air.

'Have you told her how you feel? You have to take the time
to explain to her.'

But Maggie didn't need explanations. She stumbled back
from the doorway, so distraught she barely noticed when her
ice-blue scarf snagged on a climbing rose.

Khalid had made himself abundantly clear. She couldn't
face any more.

The desolation in his voice left no room for doubt. The con-
firmation that he missed his first, beloved wife so much tore
what was left of her heart to shredded ribbons.

She groped her way out of the courtyard, one hand outstretched to the stone wall, the other supporting her heaving
belly. She had to get away, somewhere she could breathe.
Even here in the courtyard the air was too close and thick,
choking her.

She stumbled through a threshold and found herself in the
entrance yard. Ranks of four-wheel drives were lined up
where once there'd been battle horses.

Maggie looked at her watch. She'd need to leave now if she
wasn't to disappoint the locals who'd so shyly offered their
hospitality. Khalid…her heart drummed painfully…Khalid
had clearly forgotten the appointment. Should she search for
someone else to accompany her? The last thing she wanted
was a minder.

Apparently the village was an easy fifteen-minute drive. It
was broad daylight and she was used to driving on gravel
roads, or she had been till she'd become a royal princess.

Khalid would know where she'd gone. He wouldn't worry.

She pushed back her sagging shoulders. She would *not* hide in a corner and fret over what she couldn't change. Wasn't that what she'd promised herself when she'd confronted Khalid? She had to move on with her life.

She made for the vehicle closest to the open gate. Three minutes later the engine roared into life. Without a backward glance she drove out, across the narrow bridge and onto the mountain road.

She'd driven four kilometres when she saw the turn-off Khalid had pointed out. She turned into it, glad to escape the claustrophobic confines of the castle that was Khalid and Shahina's. Where Maggie would always be an intruder.

Work had always been a necessity and a solace. That was what she needed. To focus on her baby and her work with the Shajehani women. If she kept busy enough maybe one day the pain of unrequited love would ease. Then she could think of Khalid and not have tears blur her vision and choke her breathing.

She rounded a blind curve and her heart jolted as a couple of goats raced across the road metres away. She slammed on the brakes, then cursed as the wheels locked and the vehicle slid sideways in the gravel. Her reflexes were slow and her hands slipped on the steering wheel as she tried to turn into the skid.

The seconds stretched out impossibly as the vehicle headed for the edge. A deep gutter and a cutting of sheer rock loomed beside her as she struggled with the wheel.

It was impossible.

The impact threw her forward with a jolt that shook her teeth and bruised her body. She curled her arms around her belly, trying desperately to protect her baby.

There was a terrible, blood-curdling screech, banshee-loud, as metal scraped on rock. The vehicle tipped half over in the ditch and kept sliding. Maggie barely noticed. She'd knocked her head on the initial impact.

At last the ear-splitting shriek of tortured metal ceased. The vehicle thudded to a halt at a forty-five-degree angle against a ridge of solid rock.

Eventually she summoned the energy to reach up and switch off the ignition. The only sounds were the tick, tick of hot metal and her rough panting breaths as she fought pain and the dizzying tug of unconsciousness.

She allowed herself the luxury of closing her eyes, just for a few moments. When she opened them it was with a jolt that told her she'd nodded off.

Far too dangerous. She had to get out of the vehicle. She couldn't smell fuel but she wasn't taking chances. Suddenly Maggie realised in horror that she couldn't discern even the slightest movement from her baby.

Fear and guilt slashed at her. She should never have come alone. It didn't matter that she was a competent driver, well used to the roughest of roads. Fresh tears gathered, burning hot at the backs of her eyes, and she blinked them back. She had to move. Now.

Grasping the door handle up above her head, she tried to lever herself up.

Two things happened simultaneously. Pain shot through her left leg, strong enough to make her sway and the world recede for an instant. And she felt something else—a warm gush of liquid between her thighs.

Tentatively she reached down, dread icing her veins. But there was no mistaking it. Blood. Lots of it. She was bleeding and her baby was in danger.

Heedless of the pain that made her head reel, she reached out and hauled herself high enough to grasp the steering wheel. She jammed her fist down on the horn and kept it there.

CHAPTER FOURTEEN

HER impressions were jumbled. Above all there was pain and fear. Maggie heard voices, desperate, urgent voices, and felt hands, strong and sure on her body. There was a burst of sudden agony and nothing more.

Sounds roused her, the rapid thud, thud, thud almost deafening her. Was it her heartbeat pumping out the precious blood that her baby needed? Or was it a helicopter? Rescue? Maggie opened her mouth to ask, aware of a voice urgently calling her name, again and again. But no sound came and she slid back into the void of darkness.

It was pain that roused her once more. The pain of her fingers being squeezed so tight they would surely fuse together. Heat encompassed them, the living heat of a large, roughened hand. *Khalid*. He was there. He'd found her. Everything would be all right now.

Maggie struggled through the fog that trapped her, trying to reach him, give some response so he knew she was aware of him.

Voices reached her. Staccato orders from a voice she didn't recognise and, clashing across it, Khalid's hoarse, urgent tones. 'Do what you must. Anything you must, but save my wife. That's all that matters.'

For a brief moment longer Maggie fought to reach him, to connect with him, but the sounds of life slid away and she fell once more into the void.

When she finally came to, she felt…nothing. No hurt, no discomfort, nothing. She lay flat on her back. Her hand was warm where fingers held hers loosely.

Khalid. It was true, she thought muzzily. It hadn't been a dream. He'd been with her all this time.

Her limp body suffused with heat and something she was too weary to define. Relief? Love? Hope? She let the sensation wash through her, content that he was here.

Gradually her senses grew more alert as her body woke. Her eyelids flickered and her mouth twitched. She wanted to say his name, hear it powerful and real on her tongue.

Finally she found the energy, swallowing to moisten her dust-dry throat.

'Khalid,' she whispered. His name was like a talisman, the sound of it lending her strength to open her eyes.

'Maggie! Maggie, sweetheart, you're awake.' But it wasn't Khalid's velvet tones she heard. It was Zeinab.

Turning her head a fraction, she found her friend's face, watching her intently. The older woman seemed to have aged overnight and weariness lined her face.

'Everything's fine,' Zeinab assured her, though her eyes were shadowed and overbright. Maggie felt a thrill of instinctive fear claw at her. 'You're safe now.'

'The baby?' Her voice was a raw croak but Zeinab understood. She tipped her lips upwards in a taut smile.

'You have a little daughter, born by Caesarean section. She's in neonatal intensive care.'

Maggie's heart plummeted, a leaden weight as fear gripped her.

'How is she? *Really*?' Guilt racked her. It was her fault her baby had been born too early.

'She's small, so she needs extra attention. There were complications during the birth. But she's improving, growing stronger by the hour.'

Maggie stared into her friend's troubled eyes, trying to discern truth from optimistic assurance.

'Khalid has been with you all the time,' Zeinab said. 'He wouldn't leave your side. He's just gone to see the baby.'

But the platitudes didn't ring true. Tense as she was with fear for her daughter, her body exhausted, Maggie couldn't even summon the strength to be disappointed.

Khalid wasn't here and no amount of well-meaning assurances could hide that. Had Maggie really expected him to be at her side when she woke? She knew where his priorities lay, and that was with their child. It had always been the baby only that mattered to him.

Moisture gathered at the corners of her eyes and she turned her head towards the pillow, too weary to raise a hand and wipe it away as hurt filled her. Her heart squeezed, catching her breath against a pain that defied even the drugs filling her system.

She must have imagined the firm touch of his hand wrapping around hers. And his desperate voice imploring the medicos to save her.

Funny what the human brain could invent, wasn't it?

'Maggie.' Zeinab's voice was low and soothing. 'You and your little girl are safe in excellent hands here.' She paused as if searching for the right words. 'Khalid will be thrilled to see you conscious. He's been frantic about you both. But everything will be all right. You'll see.'

Maggie offered her friend a weak smile, but didn't say anything. What was there to say?

It was shatteringly clear that things would never be right, even if Zeinab was correct and her baby was safe. Oh, how she prayed Zeinab was right about that.

This marriage could never be fixed.

She closed her eyes and let herself slide back to that place where there was no pain and no disappointment, only the empty haven of darkness.

* * *

Khalid stood in the shadows of the dimly lit room and looked down into his wife's pale face.

The doctor's assurance that she'd already woken and was responding well didn't convince him. Fear gripped him in a vice. He wouldn't believe it till he saw for himself that she was recovering.

Only the exercise of supreme control held him still, knees locked, feet planted wide and hands clenched together behind his back.

He wanted to cradle her in his arms, kiss her back to consciousness, nuzzle the silken softness of her hair and whisper his regrets and his apologies. But he couldn't.

Guilt tore at him with razor-sharp talons, gnawed at his innards till only obstinate willpower kept him standing. *He'd* done this. Because of him Maggie had almost died, and their child with her.

He was to blame.

He'd thought he remembered the pain of loss but he hadn't been prepared for the ripping agony that had shredded him when he'd thought he was losing her. He should have been there to drive her, keep her safe.

More, he should never have agreed to a separation. He should have smashed through the barriers that divided them. Especially his own shameful denial of his feelings. He'd conditioned himself to believe he'd never again experience such emotions. He'd been a coward, afraid at the possibility of loving and losing again.

The rescue had been touch and go. It could easily have ended in disaster in that rugged terrain. The surgery had been a frantic attempt to save them both. Through it all Khalid had been useless, unable to do more than hold Maggie and cajole, plead, demand that she stay with him. The possibility that fate would steal her away had almost unmanned him. Even now fear trembled in his belly and hammered his pulse.

Her lashes moved, the shadows on her face shifting. Was she waking? He took a pace forward, then slammed to a halt as golden-green eyes fixed on him. The oxygen he'd inhaled disappeared and he grew dizzy with relief and remorse. She looked so fragile, so wan and helpless. He clasped his hands so hard they shook. But at least he was able to maintain a necessary distance. He had to respect her feelings, not bulldoze in and sweep her into his arms as he yearned to do.

'Khalid.' Her voice was bruised, a dry choking sob. He lunged forward and poured her water. She needed him. Any excuse to obliterate the distance between them.

'Here, *habibti*. Drink this.' He slid a hand behind her shoulders to lift her. She shuddered in his embrace and he hoped fervently it was from the physical effort. Not distaste.

Her lids lowered, her lashes concealing her expressive eyes as she then sank back. Reluctantly he eased her against the pillows and slid his hand away. His fingers flexed, warm with the feel of her delicate-boned body. He put the paper cup on the bedside table and forced himself to step away.

'How do you feel, Maggie?'

Her lips tilted up in a smile that wasn't a smile. 'Alive.'

'You had me worried.' The words burst from him. Worried…he'd been terrified!

Her eyes widened, rising to meet his. Then her gaze slid away. 'Yes, the baby. How is she?'

'Getting stronger all the time.' He'd been amazed at the tiny mite's resilience. It had given him strength when his own had begun to fail him. 'Beautiful like her mother.'

Again Maggie's eyes met his, just for an instant, and he read astonishment there.

'Really? She's safe?' she whispered.

Khalid nodded, seeing the echo of his own worry in her face. 'I promise. It hasn't been an easy start for her, but the signs are excellent and she's responding well. Here.' He allowed himself to step closer, fishing out his mobile phone. 'You'll want to see these.'

He flipped open the slimline phone and called up the photos he'd just taken. He handed it over, his momentary pleasure withering as he watched the way she studiously avoided touching him.

Ice clamped round his chest. He'd hurt her so badly, enough to make her run from him. He felt sick when he thought of her alone on the treacherous mountain road. Would she let him make reparation for his mistakes or was it too late?

No, he refused to countenance that possibility.

Her eyes fixed on the phone and her mouth opened on a sigh of astonished delight. Tenderness filled her eyes.

'She's gorgeous. And so tiny. Are you sure she'll be OK?'

He nodded. 'The doctors are very pleased with her progress.' No need to mention those first hours when the outlook had been grim indeed.

'I want to see her,' she whispered.

'You will. Soon.' He stood, frozen by the knowledge that he could have prevented this. If he hadn't let Maggie down, the pregnancy would have gone to term. She wouldn't have had to fight for her very life.

He hadn't been there. He hadn't earned her trust. He'd let their marriage disintegrate. No wonder she'd pushed him away. He'd taken her passion, her affection, even her innocence, and given nothing of substance in return. Nothing that truly mattered. No wonder she'd sought a chance to go out alone, escaping his company.

He was criminally culpable. Even if she could be persuaded to forgive him, he could never forgive himself.

Slowly he sank onto the seat by her bed. Was it imagination or did she lean away?

'Here. Thank you for showing me.'

She held out the phone and he shook his head. 'Keep it till you're able to see her.'

'Thank you.' Her voice was stilted as if she spoke to a stranger.

Khalid could bear it no longer.

'Maggie.' He reached for her hand, closing his fingers around it and holding firm though she tried to tug out of his grasp. His hold tightened reflexively. He never wanted to let her go.

Even now, here in the best hospital Shajehar boasted, he was terrified of losing her. He relived those moments when his world had tilted out of kilter and stopped. Maggie's scarf snapping from a rosebush like a banner in the breeze. The swelling roar of a vehicle engine as it departed the fortress. The metallic taste of terror burning his mouth as he realised Maggie was alone on the precarious mountain. The helplessness of waiting, praying for the chopper to arrive, knowing all he could do was hold her in his arms and not give up hope.

Echoes of the past had swamped him. He'd been terrified history was repeating itself.

'You're hurting me.'

Contrition filled him. Yet he couldn't release her. It was too much to ask.

'I'm sorry,' he murmured, lifting her hand and pressing tiny, fervent kisses to the back of it. She trembled in his hold.

'Please, Khalid.' She drew in a shaky breath so hard it rattled her chest. 'Please, don't.'

Her eyes were bright with tears and her mouth worked. Guilt scorched him. He didn't want to hurt her anymore.

'Don't cry, Maggie.' He turned over her hand and kissed her palm, inhaling her unique fragrance, recognisable despite the antiseptic hospital smells. He shut his eyes and breathed it in, then flicked out his tongue and tasted her. Reaction shuddered through him.

His woman. His. He would do anything for her but he wouldn't let her go. That was asking the impossible.

* * *

'I failed to protect you. Failed to protect my family.' Khalid's voice was tight, roughened as she'd never before heard it. His hand held hers in a steely grip and his face was grim.

His demeanour was starkly proprietorial. She sensed his control was skin-deep, a veneer of civilisation barely covering far more primitive instincts. Heat flared at that glimpse of un-trammelled masculine possessiveness. But it wasn't for her. Would never be for her.

He'd feared for the baby. As she had. It was their one real emotional link: love of their child.

'It's all right, Khalid. It's over now. The baby is safe.' She didn't for an instant question the need to comfort him. She loved him, no matter that he didn't reciprocate her feelings.

'*You're* safe.' His voice was choked, thick with emotion and unfamiliar. 'I thought I'd lost you both.'

He raised his head and she was shocked by the raw emotion in his face. He looked ravaged by pain, the lines around his mouth scored deep; his eyes shimmered bright with anguish.

Her fingers curved around his, unhesitatingly offering comfort. She couldn't bear to see him in such agony.

'Seeing you there, unconscious.' He shook his head. 'It was like every nightmare of the past come to haunt me.'

The past? Of course, how could she have forgotten?

'Shahina,' she murmured dully. The accident must have sparked memories of his first wife's death.

He nodded, his mouth a line of twisted grief. 'How could I have let it happen? She died not ten kilometres from where you went off the road.'

Horror dried Maggie's mouth at the news. No wonder Khalid was distraught. What must he have gone through as he waited for help, wondering if the chopper would be on time?

'I should have known better than to take you into the mountains. Should have known it was too dangerous, especially for a pregnant woman. Too far from medical help.' He burrowed his fingers through his hair.

Maggie's distress and guilt seemed nothing to the agony she read in his eyes. Her heart twisted, wrung out by the emotion revealed there. Always Khalid had been controlled. Now she saw him stripped naked and grieving.

Instinctively Maggie lifted her hand to cup his jaw. Instantly he turned his face to nuzzle her palm, his long dark lashes sweeping down to hide his eyes. The rough texture of his chin grazed her and his moist hot breath hazed her sensitive skin.

'I don't deserve you, Maggie.'

Faced with his bone-deep pain, Maggie couldn't find it in her heart to be angry that he couldn't love her. Love wasn't a choice. It had come upon her out of the blue. She couldn't blame him for the fact that he'd given his heart years ago to another.

'I will never forgive myself. How can I expect you to forgive me?' His voice was a hollow groan. His lips moved against her skin as he anchored her cradling palm against his face with his hand.

'Khalid—'

'But I have to ask. I *must*.'

'Khalid, there's nothing to forgive.'

'Isn't there?' His eyes snapped open to ensnare hers. 'What about our marriage?'

'Please, don't,' she begged, trying to keep her voice steady. She didn't have the stamina to hear him put it into words. That their marriage was a mistake. That his heart belonged to his first wife.

Had he changed his mind about divorce? Legally she'd be free then. But Maggie knew in her aching soul that she'd never be whole again.

His eyes didn't leave hers. 'I must speak, Maggie. I have been remiss. Worse than that. I made you miserable.' He gathered in an enormous breath that hefted his shoulders and chest high.

'I've been content for too long to enjoy the benefits of marriage, the benefits of you—' his eyes narrowed '—without giving all of myself in return. I've been utterly selfish. I kept my emotional distance because I didn't believe I could love again. You deserve more than that.'

He was about to give her the freedom she needed. So why did she feel like a doomed prisoner, awaiting a death sentence?

Hot tears glazed the backs of her eyes and she tried to tug her hand free of his grip. She needed space. She needed to be alone.

But he wouldn't relinquish his hold.

'It wasn't till you stood up to me, till you denied me your body, *more*, your affection, that I realised what I'd done. That's when I understood what I felt for you.'

Maggie's breath came in short, sharp pants as her chest constricted. Yet she was powerless to turn away from his dark-as-night eyes, so brilliant and intent.

'I'm ashamed, Maggie. Truly ashamed, that I didn't understand before.' He shook his head. 'I hid from the truth, too cowardly to see beyond the narrow limits I'd set. I should have realised how badly I treated you.' His hand tightened on hers as his voice cracked.

'Khalid. No more. Please. I know how you feel; you don't need to say any more.' Already her heart was splintering as pain lanced her.

'Then you are far more insightful than I am, *habibti*. It took me too long to understand what you meant to me. How I'd grown to love you for your strength and beauty, your charm and tenderness, your warmth, your determination, all the things that make you the special woman you are.'

Maggie could only stare, meeting Khalid's eyes and seeing the honesty etched there.

'I thought it was convenience, liking, respect, even cataclysmic sexual need, that kept me wanting to be with you,' he continued. 'Anything except love.'

Love?

Maggie gaped, bereft of words.

'It was easier to tell myself I desired you because you were so sexy, any man's fantasy,' he murmured between fervent kisses to her palm. 'Or that you were good company, able to listen and give another perspective on problems. Or that I respected the way you adapted to the demands of life in a new country.'

'Or that I carried your baby?' She couldn't accept his wonderful words, despite the hope burgeoning inside her.

He nodded. 'That was another logical reason, that you were pregnant with our child. After all, it was the excuse I used to force you into marriage.'

'Excuse?' She frowned.

'I'd already decided I wanted you in my life. Your pregnancy forced my hand, but I didn't regret it.' He smiled, a flash of sheer exuberant masculine pleasure that rocked all her senses. 'I knew after one night I wanted much more from you. I had no intention of being denied. That's why you were brought to Shajehar. I had every intention of seducing you into my bed again and again.'

Heat flared in his lustrous eyes and Maggie felt an answering spark deep inside. But it was too much to take in. Too much to believe. She turned her face away.

'No, Khalid. There's no need to lie, to hide the truth.' He was trying to build something between them that just wasn't there. Presumably for their baby's sake.

'The truth? The truth is that I adore you, *habibti*. I have done for months, but I was too blind and obstinate to see. Hussein knew. And Zeinab. But they kept their counsel until Hussein confronted me at the fortress.'

'Hussein said he'd seen you and Shahina together and that I deserved to know the truth.' There. She'd said it, brought the spectre of his one true love into the open. She stared at her free hand, pleating the edge of the sheet.

'Ah, so you heard that?'

Miserably she nodded. 'You said I was different to Shahina. That you felt the difference every time you saw me.'

She sank her teeth into her cheek to prevent her jaw from wobbling. She would *not* break down.

'Exactly so, my sweet.' His hand was a hot caress tilting her chin up. Through the haze of her pain Maggie registered the tremor in his fingers.

'Shahina was my first love. We'd known each other all our lives and fell into romance almost as part of growing up. What we had was special and I never thought to experience love for another woman again.'

She could barely breathe when he looked at her like that.

'I never expected to be swept away by a love so powerful it played havoc with my common sense, as well as my libido. To find a woman who means more to me than life itself.' His fingers stroked, feather-light, across her lips. 'Yes, I loved Shahina, but you made me realise that I had to move on from the past. I love you, Maggie, with all my being. This is like a lightning bolt that has pierced my heart. I'm no callow youth and I know what I want in my life.' He drew in a shuddering breath.

'I want you. Always. For ever. Is it possible you feel something, *anything*, for me? Enough to accept my apology and stay?'

Her eyes glazed with tears. She so wanted it to be true. 'That's shock talking. The accident reminded you of Shahina.'

The horror on his face stilled her breathing. 'No, my love. Never say that! Despite the memories, my fear was all for you. And our child. What I feel for you is real and true.' He swallowed convulsively. 'Without you, I am nothing. I am the dust beneath your feet.'

He leaned in and pressed his lips to hers, in a tender kiss that made her heart flip over. 'But I heard—'

'You heard my uncle berating me for letting our marriage continue in stalemate. I'd only just realised my feelings for you. And understood how little I'd given you in return for your faith and loyalty and passion. I was racked by guilt.' His gaze held her spellbound for so long she was sure he could read her emotions clear in her eyes.

'I knew I was in love, that you were the most precious thing in my world. That I could never bear to lose you. The knowledge scared me witless. You'd withdrawn from me, with good reason. I had no idea how to persuade you to trust me, to give me another chance.'

He cupped her face with both hands. 'I wish I'd done it differently. I would have courted you properly, told you I loved you. Instead I was paralysed, fearing I'd pushed you too far. That I didn't have a hope of winning you.' He shuddered and closed his eyes.

'Khalid.' His name had never tasted so perfect on her lips. She stared, wondering, at the man who for the first time revealed his innermost fears and hopes in his unguarded eyes.

'Can you forgive me, Maggie? For not deserving you? For not offering you my love earlier? I hurt you so badly.' Desperation coloured his voice. A stark fear that matched the blaze of emotion in his eyes.

'Hush.' Her fingers were unsteady as she pressed them to his lips. Inside she felt a warmth unfurl and spread through her whole being. The warmth of love such as she'd never known in all her days.

'There's nothing to forgive, Khalid.'

His gaze trapped her, so intense it branded her.

'Maggie. You can't mean that.'

Tentatively she smiled, blinking back tears as she met his hopeful, longing look.

'I do.' It was all she could manage as her throat closed.

'Then tell me. Tell me what I need to hear.' There was a hint of his old autocratic tone in his velvet-deep voice as he stared down at her. A hint of imperiousness in the tilt of his head. But the uncertainty she read in his eyes belied his show of arrogance. It convinced her as no words could have done.

'I love you, Khalid,' she said for the first time, hearing the joy and wonder of it in her voice, seeing it reflected in his loving expression.

Then he pulled her close and there were no more words for a very long time.

CHAPTER FIFTEEN

MAGGIE bade farewell to the last of the tribal women at the door of the walled garden. The meeting had gone well and they'd been enthusiastic about the new school in the valley. One of them had even broached the possibility of a literacy programme for adults. Maggie smiled as she turned and made her way back through the scented garden.

Khalid had already battled hard to ensure that the more traditional local elders hadn't vetoed the idea of girls attending the school. He would have to be his most persuasive to convince them that their wives should also learn. But Maggie had no doubts her husband would prevail. He could be so persuasive when he wished. Or downright autocratic if the occasion demanded.

A frisson of delicious heat spiralled through her and she paused, sidetracked by the idea of him being persuasive.

'What are you smiling about, *habibti*?'

She turned to find him emerging from the shadows. The sun glinted off his hair with the blue-black sheen of a raven's wing. It gilded his compellingly handsome features and highlighted the tiny laughter lines around his mouth and eyes. She loved his laugh, rich and so mellow it always seemed to rumble right through her.

Her gaze traced his lean, sculpted features, his powerful

shoulders and dropped to the burden he cradled so easily yet so protectively in his arms.

Jasmine was six months old, round-cheeked and button-nosed. She had dark hair like her father and a rich little chuckle that suited her sunny temperament. Right now she had the fidgety look of a hungry baby.

As ever, the sight of them together, the two people in the world who meant everything to her, made her heart turn over in her chest.

She watched Khalid tuck their daughter further into the curve of his arm and knew how lucky she was. He was everything she wanted in a man, a husband, a lover, a father for her child.

'I was just thinking of how good you are at getting your own way when you want something, Your Majesty.' She lowered her eyes in a deliberately flirtatious move.

'That's it. Pander to my fantasy that I'm in total control of my own household.' She heard the amusement in his voice. 'But it seems to me that you're the persuasive one. Who was it that decided we should spend a few months each year here in the mountains?'

She looked up. The warmth of his gaze squeezed her insides as it always did when he looked at her with love in his eyes.

'Do you regret it?'

He shook his head. 'No. You were right. I can't keep you and Jasmine coddled in cotton wool, much as I'd like to.' He drew Maggie close with his free arm, his lips a temptation to surrender as he nibbled at her neck.

'Khalid!'

'Hmm?'

Maggie tried in vain to ignore the glorious sensations his caress engendered. She reached for Jasmine, who gurgled her approval. The warm baby scent filled her nostrils as Maggie cradled her.

'This isn't the time or the place,' she said, trying to sound sensible.

'Perhaps you're right.' He glanced down as Jasmine plucked hungrily at the silk of Maggie's bodice. 'This isn't the time. But after you've fed Jasmine, perhaps you'll let me practise those skills of persuasion on you.' His sleek brows tilted up in a lascivious waggle that did nothing to detract from his sheer physical magnetism.

He curved his arms lightly around her and Jasmine, holding them in his strong, protective embrace.

Maggie sighed with pure delight. She'd found the love she'd never thought would be hers. She had everything her heart desired.

Dreams really did come true.

MILLS & BOON®

are proud to present our...

Book of the Month

Sins of the Flesh
by Eve Silver

from Mills & Boon® Nocturne™

Calliope and soul reaper Mal are enemies, but as
they unravel a tangle of clues, their attraction grows.
Now they must choose between loyalty to those
they love, or loyalty to each other—to the one
they each call enemy.

Available 4th March

Something to say about our Book of the Month?
Tell us what you think!

millsandboon.co.uk/community
facebook.com/romancehq
twitter.com/millsandboonuk

One night with a hot-blooded male!

18th February 2011

18th March 2011

15th April 2011

20th May 2011